WARRIOR COVEN

In the hallowed ranks of the Ordo Xenos – Inquisitorial masters of the elite alien hunters known as the Deathwatch – there are many dark secrets. When Captain Octavius of the Deathwatch and his battle-brothers are called away on a mission, he learns of an ancient pact. In return for advanced intelligence on the forces of Chaos, the Inquisition has agreed to aid the alien race known as eldar – but can they really be trusted? The Death-watch must battle against insurmountable odds if they are to achieve their mission and prevent a terrible evil from being summoned into the universe!

More C S Goto from the Black Library

The Dawn of War novels
DAWN OF WAR
DAWN OF WAR: ASCENSION

The Deathwatch series
WARRIOR BROOD

Necromunda
SALVATION

A WARHAMMER 40,000 NOVEL

WARRIOR COVEN

C S Goto

A Black Library Publication

First published in Great Britain in 2006 by
BL Publishing,
Games Workshop Ltd.,
Willow Road, Nottingham,
NG7 2WS, UK.

10 9 8 7 6 5 4 3 2 1

Cover illustration by Phillip Sibbering.

© Games Workshop Limited 2006. All rights reserved.

Black Library, the Black Library logo, Black Flame, BL Publishing,
Games Workshop, the Games Workshop logo and all associated marks,
names, characters, illustrations and images from the Warhammer
40,000 universe are either ®, TM and/or © Games Workshop Ltd 2000-
2006, variably registered in the UK and other countries around the
world. All rights reserved.

A CIP record for this book is available from the British Library.

ISBN 13: 978 1 84416 365 6
ISBN 10: 1 84416 365 2

Distributed in the US by Simon & Schuster
1230 Avenue of the Americas, New York, NY 10020, US.

Printed and bound in Great Britain by
Bookmarque, Surrey, UK.

No part of this publication may be reproduced, stored in a retrieval
system, or transmitted in any form or by any means, electronic,
mechanical, photocopying, recording or otherwise, without the prior
permission of the publishers.

This is a work of fiction. All the characters and events portrayed in this
book are fictional, and any resemblance to real people or incidents is
purely coincidental.

See the Black Library on the Internet at
www.blacklibrary.com

Find out more about Games Workshop
and the world of Warhammer 40,000 at
www.games-workshop.com

IT IS THE 41st millennium. For more than a hundred centuries the Emperor has sat immobile on the Golden Throne of Earth. He is the master of mankind by the will of the gods, and master of a million worlds by the might of his inexhaustible armies. He is a rotting carcass writhing invisibly with power from the Dark Age of Technology. He is the Carrion Lord of the Imperium for whom a thousand souls are sacrificed every day, so that he may never truly die.

YET EVEN IN his deathless state, the Emperor continues his eternal vigilance. Mighty battlefleets cross the daemon-infested miasma of the warp, the only route between distant stars, their way lit by the Astronomican, the psychic manifestation of the Emperor's will. Vast armies give battle in his name on uncounted worlds. Greatest amongst his soldiers are the Adeptus Astartes, the Space Marines, bio-engineered super-warriors. Their comrades in arms are legion: the Imperial Guard and countless planetary defence forces, the ever-vigilant Inquisition and the tech-priests of the Adeptus Mechanicus to name only a few. But for all their multitudes, they are barely enough to hold off the ever-present threat from aliens, heretics, mutants – and worse.

TO BE A man in such times is to be one amongst untold billions. It is to live in the cruellest and most bloody regime imaginable. These are the tales of those times. Forget the power of technology and science, for so much has been forgotten, never to be re-learned. Forget the promise of progress and understanding, for in the grim dark future there is only war. There is no peace amongst the stars, only an eternity of carnage and slaughter, and the laughter of thirsting gods.

CHAPTER ONE:
TRAITORS

THE TWO FIGURES moved in utter silence and with incredible speed. They were only suggestions of images, lingering on the edge of visibility like the shadows of a lurking death. They flicked and whirled with motion, flashing like darkness in the deep shade of the dimly lit corridor. Moments of deepest quiet darted out from their movements, as though they were emitting shards of nothingness, covering themselves with a shower of imperceptibility. The total silence in the corridor hissed with unnatural menace, as though it were an aberration, and the dark figures bathed in it like composers in their own symphony.

As the two dark eldar wyches worked, the air between them started to shimmer and liquefy, as though curtains of watery darkness were being drawn across the corridor. Sparks of light from the glowing veins that ran through the mysterious, shimmering substance of the ceiling and floor caught the unearthly ripples like bursts of starlight. As the liquefaction intensified, so the shadowy motion of the wyches was cast into even deeper darkness, silhouetted against the erratically glimmering curtain. They dashed from one side of the corridor to the other, making adjustments to the devices that they had already fitted to the walls, touching their fingers to buttons that did not compress or click but which glittered as the wyches' flesh approached.

At an unspoken and invisible signal, the two wyches snapped into stillness and then dropped to their knees, bowing their heads towards the warp field that they had just created in the bowels of the vast Ulthwé craftworld. The rippling field started to pulse with waves, scattering droplets of dark-light over the kneeling figures. The waves rose and gathered momentum, crashing into interference patterns that sizzled with unspeakable power.

Somewhere in the maze of corridors behind them, the wyches could hear the metallic trampling of running feet. They presumed that the effete Ulthwé had finally realised what was going on. Pathetic: it was about time. Involuntarily, both of them snarled their upper lips in disgust at their feeble and distant brethren, but they did not move. They had no fear of the eldar guardians – the lightlings. They knew what was about to emerge from the warp gate that they had constructed in front of them, and in comparison the closing eldar were insipid, puny and spineless.

Having seen the horrors at the command of the haemonculi, fear took on a whole new meaning, and there was nothing that the Ulthwé could do to perturb the wyches. Despite themselves, the two interlopers smiled, letting the dim light spark off their black teeth; knowing that their own superiors would happily exact more terrible suffering on them than their enemies could possibly imagine liberated them for the fight to come. There was always a small chance that they would suffer even if they returned triumphant, but part of their souls rejoiced in this masochistic prospect. The gentrified and pompous eldar had no idea what the gods had cast into their future. They didn't even know that their gods were dead, the short-sighted fools.

As the footsteps grew louder, so the ripples and waves in the warp field grew more violent. Refusing to look up, Kroulir and Druqura held their gazes into the polished deck, letting the reflections of the warp dance and flash beneath them, watching the erratic and spectacular patterns gradually resolving themselves into familiar shapes. Fragments of the field splattered out of the gate, spitting icy pain over their backs as they remained bowed in patient deference.

Behind them, the sounds of footfalls shifted in tone, as though they were no longer muffled by walls or corners in the corridor. It seemed that the eldar guardians had finally reached the two wych raiders. As if to confirm their calculation, a cloud of tiny projectiles whined past the bowed figures, slicing into their scant, sculpted armour, peppering the devices that they had implanted into the walls, and splashing into the immaterial substance of the warp field itself. With suitably masterful timing, tendrils of warp started to reach out of the shimmering pool, questing into the thick, soupy reality of the craft-world passageway. They snaked and grew, reaching and thickening, intertwining and interlacing, oblivious to the hail of shuriken fire that sizzled out from the eldar guardians who were charging down the corridor towards them, behind the bowing wyches.

The running eldar guardians were shouting, sending blasts of sound and psychic noise thundering down the passage. Kroulir could hear the fear in their voices and sense the urgency in their thoughts. As tiny shuriken shards of toxic pain bit into her back she grinned, running the tip of her tongue around the glistening points of her upper teeth. Not long now. She could feel the saliva moistening her mouth in anticipation as she stared fixedly down into the deck, still unmoving.

Finally, the warp field before the wyches erupted, as though struck from the other side by a tsunami of energy. Waves of sha'iel – warp energy – broke and crashed out of the gate, washing over the two dark eldar wyches like an ocean over rocks, covering them in freezing pulses of agony. Kroulir thrilled. Behind her she could hear the gasps of the eldar guardians and sense them fighting against their own panic – it was humiliating to think that those pathetic lightlings shared anything in common with her.

Another rush of sha'iel flooded out of the gate, swamping the deck with immaterial pools. Then a curdling shriek pierced the icy air. It was a single, tremulous tone, like a tortured soul. Another joined it, and another, until in an instant there was a chorus of agonising sound searing out of the warp gate, filling the corridor with memories of pain and thoughts of misery. Inchoate yells and screams ricocheted around the corridor, the warcries of the approaching eldar guardians blending into the curdling shrieks that emanated from the warp gate. Kroulir could hear a couple of the Ulthwé stumble.

There was a clatter as weapons were dropped, and Kroulir could imagine the guardians clutching at their oversensitive ears like weakling mon-keigh, howling like children. She stole a glance over at Druqura, and saw that the young wych had not moved at all; she remained stooped in a reverential bow, and there was a faint glint from her bowed face as the dark-light of the warp reflected from her eyes and the tips of her pointed teeth.

A sudden rush erupted through the air above the heads of the wyches, but neither of them had to look. They knew what was emerging from the warp gate. They could hear its signature in the way that the screams of the eldar changed, stopping abruptly. Only Quruel, mistress of the beasts, could bring such a shocking silence into the cacophony of battle. The wyches grinned, finally unfolding from their reverential bows and spinning into pirouettes as they unsheathed their blades and turned to face the eldar behind them.

Still dripping with sha'iel from the warp gate, Quruel stood in the centre of the corridor between the wyches and the eldar guardians, her hair a snaking nest of fiery tendrils, with a warp whip crackling darkly in one hand and a staff-mounted talon spinning in the other. She was flanked on both sides by ungodly, barbed and scaled beasts. They were like small dragons, gnashing and thrashing around Quruel's legs, spitting fragments of sha'iel like saliva. Their ruddy, rust-red scales seemed to swim and shift over their bodies, twinkling with black stars, as though they were tiny, refractive windows into the immaterium itself. And their eyes burnt like pitch, deep and soulless. The only parts of them that looked material and real were their green claws, their yellow teeth, and the barbed silver spikes that ran from the crests on their heads to the very tips of their lashing tails. They were horrifyingly real.

A FORMATION OF black and red Reaver jetbikes flashed out into the jungle clearing, sprays of projectiles hissing out of their nose mounted splinter rifles. The dark eldar riders were craned forward over the controls, leaning along the scaled nose cones of their vehicles with their wild, long hair flooding out behind them like jet-streams. They were howling like warp beasts, and their eyes glinted with maniacal passion. As they sped into open ground, a volley of fire smashed into the front of their line, shattering their formation as the riders peeled away to avoid the onslaught.

The leading rider pulled up short, smoke and debris pluming out of his ruined Reaver. Just as the machine's engine core detonated, the rider vaulted to the ground, flipping neatly and turning a crisp somersault before landing with his splinter pistol already drawn. Before he could get off a single shot, his body was punched and riddled with a tirade of fire, throwing him shredded to the ground.

The eldar of Ulthwé's Dark Reaper Aspect Temple, dug into their bunkers around the edge of the clearing, tracked the flight of the speeding Reavers with their reaper launchers, lashing flurries of rockets out through the foliage as though it were paper. They stood with their leg stabilisers planted firmly against the massive report of their fearsome weapons, unleashing an inferno that even the dark eldar should fear. Ulthwé may not host as many of the Aspect Temples as some of the other eldar craftworlds, but they had always provided a home for the sinister Dark Reapers.

So close to the lashes of the Eye of Terror, the Dark Reapers of Ulthwé were constantly vigilant for signs of the return of their Phoenix Lord, Maugan Ra, the Harvester of Souls, who had vanished into the great Eye when the lost craftworld of Altansar had been swallowed whole. For now, Ulthwé was the closest place to home.

Truqui roared his fury into the wake of the speeding Reavers as they skirted the circumference of the glade, darting between the streams of fire that flooded out from his fellow Aspect Warriors. His reaper launcher was a formidable weapon, especially at range, and its constant recoil was driving his braced feet steadily into the ground. He yelled again, willing the tiny rockets into ever increasing ferocity, driving them after the treacherous raiders as though convinced that his hate for the darklings was a weapon in itself. But the rear afterburners of the Reavers were becoming faint as the dark eldar penetrated more deeply into the jungle climate of Ulthwé's forest-domes.

Without lowering his weapon or releasing the trigger, Truqui spat in disgust. 'Reapers!' he yelled, keeping his eyes fixed on the vanishing darklings, watching the threads of reaper rockets tracing their path behind them. Before he could utter another word, his command seemed to be fulfilled: a black Wave Serpent drew out of the tree-line behind him, hovering a metre above the earth, its twin linked shuriken catapults and cannons sizzling with constant fire.

Without turning, Truqui released one hand from its brace along the elegant barrel of his singing weapon and snatched it into a signal. At the sign from their exarch, the squad of Dark Reapers broke their firing lines behind him and vaulted into the anti-grav transport tank. The Wave Serpent accelerated forward, speeding after the rapidly disappearing Reavers. As it flashed past him, Truqui reached out his free hand and caught hold of a brace on the side of the vehicle, lifting himself up onto its hull without taking his eyes off his distant prey.

The massive guns of the Wave Serpent coughed and spat shuriken fire after the Reavers, but the dark eldar jetbikes were too fast and too manoeuvrable to present effective targets weaving erratically between the trees. From the tank's roof, Truqui trained his eyes on the darklings, letting his reaper launcher twitch and scan automatically with his line of sight. He knew that the guns of the Wave Serpent would not be precise enough from this range, but he was an exarch of the Dark Reapers and he lived for moments like this. Squinting his eyes in momentary concentration, Truqui released a volley of rockets from his weapon, targeted into a small, empty clearing in the trees in the distance. There was nothing there.

Whether by divination or calculation, the reaper rockets arrived at exactly the moment when a dark eldar Reaver streaked into the clearing. The warheads punched into the exhaust tubes that protruded out of the back of the jetbike, shattering the rear of the engine block and detonating inside the energy core. The Reaver was wracked with explosions along the line of the exhaust, and then it erupted into a sudden fireball as the engine caught, incinerating the bike and the rider instantly.

Truqui held his gaze on the dying flames for a second and then started to track his next target, realising in dismay that the Reavers were much too fast to be caught by his Wave Serpent. Just as the realisation dawned on him, a bank of Ulthwé guardians slid up alongside the transport tank on gleaming black and silver jetbikes. Truqui turned to acknowledge the timely reinforcements, and the squadron leader nodded in recognition, before gunning her bike and streaking off in pursuit of the Reavers, a squadron of glittering jetbikes falling into formation behind her.

Watching the jetbikes streaking off in pursuit of the vile infiltrators, Truqui cursed beneath his breath, unwilling to accept that his Dark Reapers could not finish the job themselves. Beneath his feet, he could feel the Wave Serpent decelerate, as though attuned to the disappointment flowing from his mind. Then, with a sudden start, it lurched back into acceleration and Truqui grinned. The vehicle banked sharply, angling away from the chase and plunging into the deep jungle like a shark into water. This was not over yet.

THE TWO INQUISITOR lords sat in silence, their features almost invisible in the half-light, hidden in the deep shadows cast by their heavy hoods. Vargas peered over his steepled fingers at the concerned expression on the face of his oldest acquaintance, his eyes glinting with untold pain.

'We have heard nothing for centuries,' muttered Seishon, as though merely voicing his thoughts.

'Perhaps there has been nothing to hear?' offered Vargas, but even he was unconvinced.

'You are too charitable, my old friend.'

'We have no reason not to trust in our arrangements. They were made by devout servants of the Emperor with the glory of the Imperium in mind. We must not doubt ourselves, especially not in such testing times,' replied Vargas, his voice tinged with defensiveness.

Seishon unfolded himself from his chair and stalked over to the viewscreen that dominated the wall. A million stars twinkled back into his bright eyes, filling his mind with expansiveness and icy void. The image was steady and crisp; the old inquisitor might have been looking out of a window at a local starscape, instead of off into the terrible distance. The joint Inquisitorial substation, Ramugan, was positioned as close to the Eye of Terror as was safe, but it was still a very long way away.

'Yes,' he whispered, half to himself. 'These are indeed testing times.'

As he spoke, Seishon leaned closer to the screen, letting his proximity trigger the zooming mechanism that scrolled the designated quadrant into closer focus. A deep red mist was faintly visible around the minor constellation of Circuitrine. The red colour had been deliberately lightened and enhanced on the screen, but the mist was real enough. It was a red so deep that it was almost indistinguishable from the blackness of space around it. Not for the first time in the last few weeks, Seishon wondered whether anybody else had yet noticed it.

'Re-phase and unfilter. Bring up the Eye.' Still seated at the long table in the centre of the room, Vargas snapped the command to an unseen servitor.

The screen flickered and then flashed with colour, forcing Seishon to step back and shade his eyes from the sudden burst of light. The speckled darkness was instantly replaced by a supernova of colours: bright reds and pinks burst out through clouds of blues and purples, riddled with explosions of dark green and rings of yellow. It was as though an impossible quantity of toxic chemicals had suddenly erupted into flames and set the galaxy itself ablaze.

'It is utterly invisible in the lashes of the Eye of Terror,' observed Vargas, as though reading his friend's mind. 'I would be surprised if anyone else has noticed it.'

Seishon nodded slowly as he stared into the blinding maelstrom of warp energy that defined the Eye of Terror on the screen. It was certainly true that the gentle red mist around Circuitrine was imperceptible against the massive rush of energy discharged from the Eye every second.

'I do not share your optimism, old friend,' he said, finally, turning back to face Vargas at the table. 'If we can see it, I am sure that there are agents in the Ordo Malleus who can also see it very clearly. They will not be dissuaded of its importance simply because we have not heard anything about it from the aliens…' Seishon trailed off, realising that he had gone too far. He and Vargas may well be inquisitor lords, and they may be secreted away in the Ordo Xenos sanctum of Ramugan, but walls nearly always had ears, especially in a facility of the Inquisition. And Ramugan was no ordinary facility.

'If it were a major storm, we would have heard,' insisted Vargas, carefully avoiding vocalising the identity of the agents from whom they would have heard. 'Look at where the emissions and eddies are, Seishon! They are pluming out around the Circuitrine nebula. You know full well that our… associates have been based there for untold centuries. They would have told us if there was anything to concern us – that is the very meaning of the coven, after all!' Vargas chose some of his words carefully, but his confidence betrayed him.

'Perhaps,' replied Seishon, as he turned back to the viewscreen. 'But we have heard little from these associates since the coven was formed. I am not sure that we can trust them. I am not even sure that they will remember us at all, when the time comes.

'If the Ordo Malleus have not yet seen this, and if they discover that we have known about it for weeks, there will be questions, Vargas. This is their territory, after all. Why should we be monitoring that quadrant so carefully? Why didn't we share our intelligence with them immediately? These are not questions that I would be prepared to answer before a Hereticus Commission.'

'There will be no questions. Who would dare to interrogate two inquisitor lords of the Ordo Xenos? When was the last time that we received any intelligence from our associates in Malleus, or even Hereticus? Sharing is not what the Inquisition does best, Seishon, not even here in Ramugan,' replied Vargas dismissively. 'Besides, we have nothing to hide, Seishon. Our souls are untarnished.'

'I hope that you're right, old friend,' said Seishon sombrely. 'I hope that you're right.'

EVERY FACE IN the council chamber turned to gaze on the beautiful features of Eldressyn, her translucent white robes cascading freely around her elegant form, as though caught in a divine breeze. She had uttered the words that none had dared to voice for untold centuries, and her startling blue eyes shone with a radiance too terrifying to comprehend.

'There is not strength enough amongst the Sons of Ulthran,' she repeated quietly but with such force that they seemed to penetrate directly into the minds of the eldar on the council. 'We cannot face this threat alone.'

'What you imply is a kind of sacrilege,' hissed the angular and pale face of Ruhklo. He was by far the oldest seer on the council, and his sibilant voice carried the liquid gravity of the years. 'Do you presume that this council did not foresee these events many centuries before you had even seen this chamber? Do you really want to suggest that we are not prepared?'

There was a murmur of assent from the others. It was unthinkable to believe that incidents of this magnitude would have gone unnoticed by the Seer Council. The mighty Eldrad Ulthran himself should have seen them on the horizon from a distance of several millennia.

'If we are so well prepared, Ruhklo of the Karizhariat, then why are our forces so ill-equipped to deal with the darklings?' Eldressyn turned her glorious blue eyes on the veteran seer, peering into his soul and testing his heart.

The old eldar recoiled, as though touched by beautiful, icy fingers.

The grand council chamber of Ulthwé was located in an elaborate dome, high up amongst the peaks and towers that rose gloriously out of the top of the massive craftworld. It was shrouded in a cloud of sha'iel, which made the dome pulse in and out of material existence – only members of the council itself could be guaranteed to find the chamber in phase when they approached its ancient, wraithbone doors. Other visitors might pass through the legendary doorway and find nothing but void on the other side of it. For the uninitiated or the uninvited, the doors to the Seer Council were literally a gateway into the tortured void of the warp itself.

Even though the dark eldar incursions were happening in the very bowels of the craftworld, countless thousands of metres below them, the seers in their grand hall could hear every shuriken burst and feel each shudder of sha'iel released in the various combats that raged. Inside the hall of the Seer Council, the rulers of Ulthwé could bear witness to any event taking place in their massive, sprawling, semi-organic vessel. The infinity circuit itself could be tapped from Ulthran's Dais, the altar in the heart of the chamber, and its labyrinthine expanses reached into every flickering speck of life in Ulthwé.

Hence, even from the sanctuary of the ancient chamber, the councillors were well aware that Eldressyn was not entirely overstating the danger posed by the recent and ongoing raids of the dark-lings.

'Preparation may breed success, young Eldressyn of Ulthroon, but it does not guarantee it. You may bear witness to the ending of time itself, but what would you have us do in order to prepare for it?' The voice of Eldrad Ulthran himself eased into the air, as if from everywhere at once. The sound was so deep that it was almost inaudible.

'Are you saying that this is the end?' answered Eldressyn quickly, forgetting the courtesy owed to the great farseer in the heat of her passion. She glanced suddenly towards the elevated podium in the centre of the chamber, where the shimmering image of Eldrad Ulthran had smoothly faded into existence.

Eldrad's face creased into a complicated smile, mixing paternalism, patience and condescension into a single expression. 'No, my child, I am making no such claims. Events without choices are rarer than the crest feathers of a Phoenix Lord. The end is something we create; it is not something that happens to us. I mean to suggest merely that there are some things that *cannot* be avoided, as well as some things that *should not* be avoided. An ending is nothing more than a failed beginning. We must not fail now.'

'My lord,' replied Eldressyn, recovering herself. 'You are saying that choices must be made–'

'Do not presume to tell Eldrad Ulthran what he means,' interrupted Ruhklo, his voicing hissing through her words like a serrated dagger through flesh.

'He can speak for himself, Ruhklo,' shouted Eldressyn, snapping her glowering eyes round to face him. But, when she turned back, the voice of the great farseer had fallen silent and his glittering image had already faded from the raised dais in the heart of the chamber.

'It seems that he has already spoken enough,' hissed Ruhklo with an acid smile.

For a long moment there was a heavy silence in the cavernous chamber. The shadows that laced the ornate, domed roof like snaking frescoes seemed to slither and twist, as though writhing in the discomfort of the hostile atmosphere. The council chamber of Ulthwé was more than accustomed to this kind of heated debate, as the seers argued and railed about their divergent interpretations of visions, and, over the millennia, the tortuous energies exuded from the eldar seers had gradually seeped into the structure of the chamber itself. Every few thousand years, the hall had to be ritually purified by Eldrad Ulthran himself in order to prevent it from exerting its own violence on the council of seers that met within its hallowed walls.

Eldressyn sighed and glanced around the assembled councillors. She was relatively new to this chamber, and she was one of the youngest seers to be appointed to the ruling body of Ulthwé for generations. It was rumoured that her appointment had been forced through by Ulthran himself; such a rumour was enough for some eldar to fear the role that fate held in store for the beautiful, young female, and it was more than enough for others to hate her youthful brilliance. Ruhklo, an ancient seer from a family of seers that stretched back for millennia, was certainly to be counted amongst the latter. Nobody knew Ulthran's own opinion on the matter – it was often hard to understand his opinion on anything.

There are many things unclear, said Thae'akzi, reluctant to break the silence and so speaking directly with her mind. *But one thing that cannot be hidden from even the least sensitive of minds is the turmoil in the Eye itself.*

The others nodded, relieved that the maturity of the Emerald Seer had returned calm to the council once again. None of them could remember a time when Thae'akzi had not been on the council – not even Ruhklo. She was a constant presence in the collective mind, soothing and calm, like a psychic balm. In the absence of Eldrad Ulthran himself, it was to Thae'akzi that the councillors looked for leadership and guidance. For the last few decades, Ulthran had been increasingly absent from the council, present only as a ghostly apparition and a resonant voice. The reasons for his absence were unspoken, but the council accepted on faith that his actions had the welfare of Ulthwé at heart. The seers whispered that he was preparing himself for something in the future – something unavoidable that loomed like a menace just over the temporal horizon, just beyond the restrictions of their own sight.

Eldressyn bowed her head slightly, acknowledging the wisdom of the older seer. They were the only two females on the council, but their bond was far more profound than the vulgar simplicities of gender. Their bond appeared to reside in their mutually complicated and unspoken relationship with Eldrad Ulthran himself. In different ways, he had chosen them both personally – to one he had granted the emerald robes of seniority, and to the other he had given a place on the council, honouring her in advance of her years. They were the chosen ones, and they felt their commonality even in the absence of any discussion about it. They took it on faith that Ulthran would not have brought them together on the council without a reason.

Yes, Thae'akzi of the Emerald House, it is true that the Eye's stare has become unusually fierce. The darkling raids are a menace to Ulthwé, but the swirling torrents of sha'iel that spill out of the Eye with them represent something far more terrible. Not since the loss of Altansar have we witnessed signs like this. The heavens are full of agony, and the stars weep like children. The ancient Bhurolyn, bedecked in glorious sapphire robes that were edged with a phosphorescent black, seemed calm, but his thoughts were tinged with an anxiety that was shared by them all.

Something is emerging from the future, bearing down on us like the sky itself. It is too huge to be distinguished, but we can even now feel the gravity that its existence exerts on the present, continued Bhurolyn, the tinge of anxiety germinating into a hint of hysteria.

Yes, Bhurolyn of the Sacred Star, the future contains something beyond the ability of this council to comprehend. It looks like an ending, beyond which there is an expansive nothingness that sucks the soul from our breasts and the breath from our lips. But that future lies invisibly on the other side of our choices in the present. Eldressyn's thoughts were calm and smooth, like strong fingers in a velvet glove.

We must shed light into our future through our actions now. The darklings raid our craftworld at will, darting through the lower levels of Ulthwé and stealing away our eldar brethren as prisoners. We cannot allow this to happen. The darklings must be stopped. Her thoughts were gathering passion once again.

I do not understand why Ulthran would allow Ulthwé to occupy a timeline that passed through this present. We have always survived in the past by navigating around crises of this nature – by avoiding all of the presents that represent a threat to our future. This present looks like a disastrous mistake–

Compose yourself, Bhurolyn, interjected Thae'akzi, cutting him off. *Lord Ulthran does not control the stars or the rivers of time, he merely navigates a path through them. There is not always even a single route clear of storms–*

And sometimes you must weather a storm to reach the safety of port, offered Eldressyn, as though concluding the older seer's thoughts.

'What do you suggest that we do?' asked Ruhklo bluntly, breaking the psychic communion and shattering the silence of the council chamber. He could see where the conversation was heading, and he was damned if he was going to let it get there without a word of protest.

Eldressyn turned her implacable eyes back to the Karizhariat Seer. 'Ulthwé is ill-equipped to confront the darklings on its own. We must call for aid.'

'And who will come to our aid?' asked Bhurolyn, his tone suggesting that he could think of nobody. 'Altansar was lost long ago, and the other craftworld eldar are scattered throughout the webway. They are too distant and care not for our safety. And the harlequins have no force that could be of assistance to us now, breathtaking though they may be.'

'The mon-keigh will come,' stated Eldressyn simply, as though oblivious to the shock and outrage that such a suggestion would provoke.

'You realise that you could be thrown off the council for such sacrilege!' boomed Ruhklo. 'Ulthwé will never stoop to request aid from those animals. It would be unprecedented. I am sure that Lord Ulthran would never stand for such a heinous idea.'

'You would be wrong to make such an assumption, Ruhklo of the Karizhariat, and you are well aware of that. Many millennia ago, Eldrad Ulthran himself made a covenant with the mon-keigh. You yourself were there. The Coven of Isha still stands to this day. We could call on the mon-keigh for aid… if the council is in agreement,' explained Thae'akzi calmly but with some hesitation.

Ruhklo glared at the Emerald Seer, his eyes burning with suppressed fury, as though she had just insulted him terribly. 'The council does not agree, Thae'akzi of the Green Robes. Not now, and it did not agree in the past either, as you well know. Ulthwé needs no help from the stinking, ruinous, primitive "Imperium of Man".'

As the words slid out of his throat, a shrill scream drew itself across the collective minds of the council, as though a jagged blade were being dragged against a metal plate. Involuntarily, the council shivered, wincing at the psychic violence that convulsed through the infinity circuit of their craftworld. Deep in the bowels of Ulthwé, death was clawing at the souls of their eldar brethren.

BEFORE HE TURNED the last corner in the passageway, the Ulthwé warlock, Shariele, could already hear the screams of the eldar guardians. There was a flood of psychic agony in the corridor, making the atmosphere thick and toxic, as though the souls of his kinsmen were already decaying in the fecundity of the craftworld's bowels. Even before he turned the corner, he knew what he would see and his blood boiled with hatred and pain at the prospect.

The guardian squad had already been reduced to three beleaguered eldar warriors. Their comrades, broken and twisted beyond recognition, as though tortured to death by visions of their own personal hells, lay dead, scattered across the floor like slaughtered animals. Darting between the corpses, feasting on their decomposing flesh, flashed creatures of another realm. Their yellow teeth glinted with decay even as they plunged into the pale skin of the slain eldar, slobbering toxic saliva into the puncture wounds. Their green claws pawed at the bodies, shredding the pallid flesh like tenderised meat. And when Shariele rounded the corner to face them, their pitch-black eyes snapped instantly to meet his own, singeing his thoughts with visions of hell as a dim light sparked off the barbed silver spikes along their spines.

Crunching his eyes into starbursts of hate, Shariele immediately reached forward with his arms and unleashed roiling blasts of psychic lightning from his open hands. The flames of sha'iel crunched into the faces of the two warp beasts, blasting them clear of their prey and sending them skidding over the blood-sheened wraithbone deck. They crashed up against the legs of a breathtaking darkling wych, who howled at them in disgust. She cracked her cackling warp whip across their backs, making them rear in agony and shriek with terrifying force. Then the beasts scrambled back to their feet and lurched forward again, bounding and leaping towards the eldar warlock, as though more afraid of their mistress than their enemy.

For a fraction of a second, Shariele flicked his eyes to the scene beyond the figure of the dark eldar beast mistress. He could see the shimmering curtain of a warp gate stretched across the corridor, unspeakably dark images roiling and swimming towards the surface from its ineffable depths. In an instant he realised that the gate had to be closed – it was a portal from the dark realms directly into Ulthwé itself.

As the two warp beasts charged towards him, snarling with uncontrollable hatred, Shariele also noticed the rest of the scene in the corridor around him. The three remaining Ulthwé guardians were spinning and yelling, firing their weapons in all directions at once, as though driven mad by the turmoil that seethed around them. Finally, the warlock noticed the suggestions of two shapely figures dancing through the shadows with incredible speed. Flashes of dark blades caught his eye as another of the Ulthwé guardians collapsed to the ground clutching a gaping wound across his neck. Wyches, realised Shariele, his thoughts knotted in disgust.

As the warp beasts pounced, Shariele stood his ground. He reached his burning hands forward with his fingers spread wide, holding them out like pathetic shields against the bestial fury of the vile creatures. But as the warp beasts reached their jaws around his arms, a convulsion of purple energy ripped through the warlock's body, radiating power like a dying star. The yellow teeth dug through Shariele's psychoplastic armour, but as they touched his skin they sizzled and vaporised instantly.

Like a potent venom, the thrill of Shariele's touch spread rapidly through the bodies of the two beasts, transforming each into a stinking cloud of vaporised warp-energy. In less than a second, the clouds lost their shape and all evidence of the warp beasts vanished from the material realm.

The hate riddled wail of the darkling beast mistress was incredible. It rippled throughout the whole of the craftworld, sending waves pulsing through the spirit pool itself. She strode forward, cracking her warp whip and spinning the immense talon that served as a halberd. As she advanced towards Shariele, the two wyches that had been plaguing the remnants of the guardian squad appeared at her side, spinning their vicious blades with deathly grace.

Meanwhile, the two remaining guardians regrouped at Shariele's shoulders and braced their shuriken catapults for a final battle over the corpses and souls of their brethren. For a moment, both sides paused as though weighing up the confrontation between the ancient and disremembered kin. Both sides had heard legends of the time when the eldar and dark eldar were not as different as they were now. For both, the thought merely inspired even greater hatred for the other. After less than a second, both sides let out curdling cries and charged.

THE GAP WAS closing quickly. Dhrykna's squadron of guardians knew the jungles of Ulthwé's forest domes down to the last tree and their jetbikes flashed through the foliage as though completely unobstructed. Although they were fast and manoeuvrable, the Reavers up ahead had never been this far into Ulthwé before. The darkling riders were relying on their impressive reflexes and instincts to thread them through the dense jungle.

Without turning, Dhrykna knew that Exarch Truqui and his Dark Reapers had abandoned the chase; there was no way that their Wave Serpent could keep pace in this terrain. Besides, formidable though the Dark Reapers may be in ranged combat, they were not at their best in high speed chases through confined environments. Dhrykna was sure that Truqui would find a more appropriate way to engage these raiders, and she was not disappointed.

Blasting out of the tree line in pursuit of the streaking red and black Reavers, her shuriken cannons flaring with fire, Dhrykna grinned. Up ahead, arrayed across the access tunnels that peppered the boundary wall of the forest dome, she could clearly see the shining black form of the Dark Reapers. Truqui had left the Wave Serpent blocking the main tunnel mouth, with its long gun barrels angled forward into the forest. As soon as Dhrykna had broken the tree line, she could see the reaper cannons firing on the Reavers that screamed forward towards the tunnels, directly towards the waiting line of Aspect Warriors. Truqui had established a crossfire.

The darkling raiders showed no signs of slowing. Instead, the remaining Reavers started to twitch and swerve even more erratically, roaring towards the bank of fire at greater and greater speeds. Dhrykna lay low over the fuel tank in front of her, pressing her body down against the humming machine beneath her as she willed it to catch the speeding enemies, a stream of shuriken fire lashing out of the nose batteries of her jetbike.

One of the Reavers spluttered and decelerated rapidly, smoke pluming from its engines where the jetbikes of the guardian squadron had riddled it with fire. Dhrykna had to bank abruptly to avoid the wreck as her bike flashed past it in pursuit of the rest of the raiders – the interval between hunter and quarry had been reduced to less than a second. As she zipped past the ruined Reaver, she glanced at the figures of two eldar hunched over the saddle. One was a semi-clad, wild haired darkling, grinning and whooping insanely as his Reaver splintered and vaporised beneath him, but the other was sitting in calm silence, her gentle beauty so incongruous that it was startling. In an instant,

Dhrykna realised that the second figure was an Ulthwé eldar – probably an artist or a dancer, judging by the elegance of her robes. Were the dark ones taking prisoners?

In the fraction of a moment that it took her to consider turning back, the ruined Reaver was wracked with heavy fire from the Wave Serpent's cannons, transforming it into an explosive fireball that incinerated all organic matter within a ten metre radius. Whoever she was, the Ulthwé artist was now a casualty of war.

Two more Reavers plumed into smoke and dropped behind the leading pack, run through by volleys of staunch fire from the waiting bank of Dark Reapers. Dhrykna kept focused on the fastest of the raiders, watching it weave and thread itself around the tirades of fire that erupted from the Aspect Warriors up ahead, ignoring the rapidly increasing casualty rate amongst the other dark eldar riders.

After only a matter of seconds, the leading Reaver reached the bank of Dark Reapers. Dhrykna could see Truqui tracking the darkling, spraying out a hail of rockets as it flashed through the Aspect Warriors' position. But the Reaver was too fast to be tracked at such close range, and it roared through the eldar emplacement without receiving so much as a scratch, vanishing instantly into the shadows of the access tunnels beyond. Moments later, two more Reavers flashed through the line of Dark Reapers, shrieking into the tunnels in pursuit of their leader.

Lying almost completely flat against her jetbike, Dhrykna gunned the engine and roared past Truqui for the second time that day. This time she did not pause to share a greeting, but she rolled her bike on its axis as she passed the Dark Reapers, suggesting both a salute and a reproach for letting the raiders through. The rest of her squadron sped into the access tunnels behind her, desperate to stop the Reavers before they could make their escape with the prisoners.

Truqui watched them go and cursed, muttering an incantation to Maugan Ra, reproaching him for the failure of the Dark Reapers, but beseeching him to give strength to Dhrykna's guardians. The Harvester of Souls should not permit the souls of the eldar to be harvested by anyone else.

THE IMAGE OF the deep red mist filled the wall of Inquisitor Lord Seishon's chamber. A feed from the main image amplifiers had been connected to Seishon's personal quarters so that he could keep an eye on developments as they happened. The dull, ruddy light of the gathering cloud filled the apartments with long, dark shadows, since the inquisitor had not activated any of the other light sources. He was sitting in the near-darkness in silence, gazing at the mist, considering his options, and resting his head against a tube of paper that had just been delivered to him.

He already knew what was written on the message scroll. He had heard the rumours and the reports circulating through the intricately bugged, anti-bugged and de-anti-bugged corridors of Ramugan. If there was one thing that could be relied on in a substation shared by more than one branch of the Inquisition, it was that nobody could keep a secret.

Seishon shook his head involuntarily and sighed. What a perfect place to keep a secret, he thought. Right under the noses of everyone who would be interested in it. Nobody would dare to suppose that a secret coven was housed in a facility that provided a base of action for all three arms of the Inquisition simultaneously. Ramugan was the last place that such an institution should be found, which made it the perfect home for the Coven of Isha.

It had been there for centuries, since its inception. In truth, the existence of the coven lay at the foundations of the rationale for the substation's very existence. What could possibly have convinced the three services to co-operate on the development and maintenance of a station so close to the Eye of Terror? The expense of such a facility was astronomical, and the psychic shielding required to keep the residents sane was absurd. It was the worst possible place for a base of operations. It was the most troublesome possible location. Only together could the Inquisitorial services sustain the station.

After Ramugan had been built, people stopped wondering about its rationale. Existence has its own weight. People accept things once they exist, once they have invested in them. So it was with Ramugan: the substation was created to service the Coven of Isha, but as time passed and the coven was never activated, everyone forgot about it and it passed into legend. Legends are quickly forgotten or buried in the vaults of massive libraries with infinite aisles of books and numberless pages of documents. Soon, nobody can remember them at all.

Seishon could remember. Vargas knew. And there were a few others in the Ordo Xenos who were initiated into the coven after they had proven their worth and been seconded to the substation of Ramugan. For most junior Xenos inquisitors, a posting to Ramugan seemed like a nightmare assignment. It was now well-known as an Ordo Malleus stronghold, and for good reason. Its proximity to the Eye of Terror meant that the station could serve as an early warning post if anything started to spill out of the maelstrom. More than once it had been used as a base of operations for the Grey Knights Chapter of Space Marines. And it suited the secrecy of the coven to allow the local sub-sector of the Ordo Malleus to invest Ramugan with its own identity.

Nodding faintly, Seishon flicked open the scroll and scanned the text that had been handwritten onto the parchment.

Inquisitor Lord Seishon of the Ordo Xenos, Ramugan sub-sector.

A matter has come to my attention that requires your wisdom. I dutifully request your presence at an Inquisitorial concert in the Chambers of Conference. Although it is principally a matter for the attention of the Ordo Malleus, it appears that you may also have some interest in these circumstances. For this reason, and for the glory of the Imperium itself, I trust that you will satisfy my request.

In service and in faith,
Glorina Caesurian, Inquisitor Lord, Ordo Hereticus,
Ramugan sub-sector.

It was as he had expected. Despite his anachronistic revulsion to the way Glorina had adopted the traditionally male honorific of 'lord,' Seishon knew better than to doubt her resolve or power. He stood and smoothed his cloak, before turning and breezing out of the door.

THE WARP GATE oscillated at their backs, sending crestless waves rippling across its surface in a curtain of sha'iel. Kroulir and Druqura thrilled, spinning their short blades in their hands and grinning. Quruel, the mistress of the beasts, was alive with fury in front of them, lashing out with her warp whip and daring the effete eldar to approach her talon tipped halberd. The three wyches moved with a sickly grace, as though oozing through the tension filled atmosphere.

Only a few metres down the corridor, the eldar guardians persisted in their feeble attempt to defend the lowest reaches of Ulthwé. Two warriors were braced with their species' characteristic weapon – the shuriken catapult – spraying out clouds of monomolecular projectiles that hissed and whined with toxicity as they sizzled through the air. The third figure, standing in mock defiance between the other two, was a weakling warlock. His cloak billowed out behind him with dramatic effect, but the jagged blasts of warp energy that jousted from his fingers were no match for the power of the beast mistress.

Quruel was actually laughing as the warlock's energy engulfed her form. Her head was thrown back and she was howling with sickening pleasure as her body was wracked with pain and burning agony, her feet slowing lifting off the ground.

Somewhere behind the tumult of battle, Kroulir could hear the distant roar of Reavers and the staccato percussion of rocket fire impacting into the substructure of the craftworld itself. Even as she spun and pirouetted around the shuriken fire from the guardians before her, Kroulir could make out the cackling cry of the raiding party as their signatures pierced the psychic soup of the corridor. They would be there soon, she grinned.

Stooping and spinning, she kicked up into a graceful arc, spiralling forward towards one of the clumsily immobile lightlings, letting the weight of her outstretched blades carry her forward. At the last moment, the lightling guardian staggered back, his shuriken catapult still spitting its lethal projectiles as he struggled to keep his feet amongst the fallen corpses of his kin. But Kroulir's momentum carried her, and her blades sliced down through the eldar's weapon, paring the barrel in two and rendering it into a useless mass of sparking connections.

Before Kroulir could turn again and force her blades to kiss the flesh of the reeling lightling, a blast of energy struck the side of her body, lifting her off her feet and smacking her against the side wall of the corridor. She shrieked with frustration as she slid down the wall, snapping her glowering eyes around to face the warlock that had dared to interrupt her killing dance. The fingers of his left hand still crackled with flashes of sha'iel, while the right maintained its torrent against Quruel, holding her aloft like a burning icon.

Narrowing her eyes with hate, Kroulir clambered back to her feet. How dare the lightling warlock interfere with the plans of the wych queen? Who was he to stand in the path of fate? Did he really think that his cheap tricks could hold back the tide of the future? She spat in disgust, drawing the back of her hand across her mouth to wipe the saliva from her lips, but as she did so she cut a deep gash into her forearm with her teeth and sliced a bloody tear into her lips with her dagger at the same time. Her face shimmered with blood and hatred as she glared at the eldar warlock.

Druqura had engaged the second guardian, who had abandoned his catapult and produced a long, curving sword, which he flourished with some skill. The beast mistress herself was still held in the flood of warp energy that gushed out of the warlock's other hand. Kroulir could see Quruel's teeth flashing and arcing with power as she drank in the warlock's power like a desert absorbing rain. It had been a long time since Kroulir had seen her mistress so happy, and for a moment she even pitied the hapless lightling warlock, who probably thought that Quruel was suffering terribly in the onslaught.

A sudden blast of noise shook the corridor, as though something had just exploded, sending shockwaves throbbing through the wraithbone structure. An instant later, and a plume of flame billowed into sight, expanding down the corridor towards the combatants and the shimmering warp gate, consuming the air and filling the space instantly. As one, the eldar and dark eldar ceased fighting and turned to face the fiery tide.

A dark shadow appeared in the heart of the inferno, as though something were rushing through the flames. Then the roar of a Reaver engine flooded into the confines of the corridor and a black and red jetbike erupted out of the fireball, its splinter rifles hissing into life as the rider spotted the eldar guardians and the warlock ahead of it.

Kroulir watched the lightling eldar scatter for cover as the remnants of the Reaver raiding party and the fire flashed through the corridor. The feeble warlock even released Quruel.

Running the tip of her tongue around her bloody lips as the flames caressed her exposed skin, Kroulir smiled. The wych queen would be pleased, and that could mean a symphony of exquisite pain when she returned.

The Reavers ploughed on, plunging into the shimmering curtain of the warp gate and vanishing instantaneously from the bowels of Ulthwé. With a brisk nod to the two wyches, Quruel flipped backwards into the portal and vanished, as though she were merely diving into a deep, dark pool. Kroulir and Druqura shared a look as the lightling jetbikes emerged from the smoke and dissipating flames in the corridor, roaring in pursuit of the already vanished Reavers. The lead rider's eyes were set with ferocious intent, focused intensely on the warp gate ahead of her.

With a swift sequence of elegant movements, Kroulir and Druqura spun and flipped to the sides of the corridor, flicking and twitching their fingers over the devices that they had established so recently, reversing the sequence with effortless speed. The curtain of sha'iel between them started to flicker and pulse, as though losing its already dubious stability. It flashed and strobed as material reality started to repel its immaterial structure.

Druqura dived quickly into the fading portal, plunging after her escaping kin. But Kroulir paused for a moment. She turned her back to the collapsing warp gate and stared into the eyes of the charging jetbike rider, watching the desperation piercing the squadron leader's mind. *You are too slow*, muttered Kroulir into the thoughts of the lightling rider.

With ostentatious and deliberate slowness, Kroulir stepped backwards and blinked out of existence. Instantly, the warp gate collapsed around her, making the space it had occupied implode in on itself. Less than a second later, Dhrykna's silver and black jetbike flashed through the location of the vanished portal, missing its mark by the tiniest of temporal distances and skidding to a halt just millimetres from the solid wraithbone wall beyond.

CHAPTER TWO:
THE COVEN

IT WAS HIGHLY unusual for senior ranking representatives of the three branches of the Emperor's Inquisition to occupy the same station; it was almost unthinkable that they would sit in the same room. Hence, the Ramugan Chambers of Conference, which had been specially constructed for exactly this purpose, were so rarely used that a special detachment of menials had to be sent to prepare them before the Inquisitorial conference could commence. Following the departure of the bustling sanitization team, a bank of cloaked Inquisitorial mystics was deployed around the perimeter of the great hall, where they dropped to their knees and began to chant litanies of purification. After a few minutes the chambers were filled with the resonant, rasping voices of the mystics and the thick, smoky reassurance of incense.

The main chamber had three great archways, one cut massively into the adamantium structure of each side of the triangular room. On the centre stone of each archway was the emblem of one of the branches of the Inquisition, cut in tiny but intricate precision, all but invisible to the casual observer. In the heart of the triangulated, domed ceiling of the main chamber, a massive Inquisitorial icon had been carved in relief, dominating the room. Beyond the archways were three identically constructed antechambers, entrance to which was provided by three identical doors.

At exactly the same moment, each of the three entranceways opened and the Inquisitorial retinues slipped into the sub-chambers, establishing themselves around the circular walls and securing the space within. Only the inquisitor lords themselves would be permitted to pass through the archways into the main chamber – their retinues would have to wait in the antechambers. But after long decades of service in the Emperor's Inquisition, their lordships were not naïve enough to appear before even another servant of the Emperor without first making plans for every possible contingency. Their retinues served as much for security as for ceremony.

The Chambers of Conference had been specially designed to accommodate the mutual, internal suspicions of the Inquisition without heightening them. The triangular room, which offered precisely equal space and position to each of the arms of the service, was a masterpiece of diplomatic architecture. The elaborate archways, which bristled with every kind of alarm and sensor known to the Imperium, but which disguised each and every one as a decoration or tribute to the lords who might pass through it, were the epitome of refined, elegant distrust. The readouts from the various sensors could be read from the monitors in each of the three antechambers – hence, the retinues of each inquisitor lord could keep each of the other retinues under continuous surveillance.

The only glitch in the design was one of timing: if any of the retinues entered before the others, it was theoretically possible that a stealthy and lithe assassin or death cultist could slip through the archway and secrete herself in the main chamber without the other retinues being able to note the sensor displays. Custom had conspired to solve the problem by dictating that all three retinues must enter the chambers simultaneously. If this custom were breached, then the aggrieved parties would have indisputable grounds to call off the conference.

The mystics that lined the main chamber were specially selected from all three arms of the Inquisition and subjected to egregious cycles of hypnotherapy by each of the services. Their minds were carefully picked apart by interrogators and explicators, who worked to ensure that the psychic potentials of the mystics remained potent but that their capacity to innovate or create the impulse to employ those abilities for themselves was entirely eradicated. By the time they were permitted to enter the Chambers of Conference, they were little more than psychic menials, producing a constant atmosphere of purity and calm, effectively blocking out the various formidable psychic powers of some of the inquisitor lords themselves.

Inquisitor Lord Seishon stood in the doorway to the circular antechamber of the Ordo Xenos, watching his retinue spread out around the walls with practiced efficiency. He shook his head in faint despondence, disappointed yet again by the elaborate ceremony of distrust enacted between ostensible comrades. The Inquisition was a vast and complicated institution, and it was certainly not monolithic, but it saddened him that there could be such passionate distrust amongst the agents of the Emperor even there on Ramugan.

As he took his first step into the ancient chamber, he laughed quietly, realising that the distrust was entirely justified, there more than anywhere – Zhaul, Seishon's Vindicare assassin, was the first member of his retinue to enter the chamber. In the past, he had sent her to hide in the domed ceiling vaults of the main chamber days before a conference, just in case. This time, he had not had sufficient notice for such precautions, and it worried him. After all, he didn't even trust Vargas.

He strode through the circular room, paying no attention to the banks of monitors that flashed and bleeped against the wall. There was really no point in worry about the alarms and sensors: if an alarm sounded, then the threat was too clumsy to worry about; if an alarm failed to sound, it was already all over. For a moment he wondered whether his compatriots in the Ordo Malleus and Ordo Hereticus were really reassured by the presence of the alarm systems. He suspected that they were not.

What a ridiculous set-up, he reflected as he passed into the grand, triangular conference chamber.

Pausing for a moment, he noted that cloaked figures were already waiting under the other two archways: Lord Aurelius from the Ordo Malleus and Hereticus Lord Caesurian. He nodded to them and walked forward towards the conference table.

IN THE ICY shadows of the mountain pass, a tiny starburst of light sparked out of the librarian's eyes as he knelt softly by the shoulder of his fallen battle-brother. He appeared to be checking his comrade for vital signs, holding his palm over the shattered Marine's face as though attempting to feel life itself emanating from his frazzled mind.

The kneeling librarian paused, as though noticing a noise on the edge of hearing. Slowly, he turned his head under the deep folds of his heavy hood, bringing his glittering eyes around with patient deliberation.

How can I be of service? Before he had even turned, the thoughts were already out of his head and pushing implacably into the minds of the two Marines that stood waiting for his attention.

The two towering, black armoured Marines showed no outward signs of surprise. Their helmets and heavy visors obscured even the faintest hint of human emotion. They simply nodded a silent greeting towards the librarian, who remained stooped over his comrade with one hand resting delicately over his bleeding face. Only the librarian's burning eyes were turned towards the newcomers.

A rattle of explosions shook the mountain pass, shaking rockfalls from the cliff faces above and below, and sending avalanches of snow cascading down into the valley. The two Deathwatch Marines did not even flinch, and Librarian Ashok of the Angels Sanguine hardly seemed to notice.

'As you can see, you do not come at the most convenient of times,' said Ashok, his voice hardly more than a whisper as he rose to his feet. He paused and then gestured up the rock face behind him. 'The orks have been driven into the mountains, but they are not yet a spent force. They will regroup if they are not broken now.'

'The orks are not our concern, librarian,' replied one of the Marines flatly, as another boom of ordnance smashed into the narrow pathway, showering them with fragments of stone and ice. A single patch on the Marine's right shoulder had been left uncovered by the pitch-black colouring of the Deathwatch, and Ashok could see an emblem that identified the Marine as a chaplain of the Reviler Chapter, a successor of the Raven Guards. Despite himself, the librarian's jaw clenched in agitation.

Ashok knew that there was nothing he could say. He knew that there was nothing he *should* say. He had been initiated into the Deathwatch many years before, after he had conquered his rage on Hegelian IX, leading the remnants of the Angels Sanguine Death Company in a tyranid hunt through the catacombs. Since then, he had been called upon to serve the sacred Emperor's Inquisition a number of times, and on none of those occasions had he been *asked*. The Deathwatch did not ask. He had been sworn into service, and it would be his honour to perform his duty. Why else did all initiates into the elite service leave their armour painted black, even when they returned to their home Chapters, even at the risk of offending the machine-spirits of their armour, leaving only one shoulder guard to proudly display the emblem of their own Chapters? To have been in the Deathwatch even once meant that you must be ever ready for its call again. It was the greatest honour that a Space Marine could be awarded.

As though reading the librarian's mind, the chaplain continued. 'The Emperor's will does not await the leisure of his servants, Librarian Ashok.'

Ashok turned slowly away from his fallen brethren, bringing his shadowed face around to fully confront the Deathwatch Marines for the first time. The chaplain's words had stung him unnecessarily, and, for an instant, his eyes flickered with a primal, red fire. He was more than aware of his duty, and he certainly did not need to be reminded of it by this Reviler. He was the bearer of the Shroud of Lemartes, the Guardian of the Damned; there was nobody whose soul had been through more in the name of the Emperor.

'This Marine can yet be saved,' he said, controlling his ire and indicating the Angel Sanguine who lay broken on the ground behind him. Ashok had deliberately turned his gaze on the second Deathwatch Marine, who had remained silent until now. A burst of blood-red on his auto-reactive shoulder plate told him that the Marine was a Blood Angel, and Ashok was confident that he would not want to see their common gene-seed wasted in this arbitrary display of authority and duty. They both knew that the blood-line had grown perilously thin over the last few decades.

There was a moment of hesitation before the Deathwatch Marine of the Blood Angels spoke. 'Very well,' he said simply. 'We will take your battle-brother back to a med-station. But we have no time for the orks, librarian. The orders of the Ordo Xenos are not to be taken lightly, and we must make haste. It has taken us longer than expected to find you, detached from your squad and so high in the mountains. The Angels Sanguine Death Company will be more than a match for the orks here on Trontium VI, even without you, I am sure.'

'Thank you,' nodded Ashok with genuine gratitude, as the red fires in his eyes faded to a fathomless black.

THE FAINTLY PULSING image hovered like a mythical bird, floating effortlessly over the wraithbone dais in the hidden sanctum of the Coven of Isha. The small, circular chamber occupied an unusual space within the substructure of the Ramugan station. It would have been impossible to mark its location on a schematic, since it was not entirely present in the material realm. In the forgotten past, when the station had first been constructed, Farseer Eldrad Ulthran of the Ulthwé craftworld had supplied the chamber for the coven himself, presumably fore-seeing that its secrecy would be important in the years to come. Now, the wraithbone chamber teetered on the edge of material reality, almost entirely enveloped by the tortuous and incomprehensible currents of the warp, from which it was protected by the mysterious eldar materials and craftsmanship.

Inquisitor Lord Vargas sat in the ceremonial throne that was cut into one of the interior walls of the sanctum, watching the flickering holograph of Farseer Ulthran gradually materialise above the podium in front of him.

Vargas had been the keeper of the coven for more than thirty years, but never once in that time had he come into contact with Ulthran himself. Never once in that time had the coven been invoked. Indeed, the records of past coven-keepers, hidden away in a small librarium that was kept out of sight and out of reality by being dipped entirely into the otherworld-liness of the warp, suggested that the coven had never been activated in its entire history. Not once.

The eldar had provided information to the coven-keepers of the Ramugan Ordo Xenos, but they had never asked for anything in return. And the infor-mation itself had usually proven ambiguous or even dangerous. Records in the coven librarium traced intricate and mind-bending links between these intelligence reports and apparently disastrous events in the history of the Imperium such as the Sanapan Scouring, the Mortis Annihilation, the Third Com-ing of Orian and even the epic Battle of Armageddon.

As a consequence of the relative inactivity of the pact, even Vargas himself had fallen victim to moments of doubt about its authenticity: perhaps it was only a legend after all? It was only his direct experience of the sanctum and the librarium that reassured him of the coven's continued existence: there was simply no other explanation for the secret presence of the largest wraithbone construction in the Imperium, nor for the existence of a force shielded tentacle that prodded out from Ramugan into the webway, attached to a little librarium that was filled with the scribblings of generations of inquisitor lords.

Just keeping these things secret from the rest of the Inquisition was a terrible heresy, although secreting away xenos technology for reasons of research was part of the raison d'être of the Ordo Xenos. It was an open secret, although even that was frowned on by some of the more puritanical inquisitors. There were even members of the Ordo Xenos who did not approve of attempting to make use of alien technology at all. The late Lord Agustius, for example, had been so adverse to all types of technology that he had even refused to accept bionic implants in his crippled legs, preferring instead to trundle about in his wheelchair.

Thankfully, inquisitors of Agustius's persuasion were rather rarer in the Ordo Xenos than in the other arms of the Inquisition – the Thorian Puritans, for example, had very few members amongst the alien hunters. It was difficult, after all, to reconcile the need to hunt the alien without simultaneously developing an appreciation for their technologies.

Particularly *eldar* technology, mused Vargas as he gazed around the wraithbone chamber once again. It never ceased to amaze him. He was sure that the Adeptus Mechanicus would risk a small war to appropriate this chamber, just to take it apart and see what made it tick.

Unfortunately for Vargas and the other keepers of the coven, although puritanical inquisitors might be relatively scarce within the Ordo Xenos, in this sub-sector at least, the alien hunters were not alone on Ramugan. The local Ordo Malleus and especially Ordo Hereticus were riddled with the kind of self-righteous Puritanism that drove Vargas to distraction.

Some of them must have heard the rumours and legends about the coven, but it was beyond their wit to locate the sanctum or librarium, and they must have considered it ridiculous to believe that such an institution could have existed for all these long millennia without taking any action whatsoever. Even for those who had heard the stories, the Coven of Isha was little more than a fantasy ascribed to the mythical figure of Eldrad Ulthran, on whom the inquisitors of Ramugan liked to pin responsibility for any unexplained disasters in the quadrant. Hardly anyone even thought that he was real – he was just an emblem, a caricature of the cunning, manipulative and merciless eldar.

Yes, thought Vargas, watching the ineffably elegant figure of the eldar farseer materialise before him, the coven is safer here than it might be anywhere else in the Imperium.

Greetings, Lord Vargas… As they flowed into his mind, the words were cold and fathomless, like currents running along the bottom of a deep ocean. They seemed to wash back and forth, trailing off as though forgotten in mid-sentence. The sanctum glowed and pulsed with life as Ulthran's mind made its presence felt.

Vargas nodded uncertainly. He was not a great psyker himself, and was unsure how to communicate with the eldar apparition. Part of his mind thrilled at the contact from so eminent a presence. He had never dared to dream that he would come into direct contact with Eldrad Ulthran himself. Now, it seemed, the ancient farseer even knew his name.

You may speak. I will hear you, lord. The thoughts warmed slightly, as though trying to reassure Vargas's mind with a new atmosphere of comfort. Despite himself, Vargas smiled at the use of the word 'lord.' He was a vain man, and not beyond flattery, even by aliens.

'You honour me with your... presence, Lord Ulthran,' managed Vargas, uncommonly flustered in his speech. He felt like an excited child.

Yes, replied Eldrad simply. It was true. *I am pleased to see that the Coven of Isha remains honoured amongst the servants of... your Emperor.* There was a pause before the farseer spoke the exalted title, as though he were going to say something else. Vargas gasped, anticipating the revelation of a personal name; he had heard the rumours that Ulthran and the Emperor were not strangers to each other. But, he was disappointed.

'It has been carefully and patiently maintained, my... Lord Ulthran,' replied Vargas honestly, fighting the sudden impulse to address the farseer as his own lord. 'We stand ready to fulfil our side of the coven.'

That is good, Lord Vargas, for the time has come at last, as we knew that it must. The tides of time and space have been swept by ill winds to bring us to this place. But we are here, and it is only with the present that we cannot argue. Although it is only in the present that we may fight. And fight we must, servant of the Golden Throne. Fight you must. Doom skirts the horizon like a rising star, and Ulthwé has need of your warriors to prevent its ascension into the heavens. As it says in the Coven of Isha, it is for me that you do this, and it is for... your Emperor.

Despite himself, Vargas bowed his head in deference to the farseer. When he looked up, the holograph had vanished and the wraithbone chamber was darkly silent once again.

THE MASSIVE VIEWSCREEN that filled the wall still glittered with stars, holding the slowly expanding mist of deep red in its centre, filtering out the chaotic blaze of the Eye of Terror itself. Seishon stood facing the sparkling images, watching the infinitesimal developments in the cosmos with studied care. His back was to the door when it slid open noiselessly.

'Vargas,' he clipped, recognising the sweep of air that eased into the room without turning around. 'Thank you for joining me. We need to talk.'

'Yes, old friend,' replied Vargas, walking towards the table in the middle of the room with unsteady steps, unwilling to look over at the cloaked back of Seishon. 'There is much to discuss.'

Abruptly, Seishon turned, whipping his cloak around in a swirl of drama. He stalked towards the seated Vargas and leaned forward onto the table. 'I was summoned to the Chambers of Conference, Vargas. Lord Caesurian called for a meeting – and she summoned *me...*' He let his voice trail off, as though the ideas he was implanting in Vargas's mind should have weight enough already.

Vargas steepled his fingers in front of his face and then looked up slowly, meeting Seishon's eyes for the first time. He could see the humiliation and the tinge of fear crackling around the inquisitor lord's irises like the fringes of a storm cloud. 'I know, Seishon. I also received a summons.'

'What? But you were not there! There is no place in the Chambers of Conference for two lords from Ordo Xenos... Did you attend separately? What did you tell them, Vargas?' Seishon's mind was racing with questions and leaping to answers of its own, his customary composure lost for an instant. He had known Vargas for many years, and he knew that he could be trusted in his own way – but he also knew that the old inquisitor was unusually naïve about the intricate and complex workings of the Inquisition. He could betray himself without even knowing it.

'No, my old friend,' soothed Vargas, his voice even and calm, 'you misunderstand me. I was not summoned to the Chambers of Conference, but rather to the...' He paused, as though mustering drama or simply unwilling to give voice to the word. 'I was summoned to the sanctum,' he finished.

Seishon stared at the composed old man before him, sitting at the table with his chin propped up on interlaced and steepled fingers. His eyes were clear and steady, as though his mind was mixed with wonder and certainty.

'What happened?' asked Seishon with slow deliberation, letting the syllables roll as though coaxing a child.

'Eldrad Ulthran himself appeared to me, Seishon. He has called for our aid. He has identified this as the moment for which we have been waiting all these long years. The Eye of Terror is weeping torrents of Chaos into the galaxy, and Lord Ulthran has requested our aid to turn back the tide. This is the final realisation of the coven that we have protected for so many generations…' Vargas trailed off, as though lost in a private reverie.

'Vargas,' snapped Seishon, fearing that the old inquisitor had fallen under some kind of spell. 'How can you be so trusting of this… alien?'

The last word stung Vargas like a slap across his face.

'Why else have we hidden the Coven of Isha in the shadows of Ramugan for millennia? Why else have we put our lives and our souls on the line, before the very eyes of those who would happily burn us as heretics and wyches? This is the moment that we and our forbears have waited for. How can you be so sceptical even now? Have you not sworn to uphold the coven? Is that not why you are here?' Vargas's voice was tinged with venom and reproach, even as his eyes glazed slightly with the romance of his accusations.

Lord Seishon lifted his hands from the table and turned away, walking back over to the viewing wall in silence. He gazed up at the billowing red mist that was oozing out of the Eye, and he sighed.

'You are right, Vargas. This is why we are here,' he confessed. 'Yet, I cannot bring myself to trust the aliens as you do,' he continued as he turned back to face his old friend. 'The existence of the coven does not in itself make every call from Ulthwé into its realisation. The eldar are a cunning race, Vargas, and it would not be below them to call on us for reasons of their own. How can we know that this is the moment that was seen all those millennia ago?'

'The signs are clear, Seishon,' replied Vargas softly. 'You can see the emissions from the Eye for yourself. The call from Lord Ulthran merely confirms the suspicions that we already had.'

It was true, reflected Seishon silently. They had already been concerned by the red mist that roiled around the quadrant in which they knew Ulthwé cruised the space lanes. But he could not shake the feeling that something was not right.

'That is the second time you have called the alien farseer a lord, old friend. You should be careful with your words, lest they lead you along a path to damnation. The eldar are a slippery and treacherous race, and Eldrad Ulthran is the best and the worst of them. He is not to be trusted, even when he is right. Do you understand?' Seishon peered through the half-light, trying to discern the intent hidden in Vargas's eyes.

'We must send a Deathwatch team immediately,' stated Vargas without moving, as though dismissing the cautions of Seishon as the conservatism of an over-protective parent. 'Captain Octavius has just returned to the Watchtower Fortress of Ramugan. He should lead the team.'

Seishon watched his old friend's eyes for a moment longer and then nodded his assent. 'Very well, Vargas, we will send a kill-team to assist the eldar. But the mission must adopt the greatest secrecy. Nobody must know of it. Hereticus Lord Caesurian is already suspicious enough about our activities. Malleus Lord Aurelius has detected the Eye's unusual discharge, and he is considering dispatching a squadron of Grey Knights to investigate. Ramugan is not unaware that the warp signatures are shifting. If our team is discovered, it will look like the worst kind of heresy – we dispatch aid to the aliens whilst lying to the agents of the Inquisition. We are placing our very souls on the line, old friend.'

'We are doing nothing more than fulfilling an Imperial oath, Seishon. It is our duty to the Emperor and to the Imperium of Man. If we failed to dispatch aid, we could be leaving the galaxy to burn. Our souls would be an insignificant price to pay to defend the realm.'

'You are an idealist, Vargas, as is your choice of Deathwatch captain. We will recall Librarian Ashok from the Angels Sanguine for this mission. He will join the valiant Octavius's team. They have fought together before. As for the rest of the team, we will permit Octavius himself to construct one from the Marines currently based in the Watchtower – there is no time to go out hunting for others. This mission must succeed before the Grey Knights are dispatched, if the honourable Aurelius decides to send them. It would not do for those Malleus Marines to find a black Deathwatch frigate already coasting around Circuitrine when they arrive – they would not... understand. It is bad enough that they know we are watching that sector at all. We must do our best to stall Lord Aurelius.'

WITH HER LONG black hair tied back tightly in a semi-conscious echo of her disciplined existence,

Dhrykna strode into the Seer Council's audience chamber and dropped immediately to one knee. She pushed her fist against the shining wraithbone on the floor and closed her eyes, waiting to be acknowledged.

There was a long pause.

'Rise, Guardian Dhrykna of the Shining Path.' The voice was gentle and strong, soft like that of a mother goddess. Dhrykna recognised it at once as the voice of the Emerald Seer.

The young guardian had encountered Thae'akzi of the Emerald Robes many times before, but she was still flattered that the senior seer would remember something of her own history. The reference to the Shining Path recalled Dhrykna's time in the service of the Aspect Temple of the Shining Spears, a rare and secretive Aspect with a tiny, well-hidden shrine in the lowest levels of Ulthwé.

Thae'akzi had been consulted when Dhrykna had requested ascension to exarch of the temple, and the Emerald Seer had raised a number of objections, which is why the guardian had been forced to leave the temple and rejoin life in the rest of the craftworld. Unable to settle into any of the other ways of life offered in Ulthwé, Dhrykna had dedicated herself to the way of the warrior under the auspices of the permanent core of Ulthwé's Black Guardians. Because of her skill on a jetbike, she had quickly risen to a position of command in the jetbike service that constantly patrolled the lower levels of Ulthwé, searching for raiders and signs of infiltration. She may have abandoned life as an Aspect Warrior, but it was still not clear that the life of a Shining Spear had abandoned her. Thae'akzi's reference to the Shining Path made Dhrykna's heart thrill, sensing in it the possibility of a return to that pristine temple.

'As requested, Seer Thae'akzi, I await your leisure,' said Dhrykna in an even voice, lifting her eyes but leaving her fist and knee touched to the ground.

'I understand that you have much to attend to, commander. We will make this brief.' *What did you see?* The words and thoughts slipped into Dhrykna's mind as one, and she could not differentiate between sounds heard and those merely known.

'The darklings executed a well-planned raid, my lady. It is not clear how they gained access to Ulthwé, but it is certain that at least two teams orchestrated the strike. One worked to construct a portal in the lower levels, seeking to provide an extraction point for the others. Meanwhile, the others raided an artists' colony on the cusp of one of the minor forest domes. They took a number of prisoners before being discovered and driven out of the encampments. Most of the raiders were destroyed, but more than a few escaped into the portal. Several Ulthwé eldar vanished with them as captives, while others died in the pursuit. Where possible, the way-stones of the fallen have been recovered. Clearly, the souls of those who where thrown through the warp gate are in the greatest jeopardy.'

As she spoke, Dhrykna broke eye contact with the beautiful seer, forcing her own gaze down into the writhing energy patterns that swam through the wraithbone beneath her knee. Her heart burnt with the passion of vengeance and humiliation. The dark eldar would pay dearly for the offence that they perpetrated against the eldar of Ulthwé. The Black Guardians may not be the most numerous force in the galaxy, but they were feared throughout the Eye of Terror, and rightly so.

'Your account is consistent with that of Shariele, Warlock of the Undercouncil, young Dhrykna.' *Can the Black Guardians repel this enemy?* 'The Seer Council has already met to discuss a response to this latest batch of raids by the unspeakable ones.' *Do you trust that you can do it alone, Dhrykna of the Shining Path?* 'What role was played by the Aspect Temples?' *How did Exarch Truqui fare in the battle with the darklings?*

Thae'akzi's words slipped into Dhrykna's mind from all directions at once. Sometimes pouring in through her ears, but often spiking directly into her thoughts. The effect was intense and dizzying, like being trapped in an echoing cathedral. In the end, there was nothing but truth on the guardian's lips.

'The Dark Reapers fought valiantly, my lady. But…'

But?

But, their abilities are not well suited to this kind of battle. The Reapers are formidable warriors and their ferocity is unparalleled when Ulthwé requires a ground assault. In the confines of the ventilation shafts and in the intricate organic mazes of the forest-domes… They are Khaine's hammer, my lady, and we are in need of his spear. It was as though she could not bring herself to speak such criticisms out loud, but even giving the words form in her mind made her soul shiver with perceptions of treachery.

'I see,' said Thae'akzi, breaking the silence and returning the tone to the mundane. 'And what of the Spears themselves?'

Dhrykna had been waiting for this question. Unlike the bellicose craftworlds of Biel-Tan or Saim-Hann, Ulthwé did not host all of the Aspect Temples. For some reason, the eldar of Ulthwé tended to shy away from the ways of war, preferring instead to immerse themselves in the long and subtle path of the seer. It was because of this psychic intensity that Ulthwé could manoeuvre the webway with such success, skirting the various evils and calamities that might have befallen the less wary. There would be no need to fight if the enemy could be avoided at every turn. However, evasion is not always possible, and it is not always desirable; some of the most glorious futures lay in wait on the other side of war. And certainly not all Ulthwé eldar were unfamiliar with the paths of the warrior.

On the other craftworlds, the Dark Reapers were viewed with suspicion and awe. Their sinister dark armour was adorned with ancient symbols and glyphs of death and destruction, and their loyalty rested unequivocally with Maugan Ra and the lost craftworld of Altansar, once the sister of Ulthwé as a guardian of the great Eye. Their numbers were usually small and their reputations dubious. But on Ulthwé herself, the Dark Reapers were the most abundant of the Aspect Warriors. Where all warriors are viewed with suspicion, pity, and gratitude, the idiosyncrasies of each Aspect makes little difference. On Ulthwé, the Reapers thrived.

The Shining Spears were an entirely different matter, as Dhrykna knew well. They were a tiny and elite presence on only a few craftworlds, including

Ulthwé, but they were universally prized as the
embodiment of Kaela Mensha Khaine's spear, which
struck with the power and speed of lightning. There
was nothing dubious or dark about the Shining
Path. It was a glittering exemplar of the warrior way,
and its jetbike mounted warriors were well suited to
the internal security needs of Ulthwé.

'I did not see the Spears, my lady,' replied Dhrykna
at last, able to vocalise her disappointment because
it was a self-recrimination as much as a complaint.

Why would they not come?

*I do not know, my lady. Their numbers are dwindling,
and they are leaderless, as you know.*

*You will return to them, Dhrykna of the Shining
Spears, and offer them direction.*

The thought made Dhrykna's heart pound. The
Emerald Seer was directing her back to the Aspect
Temple from which she had been expelled many
years ago. Her soul had been calling out for such a
return ever since her departure, funnelling her into a
life that was really a pale imitation of the strictures
of that Aspect. Instead of embracing the Shining
Path with its pristine, white jetbikes, she had accustomed herself to the black and silver of the guardian
jetbike squadrons, swapping her laser lance for a
shuriken pistol.

*I have been watching you, Dhrykna, as has the Temple.
Since you made your request for ascension to exarch, we
have been watching you. It is clear to us now that your
soul is true and that your path is inextricably bound to
the Shining Way. You will return to your shrine and don
the ancient armour of your people. We have need of your
skills now, as never before.*

Warlock Shariele of the Undercouncil agrees with your assessment that the Black Guardians are insufficient to meet this threat, and that the Dark Reapers are unsuited to the task. The council has called for aid from the mon-keigh, but we were... reluctant to do this. If the Shining Spears will stand for Ulthwé in this matter, it will be to their great honour, and ours.

The delicacy of the situation was clear from the chill that accompanied the Emerald Seer's thoughts. There was discomfort in her mind, and it sent shivers into Dhrykna, despite her elation.

'I will have to stand with the mon-keigh, Seer Thae'akzi?' asked Dhrykna with incredulity. She did not understand. She had assumed that she would be returning to partake in the rights of ascension, to take her place in the exarch's gleaming sanctum. How could the exarch be separated from its Temple? How could it be expected to stand with the bestial mon-keigh. It would be heresy.

'Yes, child, you will stand with them.' It was as simple as that. *You are not the exarch yet.*

DESPITE THE BRIGHT lights in the briefing chamber of the Watchtower Fortress, everything looked dark and sullen. The light sank into the matt, unreflective blackness of the walls, floor and ceiling, falling into the structure of the room as though it had never been there at all. Even the Marines who punctuated the wide space with their massive bulks offered little levity or light, their blackened armour only adding to the oppressive air. The only points of glossy differentiation were the right shoulder guards of each Marine, which displayed the glorious symbols of their various Chapters of origin.

The silence was as striking as the shadow. The Marines stood or sat in perfect stillness, neither interacting with, nor ignoring each other, always aware but never threatening or frivolous. There was a dense aura of respect dominating the atmosphere, but it was not without hints of suspicion and cynicism. The Marines of the Deathwatch were united by the strongest and most powerful of vows to the Emperor and His Inquisition, and they recognised that their battle-brothers were being honoured equally with themselves, but they were also fiercely loyal to their home Chapters and deeply suspicious of all outsiders.

Being seconded into the Deathwatch was one of the most profound challenges that a Space Marine could face. It not only meant that he would be dispatched on the most dangerous of missions to hunt down the alien menace – in many ways that was the simplest aspect of the position – but he would also have to resolve deep rooted and fundamental psychological tensions between his joint loyalties to the Emperor's will as interpreted by his Chapter and the interpretation espoused by the Ordo Xenos. Added to the mix would be the multifarious interpretations of the other Chapters, and the occasionally radical departures made by specific, idiosyncratic inquisitors.

More often than not, these differing world-views fell into a rough harmony; after all, they were all servants of the Undying Emperor. But from time to time the world-views would diverge or clash, and then a Marine was left to resolve the crisis in his own conscience. Joining the Deathwatch may be the greatest honour that could be afforded a Space Marine, but it was also the greatest challenge to his body and soul: victory and defeat, loyalty and heresy could become muddled together or fragmented into myriad aspects. More than any other assignment that a Marine might be asked to take, a secondment to the Deathwatch was a test of his character: duty before all else, but what happens when the meaning of duty is suddenly thrown into question by competing visions?

Sitting in silence on the floor in the corner of the room, almost unnoticed by the others, Ashok folded his well-muscled arms around his knees and let his hood drop down over his face. He was the only Marine in the room who had chosen not to wear his armour for the briefing. Instead, he was clad in a simple black smock that hung loosely over his frame. The hood had been fashioned out of the Shroud of Lemartes, which had been presented to him as a sign of his self-mastery following the incident on Hegelian IX. The rough sensation of its fabric against his skin offered him reassurance, keeping his mind fixed and focused. For that reason, the hood was always folded over his head, casting his fathomless black eyes into deep shadow.

Since being awarded the shroud, Ashok had never worn the elaborate librarian's helmet to which he was entitled by rank and status. Even in full armour, his head was exposed to the elements and his face was hidden under the shadows of the shroud. But he did not like even to wear his armour. He suspected, moreover, that its machine-spirit did not like to be in his presence. Together, he and his armour were terrible to behold, and Ashok felt that he needed to be rid of it when he was not actually in combat. There was no peace to be found in that ancient spirit of war, and Ashok had to strive constantly for balance in his mind.

Like the other Marines of the Angels Sanguine, who shared the gene-seed of the Blood Angels, one of Ashok's primary concerns was to stave off the insanities of the Red Thirst, the primordial rage that hungered for blood in his soul. Unlike most of his battle-brothers, Ashok had passed through the affliction of his brethren and emerged a master of himself and his passions. In the process, he had done unspeakable things to his brothers and to the servants of the Emperor, and the scratching irritations of the Shroud of Lemartes ensured that these actions were never far from his mind.

On the other side of the briefing room, a door clicked and hissed open, revealing the outline of another Marine standing dramatically in the flood of light. Ashok's eyes glinted in the rush of light, but he did not look up. He knew who it was already. The other Marines in the room drew themselves up to attention, and awaited the inspection of the great captain. All of them had heard about Captain Octavius of the Imperial Fists during their training at the Watchtower Fortress. Since his exceptional performance on Herodian IV, he had become one of the very few Marines to be given the honour of a permanent secondment to the Deathwatch. The Imperial Fists missed their eminent captain, of

course, but it was a great tribute to them that the
Ordo Xenos of Ramugan would desire to keep one
of their finest sons in permanent service. It was a rare
honour, and Octavius was a rare Marine.

Without looking up, Ashok watched the rest of the
team assemble. He noted with barely suppressed
disdain the presence of the Reviler chaplain who
had been sent to Trontium VI to recall him to the
Deathwatch, and with disappointment he realised
that the Blood Angel was absent from the group.
Typical, he thought. He recognised the emblems of
the other Marines immediately, including the emerald and gold claw of a Mantis Warriors Assault
Marine – the Mantis Warriors were a Chapter with
whom Ashok had served before under questionable
circumstances. There was a second Assault Marine –
a Black Consul – whose grizzly features and cluster
of service studs betrayed decades of service. The half-
mechanised form of a Red Talon techmarine was an
unmistakable addition to the group.

However, there was one insignia that he could not
recognise: it was a black raven on a bone-white background, with a single droplet of blood-red through
its heart. For a moment he thought that it might be
a Blood Angel cousin, but it also looked like one of
the conniving Raven Guard. Whoever it was, he was
a librarian and he emanated a latent psychic field
that glowed like a star for anyone with the ability to
see it.

Octavius strode confidently into the room, letting
the door hiss closed behind him, shutting out the
light and allowing the eyes of the Marines before
him to make out his face for the first time. The face

was struck through with a deep scar that ran from the jaw line on his right to his left temple. Fine hair fell loosely over its forehead, partially obscuring a row of golden service studs. However, it was the eyes that caught everyone's attention: pale blue and startling, as though providing windows into a soul wracked by terror and beauty in equal measure.

'Greetings, sons of the primarchs. You, each of you,' he specified carefully, 'honour this hall with your presence. The hour is dark and our resolve must be swift. We will depart immediately for the Circuitrine nebula, where we will rendezvous with the eldar craftworld of Ulthwé. Once there, it is likely that we will fight alongside the aliens against a common foe…' His voice faltered very slightly, as though he found the words that he was speaking distasteful. Ashok looked up at last, fixing his eyes on the captain. More than one of the other Marines shifted uneasily. 'We are not yet aware of the identity of this foe, but it seems probable that it is an agent from the Eye of Terror.'

Octavius paused, letting the weight of his words sink in as he looked around the faces of the assembled Marines. He had chosen the members of the team himself, drawing them from those currently stationed at the secret Watchtower Fortress near Ramugan station. He had seen them all complete the elite xenocide training routines, augmenting their already formidable combat skills with specialised alien hunting techniques known only to the Deathwatch. They were primed and waiting for a mission. Only Pelias, the battle hardened assault sergeant of the Black Consuls had served in the

Deathwatch before, but the team was rich with experience and talent nevertheless.

As he scanned the room, watching the expressions of his Marines as his instructions to co-operate with the aliens hit home, Octavius caught sight of the hunched figure of Ashok sitting in the shadows of the far corner. The librarian's hood hid his face, and his simple black smock betrayed no markings of any kind, but Octavius recognised him immediately. As the captain stared, a sheen of light glinted across the librarian's eyes, making them flash like those of a wild animal in the deepest jungle.

Greetings, captain. Ashok's thoughts pushed silently and gently into Octavius's head. *It is good to see you again.*

The captain's surprise was clear, although his composure was unbroken. He had not expected to see the Angel Sanguine in his briefing hall. Ashok had not been on service at the Watchtower when Octavius had selected his team, and the captain had not included the librarian in his plans. Indeed, he had already selected a librarian for the mission, Atreus of the Blood Ravens – a powerful psyker with extensive experience of the eldar from campaigns on Tartarus and Rahe's Paradise. It would be highly unusual for a Deathwatch kill-team to host more than one librarian.

Octavius nodded slightly, returning the greeting with a little reserve in front of the others. His thoughts betrayed him.

Lord Seishon requested my presence, captain, but I am under your command, of course. The Inquisitor Lord felt that the team would need two librarians, given the nature

*of the threat we face… and given the nature of the allies
that we seek to aid.*

The other Marines shifted slightly, becoming
aware that Octavius's pause had lengthened unnaturally. They looked around, spotting Ashok, some of
them for the first time. Atreus, the Blood Ravens
librarian whose insignia Ashok had not recognised,
was the only one that did not turn. He was already
fully aware of what was going on in the room.

'Our mission is vital and our deadline is tight. We
are acting to fulfil an ancient pact between the aliens
and the Ordo Xenos. We carry the oath of the
Emperor on our backs, Marines, so there is no room
for hesitation or doubt.' Octavius had anticipated
the revulsion on Pelias's face, but had been more
surprised to see it flicker over the features of Chaplain Luthar, the Reviler. 'We are the Deathwatch, and
duty comes before all else.'

*He who allows the alien to live shares in the crime of
its existence.* Ashok's thoughts were mocking, but his
tone lacked malice. He was quoting the famous
adage of Inquisitor Apollyon, the maxim was carved
into the centrepiece of the great arch that swept over
the assembly hall of the Watchtower. Every Marine
that entered into the service of the Deathwatch in
this sector would have those words etched into his
soul. Under the deep folds of his hood, Octavius
could see Ashok's eyes glint with the suggestion of a
wry smile. He knew that the librarian was right: at
least some of the Marines in the team would find
this mission heretical. They certainly didn't expect to
be fighting *with* aliens when they joined the Deathwatch.

'It is not our place to question the oaths of the Imperial Inquisition. It is our duty to fulfil them in the name of the Emperor. We act to defend the realm from the greatest threats to the Imperium of Man; it is not the Deathwatch that judges these threats. We are the swords of policy and it is we who execute those threats. We hold in our hands the honour of the Emperor himself, and we will not fail him.'

Octavius paused again, looking around the faces before him. He had not convinced them all, but he knew that it would take more than a few stirring words to convince a Space Marine of anything. These men were the finest warriors in the galaxy, wrought from the trials and fires of their different Chapters, each with their own ways. He knew that he could not necessarily make them believe, but he also knew that he could trust in their sense of honour and duty to the Emperor. There was no higher ideal for any of the Adeptus Astartes.

'We leave within the hour,' he stated simply, turning and striding out of the doors, leaving the Marines alone with their thoughts and each other.

CHAPTER THREE:
WYCH-HUNT

THE PATTERNS OF light danced over the polished floor like electric serpents slithering through oil. They slipped and slid, lashing into flickers as though convulsing with tension or anxiety. Shariele sat cross-legged against the wall on one side of the room, letting the waves of energy wash underneath him. Three other warlocks were positioned symmetrically around the perimeter, similarly lost in meditation, the bone-white hints of runes glinting off their black armour.

There was a faint chant infused into the air, although none of the warlocks worked their mouths and the room was shrouded in silence. But their minds were alive with song, bringing the psychic resonance in the carefully designed chamber into the realms of symphony. For the warlocks, this

divination was a kind of rapture, suspending their
souls in the violence of the abyss, letting their
essential beings ride the wave of the present, peering
constantly towards the horizon, searching for
glimmers of the inevitable storms to come. Behind
their closed lids, their eyes flashed and burnt with
flames, as beacons to their kindred spirits, guiding
them home lest they be lost to themselves and each
other forever. This ritual could never be performed
alone.

As the psychic chanting grew louder, clouds of
sha'iel started to condense into the reality of the
chamber. At first there were just wisps, just suggestions of cirrus formations taking shape near the
ceiling. But gradually the thin mist started to curdle
and thicken, drawing itself out into strips and
whirling into the suggestions of eddies. The pace
quickened and the movement broadened as the little swirls congealed and merged, slipping together
and forming a single, slowly revolving whirlpool of
sha'iel that spun around the perimeter of the room,
skirting around the backs of each of the warlocks,
bringing them into the interior of a spinning column of warp energy.

With an abrupt flash of orange fire, the eyes of the
warlocks snapped open simultaneously, flames
lapping at their irises as though consuming them.
They remained seated in concentrated meditation,
motionless and silent as their burning gazes
converged on an invisible point at the centre of the
chamber. The swirling clouds of sha'iel began to
accelerate, whipping themselves up into a tornado of
warp power, thrashing around the fringes of the room

and threatening to rip the chamber itself from the structure of Ulthwé through sheer centrifugal power.

As the maelstrom raged around them, the warlocks remained silent and calm, blazing their vision into the very eye of the storm, their eyes glazed and shinning like liquid stars. In the convergence of their lines of sight, an image started to form, flickering on the edge of existence as though unable to bear the pressure of reality. Figures started to resolve themselves at the edge of the picture. They were running and fighting, firing weapons and spinning blades, each clad in pristine black armour.

Some of the figures were massive and ugly, with cumbersome and primitive weapons. There were smaller, more elegant shapes too, dancing and springing around the hazy, flickering combat zone. And there were corpses, dozens of corpses strewn over the ground beneath the feet of the others. Hundreds of corpses, stretching out into the distance as though trapped in an infinite regression of mirrors. There were thousands of eldar corpses, millions, rolling out over the horizon in layers several deep, like the crust of a planet.

The sky above the shimmering images seemed to crack with ethereal lightning, sending souls screaming through the atmosphere and ripping through the thick, viscous clouds of darkness. A sudden crack of brightness flared like a burning spear, but then it was gone.

'Hesperax,' muttered Shariele, the single word shattering the vortex of sha'iel like a bullet through an ice sculpture. The images and the clouds of warp dissipated rapidly, repelled by the intrusion of a fragment from the material realm – the artificial purity of the Undercouncil Chamber no longer pristine enough to sustain them. And it was not just any word; the name of Hesperax had not been uttered on Ulthwé for thousands of years. It was a cursed word, as though its syllables carried death to the very tip of one's tongue.

The other warlocks broke their gazes and lowered their simmering eyes, gradually bringing their minds back into the present and back into the chamber as it appeared in the material realm. They had seen the vision as well, and not one of them wanted to give voice to the sights they had seen. They were more than accustomed to the darkness of their own souls – each had served for a time in the Aspect Temple of the Dark Reapers, immersing themselves in their own thirst for blood and battle – but none of them could ever reconcile themselves to the horrors that lurked in the souls of their lost brethren, the darklings.

Hesperax was a vision of all things unimaginable and unthinkable to them. It was a haven for the forbidden and a deeply suppressed temptation of their souls. There was a reason that the name was taboo on Ulthwé, and it was not simply because of an abhorrence for the horrors perpetrated there.

It was Hesperax, muttered Shariele, sharing his thoughts with the others. He was not looking for confirmation. He didn't need it. He simply wanted to share the burden of the word, pushing it into the minds of the others as though splitting it into separate runes for each, dividing and conquering the word like a broken enemy force. *I must inform the seers.*

* * *

'Lord Aurelius is as concerned as you are, Perceptia, if not more so. After all, it is the responsibility of the Ramugan Ordo Malleus to police the incursions of any daemonic forces into this sector.' Hereticus Lord Caesurian's voice was smooth and low, like dark velvet.

Standing formally in the entranceway to the inquisitor lord's chambers, Inquisitor Perceptia was demonstrably agitated. Her hands clasped and unclasped before her, as though she were nervous. She had old fashioned eyeglasses perched precariously on the end of her nose, and she kept pushing them restively back up towards her forehead.

'With your permission, Lord Caesurian,' began the young inquisitor, 'I would still like to take a closer look at this matter. It seems… unorthodox to me.' Her tone was respectful but frustrated, as though she felt that her superior was holding her back deliberately. Finally losing patience with her errant spectacles, Perceptia snatched them away from her face and clutched them between her tense hands.

Caesurian rose from the comfort of her lushly padded chair and inspected the youthful inquisitor from a distance. She never invited Perceptia into her chambers. The inquisitor lord found the bookish young woman unnerving, and she was keen to ensure that her private space was not infected by her peculiar brand of nervous energy. Even as an interrogator, the young Perceptia had never been a favourite student. Caesurian would certainly not describe her as her protégé. Nonetheless, she could not help feeling a certain responsibility for the woman whose career she had helped to sculpt.

'Perceptia,' she began, letting her smooth voice ease through the shadowy space between them. 'You are quite right to have faith in your instincts. The Ordo Hereticus needs inquisitors with a nose for the... unorthodox, as you call it. However...'

She trailed off as she turned her back on her visitor and walked deeper into the room. Pausing at an old wooden cabinet that rested against the far wall, the inquisitor lord slowly poured a deep red liquid into a crystal glass and raised it to her lips. 'However,' she continued, the glass poised delicately at her mouth, 'Ramugan is an unusual and carefully balanced place, as you may appreciate. The Ordo Hereticus is, of course, the paragon of subtlety at all times...' Caesurian took a sip of the red liquid before continuing. 'But, we must be particularly assiduous here. I'm sure that you understand?' The nature of the question was ambiguous, and the inquisitor lord turned her head to the side to indicate that she required a response.

Perceptia was not sure what was expected of her. 'I understand, my lord,' she said, bowing her head with more resignation than respect. 'But–'

'Aurelius would dispatch the Grey Knights if he felt that there was a reason to do so. To do otherwise would constitute a failure of duty, and I am sure that you do not mean to impugn the inquisitor lord's sense of duty, inquisitor? The fact that he hasn't suggests that there is indeed nothing with which the Emperor's Holy Inquisition need concern itself at this time. Hence, Lord Seishon's previous silence on this issue is not a matter for us to investigate.'

Perceptia stared at the back of the inquisitor lord's head, her mind racing and her frustrations bubbling just below the surface. She knew that Caesurian had never liked her. She was certainly not the old woman's favourite, there was no doubt about that. The inquisitor lord was a political animal, which was why she had been left in charge of the Ordo Hereticus facility on the Ramugan station – possibly the most politically sensitive posting in the Imperium. Perceptia, on the other hand, had no flare for diplomacy at all. Her ethical world was a binary system. There was good and, far more often, there was evil.

In her youth, the venerable inquisitor lord had been a dashing witch hunter, a woman of action. Her experience of the best and the worst of the Imperium had given her a sense of perspective. Her world was a mosaic of shadows and shades of grey. The bookish, Manichean Perceptia might have been from a completely different planet.

'Is it not possible, my lord, that...' Perceptia paused, as though aware that her chain of thought was crossing a line. 'Is it not possible that Seishon has some kind of hold over Aurelius?'

The wine glass froze at Caesurian's lips and an icy silence slipped through the room.

'Or perhaps,' continued Perceptia, falling over her words to fill the gap. 'Perhaps they have an agreement concerning that quadrant of the Circuitrine sector? Either way, isn't this something that we should be aware of?'

Caesurian threw back the rest of her wine and turned very slowly to face the young inquisitor. On the far side of the room, her face was hidden in the shadows, but Perceptia could see her expression vividly in her mind's eye.

'My dear Perceptia, there is a very fine line between intuition and foolish fantasy. This is not the place to throw about accusations. Ramugan teeters on the edge of a political knife.' Her voice was slow and even, but Perceptia could hear that its usual smoothness was now fighting an undercurrent of anger.

'But, my lord,' she protested. 'Politics should not be an excuse for heresy. There can be no excuse for heresy.' Perceptia forced the defiant words out of her mouth, despite her own nervousness about the confrontation with her one-time mentor. Her hands clasped together tightly and she wrung them as though trying to force all of the blood out of them.

The inquisitor lord said nothing for a moment and then took a step forward, bringing her face into the light. Her eyes were drawn taught and narrow but her brow displayed no furrows. Her mouth was set in a horizontal line and her jaw muscles were clenched.

'Be very careful, my young Perceptia. If you are pursuing the fires of damnation, at the very least you should expect to burn your fingers.' As though to reinforce the point, the inquisitor lord took another step forward and placed her hands over the back of her luxurious chair. One of her hands twinkled with metallic light, and Perceptia saw her augmetic limb for the hundredth time. 'By all means search, Perceptia. But search quietly, and tell nobody what you are doing. If you are discovered and you have found nothing, I will offer you no protection from the wrath of Seishon or Aurelius. I will tell them that I knew nothing of your activities. That is how Ramugan will continue.'

Caesurian paused, waiting for Perceptia to speak or show some spark of understanding, but the young inquisitor was still digesting the magnitude of the implications of the conversation.

'If I ever hear from you again, Perceptia, it will be with findings upon which we can act. Without such findings, you will never address me again.' With that, Caesurian nodded imperceptibly and the doors to her chamber slid shut abruptly, leaving Perceptia standing in the corridor outside, her nose only millimetres from the armoured, adamantium panelling of the closed door.

'THE MESSAGE HAS been sent,' stated Thae'akzi simply, meeting the disbelieving gazes of the other council members with unflinching eyes. 'Lord Ulthran himself made contact. He expects that the mon-keigh are already on their way.'

The council chamber seemed to shiver with its own sense of revulsion; little jets of light licked around the walls like the echoes of distant storms. The ambient light was dim, almost dark, matching the mood of the seers.

'Let this council record that I have objected to this move from the start,' snarled Ruhklo, his fierce eyes directed adamantly down into the polished floor in the middle of the circle of seers. The anger simmered around his features and the ground smouldered as though heated by the force of his gaze. 'The mon-keigh are not to be trusted, and they will dishonour us with their presence.'

'Had we been better prepared, Ruhklo of the Karizhariat, then there may have been no need,' said Eldressyn softly, enjoying the defeat of the bitter old seer. Her startling blue eyes shone with faintly disturbed tranquillity.

Perhaps it was this eventuality for which we have been preparing, Eldressyn, whispered Thae'akzi into the young seer's mind. *Don't be so quick to claim your victory in this council. Eldrad's ways are beyond even us.*

Eldressyn fell silent, acknowledging the secret words of the elder seer and respecting their wisdom. But in her heart she knew that Ulthwé needed the mon-keigh to win this fight, and she was certain that such a situation could have been avoided if the council had prepared properly for the future. At that moment, Ruhklo seemed like a liability – old, bitter and dark in his soul. She blamed him. It was his fault for filling the council with breaths of cynicism and malice. The very hall itself seemed to quake with his frustrations.

'The council has prepared Ulthwé for its future as best it could, Eldressyn of Ulthroon,' said Thae'akzi, smoothing the waters. 'The crisis in the Eye and the darkling raids may be but a stepping stone on the way to a golden shore. The mon-keigh will assist us, as they promised long ago. It is fortuitous that they are so bound to us now.'

'We cannot trust them, Thae'akzi of the Emerald Robes,' muttered Bhurolyn as he pulled his sapphire and black cloak around him, as though suddenly cold.

'We do not need to trust them, Bhurolyn. We just need them to come,' replied Thae'akzi softly. 'And so they come.'

There was a sudden and brief crack of light in one of the walls. It flashed and then cut its way through the wraithbone, defining a great door as it spread. After a couple of seconds, the door melted away, as though the wraithbone itself had withdrawn into the fabric of the walls around it. A dull, warm light eased through the open archway, mixing into the heavy darkness of the council chamber itself, sending hazes of interference patterns sprinkling through the air.

'My lords of the Eternal Council,' said Shariele, stooping into a deep bow on the threshold of the hall. The white runes on his black armour glinted in little starbursts as the light washed over him from behind, and his long cloak billowed and fluttered, as though the flow of light carried a breeze in its wake. 'I bring greetings from the Undercouncil of Warlocks, and news.'

'You are most welcome, Shariele of the Lost Souls,' replied Thae'akzi, turning to face the warlock and bowing slightly. Enter freely – it is your right as much as our pleasure.' She gave the impression of smiling faintly, without even a crease appearing on her smooth face.

Shariele remained in the doorway for a moment, holding his bow for an extra second out of respect for the hall and the seers therein. Then he rose and strode confidently across the patterns of light that swam through the floor beneath his feet. The Emerald Seer unsettled his heart. He had heard many of the stories about her and yet she remained a mystery to him. There was something profoundly different about their souls, and it rendered her almost impenetrable to

him. He understood that she had once passed
through the trials of the Shining Spear, in the past
before she had taken up the path of the seer. Then,
perhaps a century ago, after Thae'akzi had become a
powerful seer, Ulthwé had done battle with a force of
disfigured mon-keigh as they spilled out of the Eye of
Terror. At that time, the Temple of the Shining Path
had summoned Thae'akzi back into its sanctum: the
temple's ceremonial warlock's mask was calling for
her, bellowing her name in tones barely audible to
the sensitive eldar ear, yelling her name through the
immaterium itself.

Thae'akzi had returned to her old temple and
entered the sanctum, locking herself in the sacred
chamber with nobody to assist her and none to witness the events that followed. Days later, she had
emerged as the Emerald Seer, bedecked entirely in
the green robes that now covered her elegant form.
But the warlock's mask lay untouched on the altar in
the temple's sanctum – she had refused the call of
Khaine and turned her back on the thirst for war that
lurked in the souls of all eldar.

Unlike Shariele and the other warlocks, who had
each trained as Aspect Warriors before embarking on
the long path of the seer, Thae'akzi had made a conscious and wilful choice not to merge the paths – she
had refused to transpose her immense psychic gifts
into combative powers. Whilst it was certainly true
that not all seers who had trodden the path of the
warrior chose to combine the dual-ways into the
dark road of the warlock, it was unheard of for one
summoned personally by the spirit of Kaela Mensha
Khaine to resist the calling. The warlocks of the

Undercouncil felt a slight chill in her presence, as though she found them unhealthy, dangerous, or even weak of will. They were certain that the other seers on the Eternal Council did not understand who she was. How could they see the unfathomable strength in her soul?

As he approached the ring of seers, Shariele stopped and bowed once again. The councillors each returned his bow, paying him the courtesy of their respect. He was well known to them all.

'The communion of the Undercouncil has yielded some worrying results,' began Shariele. 'It appears that the darklings are not our only concern along this time-line.' There was a pause as Shariele awaited the inevitable questions. None came. 'The warlocks have foreseen a force of mon-keigh in the battles of the near future. They stood back to back with darkly clad eldar, poised in blood and treading on a field of our slain kinsmen.'

There was a murmur around the room as thoughts of death and doom emanated from the seers and resonated through the psychically conductive wraithbone that encased the chamber. The trails of light in the floor and walls flashed and died with increased intensity.

'The mon-keigh will be our doom – it is written,' spat Ruhklo, as though Shariele's words confirmed his fears.

'It is not written, Karizhariat! Nothing is written, as you well know. We write our future in our choices and in our blood,' snapped Eldressyn, the pristine whiteness of her delicate robes flashing starkly in the dark atmosphere. 'We *will* the future with our power.'

'What else did you see, Shariele?' asked Thae'akzi softly, ignoring the quarrelling seers at her side. 'Was it just the mon-keigh that brought blood into our future?'

'No, Emerald Seer, the darklings were also there, and the corpses were disfigured beyond the wit or inventiveness of the mon-keigh. It was… It was Hesperax.' Shariele hesitated before speaking those cursed syllables in the great chambers of council. As the forbidden sounds left his mouth, the room pulsed and lashed with a violence unseen for decades. The ground itself shook, as though repulsed.

The seers sank into silence, shocked that the Undercouncil could see what they could not. It was as though they themselves were blinded to the vision by the violence of its content. The souls of the warlocks walked in darker places, and they would not find the terror of Hesperax so utterly alien. That in itself worried Thae'akzi.

'So, the Mistress of Strife has a hand in this?' mused the Emerald Seer, nodding her understanding to Shariele as the hall flashed its own abhorrence. 'This explains the pattern of the darklings' behaviour. They are taking prisoners for the Wych Queen, so that she might harvest their souls to slake the thirst of her daemonic princess. We have encountered this foe before,' she said, turning back to face the other seers, her eyes slightly out of focus, as though remembering something from long ago.

'Yes, and we did not need the mon-keigh then,' sneered Ruhklo.

'Times change,' answered Eldressyn sharply, her presence representing vivid proof of her words.

'If the Wych Queen is collecting eldar souls, she must be seeking to manifest an agent of the Satin Throne,' reasoned Bhurolyn, his deductions adding an edge of anxiety to his words.

'Lelith's ambitions are greater than that,' said Thae'akzi, shocking Shariele by using the Wych Queen's personal name. 'She would not content herself with underlings, not even those of a daemon god.'

For a moment, the Emerald Seer seemed lost in thought. Then she turned to Shariele abruptly. 'Warlock, we must prevent the loss of any more Ulthwé souls to this darkling monster. As you are aware, this craftworld, indeed our very species, cannot afford to lose any more of its own. Worse than this, stolen souls cast into the currents of sha'iel will serve to lead the minions of the Great Enemy – Slaanesh – to our doorstep. We may presume that this explains the current, unusual discharge from the Eye. The darkling raids must be brought to an end. Do you understand, Shariele of the Lost Souls?'

'I understand,' replied Shariele simply, bowing his head. 'I can vow to be at the service of this council, as I have done many times before, but I can offer no promises of success, my lady.' He paused. 'I do not think that Ulthwé has the resources to win this fight.'

'You will not be alone, warlock. The mon-keigh have been summoned to provide aid. A small squadron of their best will be here presently. You will help them to help us, Shariele.'

A long moment passed in silence as the warlock fought against his instinctive revulsion. 'If it is the will of the council,' he replied, before turning and sweeping out of the great hall.

THE BLACK DEATHWATCH frigate, *Lance of Darkness*, was one of a select few Nova-class frigates that had been specially refitted and based at the Watchtower Fortress near Ramugan in case the Deathwatch needed to act independently of other Imperial forces. It roared through the void of real space, not daring to dip into the maelstrom of the warp so close to the Eye of Terror, where the warp currents were torrentially violent and unpredictable.

In the vicinity of the Eye, even the relatively predictable spaceways of mundane reality were treacherous. The warp could rip through the fabric of space and suck a ship back into the clutches of salivating daemons. Pockets of violent energy could erupt like massive proximity mines, exploding and showering passing vessels with fragments of concentrated Chaos; and space itself seemed to warp and shift, twisting the space lanes and bending the light of the stars themselves.

Octavius's team raced through the lashes of the Eye of Terror, engulfed in an eerie red mist that seemed to seep through millions of tiny perforations in reality itself. Warning klaxons were sounding continuously, as though the ship's machine-spirit thought that it had slipped into the warp without a Navigator to guide it. The mist appeared to be a haze of warp energy, too dispersed to penetrate or damage the *Lance of Darkness*, but dense enough to trick the vessel's sensors. The cloud was suspended in a bizarre middle realm between the material and immaterial dimensions.

'Captain Octavius,' said Sergeant Pelias, stooping through the doorframe at the entrance to the control room. As he straightened up, he nodded smartly towards the hooded figure of Librarian Ashok, noting with surprise that he was still without armour, but then the sergeant turned his attention directly to Octavius. Aside from the pilot-servitor and a skeleton crew of serfs, the three Marines were alone in the low-ceilinged space. Octavius was gazing out of the main viewscreen. He turned to greet Pelias as the rugged Black Consul Marine presented himself.

'Ah, Sergeant Pelias. Our arrival time is estimated as one hour. Please ensure the team is ready for our landing. It would not do to be ill-prepared when we meet our new associates.'

The sergeant nodded, but the grimace that snapped across his stubble speckled and scar laced face betrayed his true feelings about the etiquette owed to the aliens. 'As you wish, captain,' he growled. He turned sharply and began to duck back under the doorframe. As he did so, a series of metal implants in the back of his neck and head glinted in the dim light.

'The eldar gave him those,' muttered Ashok in barely audible tones, after the sergeant had vanished back into the body of the ship. The librarian knew that Octavius had noticed the metal plates.

'I am aware of the sergeant's history, Ashok,' said Octavius, turning back to the viewscreen without facing the librarian. No matter how many times it happened, he could still not shake the feeling that Ashok's abilities to read his thoughts constituted a discourtesy. He even wondered whether they compromised his command.

'Really?' Ashok's low, quiet voice sounded doubtful. 'Do you know what they did to him?'

'He has never spoken of it.' There was an edge of angst in Octavius's voice, as though he was drawing on painful memories. 'I would not ask him to.'

'It is best that he does not,' said Ashok carefully.

For a moment Octavius wondered whether Ashok could see the sergeant's memories. As he gazed out of the viewscreen at the dim star that they were racing towards, he wondered what it would be like to know the memories of others. He wondered whether it was as natural to Ashok as peering into the eyes of a man and seeing the courage in his soul.

Octavius did not have to look into Pelias's mind to see what had happened to him. He had been part of the same Deathwatch mission against the Biel-Tan eldar all those years before. Octavius had watched helplessly as the aliens had dragged the unconscious Black Consul into their hovering tank after the kill-team had first made planetfall. At the end of the campaign, when the planet was finally under the complete control of the eldar and the failed Deathwatch mission was being extracted, the eldar had thrown Pelias back to them, like a fish that was too worthless to be kept.

The wounds on his neck and head, which had been inflicted on the Black Consul during his captivity, had been healed perfectly by the eldar before they returned him, but the Ordo Xenos had reopened them all to make sure that nothing had been left inside the sergeant's skull. The metal plates that now covered Pelias's neck were testament to the inability of the Inquisition's surgeons to match the skill of the eldar. As for the details of what the eldar had done to him to inflict the wounds in the first place, not even the skills of Inquisitor Lord Guerilian had been able to extract them. However, the official mission report contained reference to an intelligence leak in the Deathwatch team as one of the factors that contributed to the failure of the mission. Pelias was not named in the report, but Octavius suspected that the eldar had been inside the sergeant's mind.

'He is healed. There is no threat now,' stated Octavius simply. 'Pelias is a strong Marine and a first-class sergeant. He is an asset to our team.'

Wounds like that never heal, Octavius. He harbours unspeakable pain and hatred in his mind. He may never offer his back to our eldar friends. The words eased into Octavius's mind like a whisper.

A shiver thrilled down the captain's spine and, at first, he thought that Ashok had overstepped the line. He spun to face the librarian, who remained in the shadows against the wall, his face hidden beneath the folds of his hood, with his eyes glowing faintly.

'I felt it too, captain,' said Ashok, stepping up to Octavius's shoulder and staring out into space. 'Where is Ulthwé?' he asked.

The captain took Ashok's innocence at his word and without question. The Angels Sanguine librarian was almost a complete mystery to him, but he had learnt to trust his judgement during the campaign against the tyranids on Herodian IV. Somehow, the librarian always seemed to be just outside the team, even just out of the reach of his command. But whatever else he was, Ashok was a peerless and trustworthy warrior.

'We don't have exact co-ordinates. It moves continuously and not always through real space. Our rendezvous point appears to be in the vicinity of that dim star,' explained Octavius pointing.

Footsteps sounded behind them as one of the Marines from the transportation hold entered the control room.

'He is here. He is alert to our presence, captain,' reported Atreus, the Blood Ravens librarian, striding into the control room alongside the other two to look out into the red-misted starscape ahead.

Octavius nodded a greeting, but Ashok did not take his eyes from the screen.

'Who is here?' asked the captain, addressing Atreus.

'Ulthran,' replied Ashok without turning. 'The eldar witch lord.'

'His mind fills this quadrant. It is like a giant sensor web stretched out from Ulthwé itself. He knows that we are approaching,' continued Atreus nodding and searching the myriad stars for some sign of the massive craftworld. 'It must be here,' he insisted. 'We should be able to see it.'

Octavius nodded, realising before the team had even reached Ulthwé why Lord Seishon had insisted on the presence of two librarians on this mission. 'It is probably on the other side of that large, dim star,' he suggested, pointing at the light that he had been considering with Ashok. The colour-shift affected by the mist made it look like a red giant – a supermassive star on the verge of death.

There was a moment of silence.

'That's not a star,' said Ashok in a slow whisper.

'That's Ulthwé,' agreed Atreus.

THE LOWEST LEVELS of Ulthwé were barely lit. There was just a faint pulse of light easing through the structure of the corridors, like capillaries in a body's extremities. Over the millennia, the eldar of Ulthwé had become accustomed to the darkness, and their eyes had developed sensitivities that found bright light shocking and even offensive. Theirs was a world of shadow and subtlety.

Many of the craftworld's greatest artists lived in the murky underworld. Trekhulir of the Glittering Dark, one of Ulthwé's most famed wraithsmiths, was reputed to have refused dozens of invitations to visit the sparkling heights of the upper levels. He excused himself on the basis that his work required him to cultivate the shadows; exposure to bright light would blind him to the subtleties of tone and shade. He explained that it was only in the darkness that true beauty could be found.

The crass, brashness of bright light was the domain of the clumsy, young races of the galaxy – the tau and even the mon-keigh craved the light. For the eldar, the half-light of the shadows should be home. Even more than the other craftworlds, Ulthwé had embraced this aesthetic as though it were an indisputable aspect of their existence.

Even on Ulthwé, however, the eldar path passed along many different roads. The nature of the eldar soul remained infinitely complex and multifarious. Darkness was not the only aspect that found a home

in the labyrinthine corridors of the massive craftworld. Shining like a beacon of purity in the very
deepest levels, the Temple of the Shining Path radi-
ated an entirely different aesthetic. The temple was a
glorious construction of light, as though built from
the substance of the stars themselves. Its crystalline
walls refracted the light from inside into myriad
colours, rendering it into a burst of brilliance, like a
pearl lost in the depths of an oceanic dark.

The Aspect Warriors of the Shining Spear, bestrid-
ing their shimmering white jetbikes, flashed through
the underworld of Ulthwé, policing incursions and
raids. They were objects of marvel, fear and repulsion amongst the various classes of eldar that lived
in those levels. The Shining Spears brought dazzling
light into the darkest realms, transforming the spirit
of Ulthwé for brief moments and in tiny places as
they sped through.

It was a small temple, especially compared with
the massive temple complex of the Dark Reapers,
which was based thousands of metres above in the
upper reaches of Ulthwé, where it complemented
the atmosphere of the craftworld with its sinister
blacks and dull, bone whites. Very few eldar chose to
tread the path of the Shining Spear when their souls
started to hear the whispering call of Kaela Mensha
Khaine. Most, on Ulthwé at least, chose to immerse
themselves in the shadowy mystery of the Reapers,
transforming themselves into manifestations of
Khaine in his darkest guise as the destroyer.

It had not gone unnoticed in Ulthwé or amongst
the eldar of the other peripatetic craftworlds that the
eldar of Ulthwé showed a marked tendency to pursue

the darkest aspects of their being. After millennia of skirting the lashes of the Eye of Terror, many had hypothesised that the Chaotic tears of the Eye itself had touched the very soul of the craftworld. In whispered tones, the eldar of Biel-Tan and even Saim-Hann would refer to Ulthwé as the Craftworld of the Damned – implying that it might one day follow its sister Altansar and plunge into the Eye itself, never to be seen again.

The only thing that seemed to preserve Ulthwé from its doom was its simultaneous tendency to produce unusually high numbers of seers and warlocks. Led by the mighty Eldrad Ulthran himself, the Seer Council had continuously and successfully navigated a path through the tortuous, myriad futures that spiralled out of the Eye.

Guardian Dhrykna was not unaware of the various significances of the Aspect Temple in which she had trained for so many years. She had known even before that fateful day, long years before, when she had felt the pull of the bloody hand of Khaine, his ethereal fingers beckoning her into the light. The choice of warrior Aspect was a very personal one, and it was not something in which other eldar would interfere. However, Dhrykna had been aware, even then, that she was stepping out of the usual conventions of her society. At the time of her initiation into the sparkling temple of light, only four other aspirant warriors knelt at her side, waiting to take their first steps on the Shining Path. Meanwhile, in the cavernous and echoing halls of the Dark Reaper temple, high above them, numberless ranks of eldar knelt in obeisance and shadow before the altar of Maugan Ra.

Now, at the moment when Ulthwé most needed the lightning speed of Khaine's fabled spear, the Shining Spears were a tiny force, bereft of leadership and all but forgotten in the depths of the craftworld. They had fallen into the realm of rumour and myth. Instead, where Ulthwé needed speed it had the solid power of the Reapers, where it needed mobility it had ranged fire power.

Even the Black Guardians, the craftworld's principal force, were constituted mainly of warriors that had passed a cycle of their lives in the service of the Dark Reapers. They were a small and dwindling presence on Ulthwé. The glory days of the Black Guardians, when they were known and feared throughout the Eye, were dwindling, and their training made them ill-suited to meet the challenges of the current threat.

As she casually tilted her black and silver jetbike around the last corner, almost laying the machine on its side in order to pull its nose around tightly enough, Dhrykna's pupils contracted suddenly, reacting to the flood of light that greeted her. Up ahead, half buried in the floor and half obscured by the low ceiling, the glowing, crystalline structure of the Shining Temple burst into view. It was radiant, and Dhrykna caught her breath, always awe-struck when she saw the incredible architecture of the shrine building.

In these days of darkness and shadow, it seemed almost inconceivable that Ulthwé wraithsmiths had once been able and willing to engineer such incomparable light in the bowels of their world. No matter how many times she saw it, it took her breath away each time.

Almost involuntarily, Dhrykna slowed her approach, letting the nose of her bike drop and easing off the power. She just coasted in, keeping her eyes fixed on the radiant brightness as she emerged from the darkness of the craftworld beyond. After a few moments, her eyes began to adjust to the light and she could pick out the runic inscriptions that laced the great crystal archway. On the centrepiece was the ancient rune *slavhreenur* – salvation. It resembled an arrow striving for heaven, crossed through with doubts, leaving a serpentine ignorance squirming beneath it. Its likeness was branded into the skin of the forearm of each warrior who took steps along the Shining Path; it symbolised that the warrior was one who had emerged out of the darkness and into the light.

As she approached, the brand on Dhrykna's own arm started to throb. She could feel her blood drawing her onwards.

She had not been back to the temple for years, not since leaving it so hurriedly. In her memory, she had been expelled from the order, although in truth she had simply been refused ascension to the status of its exarch. She had left of her own volition. The sacred armour of the exarch had been vacant for decades, since none had passed along the Shining Path and found themselves stuck on that road, unable to move on to one of the other myriad eldar ways. It seemed that the souls of the Ulthwé eldar were increasingly at variance with the spirit of the declining temple. Dhrykna had felt that she was different. Her heart ached for the eternal embrace of the ancient armour, in which writhed the souls of all

the previous exarchs of that exalted temple, each
absorbed into the spirit stone of the very first exarch
of the Shining Spears on Ulthwé, the radiant
Prothenulh, whose name would always be in the
mind of any exarch who donned his armour. In her
dreams, Dhrykna could sometimes hear his voice
whispering to her.

*The hour is dark at which Dhrykna of the Shining
Path returns to the Temple of Light.* The words entered
her mind with familiar ease even before her bike
pulled to a standstill and she dismounted before the
great gates. The source of the thoughts was nowhere
to be seen, but Dhrykna knew better than to expect
the temple's guardians to show themselves so
quickly.

'I return to you at the direction of the Emerald
Seer,' said Dhrykna, standing before the gates and
touching her right fist to her heart, displaying the
brand on her arm. 'Ulthwé has need of the Shining
Spears once again.'

As she spoke, the runic brand on her arm crackled
with light, like an intricate fuse. The great crystal
gates before her sizzled in response, sending pulses
of light lacing around their edges. After a second, the
gates cracked open and slid back into the walls on
either side, leaving a wide opening between. Beyond
them, in the interior of the outer temple, Dhrykna
could see the shimmering amethyst courtyard, radiant with a tranquil, lavender light. She sighed
deeply. Having resigned herself to never seeing this
sight again, Dhrykna's heart was flooded with competing emotions. In the end, however, it was a
homecoming, and she gathered herself to enter.

Know this, Dhrykna, the Shining Path permits no shadows. There is nowhere for darkness to hide in the Crystal Temple. There is nothing but eternal light in the innermost sanctum, receding off to infinity through an endless regression of refractions and reflections. Do not enter willingly. Enter because there is no other way for you to go.

The Black Guardian stood on the threshold of the Temple of the Shining Spears for the second time in her life and gazed in at the ineffable beauty of the amethyst courtyard within. The first time that she had passed through those gates, she had not known what to expect on the other side. She had only felt the inexplicable and implacable drive to enter. This time, she would take those steps onto the path in full knowledge, knowing that there was no way back into the ever-cycling life of the eldar way. These steps would condemn her to battle and bloodshed for the rest of her long life. Thae'akzi had warned her that she was not the exarch yet, but her soul screamed at her that this was her destiny.

'I understand, and I take the light into my soul. I will become the spear of Khaine. Lightning flashes, blood falls, death pierces the darkness.' With that, Dhrykna the Black Guardian stepped back into the Aspect Temple and the crystal gates slid shut behind her, sealing her into the brightness within.

CHAPTER FOUR:
GLADIATRIX

THE DARKNESS WAS intense, burning down from the swirling sky like the light of a black star. Clouds formed and roiled high in the thick atmosphere, defined against the lightless stratosphere in crisp contrast, like whirling currents through oil, smothering the myriad, grotesque stars of the Eye of Terror beyond. Despite the profound darkness, the surface of planet Hesperax appeared to be bathed in a kind of eerie visibility. It was not a world from which light had been banished by the efforts of night. Rather, it was a world forever untouched by the flaming fingers of a sun. The jagged mountains, spiked with lethal rocks and cracked through by vicious ravines, had never been warmed by the light. They were ice to their core. Darkness streamed across the surface where light should have been, cutting the scene into relief through its own, distinct visual properties. This was not simply a world devoid of light, it was a world utterly alien to it. It was not a realm of shadows, it was a world on which light had no place at all. It was a world wrought in the very image of Commorragh itself.

Once, long ago, the barren and desolate summit of Sussarkh's Peak had been the highest on Hesperax – in the days before Lelith blew the top off it to excavate her grand amphitheatre. The peak had pierced the oily clouds themselves, rising out from a mighty range of mountains near the northern pole. From there, Lord Sussarkh had reigned over the wastelands as a king, filling his subjects' hearts with fear and hatred, subjugating his dark eldar brethren just as he ruined the spirits of his foes.

The world teemed with death and its valleys ran slick with blood as Sussarkh twisted the will of his people and turned them against one another, stirring them into rebellions and counter rebellions, bringing the world to the brink of its own ruin. Meanwhile, Sussarkh the Kabal Slayer sat in mirth upon his mountain peak, watching the pretenders to his throne rip each other asunder.

It is said that the magnificent Sussarkh trusted nobody except his favoured consort, the breathtaking Lelith of the Wych Cult of Strife. One night, at the peak of his glory, even as the mountainsides were burning with the eternal flames of perpetual combat that Sussarkh himself had fanned into life, he called on his queen, the beautiful and terrible Lelith, to dance for him on the mountaintop. And she had danced.

The retinue of the Archon had arrayed itself around the rim of the summit, forming their eager eyes into the sweeping boundary of a makeshift amphitheatre, preparing a space for the exquisite performance of the young wych. Legend says that a bolt of black lightning tore through the heavens as Lelith slid her shapely form between two of the incubi warriors and stepped into the ceremonial ring, letting her long black cloak fall into the dust around her ankles.

She stood into the centre of the circle, folding her pale-skinned arms around her scarcely clothed torso, clutching a single, elegantly curving blade in each of her delicate hands. As she started to move, the heavens opened and thick black rain fell from the sky, speckling her graceful form with dashes of oil, making her shimmer and flare as she danced, with her blades flashing into sweeps and whirls of motion. The dance was beautiful and terrifying to behold.

After half an hour, Lelith's movements slowed smoothly to a halt, her glistening body coated in a layer of viscous black rain, reflecting the dark lightning that lashed through the sky above the mountain peak. She dropped to her knees before the throne of the dark eldar lord who had subjugated the kabals and cults of Hesperax, bringing the planet under his power and will, proclaiming himself the first Archon Lord of Hesperax. With one knee on the soaked ground, Lelith bowed her head and extended her arms to each side, her curving blades extending her reach as though growing out of her hands. The line of her glistening and exposed shoulder blades is said to have transfixed the gaze of the entranced and lascivious Sussarkh.

Rising to her feet and folding her arms back around her body, as though suddenly coy now that her performance had ended, Lelith grinned at the lord as he lounged in his throne. She ran the tip of her tongue over the extended points of her incisors, tempting Sussarkh to rise to his feet and take a step towards her. As he did so, he must have noticed the glint of maniacal passion that flashed in the wych's eyes, for he suddenly cast his gaze around the ring of his retinue, as though looking for reassurance.

But something was wrong. Although the incubi warriors stood exactly as they had when Lelith had started her dance, they were drenched in the dark liquids that fell as rain, but were not moving. They were not even following the breathless motions of the exquisite young wych with their hungry eyes.

Looking more carefully through the rain, Sussarkh must have realised that the liquid that slicked the armour of his bodyguards was not just rain. Their eyes did not follow Lelith, because the glint of life had vanished from them. Even as he watched, the shapes of his most trusted warriors began to shift and deform as slices and cuts began to appear all over their bodies. Limbs came away from torsos and skulls parted through the middle, slipping and falling to the ground into neatly diced heaps of their own tissue.

With a sudden realisation, Sussarkh whipped his own blade from its holster by his side and spun to face the exquisite form of Lelith. She was no longer standing coyly before the throne, her feet being caressed by ripples in the pool of the incubi retinue's blood. Instead, she was reclining sensuously in the throne itself, the tip of one of her blades touched to her bottom lip as though she were slightly embarrassed.

Sussarkh threw back his head and let out a blood-curdling cry, filling the rain drenched summit with the joyful agonies of threatened vengeance. Then he pulled his sword up to his shoulder and took a step towards the treacherous wych. But something was wrong. He tried again, his mind confused and rebelling against his apparent immobility. He remained motionless.

Horror sank slowly into the soul of the Archon Lord as he realised that his reign had finally been brought to a close. He looked down at his own chest and watched the intricate web of monomolecular cuts and slices that laced his body gradually expand as blood started to seep out of them. He watched his sword splash and clatter to the ground, his severed arms still clutching its hilt. The very last thing that the great Sussarkh saw was a puddle of his own blood lapping against the naked foot of Wych Queen Lelith of Hesperax as his head crashed down into the expanding pool before *her* throne.

Over the following decades and centuries, Lelith transformed the nature of Hesperax, forging it into the image of her own will. In the place of internecine civil war, Lelith instituted the gladiatrix auditoriums where the wyches of her realm could exercise their grievances or simply indulge their pleasures. The greatest of the amphitheatres was cut into the summit of Sussarkh's peak itself, and it was there, overlooking the rocky steps to heaven themselves, that Lelith kept the throne. She even kept the mountain's name, letting it stand as an emblem of the folly of opposing her. Nonetheless, the kabals of Hesperax had not been disbanded, and the Cult of Strife was not the only wych coven; many voices whispered in the dark about how the wych queen could have maintained control for so long. Some of the voices even dared to suggest that her power was not entirely her own, and that the winding paths of the future might one day separate her from her mysterious, shadowy patron.

A DIFFERENT KLAXON sounded, breaking through the dull, monotonous whine of the warp sensors' continuous warning with a sharp, pulsing screech. At the same time, a blue light over the *Lance of Darkness*'s main viewscreen started to flash.

'Proximity warning?' asked Atreus, dragging his eyes away from the magnified image of the immense, distant craftworld. He was still struggling to believe that a space vessel of that magnitude could really exist; knowing it in theory was no preparation for seeing it in reality. From a distance, it could easily be mistaken for a planet or even a star.

'No,' replied Octavius, turning away from the screen and striding towards one of the nearby control consoles. As he approached, the serf instantly rose out of the chair and backed away from the monitor, making space for the Deathwatch captain without needing to receive an order. 'This is a range warning. We don't have company yet, but it's on its way.'

'Ulthwé?' asked Atreus, his voice sceptical.

'No,' replied Ashok, without having moved or even turned from his position at the main screen. 'Something else.'

'He's right,' said Octavius, staring into the green images that flickered across the terminal monitor. 'Small and fast, heading out of the Eye itself. Their signatures are inconstant, as though the ships themselves keep falling out of phase.'

'Shadowfields?' queried Atreus. He had never come across a dark eldar Corsair before, but he had done his research. In common with his brother librarians from the Blood Ravens, he never went into battle without a thorough knowledge of his potential foes. The deceptive device, codified as a shadowfield by Blood Ravens researchers, enabled the Corsair to pass in and out of sensor arrays with impunity. Sometimes, if used in combination with a mimic engine, even causing the escort ships to register on monitors as friendlies.

As far as Atreus was aware, no functioning examples had ever been seized by Imperial forces, and certainly not by the Blood Ravens. Of course, he was perfectly willing to concede the probability that the Ordo Xenos had entire Corsairs holed up in research facilities somewhere, or even that other Space Marine Chapters might have captured one without reporting it. If it had taught him nothing else, his brief period of service in the Deathwatch had revealed to Atreus how little information was actually shared between the various institutions of the Emperor's will.

'Possibly,' replied Octavius, well aware of the stories of such devices.

'Atreus is right – they are eldar raiders, or dark eldar,' confirmed Ashok, his eyes closed with concentration. 'But they are not welcome. Not Ulthwé. Ulthran is aware of them. The craftworld has launched gunships.'

The Blood Ravens librarian nodded his silent affirmation.

'He's right,' said Octavius, still gazing into the ghostly green screen. 'Six Shadowhunter escorts have launched from Ulthwé and identified themselves to us as friendlies. But they do not appear to be intercepting the–'

Octavius cut himself off. Suddenly the range warning stopped and the blue light faded.

'They're gone,' he said. 'They just blinked out...' He was lost in thought for a moment. 'The Shadowhunters are closing on *our* position. They have come to escort us in.'

He lifted his head from the monitor, the lines of concern that creased his face clear for everyone on the deck to see. 'Librarian Atreus, please ensure that the team is ready. It seems that we will be meeting our new friends rather sooner than we anticipated.'

Atreus nodded smartly to the captain and glanced over towards Ashok, whose broad, unarmoured back blocked much of the viewscreen. The Angel Sanguine showed no signs of turning, so Atreus strode directly out of the control room.

'Ashok...' began Octavius.

'I don't know, captain, but I'm sure that we will find out soon. It seems that there is more to this mission than Ulthwé. I suspect that the raiders were dark eldar. Atreus would appear to agree. We must be cautious,' answered Ashok, not waiting for the captain to vocalise the obvious question.

'We are always cautious, Ashok,' nodded Octavius, smiling slightly. 'And we were certainly planning on being extra careful in our dealings with the perfidious aliens.'

Ashok nodded quietly. He had still not turned to face the captain, preferring instead to keep his eyes fixed on the image of the craftworld that was growing gradually larger as the *Lance of Darkness* closed on it. His dark eyes were half-closed in concentration, as though an effort of will was required to keep a pervasive and powerful presence at bay. After a few seconds, a series of flashes seared towards the screen and vanished behind the frigate. The Deathwatch's escorts had arrived.

'Librarian,' said Octavius, his feeling of unease about the brooding Angel Sanguine having returned. 'Please prepare yourself for our rendezvous. I assume that you will want to wear your armour.' It was the closest thing to an order that he had ever uttered to Ashok.

'As you wish, captain,' replied the librarian, turning smoothly and nodding a gracious bow from under his hood, where his eyes remained hidden in shadow. Without another word, Ashok strode out of the control room, his long cloak billowing slightly in his wake, leaving Octavius alone with the serfs on the control deck.

The events of the last few hours had unravelled faster than even he was accustomed to. In the service of the Deathwatch, Octavius was quite used to being despatched on short notice, but the incredible speed and extreme secrecy with which the current team had been assembled made him uncomfortable.

He had not had as much time as he might have liked to assemble a team that would work well together; he had done his best, of course, and he was sure that he could rely on each and every Marine that was seconded into the Deathwatch. They wouldn't be there at all if they were not the very brightest stars of their Chapters. But then, even after he had made his choices, the inquisitor lords had thrown an extra piece into the mix without telling him.

It was true that he had worked successfully with Librarian Ashok before, but the role of the mysterious Angel Sanguine in the present affair was unclear to him. In addition, the sudden and unconfirmed appearance of dark eldar Corsairs in the system made the picture look even more complicated. No mention had been made of the utterly evil brethren of the enigmatic eldar during the mission briefing, and Octavius wondered whether Lord Vargas was even aware of their involvement, if indeed they were involved. The Imperial Fists captain was no stranger to the political intrigues of high command, and it occurred to him that his masters in the Ordo Xenos might not really understand what they were sending him into.

Looking up at the giant viewscreen, Octavius marvelled at the scale and elegance of the massive craftworld as the *Lance of Darkness* drew closer to it, dwarfed like a fleck of dust next to a moon. The craftworld was as large as a planet, but beautiful like a work of artistry, more graceful than anything in nature. Despite his hardwired distrust and disdain for the aliens, Octavius could feel a sense of awe gnawing at his heart. He wondered how many humans had been this close to Ulthwé and lived to tell the tale. It was incredible.

As the gargantuan vessel filled the viewscreen, Octavius watched for the red proximity alarm to sound. But there was nothing. He waited a few more seconds, expecting the pilot-servitor to cut the engines and coast the last few thousand metres into the docking bay that had opened before them. However, the pilot showed no signs of slowing. Instead, his head was poring over a terminal, monitoring the proximity readings and trying to make sense of the docking instructions being supplied by the eldar. On the viewscreen, Ulthwé got closer and closer, until Octavius became certain that they would simply crash into it.

There was no crash.

'Pilot?' queried Octavius, letting a note of concern enter his voice.

'Captain. Eighty kilometres and closing. The engines will cut in seventy.'

Still eighty kilometres? Octavius's eyes widened slightly as he stared at the screen. He could see nothing except the glittering black and silver form of Ulthwé, completely obliterating the starscape ahead. How big was this craftworld? How many eldar survived in its massive structure? Scale was difficult to judge in space, but Octavius had never seen anything that appeared so huge even from so far away. Every instinct told him that the *Lance of Darkness* was about to crash into it.

THE QUEEN'S PODIUM was set into the sheer wall on the north of the great auditorium on Sussarkh's Peak. There was no path of approach, and the wall itself was immaculately smooth, almost frictionless. There was no way up. It was the only side of the auditorium that was not teeming with wyches or macabre ornamentation. The amphitheatre was a colossal testament to the power of the Cult of Strife, and its place of greatest honour was, naturally enough, reserved for their magnificent and terrible queen.

It was a luxurious platform, bedecked in lavish velvets and soaked through with rich, treacly blood. There was a series of gargoyles by the floor around the edge of the podium; their vomiting mouths served as inlets for the gallons of blood that were spilt into and drained from the main auditorium every day.

The ground was fecund with death, cushioning the delicate footfalls of the queen and her closest, most trusted succubi. On the most auspicious days, when the auditorium fighters were at their best, the flow of blood onto the platform would exceed the limits of comfort and it would gush out over the lip of the podium, cascading down the sheer wall like a waterfall of gore and glory, driving the wyches wild in the stands.

Lelith grinned, reclining into her throne and stretching out her long legs extravagantly. Beneath her, the bones and flesh of the throne groaned and moaned, as though pressed into a mixture of agony and ecstasy. The queen closed her eyes and smiled with the pleasure of power, feeling the teeming thronelings striving against each other for a touch of her perfect skin. The throne rippled with a kind of tortured rapture, and droplets of ruby blood oozed out from its writhing, organic structure.

A great roar erupted from the assembly, almost masking the gargled screams of the hapless victims in the arena. Quruel, the mistress of the beasts, was prowling around the perimeter of the arena like a beast herself. She was without weapons, except for the bladed gauntlets that were strapped to her forearms with threads of sinew and plaits of hair, and she patrolled the edge of the circular theatre proudly erect at one moment and then bestial on all fours the next.

Two warp beasts lurked and lashed around the open space, pausing to feed on the flesh of the fallen corpses that were strewn haphazardly over the floor, but too nervous of Quruel to linger for long. They were new to the material realm of Hesperax, summoned out of the warp by Quruel to replace the dragonettes that she had lost in Ulthwé. Their wills were not yet entirely broken, and they were not yet wholly house-trained. But they were learning.

In the very centre of the auditorium, a small number of creatures were clustered together like cattle. They had their backs to each other and their petrified faces shone out towards the three prowling predators. Their numbers were dwindling and their bravery had evaporated long ago. A couple of the men still clutched weapons in their hands, although they appeared to be using them as crutches for their courage rather than as potential sources of their salvation. They had seen their comrades picked off by the warp beasts, one by one, and they had heard the curdling, shrieking agony of their deaths. The remaining men had lost all hope of life and their faces betrayed their forlorn souls, resigned absolutely to the horror of their fate.

The abject terror that flowed out of their human victims like the very stench of death was sweet as a rich perfume to the assembled wyches, who breathed it in thirstily as though it were a narcotic. They cheered and brayed, shrieking with exhilaration, and their excitement seemed to drive the beasts and their mistress to new frenzies of violence. The warp beasts roared, rearing and snarling before pouncing towards the humans for a last storm of teeth, talons and claws. The men offered no resistance. They simply sank to their knees, sliding down their swords and staffs until their hands and feet were soaked in the blood drenched earth. If it were not for the howls and the lashing of claws, the faint whisper of futile prayers would have escaped into the darkness.

Another great cheer erupted from the crowd as Quruel strode into the midst of the feeding frenzy, dragging the beasts back away from their carrion, throwing them aside with complete disregard for their size and bulk.

The beasts shrank back, snarling and cowering in equal measures. Their eyes blazed with a thirst for death and the flesh of the dying, but they were wary of the lithe warrior that stood defiantly before them, bathing in the blood of their quarry. They paced and drooled in a circle around her until she finally acknowledged them, demonstrating her power over them, making them hers. She reached down and ripped a limb from one of the broken bodies, tossing it out towards one of the beasts. Both dashed after the flesh, clashing with each other, lashing out with their filthy claws.

That's it. But there's plenty more, hissed Quruel in a tongue that only they might understand. As her mind spoke to them, she threw a second slab of flesh and the fighting stopped. The weaker of the beasts broke away and dashed for the new scrap, dropping to the ground and gnashing at it with glinting yellow teeth. *Now*, she muttered, to herself as much as to them. *Now you are mine.*

VERY GOOD, QURUEL, MISTRESS OF THE BEASTS. VERY GOOD. The thoughts belonged to Lelith, but they resonated throughout the amphitheatre as though amplified into the minds of everyone present. The assembly turned in unison to see their queen on her feet at the edge of her podium. Her feet were placed neatly together and her hands were clasped meekly in front of her, but her hair rippled out behind her as though caught in a gale that nobody else could feel. Those who looked more closely would have seen that her feet were not actually resting on the ground at all. It was as though she were held in a breathless aura of her own darkness.

A deathly silence descended on the mountaintop.

ENOUGH OF THIS TRAINING SHOW – LET THE ENTERTAINMENT COMMENCE. BRING IN THE PRISONERS.

As the thoughts echoed around the summit, the floor of the arena cracked through the middle and the structure of the amphitheatre groaned. Slowly and with heavy deliberation, the ground started to open up, and the assembly of wyches started to chant, anticipating what was to come. Their focus was intense and unbroken.

As the floor withdrew, the blood and flesh of the dead gushed into runnels around the perimeter, from whence they were channelled up onto Lelith's podium; a great red wave burst out over the edge of her platform, breaking around Lelith herself, coating her in a glistening second skin, and conjuring an ecstatic roar from the crowd.

A second floor arose to take the place of the first, clean and smooth as though having been specially cleaned and prepared for the carnage to come, ritually purified before being ritually sullied. In the very centre of the new floor a few pale and elegant figures were huddled. Their shapes were tall and graceful, not wholly dissimilar from the wyches that whooped and brayed as they came into view, yet they appeared profoundly out of place in the grand arena of Hesperax.

As the new floor finally filled the void left by the old one, clunking solidly into place, the features of the prisoners could be more clearly seen. They appeared to be eldar, although they were not attired in the psycho-plastic armour that characterised eldar warriors. Their long, flowing robes gave them a more aesthetic air, utterly incongruous in their current surroundings. Even their facial features seemed somehow strange, as though distorted or twisted out of alignment. They appeared damaged in indefinite ways. Despite the riotous noise that echoed around the arena, the eldar prisoners remained silent and still, as though their spirits were already broken and their souls were resigned to their doom.

Sighing in undisguised disappointment, Lelith dropped her feet back down into the spongy floor as the last waves of blood lapped past, dropping down the sheer face of the arena in a smooth cascade. She let her body fall backwards. In unseemly and hungry haste, the thronelings rushed to cushion her fall, forming spontaneously into a chaise-longue and capturing the queen's exquisitely discontented body.

Skazhrealh had clearly been unable to resist tampering with the lightlings, reflected Lelith in displeasure, ignoring the squirms and chuckles of the thronelings beneath her. She had not given the haemonculus permission to damage the captives, and her lip snarled at the implied defiance. Although she could understand how Skazhrealh's thirst for the infliction of agony on the fragile and pathetically beautiful lightling bodies might have made his defiance almost inevitable, Lelith also had a taste for these delicacies.

Not only that, but there was at least one other power on Hesperax who would be anticipating indulging in the unblemished souls of the eldar, and it would not be wise to disappoint her. Lelith would not let this pass, and Skazhrealh would feel the sharp end of his own instruments of torture before the night was out – his apprentices would appreciate the practice, and even Skazhrealh would probably find some pleasure in the throes of his own agony. Lelith made a mental note to kill him before that happened.

The shouts from the assembled wyches had fallen into a rhythmic chant, gently lulling Lelith out of her tortuous reverie. She lay for a moment, enjoying the moisture and warmth of the throne against her skin, listening to the pulsing mantra that filled the auditorium, feeling it darkening her already pitch-black soul.

Reluctantly tensing the sculpted muscles of her abdomen, Lelith began to rise, but the thronelings chased after her, desperate not to lose contact with her shoulder blades or her long, black hair. The throne stretched, its bones creaking and streams of blood lubricating the joints, and Lelith smiled, shaking her head in disgust – she never felt pity for the thronelings or for anything else.

THE HONOUR OF THE SPORT SHOULD GO TO OUR YOUNG RAIDERS, KROULIR OF THE DESPERATE DARK AND DRUQURA OF THE FORGOTTEN STRIFE.

The thoughts brought silence back to the dark amphitheatre, and then an eruption of cheers intermixed with sniggers and whines of jealous disapproval and disappointment. Everyone wanted a chance to make the kills, and each resented the privileges of the others. In the midst of the din, Kroulir and Druqura vaulted down from the stands, turning deliberate somersaults as they sprang into the arena, landing softly with their blades already drawn and their eyes flashing.

Immediately, they started to patrol around the captives, keeping their distance at first as they weighed up the physiques of the lightlings, assessing the potential challenges – there wasn't much to speak of. The wyches' teeth glinted viciously in the dark light, but their eyes betrayed their disappointment. Their quarry showed almost no signs of noticing them. There were no screams, no wails of anguish, not even any futile posturing. The eldar prisoners were docile and emotionless. Hardly any sport at all. It wasn't just because they were broken; they were simply weak specimens – eldar who had never even placed a foot on that ridiculous cycle of the warrior.

As the crowd's interest started to wane, Kroulir licked her teeth and sprang forward, igniting another, weaker cheer from the watching wyches. In her mind's eye, she could still see the wretched face of the lightling warlock in the cursed craftworld; these prisoners may not be his equal, but they were still lightling aberrations and she would offer their souls to her queen. One day she would return for that warlock. An eldar waystone was a rare delicacy, even if ripped from the body of a vacuous artist such as these. It was not great sport, but there was still a worthy reward, and wrenching a soul from the wretched confines of its weak flesh was a type of reward in itself.

THE LIGHT WAS brilliant and stunning, refracting into myriad colours and sparkling with a pristine purity that made Dhrykna feel transfigured as she walked the once familiar corridors of the Temple of Light. She had trodden these passageways innumerable times in the past, transposing them into neural pathways in her brain so that she could find her way around in the dark if she needed to. But there was never even a hint of darkness in the temple, not even a single shadow sullied the crystalline walls. The

light was pervasive, and even if Dhrykna were to
close her eyes she would not be able to shut out the
dazzling presence of the temple's spirit.

The temple appeared completely deserted.
Dhrykna had been walking since the hour of Karan-
dras and yet she had not seen another face in all that
time. She was being watched; that much was clear to
her from the tension in her mind. But the temple
guardians remained hidden from her and not a single Aspect Warrior had shown himself in the
sparkling maze. Had the numbers really grown so
few, wondered the Black Guardian, her heart sinking
at the thought.

As she approached the mirrored doors to the sanctum, Dhrykna paused. She could see herself clearly
in the reflection, her black and silver armour heavy
and incongruous in the dazzling surroundings. It
was almost offensive to see herself in such a way.
Had she really moved so far from the Shining Path?
Had she really become so dark and so riddled with
gravity? The spear of Khaine was almost unrecognis-
able in her visage, and she dropped to her knees
before her own image, suddenly distraught and
weeping at what she had become.

Her tears streamed down her cheeks like sparkling
rivers, transforming her face into a reflective burst of
light. They poured onto the ground, pooling around
her knees. She had disfigured herself. The emotions
of the eldar were violent and extreme, and for a
moment Dhrykna could do nothing about her self-
reproach and despair. As she knelt, wretched and
distraught, she glanced up into the great mirrors of
the outer sanctum once again and saw her face

transformed – each tear glittering like a crystal jewel. Her eyes flashed with recognition and the doors slid open silently. Humility was a rare quality amongst the eldar, especially on Ulthwé.

Composing herself, Dhrykna rose to her feet and strode into the inner sanctum, feeling the light trickling over her face and infusing her with its own radiance. Once inside, the great mirrors slid back into place behind her, sealing her into an infinite regression of dazzling reflections. Laid out on a glass altar before her was a suit of pristine white armour. She recognised it at once as the very same suit that she had worn during her years of service in this hallowed temple. Its psycho-plastic was scarred here and there, where blades and las-fire had scuffed its surface, but otherwise it was immaculate.

Looking from side to side, expecting to see the temple guardians flanking her ready to make the presentation of her armour, she was startled to see an eternal row of Black Guardians gazing back at her, their eyes and face obliterated by dazzling lights. Their infinite line was akin to an aberration in the sanctum, heavy and black and ugly. With a start, she realised that they were all her. Her dismal and mundane existence was reflected back at her a million times, driving itself into her conscience and making her shrink back away from the horror of herself.

There was nowhere to hide in the sanctum of the temple of light. There were no shadows in which the unprepared or the cowardly could seek refuge. But Dhrykna required no shelter. She clenched her jaw in determination and turned back to the armour that awaited her on the altar. *That* was her. She had never been the same since removing those immaculate plates, but now she had returned to them, like a prodigal child.

As she took a step towards the altar, something else caught her eye in the far wall. It took a few moments for her eyes to adjust to the intense light, but she could see a shallow alcove cut into the crystal structure of the wall. Inside the recess there were two shelves, each supporting the flawless visages of helmets – two entire rows of helmets, untouched and gleaming.

Distracted for a moment, Dhrykna skirted around the altar and approached the helmets, peering closely but not touching them. They were the helms of warlocks, reserved for those Aspect Warriors who left the Shining Path of their own volition, determined to make their journeys along the long and arduous road of the seer. In times of strife, such seers might return to the Temple of Light and offer themselves back to this aspect of Khaine, turning their hard-won psychic powers self-consciously towards the purposes of lightning death and prompt destruction. Such seers would become warlocks, creating a confluence of the dual ways of seer and warrior for themselves, forging their own bloody paths into a darkly glittering future of their own making.

Not a single helmet was missing, and Dhrykna's eyes widened as she realised what that meant. She knew that the Emerald Seer had spent one of her cycles in the service of the Shining Spears, and she had heard that the great seer had received a summons to the temple during a hard-fought conflict with some distorted mon-keigh from the Eye of Terror. She had also heard that Thae'akzi had resisted the lure of the bloody-handed way and had emerged from the temple without adopting the visage of a warlock. However, it had never occurred to Dhrykna that there was not a single warlock on Ulthwé that drew their energy and inspiration from the Shining Path. The words of the temple guardian returned to her: the Shining Path permits no shadows.

Casting her mind back through the gleaming corridors of the temple, Dhrykna realised with horror what should have been obvious from the moment she entered through the great archway into the court of the amethysts: the Shining Spears were vanishing. The corridors and passageways of the temple were empty because there were no warriors to fill them.

She had been so awe-struck by the glittering majesty of the place that she had failed to notice the most obvious thing. The light of the Spears was gradually being swamped by the heavy darkness of Ulthwé – the spirit of the craftworld itself was changing, darkening still further. In a moment of horror she realised that the Undercouncil of Warlocks must be comprised almost entirely of former Dark Reapers. The thought made her shiver.

Turning abruptly, Dhrykna gazed back at the pristine, white and silver armour that had been laid out for her. Despite its sudden agonies, her soul soared at the realisation that it belonged in this majestic sanctum. That armour was hers. The light of the Shining Path flowed through her, igniting her spirit and giving her life. For the glory of the Shining Spears and the security of Ulthwé, Dhrykna reached her hand out towards the armour. How could there

be an exarch when there were not even any warriors?
The temple itself cried out for salvation, for vindica-
tion and for blood. Thae'akzi had been right to send
her back to the temple – with her soul so transfigured, she would even stand shoulder to shoulder
with the mon-keigh.

'Light flashes, blood falls, death pierces the darkness,' whispered Dhrykna, reaching for the armour.

As THE LAST of the lightling victims collapsed to the
ground, its throat slit neatly and its eyes bulging at
the last, the assembly of wyches had fallen almost
silent. In one or two sections of the amphitheatre
wyches from the Cult of Vengeance actually jeered.
Most were content to voice their disapproval
through silence, fearing the wrath of Lelith and her
Wyches of Strife should they speak out. But there
was barely a single wych who was left satisfied by the
spectacle. The pathetic lightlings had been no sport
at all; Kroulir and Druqura had dispatched them
with skill and grace, but there had been no thrill.
Blood was not enough in itself. Even pain was insufficient. The wyches craved combat in their arena, not
merely death. And these lightling artisans had provided no resistance at all. They were worse even than
the decrepit humans that Quruel had used as game
for her beasts.

The two young wyches snarled in dissatisfaction,
frustrated that their moment of glory in the arena
had been rendered so cheap by the inadequacy of
their opponents. They wrenched the glittering waystones from the corpses of the lightlings, hardly even
giving them a second glance as they snapped the

chains that held the spirit vessels around the necks
of the fallen. In place of pride at her victory, Kroulir
spat hateful phlegm into the faces of the dead.
Rather than seeing their waystones as her prize, she
saw only the fragile and contemptible weakness of
the lightlings, who genuinely thought that their
souls could escape the daemonic caresses of
Slaanesh if only they were hidden in these tiny spirit
stones. It was pathetic. Slaanesh was a worthy adver-
sary, to be sure, but there were far better, more
inventive and more interesting ways of dealing with
it than continuously hiding. Of all the dark eldar,
Lelith herself knew this better than anyone.

Cheers and jeers echoed around the auditorium
as the atmosphere on the mountaintop curdled
with sickly malediction. The two young wyches
shrieked up into the stands, defying the crowd with
the jagged points of their teeth and the tips of their
blades, daring challengers to come forth, if they
found the contest unworthy of a Hesperax wych.
Although they snarled and screeched, none in the
assembly responded and the mixture of rapture
and disgust continued to be thrown out of the
stands.

With the crowd unsilenced and the waystones
held loosely in their hands, Kroulir and Druqura
strode towards the base of the sheer wall in which
was recessed Lelith's podium. They dropped to
their knees before it, holding the tiny, glittering
jewels above their heads for all to see.

Silence descended at last as Lelith rose to her feet
and looked down at the offering. For a moment, it
was not clear what the wych queen was going to do.

The expression on her face was blank and she muttered no thoughts into the darkness. The silence of the crowd shifted imperceptibly from reverence to anticipation.

With a sudden spring, Lelith vaulted off her platform, turning and twisting through the air with exquisite ease before landing silently in front of the kneeling wyches. After a moment's delay, her retinue of succubi also launched themselves down into the arena, positioning themselves in a crescent around their suddenly exposed queen, facing out towards the assembly, daring challengers to attempt their lustful coup.

Nobody moved. The entire amphitheatre fell into a tense immobility.

I ACCEPT YOUR OFFERINGS, KROULIR OF DESPERATE DARK AND DRUQURA OF FORGOTTEN STRIFE. BRING THEM TO ME.

There was nothing that the young wyches could do to resist the queen: her delicate yet sickly fragrance intoxicated their senses from the moment that she landed before them, and her thoughts seduced their minds like sensuous lovers, promising so much more than words.

Kroulir fought with her will, struggling to raise her head enough to catch a glimpse of the taught, pale skin that covered the queen's calves. But she could not move. For nearly a minute, she could not even breathe.

Bring them to me, coaxed Lelith in an intimate tone that only they could understand, driving them wild with unexpected emotions. She crouched down before the wyches, bringing her delicately angled face into their line of sight, making their eyes bulge with self-consciousness as they realised that they had no choice but to gaze on her.

She held out her hand. *Bring them.*

Kroulir nodded abruptly and held the stones out, her hands falling barely a centimetre away from the queen's skin. She dared move no closer, although everything in her being screamed at her to reach the extra distance and touch the forbidden flesh.

VERY GOOD, announced Lelith, laughing as she stood once again. She snatched the waystones from the hands of the two wyches, just grazing their skin with her fingertips, and then sprang back up onto her ceremonial platform. She turned back to the assembly. KROULIR AND DRUQURA DO HONOUR TO HESPERAX. Then she turned again and vanished through an unseen doorway in the wall at the back of her platform.

Below, still kneeling on the blood soaked floor, Kroulir could not move a muscle. Her eyes were wide and wild as though something had been transformed in the shadows of her dark soul. There was a new blackness in her gaze and a passionate craving to touch that pale skin again. There and then, with her knees drenched in blood, she vowed to serve Lelith with her last breath.

THE LIGHTLESS WALLS of her seer chamber, high up in one of the fortress towers of Sussarkh's Peak, were marked with intricate webs of runes, ancient beyond the comprehension of all but the most erudite of wyches. The walls curved gently into a sweeping circle, with the runic panels arranged in a precise configuration, designed to focus the energy flows of

sha'iel into the very centre of the room. The architecture concentrated the warp and permitted Lelith
to open a portal into the immaterium with little
more than a thought. A secondary feature of the
careful design was that it also permitted certain enti-
ties of the warp to manifest themselves in the
chamber, at least in vaporous forms and only for a
brief time.

Threads of smoke and incense eased around the
room, whirling and wafting freely as Lelith sat in
silence. She was cross-legged with her eyes closed,
her hair falling loosely around her shoulders. Her
lips were working softly and a faint whisper curdled
with the smoke, filling the room with a delicate, daemonic spirit.

As the wych queen chanted quietly, a breeze eased
into the chamber, like a breath of humid air, swirling
the tendrils of smoke into a veil around her. Gradually, the breeze became a wind, stirring the smoke
into a mist that began to cloy against Lelith's skin.
She shivered involuntarily, jerking her shoulders as
though trying to shrug off an uninvited hand. As
though in response, the mist started to twist and
eddy in the centre of the room, pulling in the smoke
in long, spiralling tendrils that dragged shimmering
trails over Lelith's pale skin.

The atmosphere in the seer chamber shifted, as
though perforated by a mist of sha'iel itself. The
runes around the curved wall started to glow a deep
red, pulsing with an inconsistent and unsteady light.
As the slow, vague vortex in the heart of the room
began to solidify, the pulsing runes became stronger
and more intense. Threads of sha'iel began to slip

and slide between the runes, cutting the wall into a matrix of segments, as though it were being dragged out of real space piece by piece. After a few seconds, the fragmented wall convulsed and expanded, breaking apart to reveal a raging maelstrom of sha'iel in which the pieces seemed to hang in suspension.

Lelith's eyes flicked open, and she grimaced at the sight of her phase-shifting sanctum, caught half way between the material and immaterial realms. She may be the Wych Queen of Strife, but that did not mean that she enjoyed the slippery, oozing minions of the warp. They were a necessary evil – a temporary expedient – and one that she would rid herself of as soon as she could.

Glancing over towards the vortex of incense and warp in the centre of the misdimensioned chamber, Lelith shook her head faintly, waiting for the messenger to adopt its chosen form. It was taking its time deliberately, playing with her nerves. Lelith hated to be kept waiting, and her upper lip snarled involuntarily. She would not stand for these kinds of games from anything else. She would certainly have surgically removed any hands that had touched her skin in the familiar way that the smoke tendrils had touched her. Simply, the languorous fog offended her, and she bit down on her tongue to control her anger, drawing a bead of blood onto her perfect lips.

Eventually, a vague shape started to form in the mist. It was little more than a suggestion of a body with no face, just vapour. But Lelith recognised the shape at once and, despite her suppressed rage, her soul thrilled for a moment. She had not been expecting to see this body yet. The previous messenger had told her that she had not yet sacrificed enough souls to earn a glimpse of the princess. Clearly, something had changed – the campaign of raids on Ulthwé was paying off. For a delicious moment, Lelith wondered what she would see if she sacrificed the hundreds of souls that she kept stored in the spirit pool, hidden deep in the heart of Sussarkh's mountain.

The air in the seer chamber was filling with a sickly scent, a rich fragrance of death, and Lelith let it flow between her lips, leaving a tantalising taste on the tip of her tongue. She knew that the daemon princess could feel the contours of her mouth through the mist of incense, but the sensation was so gloriously sickening that she permitted the intrusion.

The indeterminate figure in the warp vortex emanated an indescribable violence, as though it represented merely the tip of an entire universe of pain. There was also an ineffable beauty in the air which momentarily confused the wych queen – was the daemonette attempting to seduce her, or was it the other way around?

I have come to offer my thanks, wych queen.

Lelith watched the vaguely defined lips with fascination. They emitted no sound, but the words caressed her mind with silky and treacherous affection.

There is no need for thanks – we have a bargain. Fulfilling it is an obligation, not a favour.

The gorgeous form shifted slightly in the whirl of scent and mist, and when it replied there was a trace of annoyance in its tone.

As you wish, wych. The tone was smooth and seductive, but its level of address had shifted as though frustrated that its ingratiation appeared to have failed. *But you would do well to remember the terms of our bargain. These pathetic, weakling souls do not give satisfaction.* There was a pause. *And if I am not satisfied by your offerings, I will have to find something else to take from you, Lelith.*

Despite herself, Lelith shivered. The duplicity of the temptress daemonette was not difficult to recognise, but it remained difficult to combat. The dark eldar had developed their own strategies for preserving their eternal souls, and Lelith was at the sharp end of one such deal. It was a more proactive strategy than that of the lightlings, but it carried great risks.

Anger started to build uncontrollably as Lelith realised that there was nothing she could do to this messenger apparition. And there was nothing that could be done about the terms of their contract. It was sealed millennia ago, written in blood and the essence of an Archon's soul.

Be gone, daemon! I do not need reminding of our bargain. The harvest is just beginning – you will get your souls. Fear not.

I have nothing to fear, wych. If you can fulfil our terms, I will feast. If you fail… I will still feast. Fear, my beautiful Lelith, should not be unknown to you.

Be gone, snapped Lelith, unwilling to consider the daemonette's words.

The face of the body in the vortex was still only a suggestion, but Lelith could clearly see the smile that cut through its features. As she watched, the body started to spin more and more rapidly, sucking the threads of fragrance and sha'iel into the increasingly dense whirlpool, the sickly smile still emanating into the seer chamber. With a sudden intake of breath, the chamber was empty and normal once again, with only the faint, lingering scent of death as an indication of what had happened.

Ah, Lelith. I have been waiting for you. A hologram flickered into sight where the vortex had been only moments before. It was clear, crisp and distinct, in stark contrast to the apparition of the daemonette. The figure was unmistakable. *Our plans are progressing as we anticipated.*

Lelith caught her breath, composing herself instantly before the eminent if unexpected guest. *Of course, old friend. The future is not such a complicated place when you work so diligently to forge it.*

CHAPTER FIVE:
CONVOCATION

THE LANCE OF DARKNESS was not a large vessel by the standards of the Adeptus Astartes or the Imperial Navy. Nova-class frigates were made for speed. It was as much a gunboat as an assault craft, which was partly why the Imperial Navy was keen to see fewer of them in the arsenals of the Space Marines; the balance of power between the services was a precarious thing. However, its unusual range of abilities made it the ideal gunship for the Deathwatch, and the Ramugan Ordo Xenos maintained two such vessels in permanent readiness. Compared to a strike cruiser, the frigates seemed tiny, but they packed more than enough firepower to punch a squad of Deathwatch Marines deep into enemy space.

Even though it was not a large vessel, the *Lance of Darkness* was still far too large to be held inside a station dock. Like its bigger cousins, it utilised smaller craft to shuttle personnel back and forth to other vessels or to the surfaces of planets, and it contained two Thunderhawk gunships for exactly such purposes.

Ulthwé simply swallowed it whole.

The immense docking bay doors yawned open as the frigate made its final approach to the craftworld. On the control deck, the viewscreens had been completely dominated by the massive vessel for over half an hour. By the time the *Lance of Darkness* was close enough to trigger the bay doors, the bridge crew could only see a tiny fragment of Ulthwé looming before them, but it loomed vast and limitless before them. The image seemed to crack and part in the middle, as massive shimmering doors withdrew from the space, as though dissolving or withdrawing into a different realm of reality altogether. Inside was revealed a cavernous space, big enough to hold a moon or a small planet.

Octavius stared. His mind was accustomed to experiencing the horrible and the terrible of the galaxy. He had watched his battle-brothers die; he had seen aliens torture his brethren, and he had tortured them in return. He had gazed into the inexplicable and infinite evil that lurked in the eyes of a tyranid hive tyrant and he had seen entire worlds burn. But the sight of Ulthwé was not something for which any of his terrible memories could have prepared him.

With his helmet tucked under his arm ready to lead the landing party, Octavius stared, unblinking, and his complex blue eyes sparkled with awe. There were dozens of ships harboured in that cavernous space, perhaps hundreds. And they were not all the tiny, rapid-strike fighters that he might have expected to see docked internally. There were larger vessels too, ships much bigger than the *Lance of Darkness*, sleek and beautiful in ways that the Imperium could neither understand nor hope to imitate.

Straining his eyes into the distance, and taxing his memory for the unusual class names, Octavius thought that he could see Aurora and Solaris cruisers in dry dock. Even further away, so far that he found it hard to believe that he was perceiving the distance correctly, Octavius thought that he caught a glimpse of a Void Stalker battleship – such vessels had only rarely been encountered by the Imperial Navy and never with favourable results for the Imperium. It was like an entire fleet, waiting to be born out into the cold void of space. Given that, why in the Emperor's name did the Ulthwé need the Deathwatch?

Standing beside him, Librarian Atreus saw the look of wonder and concern on his captain's face.

'I have heard of this place,' he began in a low voice, as though conscious that he should not shatter the magic of the moment. 'The great space-dock of Calmainoc. It does not literally exist within the confines of Ulthwé. The bay doors open into a kind of warp portal, hardwired into the structure of the craftworld itself. The portal is indistinguishable and inseparable from the main doors. The harbour, however, could be anywhere in the galaxy, or even beyond it. Only the ways in and out are in Ulthwé, which is

effectively the same as having it here all the time…'
His voice trailed off, as though in wonder, as he
recalled the ancient librarium of the *Omnis Arcanum*
in which he had read the forbidden knowledge. 'I
had never thought to actually see this place.'

Octavius nodded abruptly, ending his own reverie
and forcing Atreus out of his. 'Thank you, librarian,
but it is of no matter. We must expect that the aliens
will do things differently from us, but we must constantly keep our purpose before us. We are here to
fulfil an Imperial vow, not to marvel at the artifice of
these xenos. Their space port is of no concern to us.
Its purpose is to permit us to dock, so dock we shall.'

'Yes captain,' replied Atreus, noting the resolve that
had flooded over Octavius's face.

'The others are ready, I presume?'

Other than the serfs, the two Marines were alone
on the control deck. Even if he had not expected to
see any of the others before landing, Octavius was
surprised that Ashok had not returned to the bridge
after donning his armour.

'They stand ready.'

'Librarian Ashok?'

'He is preparing himself in the chapel, captain.
None have disturbed him.'

Octavius held the librarian's gaze for a moment, as
though searching for words unspoken. He wondered
what the Blood Raven thought of the mission's other
librarian, but he knew that the pause suggested his
own indecision. 'Very good, Atreus,' he said finally.

THE MON-KEIGH VESSEL was ugly beyond imagination.
Dhrykna had seen similar ships before, but invariably

from a distance and they were usually in flames. This was certainly the first time that she had ever seen one easing into a berth in Calmainoc's bay. It was not a very large ship, but somehow it conspired to be hulking and cumbersome, like a blunt assault on the senses. It was coloured in a pitch shade of black, but not of the depthless and utterly colourless variety familiar to the eldar of Ulthwé. This black was material and heavy, as though it were intertwined with the force of gravity itself. Despite her intense self-discipline, Dhrykna squinted in displeasure: the presence of the mon-keigh was simply offensive.

Looking to her left, the Shining Spear could see the rest of the reception committee in a loose line. Except for Thae'akzi herself, they all emanated a restrained disgust at the sight before them. Dhrykna could taste it in the air, as though it was the intense humidity of a diseased jungle. In comparison to the boxy, lumbering bulk of the *Lance of Darkness*, the group of eldar felt like angels or deities. They were like dark, slender gods, watching the approach of lesser animals.

For a moment, Dhrykna dropped her eyes to her feet and saw her new boots as though for the first time. They shone with pristine whiteness, rimmed with a line of silver-blue, glittering against the dark, shimmering wraithbone deck. In that instant, she forgot all about the approaching mon-keigh and the gathering darkness in Ulthwé, and all she could see was the brilliant light of Khaine's lightning spear. She knew that she stood out from the darkly clad reception committee like a lonely star in the void of space. Even the Emerald Seer must appear dull and tame in comparison, like a shadow of her own magnificence. The Shining Path permits no shadows, recalled Dhrykna.

A faint hissing sound drew Dhrykna out of her reverie, and she looked up to see the boarding bridge extending out towards the mon-keigh vessel. She never ceased to marvel at the way those bridges reached literally light years from the edge of the dock to the airlocks of the berthed vessels, yet they may appear to be only a hundred metres long. Even the wraithsmiths of Ulthwé had lost the techniques required to reconstruct such incredible devices, bridges that actually spanned the galaxy via a specially contained glitch in the webway. Even repairs taxed the limits of their skills – so far had the eldar fallen.

The mon-keigh vessel might really be drawing to a standstill around a distant star, but it was also dropping its landing ramp down onto the bridge in the very heart of Ulthwé. The contradictions were mind-blowing even for Dhrykna, and she smiled when she wondered how the primitive brains of the mon-keigh would struggle with the concepts involved. Fifty confident strides from the edge of the jetty to the flank of the *Lance of Darkness* may mask an incalculably large distance.

The hissing bridge clicked finally into place, locking into the side of the mon-keigh frigate just below the access ramp. Immediately, the ramp clunked and detached from the ship, lowering slowly and mechanically until it clanked against the surface of the bridge. Steam jetted out from behind the ramp, wafting up into the unreal atmosphere of Calmainoc's bay like smog from a primitive factory, blurring the stars and lights that seemed to blink throughout the dock behind. Dhrykna snarled in repulsion, and she could sense the revulsion oozing out of the minds of the rest of the reception committee. Warlock Shariele had good control of his emotions immediately on Dhrykna's left, and it was often impossible to perceive the thoughts of Thae'akzi, but the retinue of Black Guardians could not suppress their disgust and Ruhklo of the Karizhariat made no attempt to hide his detestation. The mood was dark and riddled with resentment when the mon-keigh's airlock finally ground open and the eldar caught their first glimpse of their guests.

As the billows of steam gradually dissipated, the silhouette of a heavy, powerful figure became visible in the opening. It seemed motionless, like a statue or a monument to the crude, bulky magnificence of the Imperial creed. Despite herself, Dhrykna found a spark of admiration prodding into her conscious-ness. The sheer physical presence of the mon-keigh weighed into her thoughts, impressing her with a sense of power that she had not anticipated from the primitive species. A starburst of bright yellow flashed through the vaporous air, emanating from one of the massive shoulders of the impressive Marine as he vaulted down out of the *Lance of Darkness*. His heavy boots crunched down onto the wraithbone bridge, sending waves of vibrations pulsing through its structure, as though that delicate sliver of Ulthwé was repulsed by the touch.

Dhrykna glanced down at her armoured boots once again, admiring the glittering and deceptively delicate psycho-plastic material. Even as she looked, she could feel the impact of the Space Marine's footfalls pulsing under her soles. Even their feet are heavy and ugly, she thought.

But they are strong. The thoughts were quiet, like a psychic whisper.

Yes, Emerald Seer, I can feel their power even now.

The Marine strode confidently across the wraithbone drawbridge towards the reception committee, its feet clanking and echoing throughout the unreal vastness of the dock. It did not even pause to wait for its brethren to fall into formation behind it, although it would probably be able to hear the thuds as several similar figures dropped out of its ship in its wake.

As the Marine approached, Dhrykna realised that its face was completely hidden behind an armoured helmet that appeared to be integrated into the structure of its armour. Except for the patch of bright yellow on one shoulder, the armour itself was coloured in the same primitive but menacing black as the frigate from which the Marine had emerged. As far as she could work out, the armour was adorned with various kinds of simple purity seals, holsters for weapons, and also powered servos. Despite its cumbersome design, it looked like it might be an effective tool for a warrior. She had come across Space Marines before, of course, but she had never looked at them with curiosity in her heart before, only with hate and loathing.

The leading Marine stopped short of the eldar committee, standing with its feet set solidly apart and its head held confidently, just at the point where

the bridge met the main jetty. It was fractionally too
far away from the eldar for them to deliver their carefully rehearsed greetings, and Dhrykna could detect
a slight irritation flickering through the minds of her
comrades. They suspected that the Marine was
slighting them deliberately. It was the kind of subtlety that they had not expected from the mon-keigh.

As it stood motionless, five other black-clad
Marines strode up behind it, taking up a formation
that resembled a bristling armoured wall. They were
a motley assortment of shapes, but each of them
looked powerful and solid in a way quite alien to the
eldar. One of them appeared to have some kind of
jump pack fused to its back. Another bore a bizarre
and grotesque mask that distorted its helmet into a
vision of horror. One was at the centre of a series of
twitching mechanical arms that seemed integrated
into its armour. But, standing before the eldar, each
one of the mon-keigh warriors in their power
armour appeared formidably solid and massive,
dwarfing the delicate and slender sons of Asuryan.

The Marines did not advance; they showed no sign
of trying to interact at all.

The minds of the eldar shifted uneasily, although
their bodies betrayed nothing of their irritation. As
they gazed in silence at the mon-keigh that had been
permitted to tread the sacred wraithbone of Calmainoc's dock, the eldar began to see something
unexpected in amongst the aliens.

Even Dhrykna could see the disciplined and controlled psychic halo that emanated from one of the
Marines behind the leader. She had heard that not
all the mon-keigh were equally psychically stunted,

but it had never even occurred to her that those with the power would serve those without. It seemed incredible to her, and her mind rebelled against the unreason of it. Even as she watched, another thump on the bridge made her snap her attention back towards the *Lance of Darkness*, where a seventh mon-keigh warrior rose slowly to his feet.

The Marine that strode up the causeway was ablaze with psychic energy. It just poured out of him, as though it ran through his veins and eased out of the pores in his skin. It was the only one of the aliens that did not hide its face behind the armoured panels of a helmet. Instead, a heavy hood shaded the features of its face, and a long cloak plumed out behind it as it walked.

For a moment, Dhrykna wondered how the rest of the mon-keigh could live knowing that superior specimens like this existed in their midst. The blind fools could not even see the brilliance in its soul. Its light was invisible to them. The last Marine was certainly no eldar, but it emanated a rare power that even the eldar would have to acknowledge, although it flickered with a barely contained radiance. It was of a completely different nature from the tightly controlled halo of the first mon-keigh psyker. Dhrykna had not expected to encounter such a presence, and she wondered whether the Seer Council had foreseen the involvement of two mon-keigh psykers in the heart of Ulthwé.

As the remarkable last Marine drew into formation with its brethren, behind its leader, Thae'akzi the Emerald Seer finally and softly stood forward of the eldar committee, her light robes fluttering in an invisible breeze. She nodded her head in the suggestion of a bow before straining her face into a series of unnatural contortions as she strove to give voice to the ugly, guttural sounds of the mon-keigh tongue. She knew that there was no way that the primitives would be able to approximate the elegant and musical tones of an eldar language. It was not a question of meeting them halfway; she would have to meet them almost entirely on their own terms.

'Welcome here you are,' she said, stilted and uncomfortable.

As HE STRODE across the alien bridge, Octavius tried to absorb the magnitude of the dock that opened out around him like the void of space. It was as though he was walking along a hairline gangplank between a gunship and a frigate, not striding across a docking jetty in the interior of a gargantuan craft. For a moment he caught himself wondering at the technology – what kind of material could reach seamlessly through the warp as though it were simply stretched across a docking bay?

This, he supposed, must be wraithbone, drawn out of the warp itself. He had seen small pieces of it before, of course, but he had never thought that entire architectural structures might be constructed out of it. Glancing down at his feet, he wondered what would happen to him when he crossed the invisible boundary between the distant docking space and the interior of the craftworld.

He shut the thought out – it was irrelevant to the mission. The matter at hand was the first meeting with the eldar. The scholarly and well-informed

Librarian Atreus had suggested to Octavius that he should not approach them directly, but to stop short of their position and to make them come to him. It would be interpreted as a sign of the team's resolve. It would show that they were not intimidated by the Ulthwé. If he stopped too far away, however, this might be seen as unseemly arrogance. Behind his visor, Octavius clenched his jaw, already irritated by the ritualistic subtleties of the eldar.

Glancing up to where the eldar were waiting in a line, Octavius thought that the welcoming committee looked feeble. Inside his helmet, he ground his teeth in frustrated repulsion and disappointment. The eldar dignitaries were tall, but they were slim and looked fragile. Octavius felt certain that he could break one of them in half over his knee if he had to. It was a reassuring thought, as he stopped walking a few strides short of their position.

For a few seconds, nothing happened. The eldar stood motionless, staring at him as though expecting him to do something else. Octavius just waited. Atreus had told him that it would be worse to reposition himself after stopping than simply to stop in the wrong place. To move in response to an uncomfortable silence would suggest weakness or, even worse, might be interpreted as manipulative. The Imperial Fists captain held his ground as the rest of the team strode up behind him, taking their positions in a crescent around his back. Octavius could hear their footfalls all the way along the bridge, but they checked in over the vox-links in their helmets nonetheless.

'Ashok?' queried Octavius in little more than a whisper, never taking his eyes off the aliens in front of him.

'On his way, captain.' It was Atreus. 'He was not quite finished in the chapel.'

Hidden behind the darkly tinted visor of his helmet, Octavius squinted slightly, letting his frustrations spill over onto his face for just a moment. He regretted the instant of weakness at once, immediately recomposing his features and his thoughts, conscious all the time that the eldar might not need to see his face to understand his emotions. It would not do for their hosts to perceive any problems in the team, especially when Octavius himself was not even sure whether there actually were any problems or not.

Despite his mysterious behaviour, Octavius realised that he trusted the librarian from the Angels Sanguine. Just as the thought entered his head, Octavius heard the crunch of Ashok's boots hitting the bridge behind him, and the solid rhythmic impacts of him striding up to join the others.

A slight movement amongst the assembled eldar drew Octavius back into the uncomfortable reality of the situation. He could not tell which of them had moved, but they seemed to emanate an aura of agitation, as though they were shifting their feet without actually moving. The line contained an interesting array of classificatory types: Octavius recognised the image of an eldar witch-seer in long flowing, green robes – a 'seer'. There was another seer, a male, garbed in a cloak that Octavius struggled to resolve in the dim light – it might have been black or midnight blue, and it made him uncomfortable to look at it for too long; there was a male war-witch, or 'warlock,' dressed in sinister black armour which was decorated with hundreds of eldar runes and there was a line of warriors, set out in the black and gold armour that characterised the so-called 'Black Guardians' of Ulthwé. Only one of the group was not shrouded in dark colours or oppressive auras, and she stood to one side of the line, stunningly beautiful and radiant in pristine white and silver-blue. She was like an angel in the darkness, and Octavius had to force himself to cast his gaze away from her as the emerald seer stepped forward.

Octavius watched as the seer closed the gap to a single stride. Then she stopped, satisfied apparently that they were now close enough for the greetings to commence. She narrowed her eyes in what looked like disdain or pain, and then she spoke with such an inhuman voice that it sent a chill to the back of Octavius's eyes.

'Welcome here you are.'

'We are not here for your welcome, nor are we here at your pleasure. We are here out of duty,' replied Octavius dismissively, as his mind reeled against the incongruence of the eldar's words. It had not even occurred to him that the eldar would be able to speak in the tongues of the Imperium, and he realised at the same time that he had given no thought to the problem of communication. Perhaps Librarian Atreus had a command of the Ulthwé tongue, he wondered, realising that the eldar's linguistic knowledge put his team at a disadvantage.

'Then your duty us honours,' answered the seer with a slight, stiff bow. She was clearly trying to make this encounter as smooth as possible.

'Yes,' nodded Octavius curtly. She was right, he thought. The presence of the Deathwatch does far too much honour to the eldar of Ulthwé. He was not about to deny it, not even for the sake of diplomacy. If the mission had called for a diplomat, Vargas would have sent an inquisitor with them. Diplomacy was not what the Deathwatch did best.

The green eldar witch grimaced slightly, as though trying to smile. Her half-closed eyes flashed between long eyelashes. At the same time, the other eldar seemed to twitch and shift their feet. A couple of them turned their heads to look back into the interior of the craftworld, as though eager to leave. Octavius shivered, feeling a pulse of iced electricity shimmering through his spine.

'Captain,' hissed Atreus's whispering voice into Octavius's ear. 'I feel it too.'

'What is it?'

'I'm not sure. It may be some kind of alarm.'

A violent spike of cold jabbed into Octavius's body, making him stagger slightly. A strong hand gripped his shoulder, steadying his balance and filling him with reassurance.

'It is an alert, captain.' The deep voice and firm grip belonged to Ashok. 'The eldar have detected an intrusion. We may discover our purpose here sooner than expected.'

Abruptly, the Black Guardians that stood amongst the welcoming committee nodded swift bows before turning and running back towards the huge elliptical doors that sealed off the docking bay. As they approached, the doors slid silently open, revealing a bank of jetbikes waiting on the far side. As one, the eldar warriors vaulted into the saddles and kicked their vehicles into life, flashing off into the interior of Ulthwé, gone in an instant.

'Well?' asked Octavius bluntly, directing his inquiry towards the emerald seer who remained before him. 'Is there anything you think you should be telling me?'

The female seer hesitated for a moment, apparently unsure whether to explain what was happening. She looked back over her shoulder at the two jetbikes that remained just beyond the docking bay doors.

'Violation lower levels we have detected,' she said, turning her face back to Octavius. *Your psykers detected our alarm?* She added, pushing the thoughts gently into the captain's head. She was surprised, and then she was shocked. *You also felt it?*

'Is this why we are here, eldar?' asked Octavius, ignoring the intrusions into his mind. He did not want to become embroiled in eldar mind games. If this 'violation' was why he had brought his team into the clutches of these aliens, then he wanted to see his duty done.

'It is not… and it is, human,' answered Thae'akzi, cocking her head slightly to one side, as though curious about the motivation of the mon-keigh. Her deep green eyes gazed at the captain's visor, and for a moment Octavius wondered whether she could see straight through it.

'Which is it?' he asked.

The seer did not reply. Instead, she smiled faintly and turned to face the glittering white warrior behind her, muttering something unintelligible. She then addressed some quick remarks to the warlock in the retinue. Both bowed deeply, turned and strode off towards the last remaining jetbikes.

'If vehicles you have able to keep up, follow Dhrykna and Shariele. Show you the violators they will,' said the seer, turning her eyes back to Octavius.

Octavius made no direct response. He simply turned and strode back towards the *Lance of Darkness*, followed by the rest of the Deathwatch kill-team. They climbed back up the loading ramp, which clanked shut behind them. After a few seconds, a huge hatch cracked open in the side of the frigate and a long, heavy ramp rumbled out towards the wraithbone bridge. Steam and vapour clouds billowed out, and then an immense roar of power erupted from within the Nova-class frigate.

Standing with Ruhklo on the jetty of Calmainoc's dock, Thae'akzi raised an eyebrow as she watched the first black assault bike lurch out of the monkeigh vessel, clearing the ramp as it growled through the air, crunching down onto the walkway, its fat tyres almost as wide as the wraithbone bridge itself. Several more bikes roared out of the *Lance of Darkness* in the wake of the first one, and a hovering land speeder took up the rear.

'We will keep up, but we will not wait for your guides, eldar,' snarled Octavius as he slid his bike to a halt next to the green-robed seer, while the rest of his team pulled up in formation around him, the powerful engines of their bikes growling and snarling like beasts straining at their leashes.

MYRIAD EMOTIONS SPIRALLED through Dhrykna's mind as she flashed through the passageways just outside Calmainoc's bay. Her heart felt satisfied, hungry and nauseated all at once. She was astride one of the glittering white jetbikes of the Shining Spears, burning like a beacon of hope in the dark corridors, flanked by the black and silver form of Shariele's bike, which appeared as little more than a shadow of her own. This was her, and she was true to herself as a manifestation of the light of Khaine, but there was something hollow about her context, as though she were rattling around within the emptiness of an Ulthwé devoid of substance.

She hungered for the time when the eldar of this craftworld would no longer hide in the shadows, and her spirit swam in her species' memory of a distant past when the eldar stood proudly in the light, shrinking from nothing. But her reveries were shattered by the blunt, roaring gravity of the mon-keigh that sped along in her wake, throwing their stinking, primitive machines around the sweeping bends and tight corners of Ulthwé's labyrinthine corridors. Could there be a more stark reminder of what Ulthwé had become? It made her sick just to think about it.

Up ahead, around a couple more corners, Dhrykna knew that the Black Guardians would have activated Ghreivan's Gate, one of several hundred such portals that were strewn throughout the immense structure of the craftworld. It was an access point into the intricate lattice of warp routes that the original architects of Ulthwé had hardwired into the infrastructure, permitting those who understood the complexities of its function to travel almost instantaneously between different parts of the vessel.

It was another example of a technology that the wraithsmiths of Ulthwé could no longer duplicate. They knew enough to utilise the functions of the matrix, but not enough to expand it into newly constructed areas of the craftworld. Dhrykna had heard that passing through these internal portals actually immersed travellers in the infiniteness of the Ulthwé spirit pool – the infinity circuit itself. She shuddered as she realised that the mon-keigh chasing her through the shadowy passageways would probably become the first ever to touch the fabric of Ulthwé's soul, and they had no idea of the magnitude of their honour or of the terrible pollution that they brought into the very heart of her world.

The Shining Spear pressed herself lower against the chassis of her jetbike, streamlining herself until she seemed indistinguishable from the bike, as though they were together the brilliant spear of Khaine himself, flashing through the darkness. She willed her bike up to an incredible speed, feeling Shariele fall slightly behind to her right, and hoping all the time that the mon-keigh would not be able to keep up. She knew that the Seer Council had instructed her to guide them, but her very soul screamed in defiance at the thought that they would pass into the spirit of Ulthwé. To her considerable irritation, she realised that the crude, roaring mon-keigh bikes were keeping pace.

She rolled her bike along its axis as it banked around the last corner, bringing Ghreivan's Gate into view at the end of the corridor. It was roughly circular in shape, although its frame was decorated with ornate runes and twisted as though stretched through several dimensions at once. Within the frame was a curtain of liquid night, shimmering and oily. As the nose of her jetbike broke its surface, submerging as though into a pool, Dhrykna caught a glimpse of the scene on the other side, distorted by the interdimensional refraction and riddled by the surface ripples. She could see the Black Guardians engaging the darkling raiders down in the lowest levels of Ulthwé – they were not winning.

There was not even a splash as the pristine jetbike plunged through the gate and vanished from the corridor.

As USUAL, THE room was barely lit and Inquisitor Lord Seishon sat quietly in the middle of it, as though in meditation. His eyes were half open, but even those who knew him well would not be able to tell whether he was sleeping or awake. Most of the light in the room was tinged with red, as though filtered through a pool of blood. It was a weak light, little more than a glow emanating from the viewscreen that dominated the far wall.

Ever since they had first spotted the anomaly in the Circuitrine system, Seishon had kept a watchful eye on the lashes of the Eye of Terror, as the ruddy, red mist wisped and plumed through the nebula. On the screen, it looked like little more than a pattern of ink swirling through a tank of water. Seishon exhaled and shook his head: how incredible to believe that the swirling tendrils of ink engulfed hundreds of stars.

It was not just the maelstrom of the Eye that clawed at Seishon's soul as he watched the image on the viewscreen zoom through an incredible ratio of magnification. The last communication from Librarian Ashok before the Deathwatch team had finally vanished into the massive docking bay of the eldar craftworld had sent Seishon's mind reeling. He had been concerned about the trustworthiness of their erstwhile allies even before he and Vargas had reached the decision to despatch the Deathwatch, but the latest news had added whole new levels of suspicion and doubt.

Ashok had suggested that the dark eldar might also be involved in the plot, and that was not an eventuality for which Seishon had been prepared. He was absolutely certain that Vargas would have given it no thought whatsoever, and he was equally certain that the cunning, arrogant and insightful aliens would have expected the human keepers of the Coven of Isha to ask few questions. Vargas, imagined Seishon with a faint disgust edging into his thoughts, probably asked no questions of the messenger at all. Vargas had claimed that the messenger had been Eldrad Ulthran himself, but Seishon was beginning to doubt even that. Vargas would believe anything. And how could that ancient sorcerer still be alive after all these millennia? Eldar may be long lived, but this Ulthran would have to be virtually immortal.

A faint chime sounded from the main door into his chambers, but Seishon ignored it for a moment, endeavouring to compose his thoughts. It would not do to confront an agent of the Inquisition in this unbalanced frame of mind. This was one of the many drawbacks of being based on Ramugan – no matter where you went and no matter to whom you spoke, there was always a chance that they would twist your actions or words into those of a heretic. Heresy was everywhere, and it was only a small leap of logic to reach the conclusion that heresy was also everything.

'Enter,' he said at last, keeping his back to the door as it slid smoothly open. He knew it was Vargas. The dulled, almost impotent psychic stench oozed into the room even before it opened.

'Seishon–' started Vargas, breaking into voice even before the door had sealed closed. Seishon silenced him by slicing his hand out to one side, before turning to face his honoured guest.

'Careful, old friend,' he cautioned, indicating the door with his eyebrow. For a moment, and not for the first time, Seishon marvelled at the fact that Vargas had risen to the exalted rank of inquisitor lord. They had known each other a long time, and Seishon could not remember a time when Vargas had demonstrated the kind of political edge or subtlety demanded of his position. And he was one of the very few senior inquisitors in this sector that had almost no psychic ability at all. He made no secret of it.

'Oh, of course,' replied Vargas hastily, shuffling into the room and slumping down into one of the chairs around the table in its centre. He looked up at Seishon, flustered and clearly exhausted, before letting his gaze drift to the image on the giant viewscreen.

The door closed and Seishon activated a series of purity seals with a casual wave of his hand. They would not keep out the most determined of spying devices, but he had any number of more painful ways to deal with anyone or anything that actually dared to breach the integrity of his chambers.

Taking two weary steps, Seishon joined Vargas at the table, lowering himself stiffly into the chair opposite his old friend, watching him rattling a glass against a crystal carafe as he tried to pour himself some wine. A cunning thought occurred to him at that moment, and he kicked himself mentally for not having thought of it before: perhaps all of this bumbling innocence was just a front? Perhaps Vargas just used this image to disarm his adversaries?

He would not be the first to attempt such a ruse, reflected Seishon, narrowing his eyes as the logical implications of the theory started to play out in his head. If this personality was a ruse, which seemed necessary as an explanation for Vargas's position and rank, then the chief victim of the ruse was probably Seishon himself, since he had known Vargas longer than anyone. Not only that, but Seishon had taken the old fool into his confidence. If Vargas was not who he purported to be, then Seishon's already precarious position regarding the Coven of Isha was even more precarious than he had realised.

'Seishon?' inquired Vargas. His wine glass was already drained and he was busily pouring himself another, a concerned smile playing over his lips.

'Yes? Oh, yes, sorry,' replied Seishon, composing himself, immediately aware that he was making exactly the mistake he had striven to avoid for decades on Ramugan. It was all well and good to be suspicious – indeed, it was essential to be suspicious – but it was no good to *show* your suspicion, and it was even worse to let your suspicion compromise your attentiveness. The stress of the situation was clearly having an effect on him.

'Are you sick?' asked Vargas, his voice tinged with what appeared to be genuine concern.

'No. I'm fine, Vargas. Thank you. I am merely concerned about this... situation,' he finished, flicking his head to indicate the image on the screen behind him, before reaching for the carafe.

'As am I, old friend. There has been no further word from Lord Ulthran.'

'Did you expect to hear more?' asked Seishon, raising an eyebrow and then sipping his wine.

'I am not sure what to expect, Seishon.'

'Expectations are not always the allies of faith, old friend.'

Vargas nodded thoughtfully, but Seishon felt sure that he had not understood him.

'I have reason to believe that the dark eldar are somehow involved in this affair, Vargas,' he continued, watching the other's face for some sign of recognition.

'Really? Why?' It appeared to be genuine surprise, although not necessarily alarm.

'Librarian Ashok sent a communiqué from just inside the Circuitrine nebula. The *Lance of Darkness* detected small, fast gunships emerging from the Eye of Terror as it approached, possibly fitted with shadowfields.'

'Did they engage?'

'No. The flyers fled when Ulthwé launched its own escort vessels to guide the *Lance* home.' Seishon's mind was racing again, shot through with a tirade of implications and possibilities. 'The alien witch said nothing about his dark brethren, I suppose?'

'Nothing,' answered Vargas a little too hastily. His mind was already wandering into new areas. 'These gunships, were they large enough to be detected by the Malleus sensor arrays?'

'I doubt it, Vargas – the distance is too great. In any case, as you must know, the *Lance of Darkness* had to time its run in counterphase with the sensor sweep, otherwise we would have had Lord Aurelius storming in here before they had even got out of this system. Anything they encountered on that route would be invisible to us, I hope.' Seishon was getting sick of explaining things that Vargas should already know.

'I have heard from Aurelius,' said Vargas, almost incidentally.

'What?'

'He asked me why you are so interested in the Circuitrine nebula.'

For a moment, Seishon was at a loss for words. 'And what did you say to him, Vargas?' A heavy, sinking feeling had settled into Seishon's stomach. He should have been able to anticipate that Caesurian

and Aurelius would have approached Vargas to confirm his story. He would have done the same thing,
especially considering the apparent likelihood that
Vargas would spill his soul. 'Was Caesurian with
him?' The Hereticus lord was far more dangerous to
him personally, if not to the mission itself.

'I told him that I was not aware of any particular or
special interest in that nebula, and I implied that I
would naturally be aware of any such interest if
indeed it were to exist. I assured him of our co-
operation with the Ordo Malleus here on Ramugan,
in keeping with the conventions of the eons.'

Seishon nodded, his mind elsewhere. 'A good
answer, Vargas.'

'And no, Caesurian was not with him. He did,
however, mention a young Hereticus Inquisitor Perceptia. Evidently she has been asking some
questions of junior interrogators in the Malleus
compound. This is why Aurelius came to me.'

'Perceptia? Never heard of her,' sighed Seishon, a
note of relief easing into his voice.

THE FRONT OF Octavius's bike burst out of the liquid
curtain of the infinity portal, roaring like a wild animal hungry for a kill. As the fat tyres crunched down
onto solid ground once again, the captain shook his
head rapidly, scrunching his eyes shut and trying to
reorient his senses. Flashing through the fringes of
Ulthwé's infinity circuit, or wherever it was that
those portals went, was not something for which the
untrained human brain was well equipped. It took a
couple of seconds for Octavius to regain crisp vision
and proper balance.

Before he could see what was going on around him, he could hear it. The noise was incredible. There were yells and screams, shouts in languages that Octavius had never heard. Terrible, shrill wails tore through the air, slicing through the other sounds as though cutting through water. Explosions shook the ground, and the unmistakable sizzling hiss of shuriken fire was pervasive in the background.

Hitting the brakes, Octavius slid his bike to a halt, not willing to charge forward blindly. In less than a second, Ashok skidded his own bike around, bringing it to rest less than a metre from his captain's, but he was already blazing with fire, his staff alive with power. Almost instantaneously, Atreus pulled his bike up on the other side of Octavius, his own staff spitting with a constant stream of blue energy. Immediately, Octavius realised that the librarians were better able to adjust to the oddities of travelling around Ulthwé and he was again thankful that Seishon had insisted on them both. He also realised that the two librarians were flanking him to protect him from the enemy while his senses returned to normal.

With a roar, Octavius unholstered his bolter and let rip into the semi-resolved haze before him. 'Primarch – Progenitor, to your glory and the glory of Him on Earth!' No son of Rogal Dorn needed the protection of another Marine.

In a matter of seconds, the Deathwatch team was assembled, and it found itself in the midst of a fierce battle between a bank of Ulthwé eldar on one side and a scattering of dark eldar on the other. Even after his sight had returned, it took Octavius a moment to work out which side he was supposed to be on. Both groups looked like eldar to him. Both were dressed in dark armour and firing tiny projectiles from hissing weapons. He noticed that Atreus and Ashok showed no hesitation at all – they immediately directed their fury towards the scattered distribution of aliens to the left. The others in the team took their lead from the librarians: Chaplain Luthar suddenly gunned the engine of his bike and powered off to one side, trying to out flank the dark eldar and get around behind them. Kruidan of the Mantis Warriors took his valour in his hands and roared forward directly into the heart of the dark eldar formation – as he closed on their line, his jump pack ignited and he blasted up away from his bike, sending it careening into the aliens, where it exploded into a massive fireball.

Sulphus, the Iron Father of the Red Talons, manoeuvred his land speeder with two of his arms, punching the trigger for the front mounted heavy bolters, while his other arms unleashed volleys of fire from bolt pistols.

Only Pelias stood at Octavius's shoulder. He seemed to hesitate for a moment, glancing back towards the formation of Ulthwé warriors who were even now beginning to disengage from the battle, as though assuming that they no longer had a role to play in this encounter. Octavius watched the scene unfold, calculating his next move. The dark eldar force was not as powerful as he had thought at first – the aggression of his team had already splintered it. Kruidan had wiped half of it out by himself with his bike stunt – at least, half of what had been left of it after the onslaught from Ashok and Atreus. The Mantis Warrior fought as though he had a point to make.

Watching closely, Octavius could see that the dark eldar and the eldar of Ulthwé did appear slightly different from each other. The former seemed less organised and more anarchic – lashing out with barbs and blades as though fighting entirely for themselves, or perhaps out of a desperate fear of an invisible master. They laughed and brayed, shrieking with reckless abandon. Their armour was artistic and stylised, as though designed as much for their own sensory pleasure as for protection – some of them, particularly the females, displayed more skin than armoured panels. They seemed to decorate themselves with flashes of colour – usually red headbands, bracelets, anklets or scarves.

Looking more closely, Octavius could see that the decorations were red with blood – some of them still edged with bone or finished with shrunken skulls. And they seemed to show a marked preference for bladed weapons, particularly the females who danced and spun with such breathtaking precision. They were like dancers of death.

The Ulthwé, on the other hand, were disciplined and coherent. Their armour was almost like a uniform, immaculate and polished, baring strange runic markings that seemed to bind them together as a single force.

Most of the warriors looked like males, but it was difficult to tell under the seamless black armour, since both genders were slim and elegant creatures. They seemed to prefer projectile weapons and most sported long rifles, which they fired in banks and disciplined volleys. These eldar did not look like the ones that greeted the Deathwatch team up in Calmainoc's dock. The only figures that Octavius could recognise were the dashing forms of his two guides: one was a flashing streak of brilliant white, darting through the scattered dark eldar, cutting down her foe with javelins of lasfire; the other had long since abandoned his jetbike and was standing defiantly in the heart of the combat zone, lashing out at his dark brethren with crackling bursts of lightning from his fingertips.

Despite himself, Octavius nodded his approval. He was learning a great deal from this first encounter. It was a rare opportunity for a Deathwatch captain to see the eldar and dark eldar pitted against each other, and he felt that he was beginning to get a sense of some of their differences, at least in battle. But he was also beginning to realise that the eldar of Ulthwé themselves were not a homogeneous gaggle of aliens. There were depths to the actions of these creatures that he could not guess at, at least not yet.

However, the thing that struck him most was the fact that he wasn't sure why he was there. The eldar seemed to have enough firepower and enough talent to confront the smattering of dark eldar raiders that attempted to threaten their position. Of equal concern was the fact that the Ulthwé eldar seemed content to disengage when Octavius's team showed up – all of them except the white warrior and the warlock. Perhaps this was simply a test? Whatever it was, he felt certain that the eldar had not summoned the Deathwatch just to fight a handful of alien raiders for them.

SOME PEOPLE CURSE when they get angry or frustrated. Some people hit things or lash out. Perceptia was not one of these people. When she got angry, she went to the librarium and read a good book. Actually, when she got angry, she went to the hidden depths of the Hereticus librarium of Ramugan and read bad books. Very bad books indeed.

She hated talking to the subordinates of inquisitors, especially to those outside of the Ordo Hereticus. It was bad enough trying to get sense out of her own colleagues and peers; even when she had been part of Caesurian's retinue, she had never really managed to get an honest answer out of any of the others. When it came to explicators and interrogators from the Ordo Malleus or Xenos, they would often simply not speak at all, or just walk past without even acknowledging her.

It was one of the oddities of the Ramugan station that agents from each of the services would occasionally come into contact with each other. It was not peculiar to Ramugan, however, that these agents would have absolutely no trust in each other when they did cross paths. There were all kinds of questions, suspicions and competitions between the ordos – in addition, each agent wanted to assert the superiority of its own by demonstrating its casual or studied disregard for everyone else.

As an interrogator, everyone could ignore her, but now that she was an inquisitor she could at least demand a few moments of time from the junior staff of others. Inquisitors may still be able to ignore her, and inquisitor lords might not even notice that she existed, but she could pester a few explicators for snippets of information. Now, however, she hated doing it – it was beneath her to deal with these underlings. Besides, the stupid explicators in the Ordo Malleus had not understood anything. They had not even known that there was anything they did not know, which seemed like the height of stupidity. She had always hypothesised that the agents of the Malleus were probably the least intellectually able of all, and it seemed to her that she had now found proof of her theory. All brash and no brains.

So, Perceptia had given up on the living for now. Caesurian had told her not to return until she had some evidence, so she was going to find some. The lowest levels of the Hereticus librarium contained the rantings and confessions of heretics that had been caught on Ramugan station itself over the centuries. The existence of such files was hidden from just about everyone on the station, even from most of the Ordo Hereticus.

They were twofold secrets: first, because the Ordo Hereticus of Ramugan did not want to advertise the fact that they kept intricate and detailed records about personnel from the other local branches of the Emperor's Inquisition; and second, because nobody liked to admit that even a place as saturated in the sacred light of the Emperor as Ramugan – a station uniquely blessed by the Inquisitorial trinity – could grow its very own heretics in such large numbers. The latter, of course, was not much of a secret and certainly no surprise, but it was treated as a secret for diplomatic reasons, to prevent the Ordo Hereticus from being seen as a police presence on the station.

Dropping the bundle of manuscripts onto the table between the document stacks, Perceptia took one last look around the shadows that crept between the shelves, peering through her dirty glasses and the cloud of dust that billowed up off the metal desk. Satisfied that she was alone, she pushed her spectacles back up towards the bridge of her nose and sat down.

She brushed the dust off the loose cover and stared down at the seal that was still faintly visible in the paper, pressed in with the stamp of an Inquisitorial curator many centuries before. Next to it, even fainter than the seal, was the image of a pale and over-stylised eye. Untying the string that bound the bundle together, Perceptia leafed through the pages in between the covers, looking casually over the confessions and last breaths of hundreds of souls, each meticulously recorded, verified and filed by the agents of the Ordo Hereticus.

After several seconds, she finally found the document that she was looking for. It came as a relief, because it had been many long years since last she had seen that piece of paper. The confession, which was now over five hundred years old, had been used as a case-study during her training as an interrogator. It contained the last, garbled words of an old inquisitor lord of the Ordo Xenos. He had confessed to everything. He even confessed to a range of heresies that the interrogators had known nothing about. Before the end, he had also confessed to being a tau elemental and having fathered a half-breed child with an eldar female.

The standard wisdom was, of course, that Inquisitor Lord Herod would have confessed to anything. It seemed an undeniable fact that the poor man had gone insane.

However, a section of Herod's confession had stuck in Perceptia's mind, even as a green interrogator. Her mentors had used those passages as examples of the importance of being aware of context when conducting an interrogation. They had explained to the young Perceptia that human minds would scramble for information from their social and cultural surroundings at a time of great anxiety – or at a time of madness. They had laughed at the content of Herod's confession, hissing that it was as incredible as a children's story.

In fact, they had then produced a small, illustrated book, which was itself hundreds of years old, in which a very similar story was told. The seemingly inevitable conclusion was that Herod had gone mad, regressed back to his childhood, and finally confessed to the sins of fictional characters from the stories he had encountered in the Schola Progenium. Interrogation, the mentors had insisted, was an art, and a skilled interrogator should know the difference between a confession and a rant. They had explained how techniques had been refined considerably since the time that Herod's 'confession' had been extracted.

Perceptia leaned back away from the page, pushing the bridge of her spectacles with her finger tip. The story still seemed interesting to her. It said something about a secret society of inquisitors who were in league with the eldar. She had heard such legends before, of course, Ramugan was rife with them: the Ordo Malleus had a secret pact with the daemonic powers of the region, and the Ordo Xenos were secretly in league with various alien species that appeared in the sector from time to time. Very occasionally, such rumours turned out to have substance, or at least enough substance to warrant the purging of a soul and the recording of a confession.

Intermingled in amongst the references to hybrid children and heroic stands against the ancient necron threat, Perceptia thought that Herod had mentioned something specific, something that she suspected was not in the children's story. Something that he had added to the story from his own experience. Something that might even constitute a genuine confession.

There. She stabbed her finger down against the page, tearing its dry surface with the point of a finely manicured fingernail. Perceptia's fingernails were a point of pride. She had always insisted that she could tell a lot about a person from the state of their hands, and she was determined that hers would not betray her. Whenever she pushed her glasses up her nose, she imagined that someone was inspecting her fingernails.

She leaned her face closer to the text and blew the residual dust clear of the page. Yes, that was what she was looking for.

...After she had given birth to my son, she left me. It was terrible, I... there was nothing I could do, you understand?

Nothing. She was more beautiful than I could stand, she was… Have you ever seen? By the stars…

<<What happened after your son was born?>>

She took him back! She flashed like a star and vanished back into the Circuitrine nebula…

Pulling a little pocket-sized book out of her pocket and dropping it onto the desk next to the confession, she pressed its wrinkled pages flat and started to leaf through it. It was a copy of the *Legend of Hourian*, the story of an ill-fated inquisitor who had fallen in love with an eldar princess. Perceptia read out loud from the last page: 'After the terrible and beautiful child was born – an unholy creature of exquisite form – the princess cradled him in her arms, with her eyes full of tears. She looked up at Hourian for a fraction of a moment, her sadness written deeply in her eyes, and then she vanished, blinking out of existence like a dying star. Though he searched for years without end, Hourian never saw her again.'

'Yes!' said Perceptia, realising that her memory had not let her down. Herod had added the reference to the Circuitrine nebula. It was not much of a lead – the name of a system hidden in the ramblings of an insane, senile old inquisitor lord who had died five hundred years ago. It was nowhere near enough to take to Caesurian, but it was certainly enough to warrant further investigation. Interrogation was an art, after all.

THE SURVIVING DARK eldar slipped away into the shadows, presumably aware that they were outclassed by the Deathwatch. Only the shimmering white female gave chase; the rest of the eldar simply regrouped and retreated back to wherever they had come from, leaving the Deathwatch alone in the smoky remains of the combat zone.

'They will not be back in a hurry, captain,' said Kruidan, striding back towards Octavius as he holstered his bolter. The Mantis Warrior was clearly proud of the role he had played in this first encounter, and rightly so. Only Octavius and Ashok knew that this was Kruidan's first mission with the Deathwatch. In fact, he was the first Marine to be seconded from the Mantis Warriors since the once renegade Chapter had completed its penitent crusade. He obviously felt that he had something to prove, and perhaps he did.

'It was too easy,' rumbled Sulphus, climbing out of his customised land speeder. 'And we were too slow getting here.' There was an edge to the Iron Father's voice which suggested that he was blaming the others for the delay. He flexed his mechanical limbs as though they were significant to his argument. It may not have been deliberate, but it was enough to ruffle some feathers.

'He is right, captain,' agreed Luthar, as though the implicit criticism had been levelled directly at him. He unclasped the elaborate and terrifying deathmask that covered his face and nodded his agreement, as though accepting responsibility.

'This is not the time for self-reproach, Chaplain Luthar,' said Octavius, shaking his head slightly. 'The encounter was a victory. The dark eldar were routed. We suffered no casualties and the Ulthwé appeared similarly fortunate.'

'They were not fortunate, captain. The aliens hardly fought at all,' whispered Pelias, as though unsure whether to speak the thoughts out loud or not. 'They just watched us.'

'Not all of them,' corrected Atreus. 'The warlock and that white female – they fought well.'

'Agreed,' replied Octavius.

'They took prisoners, Octavius.' Ashok's voice was low and resonant.

'Yes.'

'It seems strange to me that the dark eldar would seek prisoners here,' continued the Angel Sanguine, indicating the uninspiring surroundings with a gesture from his head. 'They usually seek warriors for their games, Octavius. The Ulthwé of this sector are little more than peasants. Look at them.'

The Imperial Fists captain looked out through the clearing smoke and saw the eyes staring back at him from the perimeter of the zone. These were the local residents who had come to see what had happened and, sure enough, they did not look like warriors. Their builds were even more slight than those of the eldar fighters, and they had no armour and no weapons.

'We should leave,' concluded Octavius, nodding his acknowledgement to Ashok. 'We will return to the *Lance of Darkness* and appraise the situation fully. I suspect that we have not seen the last of the dark eldar, and our function here is still not clear. I wonder when the Ulthwé will deign to explain why they have called for us.'

With that, Octavius kicked his bike back into life and slid its back wheel through 180 degrees. The infinity portal was still a shimmering curtain, exactly where the team had emerged. Grimacing at the prospect of travelling back through that alien technology, Octavius gunned his engine and roared forward through the curtain.

From under the deep folds of his heavy hood, Ashok watched the rest of the kill-team vanish in pursuit of their captain. He paused for a moment, wondering whether he should follow them, but then he turned and strode off deeper into the structure of Ulthwé. He had other things to do.

CHAPTER SIX:
LEGERDEMAIN

THE DARKLY CRYSTALLINE walls seemed to vanish up into a distant sky. It was almost impossible to believe that this was an interior space, and that somewhere in the shadows high above there was a ceiling. Dwarfed like a tiny model soldier, Octavius stood in the magnificent archway that led into the massive hall, his head barely even a tenth of the way to its apex, and its apex almost insignificant in the height of the wall. He surveyed the cavernous space before him, taking in the entire scene instantly and then letting his eyes slowly scan from one side to the other, lingering in the shadows cast by each of the narrow, elegant pillars that disappeared into the invisible heavens above. It was an inhuman scene. He had been inside the grand halls of *Phalanx*, the now legendary fortress monastery of the Imperial

Fists that had once shadowed the craftworld of
Ulthwé during the first Black Crusade, and he had
even seen the epic frescoes depicting the majestic
spaces in the Imperial Palace on Terra, with Rogal
Dorn himself standing at the shoulder of the
Emperor. But he had never seen a space as expansive
as the one in front of him now.

There was a crackle of static, and then Pelias's
voice snarled into Octavius's ear. 'There's nothing
here, captain. The warlock was wrong, or he lied to
us.'

'Why would he lie?' asked Octavius, genuinely
curious. 'What would he gain?'

'Who can say what his motives might be?' hissed
Luthar. 'It is still not even clear why these aliens want
us here at all.'

Octavius said nothing, but he knew that Luthar
was right. Even after their first encounter with the
dark eldar, the Ulthwé had still not offered an explanation for their presence. Octavius had taken his
team back to the *Lance of Darkness* to reconsider
their position, expecting that the eldar would send
an envoy.

When nobody came, and after the team had
checked and rechecked all of their weapons after the
recent combat, there had been little else for the
Marines to do other than discuss their presence on
Ulthwé. They were reticent in each other's company,
which was understandable, but none of them were
pleased to be there. Pelias had been strangely silent,
and Luthar had preached to them about the importance of purity in the face of xenos pollution. None
of them had needed to be reminded, but they had

let the chaplain speak in deference to his position. Octavius himself had listened impassively, sitting apart from his men, turning the events of the last day over in his mind, and wondering where Ashok had gone.

Atreus had been the first to notice that they had a visitor. He had risen to his feet and wandered over to one of the viewscreens, clicking it into life. For a while there had been no image on the screen, as the snow of static speckled the picture; none of the *Lance of Darkness*'s instruments worked faultlessly in the bizarre, ethereal space of Calmainoc's dock. After a couple of seconds, Atreus brought up an image of the wraithbone bridge that connected the Deathwatch frigate to the jetty. A single eldar was striding along it towards the ship. They had seen the impressive figure before; he was the warlock in elaborate rune armour that had been part of the welcoming committee.

Rather than letting the alien war-witch enter the *Lance of Darkness* and risk offending the venerable vessel's machine-spirit, Octavius resolved to go out and meet him. However, after a couple of seconds, Atreus stopped the captain and reported the warlock's message. It was simple: *We have seen where the next attack will be. Follow me.*

'I do not think he was lying,' said Atreus, his tone even and reassuring. 'He meant for us to be here in time to confront the raid. His vision is not perfect, but he was confident that he was right.'

'They are always confident, librarian,' growled Pelias. 'But confidence does not make them right.'

'They are as fallible as any organic form,' mumbled Sulphus, twitching his mechanical arms.

'All life is fallible, brother. Life itself is the issue, not its material composition,' pressed Luthar, as though responding to a duty. He watched the Iron Father carefully and realised for the first time that only his head and right arm were still organically human. The rest had been replaced by mechanical limbs, organs and appendages, in the manner of the veteran Iron Hands techmarines. Sulphus must be old beyond his years – perhaps he had even trained with the tech-priests of Mars, wondered Luthar.

'Life is not all the same, brother-chaplain,' snarled Sulphus in response. 'Consider the eldar. Would you grant them the same quality of life as human beings?'

'Enough,' said Octavius firmly, but without anger. 'This is not the time for such debates.' He paused, looking around. 'Where did the warlock go?'

'Ran away and left us,' hissed Pelias, with undisguised venom.

'Atreus – any idea where he went?' pressed Octavius, ignoring Pelias.

'I do not think that he has gone, but I cannot tell where he is,' replied Atreus, without deliberate obfuscation. *I think also that Ashok is nearby, although I cannot tell exactly where*, continued the librarian, pushing the thoughts gently into his captain's mind. *We are not alone here.*

The giant, crystalline pillars that vanished up into the darkness above were almost translucent, tinged with purpling light as though constructed out of amethyst or sapphire. There were hundreds of them, but, looking closely, Octavius realised that they were not regularly spaced. There was no symmetry in the vast chamber; the pillars were positioned just slightly out of alignment, as though placed to provoke a deliberate discomfort or a specific, alien aesthetic pleasure. Octavius wondered about the acoustics in such an unusual space, realising that the intervals of the pillars may disrupt sound waves and that the impossible height of the chamber could swallow even the sound of explosions.

'I don't like this,' confessed Octavius, snapping a signal that sent Kruidan and Luthar off to one side with their backs pressed against the wall. Pelias and Sulphus went the other way, leaving Atreus and Octavius standing in the mouth of the great arch. Octavius unclipped his bolter and stepped forward.

A faint whine slid through the air. It was just on the very edge of hearing, like the buzz of a poisonous insect. They all heard it. As one, the Marines snapped their faces towards the ceiling, weapons snatched from holsters and braced for firing. After the abrupt rattle and clatter of preparation, the whining seemed to stop. There was silence once again. If it wasn't for the fact that they had all reacted, Octavius might have thought that he had imagined the noise.

There it was again, a high-pitched whine, like the sound of a power coil energising. It was louder this time, but intermittent, as though the power was spluttering or something was interfering with the sound – a whistling staccato. Because of the broken notes, it was hard to tell whether there was just one sound source or many, but the increase in volume suggested either an approach or a multiplication, or both.

High up in the sky, something dark flashed between the pillars, flickering in and out of visibility as it strobed behind the translucent columns. It was too fast and too distant to make out properly. After a couple of seconds, there was another flash, this time heading in the opposite direction, disappearing off to the left. Then there was another and another, until dozens of the rapid shapes flickered and wove through the forest of pillars high above, hidden in the lightless altitude. Whatever they were, they were gathering, and the ear-piercing whine was growing louder with every heartbeat.

A sudden flash of brilliant energy cut up through the shadows, reaching up from the ground and piercing the darkness in the heights. It was a jagged spear of warp fire, tinged with a sapphire hue. Up in the invisible reaches of the sky, an explosion erupted, shaking the magnificent columns and sending intense vibrations cascading down through their structure. Immediately afterwards, a black, smoking shape spiralled down out of the darkness, flames licking around it as though it were a falling angel. It slammed into the ground and detonated, exploding into a fireball of fragments and shrapnel.

Octavius did not watch the falling star; his eyes were tracking across the ground, searching for the source of the blast. Over on the other side of the immense chamber, he could see the silhouette of another Marine, a glowing force staff pushed out in front of him and an aura of power flickering around his outline.

Ashok, confirmed Atreus, sharing Octavius's line of sight.

The Imperial Fist nodded his affirmation.

Meanwhile, Sulphus and Kruidan had opened fire, using Ashok's sudden blast as a tracing round. Kruidan's jump pack flared with power and he rocketed up into the darkness above, spraying shells from his bolter as he went. As the fire spilt out of his jump pack, a pool of light followed the Mantis Warrior into the heights. In the fringes of the light, a flock of elegant and dark figures could be seen skating through the air on what appeared to be giant blades.

Almost as soon as the dark eldar raiders became visible, they dived out of the heights, scything down towards the Deathwatch Marines on their bladed skyboards, projectiles hissing out of the multi-bladed hellglaives that they wielded in both hands, a terrible keening filling the air. The dark eldar on the boards were similar to the ones encountered earlier, but not identical. They had long, unkempt hair that flooded out behind them like capes of darkness. Blades protruded from glinting gauntlets on their wrists and from armoured boots that came up to their knees. Other than that, their clothing and armour was minimal, revealing snaking lines of black and red tattoos all over their pale bodies. They screamed as though they were defying death itself.

Like an angel of fire amongst them, Kruidan hovered on the flames from his jump pack, spraying the flittering aliens with bolter shells and lashing out with his chainsword whenever any of them strayed close enough for him to reach. But the slippery foes were fleet, too fast and manoeuvrable to be brought down by a single Marine, no matter how furious his assault.

Streams of shells ripped up through the hall in support, ricocheting off pillars and riddling the heights with explosive fragments until the aliens could find no haven from the onslaught. A carefully placed javelin of energy from Atreus's staff crunched into a skyboard, destabilizing it and sending its rider spinning uncontrollably towards the hovering figure of Kruidan.

The collision was inevitable, and it sent the Mantis Warrior roaring back into one of the pillars, where his jump pack spluttered under the impact and failed. Together with the struggling dark eldar raider, the Marine tumbled and slid down the sheer face of the pillar, fighting to keep upright and to keep the alien beneath him. The two figures ploughed into the floor at the base of the column like a meteor striking the ground, sending a shock wave convulsing through the hall.

Meanwhile, the rest of the dark eldar raiders were swooping down on the kill-team, unleashing a rain of splinter projectiles from their unique weapons. At the base of their dives, when the proximity was tight, their hellglaives became lethal scything weapons, with multiple, sweeping blades protruding from each end of them.

The combination of ranged and then intimate attacks sent the Deathwatch onto the defensive for a moment – only Atreus's staff was as versatile as the alien hellglaive, and the librarian was making sure that the xenos creatures knew their tactics would not cow a librarian of the Blood Ravens. As Atreus parried and jabbed with his burning staff, meeting the hellglaive blades with the unyielding substance of his force staff whilst unleashing sheets of sizzling energy into the faces of the diving foes, Octavius whipped his chainsword into life and brandished it in his off-hand, his bolter still coughing in the other.

From the other side of the great hall, intense blasts of energy were still arching between the pillars as Ashok stood his ground and unleashed his psychic fury, punching his rage into the flailing bodies of the slender aliens as the force ripped them off their skyboards and sent them tumbling to their deaths.

The hall was transformed into a deathtrap, with projectiles pinging rapidly between the innumerable pillars, with bolter shells exploding into shrapnel, and great sheets of psychic fire interweaving the carnage. The surviving dark eldar responded by dropping their skyboards down low to the ground and using them to skim along the surface in rapid attack runs.

The kill-team regrouped into a circle around the pillar that Kruidan had crashed into – he was back on his feet with his bolter and chainsword brandished, and with his boots coated in the thick ichor of the pulverised alien that had broken his fall. The team kept the pillar at their backs as they fended off the swooping hellion raiders. On the far side of the hall, Octavius could see that Ashok was still standing alone, he did not have time to work out whether he should praise the Angel Sanguine for his valour or condemn him for his failure to play in the team. Either way, the librarian was succeeding in dividing the attentions of the hellions, so Octavius was pleased that he was there.

'Where is that warlock?' snarled Pelias, stepping forward of the defensive ring as he parried a swooping blade with the barrel of his bolter. In the same movement, he deflected the blade of the hellglaive down next to the feet of the hellion, driving it into the structure of the skyboard itself. The fragile vehicle sparked and whinnied, bucking its rider before spiralling off into a fireball against one of the other columns. The rider crashed to the ground at Pelias's feet and, without hesitation, the Black Consul tugged his combat knife out of the holster in his boot and drove it into the alien's throat.

'The eldar are nowhere,' growled Sulphus, three bolters coughing simultaneously from one organic and two mechanical arms.

'We should not place our faith in the aliens, brothers,' yelled Luthar over the din. 'Faith is reserved for the Emperor. Ask rather where are our souls!'

As he spoke, the chaplain took a mighty swing with his crozius arcanum, bringing it up in a powerful arc that met the front of an incoming skyboard. There was an explosion of blue power as the hellion stopped abruptly and was thrown back by the impact. The skyboard simply shattered, and its rider skidded to the ground beyond it. Even as it tried to climb to its feet, Kruidan and Pelias both levelled their bolters and shredded it with a concentrated volley of fire.

'There!' cried Atreus, jabbing the direction with the tip of his staff.

Without releasing the pressure of his trigger finger, Octavius glanced over towards the far side of the cavernous chamber. He could see Ashok running with his staff spinning into a sphere of pristine energy around him. He could see a line of speeding Reavers in front of the librarian emerging out of the shadows of a wide side passage, heading directly at him with their nose mounted splinter cannons flaring. Behind them, he could see a formation of Ulthwé jetbikes in pursuit, including the dazzling white form of the female warrior and the menacing visage of the warlock.

Even as he watched, Octavius saw Ashok sidestep the first Reaver, bringing his staff crashing down onto its nosecone as it flashed past him. Without pausing to watch the dark eldar vehicle spark and convulse with explosions, ploughing spectacularly into the deck, Ashok spun and brought his searing staff around in a wide horizontal sweep, smashing it into the path of a second Reaver, which detonated massively, obscuring the entire scene behind a mushrooming cloud of brilliant light for several seconds.

As the cloud cleared, the remaining Reavers burst out of it, weaving in and out of the pillars in the great hall, flashing through the space towards one of the arches on the other side. Even from that distance, Octavius could see that the dark eldar riders had prisoners bound, gagged and secured to the back of their vehicles, where they also served as an extra layer of organic armour. In close pursuit went the Ulthwé jetbikes; the white rider was far out in front, manoeuvring her bike with breathtaking skill and grace – she brought down two more of the Reavers before they vanished again into the darkness of the infrastructural tunnels.

Scanning back to the site of the first two explosions, Octavius could no longer see Ashok. He was gone.

THROWING HER WEIGHT to one side, she made the jet-bike bank and start to roll, but by gunning the engine she held the angle and brought the machine upright again, even closer to the fleeing Reaver that flashed in between the great pillars of Kha-landhriel's Hall. Lying flat over the fuel tank, Dhrykna willed her shining bike to even greater speeds. She could see the prone body of a ceremonial dancer from the local eldar community strapped across the back of the darkling's ride, and she was determined not to bring the wretched machine down until she had rescued the prisoner.

The darkling was good, weaving and darting between the columns with consummate ease. Despite the severity of the situation, Dhrykna thrilled at the challenge, and she could feel the air of contemptuous pleasure flooding back from the darkling in his backwash, as though he was enjoying it too. She grinned, pushing the shimmering white bike to even faster speeds and gaining another few metres on the meandering darkling. It was exactly for moments such as this that she had wanted to rejoin the Shining Path. This was what she had been born for, flashing through the shadows like the spear of Khaine in the service of Ulthwé.

As the distance closed almost to within reach of a harpoon grappler, Dhrykna looked ahead, anticipating the future course of the chase before committing herself to trying to recover the dancer. A flare of light in the middle distance caught her eye, distracting her from the chase for a moment. She cursed under her breath as she realised that the distance to her quarry had stretched even in that briefest of instants. Inhaling sharply, she willed an extra burst of speed and raced after the Reaver again, scraping past the next few pillars so closely that she left fragments of paint etched into them.

But there was something about that burst of light up ahead that Dhrykna could not ignore. Even as she focused all of her attention on the speeding darkling raider, part of her mind kept replaying the flare over and over again, as though trying to discern more details in a slow motion replay. Before she could work it out, the present interrupted her attempts to analyse the past and the Reaver in front of her suddenly coughed and sparked, decelerating sharply as though struck from the front, where an intense burst of light had suddenly erupted.

Dhrykna had to bank sharply to the side to avoid smashing into the back of the hobbled Reaver as its nose dipped and ploughed into the ground, digging a trench in the polished floor of Khalandhriel's Hall. As she rolled her bike she craned her neck back round to see what had happened to her darkling prey.

Standing in a ferocious halo of light was one of the mon-keigh warriors, its force staff still ablaze with power, the edges of its heavy hood crackling with blue flames, and its eyes alight with a terrible red glow. Even a she watched, it brought its staff down from the point where it had struck the speeding Reaver, and the mon-keigh psyker spun on its heel, bringing the staff around in a surprisingly graceful curve until it smashed into the front of another Reaver, exploding it instantly.

Although she would be giving the remaining Reavers a lead, the Shining Spear pulled her bike around in a tight curve, peeling off to the side and circling back to retrace her path through the glittering fireball that now engulfed the two downed Reavers. As she flew through the flames it became clear that the prisoners tied to the back of the two darkling vessels were dead; their bodies were broken and twisted unnaturally, and their skin was already ruined by the fire. Dhrykna's eyes narrowed as she realised that the mon-keigh had killed the dancers along with the darklings. They narrowed even further when she realised that that mon-keigh psyker had vanished. She had known from the start that the psyker was going to cause problems.

Lifting her head and pressing herself low over the body of her bike, she opened the throttle as far as it would go and flashed off in pursuit of the remaining Reavers, her fury dripping out behind her like fuel from a faulty afterburner. If she could not vent her passion against the mon-keigh, at least she could show the darklings the meaning of death.

THERE WAS so little light in the corridors that even Ashok's enhanced occulobes struggled to resolve the images around him. The narrow, winding passageways were in stark contrast to the massive, expansive open spaces in which the Deathwatch had fought its first two encounters. The librarian could see and hear the impacts and concussions of combat behind him, but he felt sure that Octavius had the situation under control. The hellions were all but defeated already, and the Ulthwé jetbikes were dealing with the Reavers. He assured himself that his absence would not be missed, even if it would be noticed.

The lower levels of Ulthwé were like a maze, riddled with ventilation ducts and service tunnels, all of them shrouded in the oppressive weight of shadows. With a whisper, Ashok set a light flickering on the tip of his force staff, spreading a bluish glow through the passageway. He paused to take in the scene and then extinguished the light – there was nothing worthy of his attention in the cramped corridor, and the light would serve only to attract the attention of others. The Ulthwé would be distracted by the raids for only so long, and Ashok was keen to have reached his target before that moment came. It was not often that one of the Emperor's librarians found himself alone and free in the bowels of an eldar craftworld.

After a few more steps, Ashok came to a junction in the passage. It split in five directions – a regular cross-roads but with an extra corridor opening out of the ceiling and heading up into the higher reaches of the craftworld's infrastructure. Crouching slightly, the Angel Sanguine sprang into the air, catching hold of the lip of the tunnel with one hand and swinging himself up into it. He needed to go up

– he was not going to find what he was looking for down in the lowest dumps of Ulthwé.

Thereafter the corridors all angled upwards, sloping up towards the interior of the alien world, like tunnels into the centre of a planet. Whenever he came to a junction, Ashok selected the route that was most steeply angled or the one that he thought headed most directly towards the geometric heart of the craftworld itself. In the back of his mind, he was drawing a complex and intricate map of his route, hoping that he would be able to find his way back down to the depths once he was finished up there. After a while, however, he began to curse. He had presumed that even the service tunnels of the immense craftworld would contain versions of the infinity portals that the Deathwatch had used to get from Calmainoc's dock. It was impossible to believe that service personnel had to travel the incredible distances through the vast vessel in the normal way – it would simply take too long, and Ulthwé would be gradually rotting from the outside in. There had to be shortcuts and portals, even in these cramped and shadowy passages.

Just as he was beginning to think that his human logic had failed him and caused him to misunderstand the rationale of the aliens, Ashok emerged into a wide, quasi-spherical chamber, which appeared to function as a confluence point in the midst of the local service systems. The mouths of tunnels and passageways yawned into it from all directions, some dropping away from the floor and others vanishing up into the ceiling. It was some kind of hub.

More interesting than the multitude of tunnels, however, were the circular pools of shimmering liquid that were held in glistening frames next to each of the tunnel-mouths. Instinctively, Ashok's hand dropped to the pouch on his belt, tapping it to ensure that he had neither forgotten nor lost anything on his way. There would be no point in continuing if he had.

With another silent whisper, Ashok sent a gentle bluish light through the spherical chamber, as he climbed down into the bowl-like floor. The liquefied portals reflected and refracted the light, filling the space with a subtle spectrum of dancing colours. In his mind, the librarian could hear the faint whispering of voices that he could not understand. They wafted out of the portals, churning and curdling the air in the spherical chamber, concentrating themselves in the epicentre above Ashok's head, as though conducted there by the architecture itself. Closing his eyes, Ashok could hear beckonings and repulsions, temptations and revulsions, each pulling at his soul and competing for the attention of his alien mind. The disembodied voices knew that he was there, and their hostility was plain, even if it was often cloaked and subtle. Their emotive mutterings had insanity and death in mind.

Shaking his head and clearing his thoughts, Ashok surveyed the various passageways and portals. One of them was bound to take him in the right direction. Checking back into the spirit pool that churned and rippled next to the tunnel from which he had just emerged, he could sense an image of flashing lights and violence ebbing and flowing in its depths. It was not the past that he saw, but rather it was the present – that direction would take him back towards the ongoing fight with the dark eldar. He nodded with satisfaction, turning and striding towards one of the pools on the opposite side of the spherical chamber. He did not want to go back, at least not yet.

In the depths of one pool he saw a congregation of eldar warriors, each kneeling to the ground with their heads bowed, and with one fist punched defiantly into the deck. In another he saw a dazzling, crystalline light, refracted and split into myriad colours but somehow organised into a palace or temple that seemed to have been constructed out of light itself.

Finally, in one of the portals that curved up into the ceiling, Ashok saw what he had been looking for. The image was muddied by a shroud of darkness and blurred by the ripples that pulsed across its liquid surface, but Ashok was certain that he perceived it correctly. There was a giant and ornate gate, surrounded on all sides by ancient runic texts inscribed into the wraithbone frame of the gate itself. He could feel a cold pulse of horror wash out of the little portal in front of him as soon as his mind turned to it. Something in Ulthwé knew where he was going, and it was not happy about it at all. Smiling slightly at the thought, Ashok vaulted up towards the shimmering pool. Catching hold of the bottom of the frame that contained it, he hung there for a moment before swinging his legs up around his head and plunging himself into the rippling image.

LEAVING THE SMOKE- and debris-filled Khalandhriel's Hall far behind, the gallery stretched on forever, its highly polished wraithbone structure reflecting itself into an infinity of regressions. It was flanked on both sides by low columns that twisted and spiralled around each other, as though they were merely threads in the weave of a giant fabric. The effect was to psychologically shrink the people that walked along the elegant corridor, making them feel like little more than microscopic organisms burrowing through the clothes of an infinitely superior being.

Striding along behind the pristine white female and the sinister warlock, Octavius surveyed his surroundings without betraying any emotion at all. He was quite used to grand locations and magnificent spaces. As a captain in the Imperial Fists, he had become acquainted with many of the most auspicious structures in the Imperium. He had maintained close connections with several arms of the Administratum and with various factions within the Imperial Navy – he had used the tremendous influence of the Imperial Fists to negotiate the fabled Truce of Gohliath, bringing a viciously evangelical local branch of the Ecclesiarchy to the conference table in the legendary palace on Gohliath IV.

It was said that Rogal Dorn himself had once used that magnificent hall for volatile and delicate talks with Guilliman and Perturabo, the primarchs of the Ultramarines and the Iron Warriors. Octavius was well accustomed to the grandeur of magnificent structures, but there was something profoundly different about this long, interwoven hallway.

As the unlikely group of eldar and Space Marines reached the midway point in the corridor, Octavius realised what had been niggling at his thoughts:

there were no pictures or frescoes along the walls or on the ceiling. In the great halls of the Imperium, all of the walls would proudly sport the portraits of magnificent, lost warriors, or would boast frescoes depicting scenes from the glorious battles of the past. The walls of the hallways of *Phalanx* were virtually invisible behind the stern and heroic faces of Chapter Masters and valiant captains. Even the majestic corridors of Gohliath's Palace and the incredible vaulted ceilings of the Imperial Palace on Terra itself were teeming with images of honour and glory. Every inch was decorated to the point of gothic splendour. But here, in the hallway leading to the Chamber of the Seer Council of Ulthwé, the surfaces were without such ornamentation. They were immaculately smooth and polished to such a lustre that they were almost iridescent. Yet they were not plain, and they were certainly not without interest. There were patterns and images swirling through the substance of the wraithbone itself, like wisps of life dancing and playing in a realm that was not quite present but not entirely absent either.

Walking through the glorious hallway was akin to striding through an aesthetic experience – the hall *happened* as Octavius experienced it. It was not a static monument, but rather an ongoing experience. For a moment, the Imperial Fists captain wondered whether the rest of his team was experiencing the space in the same way, or whether an aspect of his experience was entirely his own.

Casting his gaze to one side, he could see the confident and powerful figures of Atreus and Pelias striding along behind him, showing no signs of being affected by the breathtaking edifice around them. They were well trained.

Not for the first time, Octavius wondered where Ashok was.

Stop. The thought was a clumsy command and Octavius could feel the discomfort from his team behind him. Their boots scraped against the smooth ground, as though screwing themselves into the floor for extra grip in case further insults followed. Out the corner of his eye, Octavius could see that Pelias's hand had dropped to the hilt of his bolter.

The group had reached the end of the long hallway, and they were confronted with a door of epic proportions, tall and slender like the eldar themselves. Like the rest of the corridor, the door showed no obvious signs of decoration or ornamentation, yet it seemed to exude a kind of ineffable beauty. Looking more closely at its structure, Octavius realised that it appeared to be incredibly thin, almost like glass. He wondered how much it weighed and how much damage it could withstand. To him, it appeared that the door's primary defensive merit was a type of aesthetic enchantment – who could want to destroy such a thing? Pelias sprang to mind instantly.

Stop. The thought came again, even more emphatic than the last time.

'We have stopped,' said Octavius calmly, gesturing with his hands to indicate his indifference and mild confusion. They hadn't had any choice: they had reached the end of the corridor and the mysterious door ahead of them was closed.

For the first time, the warlock turned back to face Octavius. The two warriors were approximately the same height, and the eyes of the warlock's elaborate mask were virtually level with Octavius's visor. Although they could not see each other's eyes, they held their pose for a long moment, and Octavius began to wonder whether the alien could see his face after all. No matter, he would not shrink from anybody, especially not from an alien, and particularly not from an alien that had come to the Imperium begging for help.

You will stop. The thoughts were slow and deliberate, as though being spoken to a particularly stubborn or difficult child.

'We... have... stopped,' replied Octavius, mimicking the condescension and holding his ground. He looked the warlock up and down, sizing him up as a possible opponent. It was not often that a Space Marine had the chance to stand so close to a living eldar warlock without having to kill it, and Octavius was conscious that this was a strategic opportunity. After all, the Deathwatch were not *only* a kill-team, and the Ordo Xenos was not *only* interested in annihilating aliens – if he could discover new and innovative ways to kill more aliens in the future, then he would have done his job perfectly. At that moment he realised that the eldar obviously did not expect the kill-team to survive whatever it was they had in store for them. Why else would they risk bringing a squad of Space Marines into the heart of their craftworld?

The warlock was tall, as tall as most Marines, and his presence was tinged with a kind of gravity that even Octavius found impressive. But the alien's build was slight to the point of being slender. The

Imperial Fist realised that the impression was probably false, and that he shouldn't judge the aliens by human standards, but it seemed to him that he could snap the sinister creature in two with his gauntlets. Apart from a number of obvious anatomical differences, the warlock's build was not dissimilar from that of the shimmering, white female.

Wait. The thought was strong and undeniable, belying the relatively fragile body from which it emanated.

Octavius nodded, realising that the eldar's strength was only partly in its body. At the same time, he realised that the warlock's clumsy manner was probably a result of a lack of familiarity with human thoughts. It occurred to him that the alien was actually making an effort to communicate, which was not something that it had to do. Nodding his assent one more time, Octavius realised that the warlock was trying to honour him.

CRASHING OUT OF the portal in the ceiling and crunching heavily down to the ground, Ashok vowed that he would never enter the spirit-ways of an eldar craftworld again. He skidded across the polished floor and smacked into the back of some kind of console. When he finally stopped moving, he found a moment to smile at the ridiculousness of his last vow. It was certainly not a vow that he had ever anticipated needing to make and, to make matters worse, it was one that he was absolutely sure that he would have to break in only a few minutes' time.

Thoughts and whispered voices still spiralled around his head, as though they had bled into his soul while he flashed through the inexplicable dimensions through which the alien portals passed. Tiny lights sparkled behind his eyes, like the faint echoes of dying stars. These were not entirely alien experiences for Ashok, and they prompted his soul towards dark places that he had learnt to navigate around through years of pain and horror. There was a rage lurking in the turmoil, and it was not something to which he could surrender now. He needed to be calm and rational for this task.

For a few seconds, the Angel Sanguine did not move. He sat in perfect stillness while he brought his thoughts back to himself, dragging fragments of his soul out of his memory of the sparkling, riddled spirit-way through which he had just flown. His body was unaffected, it was his soul that felt the disorientation of submersion in the profound depths of something wonderful and terrible.

As his mind cleared, he heard voices. They spoke in a tongue that he could not understand and only partly through vocalised words. Many of the tones and nuances seemed to seep through waves of psychic resonance, as though words were spoken simultaneously through oral and psychic projections. In a moment of clarity, Ashok realised that the language of these eldar made no distinction between audio and psychic noise – both were natural parts of the tongue.

Judging from the sounds, Ashok thought that there were probably three aliens in the chamber on the other side of the terminal behind which he was hidden. He found it remarkable that they had not noticed a two-metre tall, heavily armoured Space Marine barrelling through the air and crashing into the wall less than ten metres from where they were standing.

Ashok shifted his weight slightly, turning into a crouch and repositioning his force staff, poising himself. As soon as he moved, the eldar voices stopped. They had heard him. Just the tiniest of moves and they had heard him. He froze, fighting against his natural urge to vault the terminal with his staff blazing and lay waste to the filthy aliens on the other side. His task required some subtlety and some tact. Besides which, he was still not sure how many creatures there were in the chamber. Stupidity is the flipside of courage.

How could they have heard such a tiny movement but have missed his entrance? Ashok's mind scanned back through the last couple of minutes and a sinking feeling settled over him. How long had it been since he'd crashed into that chamber? It was a blur. He could remember stars and whispered voices, but he had no sense of time. Had he lost consciousness? What had happened to him after he vaulted into that portal? Damn, he hated alien technology.

The only explanation was that when he had crashed through into the chamber, the eldar had not been there. When they had arrived, he must have been unconscious, hidden behind the terminal where he crouched now. Ashok cursed himself for being so stupid; how could he have thrown himself through an alien transport system in the heart of an eldar craftworld and placed himself at the mercy of xenos technology? He was beyond lucky not to have been caught and killed as he emerged from the portal. No, he stopped his self-reproach in mid-flow: it was not luck – it was the grace of the Emperor himself. He may be in the heart of Ulthwé, skirting the fringes of the Eye of Terror itself, but the Emperor's gaze could not be bounded.

'For the Emperor and Sanguinius! Death! Death comes for you!' yelled Ashok, his voice thundering the battle cry of the Angels Sanguine Death Company as he abandoned his pretence at stealth and rose to his feet. His heavy psychic hood sparked with power and his eyes flared red as he spun his staff over his head and unleashed a sheet of blue fire. The aliens would regret any attempts to mess with his head.

Through the blur of his righteous rage, Ashok saw two stunned eldar seers turn to face him. They had been tending to some instruments built into the side of a polished, glass hemisphere that protruded from the wall. Ashok recognised it at once, even through the red haze that had descended across his vision. It was one of the access points to Ulthwé's infinity circuit – the spirit pool of the entire craftworld. Despite his fury, a smile cracked over Ashok's face as the scythe of blue energy sliced into the two seers, lifting them off their feet and sending them crashing to the ground.

THE TALL, SLIM door at the end of the great hallway simply dissolved. An uneven crack appeared in the middle of it and then it just melted away, leaving an elegantly curving arch and a view of the council chamber beyond.

Come.

The warlock's thoughts were blunt and direct, but Octavius was now certain that they contained little malice. He nodded and strode under the archway after the warlock and the shining white female, the rest of his kill-team close behind. Something at the back of his mind made him wonder what Ashok was doing at that moment.

The council chamber was a massive translucent dome, and Octavius thought that he could see the hazy glow of the Eye of Terror itself through the almost transparent ceiling. They must have been right up at the very summit of Ulthwé. The space within the huge dome was virtually featureless – there was no ornamentation or decoration but, just like the hallway outside, it managed to emanate a breathtaking beauty. Once again, Octavius wondered whether it was some kind of enchantment, or whether the aesthetic itself was merely enchanting.

Standing in the very centre of the chamber was a group of eldar in long, flowing robes of various colours and styles. Octavius recognised a couple of them from the committee that had welcomed the Deathwatch in Calmainoc's dock. The emerald seer appeared to be the leader of the group, and she stepped forward of the others as Octavius approached.

Bow, insisted the warlock's mind as he and the pristine white female dropped to one knee before the seer, touching their fists to the ground. *Bow now.*

The Deathwatch captain watched the show of deference without embarrassment. He did not bow; he would bow to no alien.

'Greetings, captain.' The sound was unnatural and forced. Octavius could see the strain stretched over the seer's otherwise beautiful face. He simply nodded in response.

'We have remiss been in dealings our with you,' continued the green witch, her head tilted slightly to one side as though she was trying to work out whether he could understand her.

'Yes,' replied Octavius bluntly. 'You have.'

'We apologise should.'

Was that an apology or an observation of etiquette? Octavius couldn't tell, and he realised that the eldar witch's scrambled grasp of this spoken language was an asset for her as well as a hindrance.

'Yes, you should,' pressed Octavius, determined not to let the ambiguity stand.

'I am Thae'akzi, the Emerald Seer,' she said.

Was she ignoring his slight, or did she not realise that he was demanding something more from her?

Octavius waited for her to continue, but she did not. 'I am Quirion Octavius, humble servant of the Emperor of Mankind, battle-brother of the Imperial Fists, and captain in the service of the Deathwatch of the sacred Ordo Xenos.' His voice was even and calm, but his eyes narrowed as he tried to assess the impact of his words on the eldar witch before him.

'Very impressive.' Was she mocking him? 'Already you have met Dhrykna of the Shining Path,' she continued, indicating the shimmering white form of the female warrior who remained on one knee before the council. 'And already you have met Shariele, Warlock of the Undercouncil.' These were statements, not questions, and neither of the eldar mentioned showed any signs of acknowledgement. 'They will you assist.'

'Assist?' queried Octavius, wondering whether the aliens would ever explain themselves. 'Assist in what?'

'Your function, human.' The voice came from one of the other seers – an older male with hate pouring out of his eyes.

'Function!' snarled Pelias from Octavius's shoulder, his resentment simmering at the edge of boiling point.

'Forgive you will Ruhklo of the Karizhariat,' said Thae'akzi smoothly, as though her words were a kind of balm. Again, it was a statement rather than a request. 'He pleased is not you are here.'

'He is not alone is those sentiments,' said Octavius, not feeling obliged to hide his team's discomfort about the present mission.

Thae'akzi nodded and smiled condescendingly, as though she understood. 'We you summoned here because have we concern at your performance in Khalandhriel's Hall.'

Octavius thought about this for a moment. 'What?' he asked, incredulous. For a moment he had thought that the witch was finally going to tell them why the Ulthwé had activated the Coven of Isha. Instead, it seemed that she merely wanted to criticise him team's performance in the last battle.

'Failed you to protect our seers. Missing are two of them from the upper levels.' Thae'akzi's tone was serious now, and heavy with criticism.

'Seers?' asked Octavius, replaying the events of the battle over in his mind.

'Yes. Guarding they were an access point to the infinity circuit in the upper levels. Bhurolyn of the Sacred Star, old and wizened, one of the council is gone.'

'We were not in the upper levels,' stated Octavius flatly, his pride riled at the criticism of the alien witch.

'Exactly. Fight in Khalandhriel's Hall diversion was clearly. You this should have realised at once. The darklings are cunning.'

And the mon-keigh are stupid.

'We were in that cursed hall because your war-witch told us to be there–' began Pelias, his anger rising, but Octavius cut him off.

'Perhaps we would perform better if you could inform us about our "function" here, Thae'akzi, Emerald Seer.'

There was a moment of silence, in which another of the seers stepped forward. She was younger than the others and emanated an exquisite, fragile beauty from within the flowing, translucent white of her long robes.

'Captain,' she nodded a brief if respectful bow. 'I am Eldressyn of Ulthroon, and your purpose here has grown out of my thoughts–' Something unheard cut her off.

'We are concerned very about the seers, captain, especially Bhurolyn,' explained Thae'akzi. 'Your fail-ure dangerous very is. If the darklings sacrifice were to those souls, then Great Enemy will grow strong. Pow-erful are those souls. Different from those before taken.'

'How is this *our* problem?' spat Pelias. 'We fought where and when we were told.'

Octavius ignored the veteran sergeant. 'If their loss is really our fault, then we will recover them for you.' He nodded a crisp bow of affirmation. This was a complicated position for the Deathwatch captain, and he could see it even if the Black Consul sergeant could not. In the back of his mind, Octavius realised that this was why the Imperial Fists rather than the Ultramarines were the backbone of Adeptus Astartes diplomacy. The Deathwatch team was there to fulfil an Imperial oath to serve Ulthwé at a moment of its greatest need. It was not his place to access that need – although he could see little evidence of it. Rather, it was his role to ensure the honour of the Deathwatch and the keepers of the Coven of Isha.

He could give the eldar no excuse to accuse his team of failure or dishonour. Although he did not believe that the loss of the seers was his fault, it was enough that the eldar felt able to blame him for it. Communication between them was not perfect. Perhaps he should have been able to work out what was expected of him? Had he been defending the fortress of *Phalanx*, he would have ensured the security of every level and every man. Perhaps the eldar expected no less of him on Ulthwé. Why could they not simply *tell him* what they needed from him? Not for the first time, he wondered where Ashok was – the librarian would be of use at a time like this.

CHAPTER SEVEN:
RAVELLING

THERE WAS AN air of heavy discontent settling in the
armoury of the *Lance of Darkness*. The Deathwatch
Marines were checking their weapons and adminis-
tering to their machine-spirits, muttering silent
words of prayer and litanies of purification. But their
minds were elsewhere, and the tension in the relative confines of the super-armoured space was
explosive.

The team had returned to their frigate directly
from the Seer Chamber, sweeping through the
labyrinthine corridors of Ulthwé on assault bikes
and a land speeder. Relative to the overall size of the
craftworld, the Seer Chamber was actually quite
close to Calmainoc's Dock, so they had taken the
long way round, deciding not to entrust their
ancient armour or their sacred gene-seed to the alien

portal network unless strictly necessary. They had some time, so they were cruising the vast, wide, smooth corridors and boulevards of Ulthwé. The sheer scale of the craftworld was incredible. Besides, Octavius had wanted to ride. He had needed some time to clear his head and to ensure that his resolve was well-placed.

Duty was usually a simple thing, but since arriving on Ulthwé he had realised that even the most prized values of the Adeptus Astartes could be riddled and twisted by the cunning of the eldar. Just being on the craftworld made him suspicious of everyone and of himself. Why had he accepted responsibility for the loss of the two seers in the upper reaches of the craftworld, despite the fact that he had not been asked to guard them? Pressing at the back of his mind all the time was another, perhaps even darker, question: where was Librarian Ashok? Despite his deep-seated respect for the enigmatic and wild Angel Sanguine, Octavius found himself wishing that he was a casualty – that, at least, would simplify the situation.

'Captain,' said Pelias at last, breaking the silence and dropping his bolter down onto the metal workbench in front of him. The pristine weapon glinted as it caught the light. 'I must ask why you humbled us before the aliens.'

Without his helmet, it was clear that Pelias was probably the oldest Marine in the room. Perhaps Sulphus was older, but it was hard to tell in amongst all of the mechanical augmetics and metal plates. The Black Consul's gnarled face was creased and scarred, and his bright eyes were sunk deeply into their sockets. He wore years of hardship and strength across his features, but there was a hint of weariness about him, as though the relentless pain had scarred his soul as well as his body.

Octavius placed his own bolter down onto a bench and looked over at his old comrade. He had known Pelias, on and off, for several decades. They had fought together before in the service of the Deathwatch. The captain had been in command of the failed incursion against the Biel-Tan during which Pelias had been captured. Although they had fought shoulder to shoulder since then, the Black Consul had never mentioned the incident again. There had never been a single word of reproach and never even a note of bitterness. The sergeant's loyalty was unimpeachable, and Octavius never ceased to admire the resilience and power of his will. Had any of the other Marines in the Deathwatch team challenged him in this way, Octavius would not have stood for it. He knew that Pelias felt his actions most acutely, and he knew that he owed his sergeant an explanation.

'I did not humble us, Pelias.'

'You accepted the blame for their mistakes. It is a dishonour.'

'No, Pelias. It is a dishonour to accuse another when you know that they are innocent. The eldar dishonoured themselves. We have been sent to aid the aliens, and it would not become us to attempt to evade our duties by arguing about blame. If the aliens want us to recover their seers, then we will see it done,' explained Octavius calmly.

'They might simply have asked,' murmured Luthar, 'rather than attempting to manoeuvre us into a position in which we had no choice. Honour is better served through our will than through obedience to theirs.'

'Honour is best serviced through duty, chaplain, not through will. Duty before all else,' said Octavius, turning his sparkling eyes on the pale features of the Reviler. 'We do not choose our paths, we can only choose the manner in which we tread them. Decisions are reached elsewhere.'

'By the will of Corax and the Emperor,' intoned Luthar, bowing slightly to acknowledge Octavius's words.

'By the Emperor and his sons,' paraphrased Octavius, smoothing the wave of unrest that pulsed around the room at the mention of Corax, the enigmatic primarch of the Raven Guard and their successor Chapters.

'The Reviler is right,' seethed Sulphus in barely audible tones. 'Corax had a will of his own. Duty is something that human failings conspire to ruin. The flesh is weak.'

The Iron Father of the Red Talons did not look up as he spoke. He simply muttered the words into the machine parts that he was cleaning, flexing and unflexing the mechanical joints on one of his arms where splinter-fire had left scoring on the surface of the metal. As he worked, his mind was racing back through the legends of how Corax and the Raven Guard had left Ferrus Manus to his fate on Istvaan V, even as the Warmaster's massed forces mustered for battle. Ferrus Manus, primarch of the Iron Hands, the father Chapter of Sulphus's Red Talons, had been unerring in his duty – only the weakened flesh of the

Raven Guard and the Salamanders had lacked the necessary will for power. The legends were hard-wired into the memories of every Red Talon, ensuring that they should never forget the weakness of flesh.

'What was that, Talon?' snapped Luthar, taking a step towards the apparently introspective Iron Father.

Sulphus looked up. There was no hint of contri-tion or guilt on his face, which was barely visible behind the patchwork of reconstructive plates and sensory augmenters, even without his helmet. 'I'm sure that even your fleshy ears were not mistaken, Reviler.' There was no emotion in the voice at all – it was not an accusation nor even a jibe, there was no defiance in the tone. It was simply a statement.

Turning his face from the simmering gaze of Luthar, Sulphus addressed Octavius. 'Where is the Blood Angel, captain?' This time, there was genuine contempt in the Red Talon's words.

Octavius hesitated for a moment, unsure of what to say. 'You are referring to Librarian Ashok of the Angels Sanguine, Iron Father?'

'Of course.' The flat tone suggested that Sulphus saw no difference between the successor Chapter and the Blood Angels themselves. 'He also appears to have left us.'

The connection with Corax in Sulphus's mind was thus laid bare for the others to see. It was no secret that the Blood Angels were passionate warriors, amongst the finest and most devout in the galaxy, but for the Iron Father this passion looked like the irrational weakness of human flesh. There could not be a Chapter further from the ideals of Ferrus Manus than the Blood Angels.

Despite his anger at Sulphus, Luthar turned to look at Octavius. By nature, he was also suspicious of the emotionally charged and occasionally uncontrollable Blood Angels. The Revilers, like the Raven Guard themselves, were disciplined and calculating fighters. Although they could not argue with the glorious record of the Blood Angels and their successors, they could not bring themselves to condone their tactics.

Ignoring the look from Luthar, Octavius directed his response to Sulphus. 'His location is not your concern, techmarine,' said Octavius, his voice firm and full of authority. He was the commander of this mission, and even the Iron Father had to recognise that.

Sulphus nodded with only a hint of disingenuousness. He was not content with this reply, but he was a Space Marine in the service of the Deathwatch and *he*, at least, understood the demands of his duty.

If he was honest with himself, Octavius was also not content with his answer. He did not know where the librarian was and it worried him. There were various possibilities, and none of them were good. Either the magnificent Ashok was dead, captured, or deliberately avoiding the duties of the team. It was the last possibility that worried Octavius the most – it meant that either Ashok had his own agenda separate from that of the kill-team, or that he was pursuing somebody else's separate agenda. Given the unusual way in which the librarian had been included in his team, Octavius's suspicions naturally inclined towards the latter possibility.

'What is the plan, captain?' asked Atreus, turning the conversation back to the matter at hand. In truth, he was just as uncomfortable with the tension in the chamber as the others.

The librarians of the Blood Ravens were constantly in search of clues about the unknown origins of their mysterious Chapter, and one of the working hypotheses was that it was a hybrid of the Blood Angels and the Raven Guard. Although the theory was no longer taken very seriously, since it appeared to be based more on the linguistic coincidence than on sound historical evidence, Atreus was not entirely comfortable to hear both Chapters maligned at the same time. His instincts were defensive, and he wondered whether that in itself was significant. Very deliberately, he did not turn his cold gaze on Sulphus.

'We need to find out where the dark eldar raiders are taking their prisoners,' replied Octavius. 'I suggest that we take the *Lance of Darkness* hunting. Even if we find nothing, at least it will get us out of this cursed craftworld for a while.'

THERE WERE JUST too many files. Perceptia, slumped back against the tomes behind her, leaning her weight against the shelves without giving any thought to whether they might collapse under the pressure. They shook immediately, and she caught her weight, standing upright once again before the dominoes fell. Those shelves had been there for hundreds of years – it would not do for her to knock them all down in a moment of despairing resignation.

Wandering back to the little desk on which she had been working, she eyed the text of Herod's confession once again. She had laid it out next to the final pages of the *Legend of Hourian*, and it seemed increasingly clear that the long deceased Herod had drawn many of his crazed ideas from that bedtime story.

Perceptia sighed, pushing the bridge of her glasses back towards her forehead. She needed to find some other references to the Circuitrine nebula. It was certainly true that the system had some significance in the context of Herod's confession, since it was the major point of variance with an established and identifiable text. However, it was far from clear that the nebula had any relevance above or beyond Herod himself – perhaps he had spent long parts of his career in that system, or perhaps he had just recently read some kind of report about it? In these cases, Circuitrine may be relevant to him, but it may not be of any interest to Perceptia – the coincidence with the suspicious actions of Inquisitor Lord Seishon may be just that: a coincidence.

She needed to find out some more information about Circuitrine. In particular, she needed to know whether any other heretical Ordo Xenos inquisitors had mentioned it during their interrogations over the last several centuries. Unfortunately, there were rather more confessions than Perceptia had expected, and she was beginning to think that it would be impossible for one person to search them all.

She turned again and peered down the long, dark aisle between the stacks. The shelves must have been fifteen high, and they probably ran for twenty or thirty metres. That was the section in which the confessions of Ordo Xenos personnel were filed. There were simply too many; she needed to narrow the field.

'Can can I help you, inquisitor?'

Perceptia controlled the urge to jump with surprise and exhaled deeply. She turned slowly, showing immaculate composure. It was the curator of the Hereticus librarium's lower levels, Seye Multinus. Although he did not do it deliberately, he had a nasty habit of taking people by surprise as they were working. The problem was that he did not have normal feet, and they simply did not make any noise as he shuffled through the aisles. Silence was a virtue in a librarium, of course, but it was also unnerving, given the nature of some of the research that was being done, especially in these lowest levels.

'Seye – a pleasure to see you again.' Perceptia smiled weakly, a faint revulsion passing involuntarily over her features.

'Perperceptia? Of of course,' replied Seye, nodding his bizarrely shaped head in recognition. His strangely sibilant voice seemed to echo and chorus by itself.

It was not clear whether Seye Multinus was a mutant or whether he was simply the victim of an accidental genetic defect. If viewed from a certain angle, his head looked quite normal, although perhaps his face might appear oddly proportioned. However, such an impression could only be achieved from a very specific angle. For everyone else, it was clear that Seye actually had two faces. One of them was on the front of his head, in the normal place. The other appeared to have been grafted onto the side of his head, with the ear of the first face prominent on the cheek of the second. In fact, the curator had two heads, but they had grown together as one in a slightly unusual shape. There was only one brain at work behind those dual visages, although it was a most unusual brain indeed.

In the distant past, his condition may have been called craniopagus parasiticus, but that was not something commonly seen in the Imperium any more – if it could ever have been said to be common. This was not due to medical advances, but rather due to fear – babies born with obvious physical defects were often killed at birth, in case the defect was a sign of daemonic taint. Harbouring and caring for such a child might be interpreted as heresy, and the child itself would likely be considered an abomination. Death was a release for everyone concerned.

For whatever reason, Seye had survived in a farming community on the backwater world of Foth VI. It was an Imperial planet, but the glorious eye of the Emperor rarely even glanced at it. The population was small. There was little military capacity, and its only trading relationship was with Foth III, the major planet in the system. And even Foth III was little more than a blemish on the unremarkable quadrant's starcharts.

Caesurian had found him while he was still a boy. She had been hunting the leader of the infamous witch-coven of Trogeth IV, one of the neighbouring systems, and had tracked her to a hideaway in the Foth system. The young inquisitor had found the boy locked in the attic of a small wooden hut, surrounded by books, scraps of food that had been thrown through a grill in the door, and piles of human excrement that had not been cleaned away. He was a prisoner in his own house.

Instinctively, Caesurian had reached for her weapon, thinking that the abomination should be purged immediately. However, something stayed her hand. Instead, she watched the boy read, apparently oblivious of the armoured inquisitor standing in his doorway. He was utterly absorbed in what he was reading. And he was reading two books, one held in each hand, with a separate set of eyes scanning rapidly over the lines of each.

Not only was he reading both books simultaneously, but he was reading them with incredible speed, flicking the pages with his thumbs to turn them every few seconds. Even as she watched, Caesurian saw him reach the end of one book and toss it aside, his hand reaching automatically for another from the pile while he continued to read the one still held in his other hand.

The young Caesurian had brought Seye back with her and installed him in the lowest reaches of the Hereticus librarium on Ramugan. Only a handful of inquisitors knew that he was there, and most of those did not approve. From time to time, they would petition the lords to have the creature purged, but Caesurian protected him. She argued that he was not tainted but merely afflicted. She also claimed that he was not dangerous, and that he was extremely useful to the ordo in the librarium. His evident abnormalities should be tolerated, although not celebrated. For as long as he remained down in the forbidden depths of the librarium, no one would ever know that he existed or that the Ramugan Ordo Hereticus appeared to be committing a heresy by sanctioning the life of such an abominable creature.

Staring at Seye's faces, Perceptia found her eyes wandering, trying to work out where they should settle – which eyes should she look into? Not for the first time, she felt a wave of repulsion wash over her soul as she gazed at the curator, and her mind filled with hostility towards the radical tendencies of her one-time mentor, Inquisitor Lord Caesurian. It was appalling to think that this unclean animal was given access to such privileged information. At the same time, however, Perceptia realised for the first time that Seye was the answer to her prayers.

'Perhaps you can help me, Seye?'

'That'ss whyy I'm heere.'

'Yes,' replied Perceptia with evident distaste. 'I need you to look through these files.' She indicated the aisle behind her as casually as she could. 'And set aside any documents that make mention of the Circuitrine system. Can you do that?'

'Of of course.' A sickly, satisfied smile cracked across two mouths at once.

'How long will it take?'

Seye held Perceptia's gaze for a moment, while two other eyes scanned the aisle. 'Aboutout eight hours.'

Despite the revulsion she felt just at the thought of Seye's existence, Perceptia was impressed and relieved. 'Very good. I'll be back then.'

'THE SHIFT IN the warp is moving, Vargas. It is growing more powerful hour by hour, as though something is feeding it from within.' Seishon was pacing. 'This is not something that Aurelius will be able to ignore.'

'He has taken no action,' replied Vargas, sitting in his customary place at the table, the carafe of wine within easy reach.

'He has taken no action *yet*, Vargas.' The inquisitor lord stopped pacing and turned to face his old friend, his face riddled with contempt. 'How can you be so complacent? Have you any idea what is unfolding here?'

'We are acting in good faith, Seishon. Lord Ulthran has appealed to our oath, and we are honouring it. It is that simple. We have no choice in this.'

'Of course we have a choice, you fool.' Seishon was shouting now. 'Choice is not something that can be taken away from us, and certainly not by a deceitful alien. If your dear Ulthran has convinced you otherwise, then you are a greater fool than ever I thought you were.'

There was a long pause as Seishon struggled to contain his rage. He could not believe that Vargas was really so naïve. In fact, he was certain that the old inquisitor lord was not this naïve, but his certainty only served to infuriate him even more. If he were not really so simple-minded, then why was he behaving in this way? Seishon had the unmistakable feeling that there was something his friend wasn't telling him.

'Look at that, Vargas,' he continued, at last. 'Look at it, and tell me that Aurelius will just let that pass. It is no longer a mere wisp. It is no longer the straggling reach of a vaporous tendril. Look at it, Vargas – look!'

Sure enough, the cloud of red mist that had been gradually seeping out of the Eye of Terror, like an osmosis of Chaos power, had grown significantly. Not only had its reach extended deeply into the Circuitrine system, but its density had grown too. Even with the amplifier arrays and the image enhancement protocols at little more than casual settings, the well trained eye would have been able to pick out the telltale distortions of light from the local stars. And there were no eyes better trained than those of Inquisitor Lord Aurelius of the Ordo Malleus.

With slow deliberation, as though he was bored by the whole enterprise, Vargas climbed to his feet and sauntered over to stand next to Seishon. He gazed up at the image on the viewscreen, inhaling deeply as though straining his body with his eye sight. Finally, he nodded, clicking his tongue as if to suggest that he had seen what Seishon had indicated.

The mock theatrics made Seishon fume.

'You are right, of course,' said Vargas, exhaling deeply and letting the tension sag out of his shoulders. The general impression was that the old man was deflating, as though acknowledging his defeat at last. It was a performance worthy of the Shaonil theatre troupe of Behtle V.

Seishon waited as his friend shuffled back over to the table and took a sip of wine. 'Well?' he prompted. 'Is that it?'

'What do you want me to say?' asked Vargas, letting himself fall wearily back into the chair. 'Do you want me to explain all the risks that we are taking? Do you want me to labour over every concern, just to help you to feel as though you are right? Being right is not everything, Seishon. Being right is not going to help us at all – it is not our righteousness that is under scrutiny, here. The problem is one of duty. You can rail at me about how *you know* that Aurelius will spot the emission and despatch a Malleus force to investigate it, but that doesn't exonerate you, Seishon. It doesn't make this *my fault*. For the sake of the Emperor, Seishon, stop being so damned self-righteous – that's always been your problem. Part of me thinks that you *want* us to be discovered, just so that you can say that you were right that we would be. By the Throne! Where does that kind of guilt come from?'

Seishon stared back at his old friend as though he'd been punched in the stomach, the air knocked out of him completely. He couldn't believe what he was hearing. 'What are you blithering about, Vargas? Don't you–'

'Oh, shut up, Seishon! I've had just about all I can take from you. How long have we known each other? Forty years? Fifty? Maybe more? Well, there's only so much that my stomach can handle, Seishon – I think I might throw up. You have *always* been like this, and you have *always* treated me like this. I am not a fool, Seishon, and you know it. Somewhere deep down inside, you know that I am your equal, and you hate me for it. You can't stand it. It's driving you mad, you know that? You are actually going mad, Seishon – you know that, right? Even when you've screwed up, you always need to blame someone else. But you don't want to escape from the consequences by doing that. No, for some incredible reason *you want to be punished* for your mistakes, but you want everyone else to think that you are an innocent victim. Sometimes I wonder whether you'd take the blame for anything, just so long as the punishment hurt and everyone thought that you'd been wrongly accused. Why do you want to be a martyr, Seishon? Is being alive in these dark times really such a sin?'

The shellshocked inquisitor lord staggered slightly, as though under a physical barrage. He reached for the back of a chair to support his weight.

'What should we do, Vargas?'

That was what it all came down to: four simple words. What should we do?

Vargas smiled. 'Sit down, Seishon. Have a drink.'

Seishon's eyes were wild; he was teetering on the brink of hysteria. His mind was racing through the various consequences that could befall an inquisitor lord found to be acting in collusion with xenos powers. There were legends about such things, and the archives held a few official transcripts of the treatment of people like the infamous Lord Herod.

Inquisitors of the Ramugan Ordo Xenos were all exposed to Herod's myriad sins during their time as explicators – he was held up as an example of all the things that could go wrong for inquisitors who found themselves a little too enamoured with an alien species. There were even rumours that his case was used by the Ordo Hereticus as an example of signs to look out for amongst the officials of the Ordo Xenos. Whether true or not, Herod's example was usually more than enough to emphasise the importance of a pure heart, if any such emphasis were necessary, and the importance of pure action, or at least the appearance of pure action.

The tall, usually composed and elegant inquisitor lord sat down carefully in the chair opposite Vargas, his movements deliberate as though he was keeping them in check with the power of his will.

Vargas poured his old friend a glass of wine and placed it softly in front of him. 'Drink.'

'How can you be so calm, Vargas?' asked Seishon, after a couple of sips from the glass. The deep red liquid seemed to relax him immediately. 'My agents tell me that the young Hereticus inquisitor is still poking around, and Lord Aurelius has summoned Captain Mordia of the Grey Knights for a briefing about the emissions from the Eye. Our plot is unravelling before our eyes, Vargas.'

'What would you have us do? We have no power over Aurelius. If he dispatches Mordia then we may be discovered, and we may have to answer to Caesurian about our contacts with the eldar. She will not be sympathetic, and we will be executed, or worse. But consider the other possibilities, Seishon. Suppose that we prevent Aurelius from dispatching the Grey Knights. Suppose then that the outflowing of Chaos from the Eye is a serious and present threat to this sector, or to the whole Imperium. We may save our own lives by blocking action from the Ordo Malleus, but we risk the doom of millions of souls. That, surely, would be the greater heresy? I, for one, would not trade the Imperium for my soul. Before all else, I am a servant of the Emperor, Seishon, as are we all. There is nothing that we should do. It is out of our hands. Everything now rests on the broad shoulders of the valiant Captain Octavius.' Vargas's voice was gentle and kind, as though he were explaining something to an over-excited child in the simplest way that he could manage.

'You are right, of course,' conceded Seishon. He had never imagined that such a role reversal would ever occur in his relationship with Vargas, but part of him smirked at the realisation that he had been right to think that Vargas had been attempting to deceive him with fake stupidity.

'The most important consideration now,' continued Vargas, his tone hardening slightly, 'is the integrity of the kill-team.'

This was unexpected. 'You doubt the team, Vargas?'

'Captain Octavius is the finest Marine I have ever encountered – he will see his duty done. He has assembled an able and talented squad, despite the short notice. I have faith in his judgement. However, he did not choose all the members.'

'You are referring to the librarian from the Angels Sanguine – Ashok?' Seishon's voice edged towards the defensive. 'Are you insinuating that you trust Octavius's judgement but not mine, old friend?'

For a few thoughtful seconds, Vargas did not reply; he simply toyed with his wine glass. 'You are a clever man, Seishon. Of that I have no doubt. Your cleverness is there for everyone to see. I trust your cleverness.'

'That is not an answer.'

'It is not the answer you wanted, but it is my answer. The point remains, however, that Octavius did not recruit your librarian–'

'Ashok was not at the fortress to be chosen. We brought him in from outside specially, as you know. Octavius may well have chosen him, had he been aware of the option. They have fought together before, with great success.'

'Indeed. It seems, however, that your Ashok has vanished.'

The maniacal glint returned to Seishon's eyes, and panic crept back into his voice. 'What?'

'In his last communication, Octavius told me that Librarian Ashok slipped away from the squad during an encounter with a dark eldar raiding party. No explanations. He just left. Furthermore, the Ulthwé have complained about a precision attack on two of their seers, deep within the infrastructure of the craftworld, near to an access point to the infinity circuit itself. It appears that the seers were abducted during the raid. Octavius wondered whether we might know anything about that.'

Seishon said nothing. He was gazing into the gently swirling liquid in his glass, as though lost in contemplation.

'Well, old friend?' prompted Vargas. 'Do we know anything about that?'

'Perhaps he was captured?' Seishon did not look up. He appeared to be talking to himself, spilling his

concerns onto the table like wine from the glass.
'This is bad news, Vargas.'

Something about his old friend's tone told Vargas
that they were thinking at cross purposes. The significance of Ashok's disappearance was clearly
different for Seishon. He was hiding something, and
it was something that appeared to have gone wrong.
Beneath that heavy veneer of superiority and self-
righteousness, Seishon had always been a schemer,
and Vargas hoped that his old friend had not taken
a step too far this time. The Deathwatch team was
their only possible salvation.

I TOLD YOU *not to damage the lightlings, Skazhrealh.*
Lelith's thoughts were silky smooth, and they
slipped through the frantic psychic defences of the
haemonculus like cream easing through a grinder.
Did I not make myself clear?

The touch of the wych queen's thoughts sent shivers jousting through Skazhrealh's nervous system,
but the sharp, scraping touch of her long fingernail
being drawn across his lower lip was more than he
could bear. Blood gushed from the wound that her
razor-like nail had opened just above his chin, pouring into his mouth, making his breath bubble.

I did not seek to offend you, my queen. His thoughts
seemed to stutter, as though ebbing through alter-
nating waves of agony and ecstasy. *My duties are
performed only in your service.*

A sharp pain stabbed into his head and he howled,
gargling the blood that had pooled in his throat and
spitting showers of red beads up into Lelith's face.
He had often wondered what the insertion of a skull

hook would feel like, and now he knew. He had pushed them into the foreheads of various species in the past, making careful note of the particular nuance of scream that they produced. Despite the fact that the progeny of Hesperax were physiologically not dissimilar to the eldar lightlings, Skazhrealh was intrigued to hear that his own howl was rather different from the ones emitted by the last batch of Ulthwé prisoners. A sick, grotesque smile cracked across his ruined lips as he realised that even now he was performing his duty as a haemonculus. Urien Rakarth himself, the master haemonculus of Commorragh, would have been proud of his selfless industry.

The sanctorium of the Hesperax Haemonculi was dug deep into the heart of Sussarkh's Peak, sunk into the sulphurous and insufferably hot, volcanic depths. The only light was provided by the persistent, hellish glow of the lava flows that coursed through the passageways, unchecked and barely controlled by the crude systems of cracks and runnels. In the sanctorium itself, the lava runnels criss-crossed the uneven, rocky floor, sprinkled with half-submerged equipment and instruments that were made of substances impervious to heat, or made deliberately to be kept at inhumanly violent temperatures.

The walls of the laboratory were lined with the haemonculi's playthings. Some of them were dead already, left forgotten and hanging for so long that they starved or asphyxiated in the noxious atmosphere. Some of them were as good as dead, with limbs missing or egregious wounds left open to the toxic air.

The others simply wished they were dead. There were humans, a couple of lightling eldar, a collection of darklings who had made the terrible mistake of crossing Lelith at some point in their now agonisingly prolonged lives, and even a couple of massive orks hung like rotting trophies. The only thing that the broken and ruined bodies had in common was that they all retained their eyes and ears. Their eye-lids were crudely pinned or stitched open to deprive the guests of sleep and of the release of dreams, but also to ensure that they had no choice but to watch what was being done on the operating table in front of them, knowing that their turn would come.

Skazhrealh had loved to perform his art before a captive audience. He had added notes to his records about the kinds of responses that could be expected from different spectator species when he performed different operations in front of them. The humans were the most interesting – they were so easily shocked, so easily moved to fits of panic, fear or nausea. They would cry out almost as though they were being operated on themselves. The lightlings were more resilient; their threshold was much higher, but once it was reached they would howl and cry with a passion unmatched by any other species. It was a real art to bring lightling prisoners to such a level of orgiastic and voyeuristic agony. As for the orks – they never responded to anything, unless it was done directly to them. It was as though they had no capacity for empathy whatsoever. An audience of orks was no fun at all.

Now it was Skazhrealh himself that was strapped to the operating table. The privileged guests who hung around the perimeter of the sanctorium were treated to a very unusual display. They saw their torturer and captor subjected to exactly the kind of punishments that he had been inflicting on others. The gasps of horror from the captive audience had a new quality, full of a new level of terror that reflected the fact that their captors had no qualms about inflicting these punishments even on their own kind. The satisfaction of vengeance was utterly swamped by a crashing wave of abject terror.

A group of three cackling haemonculi apprentices busied themselves excitedly, probing the limits of his endurance with barbed instruments and molten-hot blades. This was the first time that any of them had been let loose on a victim without the supervision of Skazhrealh, and they were torn between the desperate desire to get it right and the exhilaration of liberty. Somewhere in the dark recesses of their minds, they had known that this day would come – how else would a great haemonculus like Skazhrealh be deposed? It was inevitable that his thirst for experimentation and pain would lead him to cross the line – it was the fate of all of them. It was a glorious and agonising symmetry: the haemonculus invariably met his end at the sharp end of techniques that he had practiced or even developed himself for centuries.

Meanwhile, as Skazhrealh shrieked and screeched his torment, the haemonculus could not help but admire the skill of his underlings; he had trained them well.

In the midst of it all stood Lelith. She was taller than the bustling apprentices by a clear head, and her flawless, white skin was unmarked by the clamps and incisions of self-mutilation. Although she stood at the head of the operating table, with her long, black hair cascading down to her hips, level with Skazhrealh's face, she appeared strangely incongruous, as though she was not really there. Her every movement, no matter how slight, was elegance made manifest. When she flicked her hair, the captives that were pinned so agonisingly and gruesomely to the walls groaned with something other than pain. This was not a sight that any of them had expected to see before they died.

If she was completely honest, however, playing with Skazhrealh was just a way to kill some time while she waited for the arrival of her new guests. But Lelith was never completely honest, and the show was distracting enough to hold her attention for a little while.

You know how lively souls need to be in the arena, otherwise they bring so little sport and so little... satisfaction. Lelith's thoughts were like whispers in Skazhrealh's ears. She caressed the skin on the side of his neck, drawing a row of deep, parallel gashes in his flesh with her nails and making him writhe in an uncontrollable mixture of ecstasy and agony. *But you broke them, dear Skazhrealh. They were no longer even amusing for us, and they certainly brought no contentment to our beloved princess.*

The haemonculus was losing the ability to form coherent thoughts. His mind was rebelling against his pain wracked body. It strove for the complicated darknesses of insanity and unconsciousness, but Lelith's thoughts held his soul dangling by a thread, keeping him swinging over the abyss, teasing him with the promise of utter annihilation.

I… they… too weak… only duty… pain, glorious pain… had to push too hard… snapped… broken, but not dead… No no, not killed.

My poor Skazhrealh, death is hardly the point. Death is a release, not a punishment, as you will soon discover. You of all people should know this, most treasured Skazhrealh, but you will experience the meaning for yourself soon enough… Although perhaps not soon enough for your liking. The real issue is power, Skazhrealh. Power – do you understand what that means? It means that if you break my toys, then I will break you.

All at once, Lelith appeared to grow bored with her plaything. She stood back away from the operating table and stared down at the pathetic form of the treacherous haemonculus. How thoughtless of him to force her to find a new one so quickly, especially when there were fresh guests en route. For a moment she considered the three apprentices, watching them busy themselves with forceps, needles and imaginatively shaped branding irons. One of those would probably do, she thought. And if not, she still had two more to work through.

At last, Lelith turned, sending her luxurious hair whirling around her, making the dying audience gasp. The tips of a few hairs glanced over Skazhrealh's cheek, and his body lurched at the touch, straining against the restraints that held him on the table as though in an auto-reflexive response. His body yearned for another such touch, and his muscles knotted in panicked anxiety as he realised that it would never come again. At the same time, a

thought slipped into Skazhrealh's soul like an
impossibly fine blade, severing the thread that
served as its lifeline: *Give my regards to the Satin
Princess.*

ASHOK'S EYES FLICKED open, revealing a burning red
inferno raging in his irises. In the centre of the
storm, his pupils flared with darkness, as though
seeking to swallow up the fury that engulfed them.
The muscles of his massive shoulders bunched and
tensed, but his arms would not move. They were
secured into some kind of harness that stretched
him out as though crucified. His legs had been
bound together and strapped to a vertical pillar that
ran up behind his back. Presumably, it attached to
the crosspiece to which his arms were lashed with a
material that he could not recognise. His feet were
held about a metre above the ground.

His body was wracked with pain. It was of a kind
that he had not felt since the ascension rituals, when
his body had been violated utterly in order to transform it into the superhuman form that it now had.
Thrashing his head from side to side, rage bubbling
in his mind and blurring his vision, Ashok could see
tiny little needles protruding from the joints in his
armour.

Whoever had inserted them had known what they
were doing. They had found all of the pain-nodes
that were accessible on a human body without
removing the Marine's armour. Presumably they had
also found the nerve chain that Marines were condi-
tioned to be able to shut down in cases of extreme
pain to permit them to continue functioning. This

was specialised knowledge of the kind prized by the apothecaries of the Adeptus Astartes, and Ashok's mind flew into a spin trying to think who else might have acquired it, and how.

Roaring with frustration, like a chained beast, Ashok threw his weight forward and thrashed his arms against their restraints. His efforts were met with lances of agony flashing up his shoulders and into his neck. But he did not move.

You should not struggle, human. You will die.

Whoever the thoughts came from, they were calm and certain. Ashok glowered through the shadowy space before him, his red eyes giving the darkness a bloody hue. As far as he could make out, he was being held at the end of a short, tubular corridor. Metallic joists ran around the walls and ceiling, as though the passageway had been bolted together in sections, and there appeared to be benches set against the concave walls.

It looked like the inside of a small ship – the hold of a small fighter or escort vessel. Closing his eyes for a moment, Ashok could hear the telltale hum of an engine. It didn't sound like any vessel he'd been in before, and it certainly did not growl with the solid power of Mechanicus engineering.

Opening his eyes again, the red glare had dimmed slightly and his mind was searching for calm havens in his thoughts. With an effort of concentration, he managed to dull the pain that coursed throughout his body, but he could not shut it out entirely. It was enough for him to regain control of his senses.

As his eyesight improved, he could see two slender figures sitting neatly side by side on one of the benches. Their heads were hooded under rich sapphire robes and angled sullenly down towards the floor. He could not see their faces but, since there was nobody else in view, Ashok assumed that one of them had to be the source of the thoughts. They did not appear to be in restraints or shackles.

Help me down. He spread his thoughts across the hold, not caring which of the figures responded.

There was no reply. Neither of the robed figures moved or showed any sign of recognition.

Help me down, repeated Ashok, more firmly this time, gritting his teeth against the pain that rose with his frustration. *Help me dow…* His mind was starting to cloud with anger once again, and he could feel his discipline slipping. Whatever his captors had done to him, they had somehow managed to destabilise decades of training and self-restraint. Despite his shackles, Ashok had not felt so unrestrained since the episode on Hegelian IX, when he had killed a brood of tyranids and a squad of his own Marines. He felt dangerous.

'Help me down,' he growled.

One of the robed figures stood up and took a couple of steps towards him. When it got to within arm's reach of Ashok, it reached up and pulled back its sapphire hood, revealing a beautiful, pale face with sparkling hazel eyes.

'Can not you help,' it said, gazing calmly up into the furious flames of Ashok's unfocused stare. 'You us help.'

It didn't make any sense. Ashok peered through the mist of his own gaze, trying to identify the beautiful, alien face before him, but his thoughts were swimming. It was as though he had been drugged, but what kind of drugs could be administered that would have any impact on the physiology of a Space Marine?

He shook his head, trying to clear the confusion through physical movement, but he succeeded only in triggering another spike of pain at the base of his neck.

The darklings have taken us, human. Rest now. Fight later.

He shook his head again, daring the pain to do its worst. It had been so long since he had felt pain like this; it was a kind of resurrection and he could feel it pulsing through his body as though rejuvenating him.

He roared again, staring straight into the face of the female seer in front of him. The muscles on his shoulders bunched massively as he strained forward, but he could not move. Intense pain took him to the edge of consciousness, and his eyes widened in defiant determination.

The female seer was not one of the two he had killed on Ulthwé. They had both been males, he was sure. Their shocked and horrified faces flashed back through his memories, framed in the fiery energy discharge from his force staff, blending into the violence of his current emotions. But there was something else in his memory, something prodding at his semi-conscious state as though triggered by it.

The spirit-ways of Ulthwé had done something to his brain; he had lost consciousness for a while before his confrontation with the seers at the access point to the infinity circuit. He could remember that now. He could remember considering whether to use the portals to get back to the *Lance of Darkness* after his business was done. He had reasoned that there was no choice and had thrown himself back through the immaterial channels. Then he could remember a different chamber, alive with rushing dark eldar. They were dragging two eldar seers to a Raider transport, dragging them by their hair. One of them had turned and seen Ashok, its pale blue eyes burning like distant stars.

He roared again, defying the pain inflicted by the hellish ingenuity of his captors' restraints. Fury filled his thoughts, dominating his soul and making his eyes burn. As he railed against his immobility, images of the dark eldar raiders spiralled through his mind and he finally fell into unconsciousness once again.

CHAPTER EIGHT:
ALIEN HUNTING

THEY WILL BE *leaving soon, Dhrykna of the Shining Path. It is as we have foreseen.* The emerald eyes of Thae'akzi gazed down on the kneeling figure of the Aspect Warrior, an earnest and pained smile gracing her lips. *You must accompany them, child.*

The Shining Spear did not look up at the Emerald Seer, but kept her face angled down into the polished surface by her knee. The seer's words were not unexpected, but they were far from welcome. She had seen the mon-keigh soldiers fight, and they were impressive enough, even if they showed little understanding of the stakes in a fight with the darklings. One of the psykers had killed as many Ulthwé captives as darkling raiders.

They are clumsy and stupid, Thae'akzi of the Emerald Robes, and I cannot control them.

235

That is why you must go with them – your path is shining and clear. You will guide them with the light of your example. It has been a long time since Ulthwé had a Spear to shatter the darkness, and we should be thankful that you are here now.

Despite her reservations, Dhrykna's heart thrilled at the compliment from Thae'akzi. It was as though the Emerald Seer had known exactly what to say to stir her emotions and to inspire her into action. The words were also those that whispered constantly in Dhrykna's own heart, taking on the voice of Prothenulh, the first exarch of the Shining Spears on Ulthwé. The vague promise of ascension to the throne of the exarch veiled her mind like a mist.

If it is the will of the council, Seer Thae'akzi, then I will see it done.

'It is our will,' intoned the softer and even more feminine voice of Eldressyn. Her tone was edged with music, and her words seduced an upward glance from the warrior kneeling before her. *The mon-keigh are here at our bidding, and it is our bidding that they must do. Their sense of duty compels them, just as our sense of survival compels us.*

There were no words for the emotions that spiralled through Dhrykna's mind as the seer's thoughts left their images free-floating in her consciousness. The young Ulthroon seer had a talent for making her ideas convincing, and her love for the craftworld of Ulthwé was beyond question. It was widely known that she was one of the favoured seers of the great Eldrad Ulthran himself, which gave her words weight beyond her years. If she was certain of the role of the mon-keigh warriors, then that was enough to ease the turmoil in Dhrykna's soul. Nonetheless, something still pulled at the edges of her thoughts, unravelling the swirling emotions and stirring suspicion in her heart. There was another voice in her head; it was a whispering presence that seemed to flow into her being, as though diffusing through the skin all over her body and then filtering into her mind.

She had felt the touch of that voice since a time before her first period of training in the temple of the Shining Spears. Indeed, she had always thought that it was a voice of calling – summoning her into the glittering service of the Shining Path. Since returning to the temple and donning the armour of her Aspect, the voice had become even more persistent, and in her heart Dhrykna felt certain that it was the call of Prothenulh, urging her to fulfil her destiny as the exarch of the Shining Spears.

Not for the first time in her life, the subconscious draw of the whispers in her mind seemed to contradict the words of the Ulthwé seers. When she had first been denied the ritual of ascension in the Aspect temple, Dhrykna had been sure that the voice in her soul was railing against the injustice and inappropriateness of the decision. At the time, she had striven to sublimate her antagonism, pushing it out of her mind and explaining it away as merely selfish and frustrated resentment. Now, however, with her body once again encased in the sacred psycho-plastic armour of a Shining Spears' Aspect Warrior, the memory of that voice seemed to shift and alter. Perhaps it had not been only the selfish ranting of her frustrated subconscious. Perhaps she had been wrong to kowtow so meekly to the judgement of the Emerald Seer at that time. Perhaps it had been the call of Prothenulh himself that she had ignored.

These were not the kinds of thoughts that the Shining Spear should have been entertaining as she knelt in supplication and obedience at the feet of the Seer Council, receiving their directions. With the mon-keigh polluting the very heart of Ulthwé and with the darklings raiding the craftworld at will, this was not the time for doubts about their judgment. However, she could not silence the unquiet voice in her soul; it seemed to be calling her in a direction different from the thoughts of Eldressyn and Thae'akzi. It was a voice of clarity and suspicion, and it shone in the darkest depths of her soul like a tiny, constant and distant star. Despite the intense gazes and intoxicating words of the breathtaking seers before her, Dhrykna was beginning to believe in her inner voice.

We will not send you alone, our Shining Spear. The thoughts were edged with a new sense of assertion, as though Thae'akzi had sensed the conflict in Dhrykna's mind. *Shariele of the Lost Souls will assist you to perform your duty with the mon-keigh warriors. His own visions about this matter have been clear and unambiguous. He will help you to see the true path.*

There was a quality about those last few words that made Dhrykna look up from her ceremonial position, glancing up at the stern yet exquisite features of the senior seer and noticing the fire in her emerald eyes. If she had needed any reminding, the power in that gaze prompted Dhrykna's realisation that the path of the seer was an intricate, terrible and mysterious one.

There was a world hidden behind those eyes, and it was a place that the Shining Spear would never be able to see or understand. For a fleeting moment, Dhrykna looked up at the Emerald Seer as though gazing upon an alien.

Only seconds before, the beautiful seer had bidden her to follow the light of the Shining Path in her dealings with the mon-keigh; but now she implied that such a path might be ambiguous or unclear, and that the guidance of a warlock would be required. For the first time in her long experience of the Emerald Seer, Dhrykna wondered what she was not being told. It seemed to her that Thae'akzi was attempting to *convince* her of the importance of her role with the mon-keigh. This was not something that the Seer Council had any need to do – they could merely direct her. Although it was not the place of an Aspect Warrior to question the judgement of the seers, it was also not the case that they should mindlessly abandon their own hard won paths in order to tread those laid at their feet by a persuasive mind.

The clarity of my path will not be determined by the guidance of any warlock, resolved Dhrykna, holding the thoughts at the back of her mind where they could not be seen. My path is radiant and clear, lit by the light of Prothenulh himself.

'Shariele is a strong warrior, and he has seen the movements of the darkling wyches in the waves of the future. In communion with the Undercouncil, he has seen the killing fields. You will both be needed if the mon-keigh are to prevail in this, Dhrykna,' said Eldressyn smoothly, her voice tinged with emotion. In comparison with the calm composure of

Thae'akzi, the younger seer seemed sincere and passionate about the mission. Paradoxically, Dhrykna always found audible voices more intimate and trustworthy than psychic communications, despite the heavy preference for the latter on Ulthwé. As though to emphasise her physicality, the young seer took a couple of steps forward and drew Dhrykna to her feet with a delicate touch of her fingers under the Aspect Warrior's chin. The two female eldar gazed unblinkingly into each other's eyes.

'The council was divided on this, Dhrykna. I can understand your concerns, but you must believe that we have exorcised them already. There were some who did not want to involve the mon-keigh in our business, even at this time of great need. There were some who would rather have perished than entrusted anything to the clumsy and ignorant humans. But, plans were laid long ago, plans beyond even the collective wisdom of the Seer Council today. Lord Ulthran himself stands as the composer, and we merely dance to the subtle music of his symphony. Your part in this is clear to us, and we would be telling an untruth if we told you that this whole affair does not rest on your shoulders. The Shining Spear will flash through the darkness once again, and your soul will dance in the glory of its light. The mon-keigh are a blunt instrument, but the spear is rapid and precise. Without you, they will fumble in the darkness. And without them, Ulthwé is lost.'

'There is no need for you to convince me, Eldressyn of Ulthroon. I cannot hide my heart from you, and I will make no attempt to do so. I have no desire to accompany the primitives, but, on your command, it will be done. Might I ask just one question of you?'

'You might.' Eldressyn did not smile, but her face was clear of hostility.

'Why just me and Shariele of the Lost Souls? Why not a squad of Black Guardians or a detachment from the Dark Reapers?'

Because this honour falls into the path of your future, Shining Spear. The thoughts of Thae'akzi slid quickly into Dhrykna's mind, before Eldressyn had the chance to answer her. *There is no other around whom the currents of time swirl with such pristine clarity, and thus no other to whom we may entrust this task.*

Dhrykna bowed her head once again. 'As you wish, Emerald Seer.' Do not think that I believe you have answered my question, she thought, only half hiding her thoughts from the seer. In that moment, the Shining Spear realised that even though she knew that she could not trust the monkeigh, she should also be careful about the words of the seers; their ways were far more treacherous than those of the warriors.

As THE LANCE *of Darkness* fired its engines and blasted out of Calmainoc's dock, Octavius thought that he could feel its machine-spirit heave a massive sigh of relief, as though it were emerging from under a huge weight of resistance. The atmosphere on the control deck lightened and the tension that had been growing between the Marines in the rest of the vessel seemed to ease slightly.

While the rest of the team administered to their armour and weapons in the armoury, Octavius and Atreus watched the main viewscreens on the control deck reorient to a rear-facing scene. The incredible structure of Ulthwé was accelerating away from them, bathed in the distortion of discharge from the *Lance of Darkness*'s engines, which were firing at nearly maximum capacity. Both the ship and the pilot-serfs wanted to get away from the craftworld as quickly as they could, it seemed. Despite the rapid acceleration, Ulthwé dominated the screen for a long time, obliterating the light of the stars and looming like a massive, intricate monolith.

There had been no time to wait for Ashok; in any case, Octavius was not sympathetic to the missing Angel Sanguine. It was not clear why the librarian had left the kill-team on Ulthwé, and Octavius did not appreciate having his command compromised by the actions of a maverick Marine, not even by the magnificent librarian. Besides, Lord Vargas had instructed him to proceed without Ashok.

The inquisitor lord's tone had been uncharacteristically stern, and Octavius had needed no further encouragement to vacate the alien craftworld. He had never left a Marine behind before, and he was not entirely comfortable with doing it now, but his duty to the Ordo Xenos, to the Inquisition, to the Imperium and even to the Ulthwé eldar forced his hand. Duty before all else. Besides, part of him suspected that, if he wasn't dead already, the unpredictable librarian had had something to do with the disappearance of the two seers from the upper levels of Ulthwé during the raid. No matter how magnificent the Angel Sanguine's combat prowess might be, Octavius could not shake the feeling of distrust that always flooded his brain when he came into contact with him. Whatever the case, the captain was not well-disposed to wasting more time on that cursed craftworld waiting for the librarian, who was either dead, a loose cannon, or even a traitor.

As they watched the diminishing image, waves of shivers passed through the bodies of the Space Marines, as though the *Lance of Darkness* itself were passing through successive boundaries of icy energy. At first, Octavius thought that his mind was simply releasing the tension that it had stored whilst aboard the monstrous alien vessel, but then he remembered the similar feelings that had wracked the frigate as it had approached the craftworld.

Atreus nodded, as though reading the captain's mind. *Some kind of psychic sensor array, captain. We are clearing its reach now.*

'If there is such an array,' began Octavius, his suspicious mind juggling the information without turning away from the screen, 'how can the dark eldar raiders approach the craftworld undetected?'

Their psychic technology is far superior to yours, human. The icy, unfamiliar thoughts made Octavius turn. They hurt his head and pushed his mind in unnatural directions. *Their presence is much more subtle; they are little more than shadows in the darkness.*

The tall, sinister shape of the eldar warlock was standing in the doorway to the control room. It had taken off its elaborate helmet shortly after take-off, revealing a perfectly smooth, porcelain white face with dark, elliptical eyes. Its head was an elegant oval, and its hair fell in long, black cascades down to its slender shoulders. Rather than appearing menacing and powerful, there was a distinctly feminine quality to the inescapable danger that emanated from the eldar war-witch.

'Then how do you detect them?' Octavius made no attempt to approach the alien, and he kept his voice low, forcing the warlock to approach in order to hear him.

There are ways that you would not understand.

Try us, interjected Atreus, honing his thoughts into deceptive daggers and pushing them slowly into the warlock's head, hoping that they would cause at least a little pain.

Shariele flicked his black eyes over to Atreus, narrowing them with a strange hatred that confused the Blood Raven. There were accusations written into that alien gaze, although Atreus could not see their form or content. The librarian was well aware of the unusual connection between the fabled Gabriel Angelos, captain of the Blood Ravens Third Company, and the eldar of the Biel-Tan craftworld, but he had never thought that he would see echoes of that relationship in the eyes of an Ulthwé warlock.

Your minds are not adequate, replied Shariele, punctuating his thoughts with moments of psychic pressure that sent ripples through Atreus's head. The warlock was making his point emphatically; it was not a challenge, but it was certainly a response to the librarian's test. The two psykers were sizing each other up.

Octavius watched the silent concentration sear through the air between Atreus and the warlock, and he realised immediately that something was going on.

'Enough,' he said. 'Atreus, we have no time for this. And you, Shaariell,' continued Octavius, not caring that he was probably butchering the eldar's name. 'You are here to assist us, not to hinder. It is no secret that we would rather be without you, and I suspect that the feeling is mutual. However, until our duty is done, we will work together to ensure the success of this sortie. Make no mistake, alien,' added the Deathwatch captain, bringing his face closer to the delicate features of the warlock, 'once this thing is over, you can test our strength all you like. But I warn you now, you will not find the Emperor's Death-watch lacking in resolve or power.'

The Ulthwé psyker held Octavius's gaze for a moment, as though trying to assess the captain's sincerity. Then it nodded slowly, aping a brief bow of deference. 'We hinder you are not here to,' it said, jumbling the alien tongue self-consciously. 'Help need you. Help you must we. Understood.'

'We do not need your help, alien,' replied Octavius without diplomacy. The eldar's lack of fluency in the tongues of the Imperium made communication difficult and unreliable, but he was certain that the implied insult had not been accidental. 'We merely require that you do not interfere with our duty.'

As he spoke, the shimmering and beautiful figure of the female warrior stepped through the doorway into the control room. She nodded respectfully, meeting the eyes of Atreus for a moment before striding past the small group to watch the receding picture of Ulthwé on the viewscreens.

Despite his disciplined composure, Octavius shivered again. He did not care that the aliens paid him so little respect; he could even understand how they might focus their attentions on the librarian. The eldar were a psychic race, and he could imagine that they viewed ungifted humans as stunted or primitive life forms. Quite what they made of librarians like Atreus and Ashok, he had no idea. Come to that, he was not even sure what he thought about Ashok.

However, it was one thing for the aliens to disrespect him personally, and it was quite another for them to behave without appropriate decorum on the control deck of an ancient Deathwatch frigate. He could only imagine the enormity of the insult being done to the machine-spirit of the venerable vessel with two aliens occupying places of honour on the control deck itself. He hoped that Sulphus would be able to tend to the vessel before it was called upon for combat.

A warning klaxon interrupted his indignance, and a blue range warning light started to pulse over the main viewscreen.

'It appears that even our primitive technology is of use, after all,' said Octavius, turning away from the warlock and striding across to one of the display terminals for the long-range sensors. Clearly visible at the top of the screen were three small marks, which the cogitator recognised immediately as emanating dark eldar signatures. 'It seems that we will have company rather sooner than we expected.'

* * *

THE CORSAIRS ROLLED and flashed around the *Lance of Darkness*, flickering in and out of visibility as though falling in and out of phase with the material realm itself. Their shadowfields clicked on and off intermittently, as though the flurries of sparking fire that spat out of the gun arrays interfered with the mimic engines.

The three ranged signatures had divided and multiplied into six as they had closed on the Deathwatch frigate, splintering into three attacking pairs that spiralled around each other and darted around the vessel, peppering its heavy armour with volleys of darkly glimmering fire.

The gun bays around the perimeter of the frigate resounded with fire, coughing out explosive warheads and slicing through the detritus with lances of lasfire. The gun-servitors were working overtime, tracking the rapid and constantly shifting trajectories of the dark eldar corsairs and rattling out fire into their wakes.

Even the control deck rocked under the fury of the frigate's defensive actions, as each and every gun turret seemed to fire simultaneously but in a different direction. The kinetic release from the massive recoils of the heavy cannons sent shock waves pulsing through the infrastructure of the frigate.

In comparison to the maelstrom that raged outside, the control room was a haven of calm. Octavius and Atreus stood in the centre of the roughly circular chamber, observing the behaviour of the dedicated serfs who operated the controls and made constant reports on damage inflicted as well as suffered. Streams of data flooded into the cogitators from around the ship, and the serfs sifted it immediately, presenting Octavius with the salient information so that he could instruct them appropriately.

The serfs aboard the _Lance of Darkness_ were amongst the most talented of their kind in the Imperium. Just like the Deathwatch Marines themselves, these serfs were drawn from the ranks of the pledge workers of a number of different Space Marine Chapters, often arriving in tow behind a Marine captain or sergeant that had insisted on bringing one or two of his own most trusted support staff.

The Ordo Xenos in some sectors still insisted that the serfs should be drawn directly from their own internal bureaucracies or should be seconded from the Imperial Navy, believing that service under the Deathwatch required special capacities that only the Inquisition itself could instil. However, many facilities, including the Watchtower Fortress of Ramugan itself, acknowledged that the serfs best suited for service under a kill-team were those who were already well-drilled in the strategies of the _Codex Astartes_ and who had served under Space Marines before.

Just as the great Watchtower would enlist and train the very best Marines from throughout the Adeptus Astartes, so a separate and almost forgotten administration scoured the Chapters for talented serfs, recruiting them, training them, and then utilizing them for limited periods of secondment, before returning them to their original service vessels to fulfil their pledges to the relevant Chapters. It would be simply disastrous to entrust the transport of the

Imperium's finest Space Marines to a second-rate crew of serfs and servitors, and the relationship was also beneficial for the separate Chapters that contributed their personnel, since the serfs would return much more experienced and capable than when they left.

'Bring us around. Point her nose back towards Ulthwé,' growled Octavius. 'Let's see whether these aliens are willing to risk the deployment of eldar support.'

The captain was gazing up at the main viewer, watching a line of explosions strafe in the wake of a pair of speeding corsairs – the gun-servitors were clearly unable to keep pace with the movement of the dark eldar at this close range. He did not direct his commands to anyone in particular, but asserted them to the control deck as a whole, confident that the crew would see it done.

'What kind of damage are those things doing?' he asked, conscious that the movement he could feel in the hull was largely caused by the *Lance of Darkness*'s own weapons.

'Minimal, captain,' came the reply. 'Their fire is not penetrating our armour.'

Octavius nodded without looking for the source of the voice. All the serfs were the same to him. As long as he got the information he needed, he did not care who gave it to him. He was satisfied that his vessel was holding up under the assault, but something in the back of his mind urged him to be cautious; dark eldar corsairs were not known for lacking firepower.

'What are they firing?' he asked.

There was no reply.

'I asked a question.' He turned his gleaming eyes around to survey the crew behind him, annoyed that he had been forced to recognise its personality. The serfs were all positioned at their terminals, heads bowed over glowing screens, deep in concentration. 'What are they firing?' he repeated.

Nobody looked up. 'We can't tell, captain. Whatever it is, it is impacting against the outer armour and detonating there. There is almost no penetration into the plates. It's as though the warheads are utterly without material substance.'

The white armoured eldar strode over to one of the terminals and looked down over the serf's shoulder, inspecting the data and making the man squirm uncomfortably. The faint green glow from the screen cast her pale skin in an eerie light. She nodded, but said nothing.

Before Octavius could say anything, his attention was drawn back to the main viewer by the sound of an explosion. He turned in time to see one of the corsairs splutter and then detonate, a line of debris and puffs of off-target shells running up behind it. Fragments spun and tumbled away from the epicentre of the explosion, ravaging the hull of the *Lance of Darkness* like shrapnel. At the same time, a chunk of debris smashed into the corsair that had been on the wing of the first, crunching through its thin armour and punching out of the other side of it, leaving a gaping hole through its fuselage.

As though responding to a signal, the other corsairs suddenly peeled away from the *Lance of Darkness* and flashed off towards the red, misty, glowing fringes of the Circuitrine system, close to the asteroid field that laced the lashes of the Eye of Terror itself.

'Don't let them get away,' said Octavius, keeping his eyes locked on the rapidly diminishing shapes of the four escorts. 'Keep up the gunnery, but leave at least one functioning – we need to find out where it is heading.'

'Be careful, captain.' The voice was harsh and shrill, echoing as though spoken by more than one person in chorus. Before it had finished, Octavius could already feel the slight gravitational shift caused by the rapid acceleration of the *Lance of Darkness* as it powered after the fleeing corsairs.

'What?' he said, turning back to face the glittering form of the female eldar. 'Are you telling me how to conduct my ship, eldar?' His annoyance, already raised by the casual manner in which the eldar had perused the readouts on the control deck, was palpable.

THE FLEEING CORSAIRS ducked and bobbed, weaving their way between and around the asteroids. Behind them, the *Lance of Darkness* roared with determination, its forward batteries spraying fire almost indiscriminately, exploding asteroids into scattering fragments and making life difficult for the remaining dark eldar pilots. Four corsairs had been reduced to three, but these were as elusive and slippery as fish in an ocean.

'There!' yelled Octavius, pointing to one side of a massive moon-like rock that was tumbling through the field. 'Take us around the other way.'

Even before he had finished the order, the *Lance of Darkness* banked sharply, firing a long series of retros

that ran down its port side to tighten its curve. The
frigate pulled itself back into line and roared past the
massive space boulder, cutting short the flight path
of the escaping corsairs and reeling them in. Immediately, and without waiting for an order, the
forward guns coughed a volley of rockets into the
heat trail of the alien vessels. Two of them struck
home, charging up behind the flickering corsairs and
punching into their exhaust rigs, detonating their
engine cores in fantastical explosions of light. The
debris of the two ruined vessels lashed out at the single remaining corsair as it spun and dived to avoid
the sudden onslaught. It ducked beneath the fury
and rolled round behind one of the larger asteroids,
vanishing from view.

'Cease firing,' called Octavius, satisfied that he had
caused enough damage to the aliens and conscious
that he did not want to lose the last ship. The remaining corsair might be their only guide to the location of
the kidnapped eldar seers. Assuming that there was
only one band of dark eldar pirates operating in this
section, it seemed more than likely that this corsair
would be heading back towards the same base to
which the craftworld raiders would have taken their
prisoners.

'Bring us up behind that asteroid and cut propulsion.
We are going to wait for that corsair to break cover.
When it does so, let it clear visible range but track it on
the long-range scanners. We need to know where it
goes, but we do not need it to watch us following it.'

'Understood,' came the anonymous reply.

'It seems that our primitive technology may be
good enough, aliens,' said Octavius, without turning

to face the warlock or Aspect Warrior who stood uneasily on the deck behind him. They had refused to take seats during the pursuit, and it seemed probable that they were not used to the rough gravitational shifts that such manoeuvres could generate in an Astartes frigate. Eldar vessels were equipped with gravitational stabilisers that nullified all the effects of such movements and were the envy of the Imperial Navy.

As he spoke, the signature of the last corsair reappeared on the monitor, accelerating rapidly away from the blind side of the huge asteroid.

'It's moving, captain.'

'Good. Wait.'

The dark eldar escort ship flashed out towards the edge of the asteroid field, accelerating continuously, putting a great distance between itself and the lurking *Lance of Darkness*. But then it stopped dead. There was no period of deceleration; it just stopped. After a tiny delay, it had reoriented itself and was rocketing back towards the asteroid, following exactly the same flight path as it had used in its escape route, accelerating all of the time.

'Captain. It's coming back.'

'On screen,' said Octavius with interest. Perhaps the flighty and treacherous dark eldar had some honour after all: were they returning to finish the fight head to head?

The main viewscreen flickered and a line of static oscillated across it, leaving the ghostly green image of the sensor terminal enlarged for all to see. The corsair signature was racing down from the top of the screen at an unbelievable speed. It was heading directly for the asteroid at the bottom, behind which lurked the *Lance of Darkness*. To everyone present, it looked clearly like a collision course.

'Arm the forward torpedoes,' murmured Octavius, his complex blue eyes transfixed by the apparently suicidal image. 'And bring us around to face the horizon of this rock. If our visitor is going to over-shoot, then we will be ready for him.'

There was no reply, but the captain knew that his orders were being fulfilled.

'Stop can not the darkling.' The white-clad Aspect Warrior stepped up next to Octavius, joining his concentration on the darting image. 'Too fast.'

For a moment Octavius said nothing. He was not sure whether the alien was telling him that the *Lance of Darkness* was too slow or that the corsair was trav-elling too fast to be able to stop before it hit the asteroid.

'We will see,' was his non-committal reply, which he muttered with an edge of defiance.

As they watched, the corsair's signature seemed to pick up even more speed before it blinked directly into the image of the asteroid and vanished. The sensors showed a spray of debris scattering out into space, and the warp sensors flashed to acknowledge a momentary rupture in real space, presumably caused by the destruction of the corsair's engine core.

'Bring us back three thousand metres,' said Octavius, his thoughts still suspicious. He had never heard of dark eldar raiders committing suicide rather than engaging in battle. Something was not right. 'If that vessel struck the blind side of this asteroid at that speed, then we should be able to detect a shift in the rock's movement.'

'Not crash,' said Dhrykna, still staring at the viewscreen. Her eyes were scrunched in disdain, as though she couldn't believe what she was seeing. Her expression made Octavius think of the way that he felt when he looked at the crude, clunking technology of orks.

'You said it could not stop.' Octavius turned to face the Aspect Warrior and drew himself up to his full height in front of her. He looked down into her alien eyes for the first time and steadied himself before their spiralling depths. 'If it didn't stop, and it didn't crash, where in the Emperor's name is it?'

'Not emperor's ship,' replied Dhrykna, her face cracking into an uneasy, alien smile. 'Gone home.'

'The asteroid's trajectory shows no signs of having sustained an impact, captain. The corsair did not hit it.' The anonymous voice carried a tone of certainty.

'Fine. I'm through with this cat and mouse game,' said Octavius. 'Let's see what's on the other side of this rock. And you,' he said, addressing Dhrykna directly, 'tell us what you know about this.'

'Your no enough good technology?' she said, raising an eyebrow in an unnerving imitation of sarcasm.

'Look, whether you like this or not, we're in this together, alien. Our primitive technology was enough to pursue and destroy five of these corsairs, which, apparently, is more than your precious Ulthwé Shadowhunters have managed to do. It has also been more than enough to deal with your own warbirds in the past. So stop with this pompous self-righteousness before I have to kill you too. If you're not going to assist, then you may as well be dead. This is not a passenger ship. The least you can do is help us to understand what the dark eldar are doing. I presume that you know?'

Octavius's tone was harsh and full of accusation. His patience with the arrogance of the eldar was growing thin. It wasn't as though they were doing him any favours – the Deathwatch were here to help them, for the sake of the Throne.

'Let they you them follow,' hissed the warlock from behind. 'Let they you them kill. Too easy. Not right is something.'

Octavius turned slowly as he fought to control his anger. He couldn't believe the audacity of these creatures.

There was silence, then one word. 'Dhrykna.'

'What? I don't have time for these riddles,' snapped Octavius, returning his gaze to the white armoured Aspect Warrior at his shoulder.

'My name,' she said softly, bowing her head. She was honouring him as a fellow warrior, acknowledging his performance even if Shariele refused to do so.

On the edge of anger, Octavius paused. He had expected the presence of the eldar on the *Lance of Darkness* to fray the nerves of some of the others. But he had not seriously considered the effect that they might have on him. Pelias, in particular, had simply retreated into the vessel's chapel with Chaplain Luthar, where he had remained for the duration of the pursuit. Sulphus had taken himself off to the armoury to administer to his various augmetics; he had hardly even seemed to notice the eldar, as though dismissing them as merely two extra bodies of flesh on the ship. The Mantis Warrior, Kruidan, had greeted them when they first came aboard, giving them the honour of a warrior. He had appeared without his armour and with his long, black hair hanging freely over his impressive shoulders, ritual tattoos snaking intricately over his chest, neck and face. Only Atreus had shown a calm self-possession, accompanying the eldar onto the control deck with the captain and then standing with quiet attention and surveying the scene. Octavius granted himself no space for personal reactions – it was all about duty – so his anger disturbed him.

Exhaling heavily, Octavius nodded in return, recovering the professionalism and composure for which the Imperial Fists were renowned. 'Greetings Draknar. I am Captain Octavius of the Emperor's Deathwatch. Let us see this through together so that we can both be rid of it.'

'Coming about,' said one of the serfs. 'Switching the viewer.'

Octavius and Dhrykna held each other's eyes for a moment longer, as though sharing a new, unspoken understanding and resolve. Then the captain nodded and turned to face the screen.

The dark side of the asteroid rolled into view as the *Lance of Darkness* skirted around an easy orbit. The surface was veiled in deep, uneven shadows, and it took a few moments for the optical enhancers to adjust.

'Atreus. Any ideas?' asked Octavius, his eyes widening at the view that confronted them. The Blood Ravens librarian was a fount of knowledge.

The centre of the asteroid appeared to have been blown out. It was so concave that it seemed to be bigger inside than out, as though the giant bowl had been scooped through the structure of the rock and then out of the other side. Around the rim were a series of small, metallic structures, which pulsed with tiny constellations of lights as though alive with power. Stretched out between them were threads of energy, like a giant web of darkly burning beams, forming a net that covered the mouth of the immense cave. The spaces between the threads shimmered and shone like a mystical patchwork, as though filled with individual, geometric pools of warp energy.

'It's some kind of webway portal, captain,' replied Atreus, inspecting the image carefully. 'The corsair must have dived through it when it hit the asteroid.'

'Gone home,' muttered Dhrykna, nodding slowly as though in agreement.

Octavius nodded smartly. 'Take us out two thousand metres and then bring us about. We may need a run-up for this. Let's find out what kind of cursed place these aliens call home.'

A VEIL OF darkness hung over the elevated podium in the centre of the Seer Chamber. It shimmered like a black, velvet curtain, silent and seductive. A rich, sickly scent seemed to ooze out of the folds, diffusing through the chamber like a narcotic, as though a dense collection of psycho-reactive drugs were simmering on the other side. The wisps of smoke and fragrance carried whispers and ideas, curdling around themselves into nauseous contradictions.

High up on the domed ceiling, angular patterns of violence started to course through the structure of the chamber.

Standing next to the podium, watching the veiled darkness billow and flow, Thae'akzi and Eldressyn were transfixed. They were alone in the grand chamber, the rest of the council having left after they had briefed Dhrykna and Shariele. The moody Karizhariat Seer, Ruhklo, had swept out of the sacred hall in disgust, with his cloak billowing dramatically in his wake, and with the other seers striding along behind him.

He did not approve of the presence of the mon-keigh on Ulthwé, and he certainly did not believe that they could be trusted with the fate of even a single eldar soul. Sending two of the craftworld's finest warriors to accompany the primitive fools just seemed like arrogance and wastefulness – not even Shariele and Dhrykna could salvage the immature stupidity of the humans. They would die alongside the mon-keigh and their souls would be lost to the infinity circuit. Sending them away from Ulthwé was almost like dispatching a gift for Slaanesh himself. Ruhklo of the Karizhariat could not understand why the council would let this happen. He could not understand how Thae'akzi had convinced Ulthran himself of the plan and he was furious that the words of the sapling seer, Eldressyn, seemed to carry a weight equal to his own on the council. He had served Ulthwé since before that wych had even been born.

Eldressyn had never seen anything quite like this before. The darkly fluttering curtains of sha'iel rippled with an alien energy, and her heart raced. The seduction of the forbidden thrilled through her body, making her nerves tingle and her eyes widen. The almost impossibly light fabric of her white robes seemed to blend with the smoke until it was difficult to distinguish where her clothing ended and the sickly emissions began.

In contrast, the Emerald Seer was calm. Her implacable green eyes stared levelly at the podium as she waited for the visitor to take a more appropriate form. She had seen it all before. Indeed, she could clearly remember the first time that she had stood before the sacred altar alongside Ulthran himself. He had initiated her into the necessity of foresight and diplomacy for a craftworld free-floating so close to the cursed Eye. Now she would initiate Eldressyn in turn. The young seer was eager, ambitious and thirsty for forbidden knowledge – yet everyone thought that she was so naïve and idealistic. She was perfect, and Ulthran had picked her himself.

As she watched, Thae'akzi narrowed her fathomless eyes. The eddying, narcotic smoke stung her senses, but it was her memory that troubled her. Always in the back of her mind was the day that she had been summoned back to the Aspect Temple of the Shining Spears. She had once been a warrior of their ranks, bedecked in the pristine whites and silver-blues that made them shine like beacons in the darkness of Ulthwé. But that had been before she had taken her first steps on the path of the seer, before Eldrad Ulthran himself had taken her under his wing and begun to mould her soul into an image of his own.

There were many rumours about what had happened on that fateful day, when Thae'akzi had returned to the temple, responding to a call felt deep in her soul. Ulthwé had been under attack by a force of mon-keigh warriors that had spilt out of the Eye of Terror, disfigured and terrible to behold. The young Thae'akzi had been riddled with doubts and despair at her own impotence. Her hard won powers as a seer appeared to offer the forces of Ulthwé little in their fight against the defiled intruders. She could see the events cascading back from the future, but she had no power to alter those events herself. With despair in her heart, she had found herself back in the great crystal courtyard of the Temple of Light; her soul was weeping.

Wandering the almost deserted, labyrinthine corridors of the temple, she had eventually found her way to the sanctum, wherein lay the untouched, ceremonial masks of the Shining Warlocks. As soon as she laid her eyes on the masks, she realised what she needed to do. Only by combining the paths of the seer and the Aspect Warrior would she be able to attain the kind of power that her soul craved. Only by becoming a warlock of the Shining Spears would she be able to assist in the battle for Ulthwé.

Yet the masks refused her touch. She tried in vain to conquer their spirits. Sitting in meditation, she battled them for three days without cessation or rest. When she finally emerged from the sanctum, although the mon-keigh assault had been defeated outside, so too had Thae'akzi, and her eyes had changed colour into a glaring, emerald green, the traditional colour of defiance and despair. In her mind, she felt as though she had battled the spirit of Khaine himself.

As her eminence on the Seer Council had grown, rumours had started to circulate about her time in the sanctum of the Temple of Light. She had done nothing to stop them. Without exception, they were all more flattering than the actual events of those three days. After a while, a consensus had developed around Thae'akzi's silence: she was too humble to sing of her own virtues, but she was in fact the only seer in living memory to have received the call of Khaine and to have refused it successfully. She had been summoned to the Temple of Light and, after three days of struggle, she had emerged triumphant as the Emerald Seer – defiance incarnate.

Her failure in the sanctum had become her greatest victory, but it had also turned her will against the rapidly diminishing, shimmering Aspect. She had used her influence and her power to ensure that the once glorious Temple of Light recruited fewer and fewer Aspect Warriors, pushing the minds of the potential aspirants towards darker places, pushing them inevitably towards the Dark Reapers. In her arrogance, she hardly noticed the effect that this was having on Ulthwé itself.

Ah, Thae'akzi. The thoughts were like a breath in her ear, whispered and intimate, easing her out of her reverie.

The veil of dark mist on the podium had faded into semi-transparency, becoming little more than a curtain of vapour. Behind it could be seen a shapely female form, writhing in what might have been either pleasure or pain. Its outline was not quite distinct, and its features were blurred behind the veil, but it emitted such an intoxicating air that it might have been the most seductive figure ever to have graced the Seer Chamber of Ulthwé.

Eldressyn inhaled sharply, as though gasping. A waft of vapour brushed against her skin, sending a shiver trickling down her neck like a bead of sweat.

And who is this beautiful creature? Have you brought me a gift, Thae'akzi?

I have already sent you a gift, Lelith. A great gift, exactly as we agreed. The Emerald Seer's composure was admirable.

Ah yes, the mon-keigh warriors. Their souls are strong. They will bring much… satisfaction, I am sure.

Despite their power, they are stupid animals. They may need some guidance.

Did you not provide any guides, Sister Thae'akzi? As she spoke, the wych queen seemed to reach a slender arm out from behind the veil to caress the transfixed Eldressyn.

I am not your sister, Lelith.

The Mistress of Strife had gone too far. With a flick of her hand, Thae'akzi vaporised the apparition of Lelith's arm, severing the wych's connection with the young Ulthroon Seer. *And Eldressyn is not part of our bargain. You will not touch her again.*

A feeling of rich disappointment flooded out of the image on the podium. It was mocking her.

Oh, you are so serious, Thae'akzi. Lelith seemed to be enjoying herself.

I have sent two guides, Lelith. Enough to reassure the mon-keigh that we are serious, but insufficient for them to be of any real help.

May I have them too? Lelith's thoughts were playful and flirtatious.

Let's call them a sign of our good will, Lelith. Take them and be gone.

Oh, fear not, my most colourless of sisters, I will take them. And then she was gone, leaving only a shapeless, amorphous cloud of sickly sweet mist to dissipate over the podium.

Eldressyn jolted suddenly, as though being dropped to the ground from a great height. *She is gone?* Her thoughts were tinged with sadness and resentment, like those of a child that had fallen asleep before it wanted to.

THE STARS FLICKERED and swam, pulsing as though on the edge of death. A dull red mist replaced the vacuum of space, as though seeping through the ruptured capillaries of the immaterium. It was as though reality itself were bleeding, besieged by incredible pressures from unearthly realms, like a diving bell stranded in the impossible depths of an ocean.

As the *Lance of Darkness* powered out of the webway portal and pushed through the chaotic, swirling fog, the warp intrusion alarms sounded continuously on the control deck, filling the ancient vessel with steadily flashing red light and an ululating siren. The ship's machine-spirit could sense the insidious violations that licked at its armoured plates, and its concern about the lack of a navigator onboard was evident. The vessel was not equipped for warp travel, and the vaporous mist of warp energy through which it passed confused its sensors. However, its warp shields held, because it was not submerged in the maelstrom of the warp, it was merely ploughing through the dense, eddying space of the Eye of Terror, like an icebreaker. The boundaries between material and immaterial space in this zone were permeable; droplets and shards flickered in and out of existence in each realm, struggling against their natures to survive in unnatural and alien dimensions. It was a field of perpetual death and life, a chaotic miasma of swirling vapours and intoxicating energies.

'Sensors?' asked Octavius, staring up at the vague, ruddy mist that obscured the scene on the viewscreen. He couldn't see anything.

'Nothing, captain.' The ships sensor arrays were as confused as Octavius's own senses.

'Keep trying,' said Octavius. 'Give me visual on the main viewer. We need to find that corsair. Switch to long range scanners. It could be anywhere by now.'

We do not need your sensors, captain. We know where the darklings have gone.

The Imperial Fist turned with slow deliberation, finding the eldar warlock standing with Dhrykna at his shoulder. They were both gazing up into the misty red image with confusion written across their faces, as though they could not believe that they were placing their lives in the hands of a species that could not see through the warp mists of the great Eye.

'You know where they have gone?'

There is a planet hidden in a cusp of this nebula, shrouded in the mists of time and sheltered in the eye of a tempest of sha'iel. Its presence is clear – it shines with the brilliant violence of a thousand lost souls. It is Hesperax, human – I have seen it.

Even as the warlock's thoughts eased into Octavius's head, a signature suddenly blinked into visibility on the terminal. For an instant it was stationary, almost as though it had been waiting to be noticed, and then it accelerated off towards the fringes of the nebula, just where Shariele had indicated.

'There,' said Octavius, preferring to place his faith in his own eyes rather than in the inexplicable insight of an alien witch. 'Let it pull away and then follow at range. We do not want to engage before it leads us home. Make sure the gunners are on alert. Sound the range warning.'

They know we are here, human. There is no surprising the wyches of Hesperax. They are leading you by the nose like a warp beast.

'They may think that we are being led, warlock, and you may even agree with them. But we are the Death-watch, and we will take the Emperor's justice to them whether they are prepared for us or not. It is not our way to hide our duty in the shadows or to sneak around it as though afraid of our destinies. We cannot be led to our prey – we are hunting it. If it is stupid enough to wait for us, that will simply make our job easier. When there is no possibility of surprise, to seek it is merely to waste time,' said Octavius, quoting a line from the *Codex Astartes*. 'And time is not something that I am prepared to waste today.' In the back of his mind, he could hear the words of Lord Vargas urging his speed.

The engines of the *Lance of Darkness* flared with power and the frigate slid heavily into pursuit of the darting corsair once again.

* * *

EVEN FROM ORBIT the planet appeared like a ghost. It had none of the qualities that the *Lance of Darkness*'s instruments had come to expect of a planet. Most notably, it was utterly unreflective. Whilst most planets shine with the reflected light of stars, burning in the heavens like miniature stars themselves, the planet that Shariele had called Hesperax just seemed to drink in the ambient light of its surroundings. It was like a black hole from which no light could escape. Without the benefit of a reflective surface from which to bounce its signal, the *Lance of Darkness*'s approach had slowed to a crawl, and its safety was put entirely in the hands of the control deck's serfs, who had to guide the venerable vessel manually, placing their faith in their own Emperor given reflexes.

Meanwhile, the lightning fast corsair had flicked and flashed around the dark planet, like a moth around a flame, before dipping suddenly and vanishing into the atmosphere. It was swallowed immediately by the thick, swirling clouds of darkness that roiled unendingly in the upper atmosphere; even the flaming spark caused by the escort ship's passage through the atmosphere itself was consumed almost instantly, leaving no clues for the hunters that prowled deliberately in its wake.

There was no hope that the *Lance of Darkness*'s approach would have gone unnoticed on the planet. Despite his indignance, Octavius was gradually beginning to believe that his eldar guests were right that the raiders had let him follow them. Military caution overrode his deep resentment of the aliens on his ship, and he had decided to deploy the kill-team in a manner befitting an anticipated ambush. He had no choice but to pursue the corsair down onto the planet, and if there was going to be a welcoming committee waiting for him, he was determined that the Deathwatch would be as ready for their hosts as their hosts were for the Deathwatch. Duty may oblige him to act, but it did not oblige him to be stupid.

In keeping with the guidelines laid out in the *Codex Astartes*, Octavius had divided his force into two Thunderhawks, splitting the risk and presenting any ground based defences with more than one target. However, in order to maximise the combat capacities of the team, it was important that the two hawks touched down within striking distance of each other. Once on the ground, the Deathwatch were most formidable as a unified team.

The vox unit crackled and hissed, functioning poorly in the tumult of the warp infested space around Hesperax. They were only on the very edge of the Eye of Terror, but already the conventions of material space were wobbling and uncertain.

'Captain,' yelled Kruidan, trying to make himself heard through the static as his own Thunderhawk powered away from the *Lance of Darkness* in close pursuit of Octavius's gunship. Although this was Kruidan's first mission with the Deathwatch, and despite the fact that he was the least senior of the Marines in the team, Octavius had given him command of the second Thunderhawk. In fact, the Mantis Warrior had navigated the treacherous tides of the Maelstrom and the Eye of Terror more often than any of the others – he carried the ritual markings of a member of the Praying Mantidae, an elite cadre of the Mantis Warriors Chapter that was charged with hunting down the remnants of the renegade Astral Claws. Hence, in the pursuit of his own Chapter's penitence, Kruidan had been hunting in the Eye many times before.

'Captain,' he tried again, but there was no response.

Your machines will not work here, human.

Octavius had decided to split the two eldar. Shariele, the warlock, was strapped into a harness in the cockpit of Kruidan's Thunderhawk, sandwiched between the hulking forms of Pelias and Luthar. Dhrykna accompanied the captain with Atreus and Sulphus.

Kruidan let the alien thoughts into his head as though tolerating torture. As a Mantidae, he was accustomed to enduring ritual and ceremonial hardships, including a kind of psychic torture that formed part of the initiation ceremony into the elite group. The Praying Mantidae operated much like a kill-team, dipping in and out of the Eye of Terror in small squads, persecuting the heretical Astral Claws wherever they were detected. Hence, the minds of the Mantidae had to resist every kind of violation and temptation, else they would go insane or, worse, they might turn against themselves. The Mantis Warriors lived in perpetual fear of self-betrayal.

'Kr… landi… secure,' crackled the vox. Octavius's voice was broken and unclear.

Through the forward screen, Kruidan could see the sudden burst of flame as Octavius's gunship ploughed into the atmosphere and then vanished into the clouds below. He watched the roiling, murky vapours as they whirled and eddied around the planet. For a moment, it seemed that the swirling patterns congealed into the suggestions of faces, dark and indistinct, eyes wide and mouths open as though screaming. Then he angled the nose of his Thunderhawk and fired the main engines, throwing the gunship into a steep dive and blasting through the atmosphere in support of his captain. 'For Redemption, for the Mantis Warriors, for the Emperor!' he muttered as the thunderous sound of a ruptured stratosphere clawed at the hull of the ship.

Intermixed with the roar of resistance, Kruidan thought that he could hear whispers and screams, as though thousands of souls were scraping at the armour of the vessel and desperately striving to break out of the atmosphere from below. Although the Assault Marine had dropped onto the surfaces of many planets within the maelstrom of the Eye of Terror, he had never heard the atmosphere of a world shriek with such agony before. Hesperax was a world unlike any other.

EVEN THOUGH OCTAVIUS'S Thunderhawk had dropped down through the mire of clouds in the lead, Kruidan's gunship crunched down onto the cold, cracked rock of Hesperax first. The Mantis Warrior was well experienced in making such drops, and he knew the importance of getting down to the ground quickly; there was more at stake than the simple paranoia of the Adeptus Astartes, who all craved the feel of solid ground beneath their feet. Once he had entered the cover of the thick, swirling clouds, Kruidan had opened up the gunship's engines and roared almost vertically down to the ground, where he had suddenly levelled up and fired the stabilisers to soften the impact. It was the closest mimicry of a drop-pod that a Thunderhawk could manage, but it had the distinct advantage that a Thunderhawk could extract the Marines later on; alone on the surface of a cursed, Emperor-forsaken planet in the Eye of Terror, neither a Mantidae nor a Deathwatch Marine could expect back-up to arrive in a hurry, so drop-pods were usually out of the question.

The instant that the Thunderhawk's hatch blew and its ramp cut into the ground, Kruidan was outside. Pelias and Luthar were close behind him, forming a defensive but aggressive triangle with their weapons primed. Bringing up the rear, striding down the landing ramp as though walking out into his garden, was the eldar warlock, Shariele. Kruidan had noticed with some satisfaction that the already pale-skinned alien had turned even paler during the high-G descent, but the warlock had now hidden his sickly features behind his ornate and sinister, rune encrusted mask. Were his visage not so full of a terrible dignity, his manner would have appeared casual as he disembarked from the Thunderhawk.

The landing site was a black crater, cut into the icy and rocky surface of the planet. Surrounding it, rising around the perimeter like a range of miniature mountains, was a ring of debris and rubble that had been gradually frozen into place over the long years since the crater was blown. As he scanned the scene, Kruidan could see no movement either within or outside the perimeter. He had hoped that the speed of his descent would have made the Thunderhawk difficult for any ground based sensors to detect it, or at least to differentiate between it and a meteor; from the look of the planet's surface, meteor strikes were not an uncommon occurrence on Hesperax.

Once they had dropped into the deep crater, Kruidan thought that the gunship might remain unseen and undetected for a while, at least from line of sight sensor arrays. In any event, it was the best that he could do, although he was concerned that Captain Octavius had dismissed his approach as unnecessarily rash and at variance with the teachings of the *Codex*: a Thunderhawk was not a drop-pod.

Looking up, Kruidan could see the faint glow of the captain's gunship, still engulfed in the dark, vaporous clouds, as it descended towards the landing site at a more orthodox speed and angle. Its engines flared with power and the roar was faintly audible already. If he could see it, reflected Kruidan as he tracked his bolter around the broken landscape, alert for signs of movement, then so could anyone else who was looking.

We are not alone. Shariele had stopped moving and was looking fixedly over towards a point on the lip of the crater.

Kruidan snapped his bolter over in the same direction and waited for something to emerge. He couldn't see anything, but he knew that the eldar's senses were different from his own, and probably more attuned to the presence of its dark and distant kin.

'They're firing,' hissed Pelias, his voice crackling with sibilance through the vox-bead in Kruidan's ear.

'What?' snapped Kruidan, glancing back at the solid figure of the Black Consul to see what he was talking about. The sergeant's helmet was angled up into the sky, and Kruidan understood at once.

As Octavius's Thunderhawk emerged from the cloud line, they could clearly see the rapid flashes of muzzle flares, and the faint report of detonations punched through the howling engine roar. After a couple of seconds, bursts of dark light started to explode across the underside of the gunship's hull as something or someone returned fire from the ground.

A sound like the explosive shattering of glass made Kruidan spin. He saw a crackling line of warp energy searing out of Shariele's hands and crashing into the icy rocks on the lip of the crater. At the same time, Luthar opened up with his bolter, snapping off a succession of shells into the steaming shower of shrapnel, riddling it with a staccato of explosions.

There was a moment of delay, and then a cloud of dark projectiles whined out of the mist, sizzling through the air towards the warlock and the three Marines. An ear-piercing shriek rose out of the muffled cacophony of the sudden violence. It was just a single voice at first, screeching out of the explosion on the edge of the crater, but it was quickly joined by more, until there was a hideous chorus echoing around the entire perimeter.

Kruidan hesitated for a moment, glancing back up at the beleaguered shape of Octavius's Thunderhawk in time to see its main engines fail as a series of warheads slammed into its rear. The stabilisers fired immediately, but the gunship rocked and dropped suddenly, falling like a massive weight of unsupported adamantium. Its weapons were still firing, even as it fell, spraying the ground with a hail of explosive shells.

There was nothing that could be done to help the captain; Kruidan reluctantly turned his attention back to the matter at hand. Luthar, Pelias and Shariele had retreated until they were back to back in the centre of the crater, just beyond the ramp of the Thunderhawk, which provided them with some cover. The Mantis Warrior took in the scene for a moment, standing just out of formation. He had seen a lot of incredible things in his time: he had watched the great daemon of Fhroxcalin drag itself into reality through a tear in the warp, he had seen entire planets consumed by the Great Devourer, and he had even seen a necron lord whip stardust into a beautiful and terrible lance of power. But he had never seen an eldar warlock fighting back to back with two Space Marines. His soul rebelled against the sight, but this was no time for moralising.

The splinter projectiles were clattering into his armour from all directions at once. The crater appeared to be completely surrounded by dark eldar warriors. It was as though they had been lying in wait for the Deathwatch to arrive. But, even if the surviving corsair had been able to warn Hesperax of their arrival, Kruidan doubted that they would have been able to organise such a perfect ambush so quickly.

He growled with displeasure and disgust, igniting his jump pack and roaring up into the air. He had equipped himself with two grenade launchers from the armoury of the *Lance of Darkness*, and he drew them both from their holsters on his legs, discarding his bolter. As his jump pack poured fire out beneath him, he spun slowly on an axis with his arms held straight out to his sides. As he ascended, he could see rows of dark eldar over the lip of the crater, their jagged teeth glinting viciously in the black light, interspersed with vehicles and hideously angled machinery. There must have been hundreds of them.

Roaring over the sound of his jump pack, Kruidan squeezed the triggers on both outstretched grenade launchers, holding them in as the weapons convulsed over and over again, releasing dozens of grenades in two wide, concentric spirals around the perimeter of the crater. The parabolas were shallow and the first grenades impacted in less than a second, divided by 180 degrees around the pit. Explosions strafed around the rim as the rest of the grenades hit the ground and detonated, forming a wide ring of fire and icy shrapnel. The dark eldar scattered back away from the crater's edge, leaping and darting out of range of the detonations like metal fragments being repelled by an electro-magnet.

As his grenade launchers whirred and clicked empty, Kruidan continued to spin, turning to the horizon and seeing Octavius's Thunderhawk crash down into the barren rocks. It crumpled as it impacted against the ground and then exploded, scattering flames and metal fragments into a sphere of destruction and sending up a massive mushroom of smoke and debris.

Below him, Pelias, Luthar and Shariele were ablaze
with fire, but already the dark eldar were leaping and
dancing over the lip of the crater and closing them
down; their numbers were thinning under the barrage, but there were simply too many of them.

CHAPTER NINE:
GLADIATOR

IT WAS INSULTING: their captors hadn't even bothered
to remove their power armour. Instead, the dark
eldar had simply shackled the ankles and wrists of
the Marines, pulling them tight against the wall.
There was not a chain or a lock in the Imperium that
could restrain a Space Marine in full combat armour,
but these shackles were made of a material that they
had never seen before – they appeared to be made
out of the darkness itself. With all of his arms
clamped back against the wall, Techmarine Sulphus
inspected the restraints with undisguised admiration.

Pelias roared, thrashing against the shackles and
smashing his fists back against the wall. Like the others, he could feel the jagged arcs of agony lancing
through his nervous system when he moved. But,

unlike the others, he had felt this pain before. The Biel-Tan had used similar nerve-pins to immobilise him when they had taken him captive. Not even the ministrations of Inquisitor Lord Guerilian had managed to remove the physical memory, and every piercing streak of pain brought back flashes of torture from his past. It was as though the pins had been pushed home in exactly the same places, sliding in between the plates of his armour and penetrating critical points in his nerves.

Hanging on the wall next to Pelias, Kruidan was barely conscious. After he had run out of ammunition above the crater, something had hit his jump pack and blown it off his back. He had free fallen to the ground and smacked into the spiked, ice hard rocks. There was a massive wound on his back where his armour had been melted by the explosion of fuel, his skin was riddled with shrapnel and a long, jagged, stone spike had been jammed through his shoulder.

Although his Larraman's organ had eventually stemmed the flow, he had already lost so much blood that he hung virtually limp from the shackles around his wrists. His vision was slightly blurred and his ears were full of Pelias's cries.

Had he been able to look around the chamber in which the Marines had been secured after they were captured in the crater, Kruidan would have seen a vision of hell. On one side of him was Pelias, writhing in his present pain and in half remembered agonies from his past. On the other side was Luthar, silent and motionless with his arms outstretched and bound to the wall behind him, strung up like a crucified criminal. Next to him was the slender figure of Shariele, with pulsing warp tainted stakes driven through his hands and feet. Sizzling streams of toxic blood hissed into pools on the ground beneath his stigmatic wounds, and his de-masked head was slumped forward onto his stretched chest. Further along the wall there were other bodies, shackled, hanging and in various states of ruin.

The chamber itself was stifling and hot. Channels were cracked into the floor, bubbling with lava and steaming with sulphurous gases. The light was faint, orange and hellish, emanating from the volcanic discharge on the ground. In the centre of the room was a metallic table, on which were strewn the broken remains of what looked like a dark eldar of some kind. Its limbs and head were restrained by hoops of dark material, although they were no longer attached to its intricately scarred abdomen.

It was difficult to tell whether the grotesque piercings and mutilations that covered the creature's dismembered body had been inflicted as part of a process of ritual torture, or whether they had already been there when the unfortunate alien had been subjected to a barbaric form of execution by dissection.

Muffled groans rumbled through the fumes, suggesting the presence of other prisoners hanging on walls that were only vaguely visible through the clouds of sulphur. One or two of the noises sounded human, but a number of them certainly were not. The deep guttural sound of a frustrated ork was unmistakable, even to a Marine in Kruidan's devastated condition.

As he struggled to take in the inhumanity of his surroundings, swimming in and out of consciousness,
Kruidan saw the ghostly figures of hunched and muti-
lated dark eldar shuffling around the chamber before
him. They passed in and out of the clouds of noxious
gas, fading in and out of visibility. Occasionally, a
scream would cut through the vague, smoky atmosphere, shattering the nauseating lull that had settled
over the Marines. A tremendous gargling roar told
Kruidan that the ork had finally been liberated from
the misery of its existence.

Opening his eyes at the sound of approaching feet,
the Mantis Warrior saw the face of his tormenter
grinning insanely into his face. The haemonculus's
eyes glittered with an intense and maniacal passion
and its tongue was curled hungrily around one of
the incisors that protruded from his upper jaw. It
was less than half a metre from Kruidan's exposed
face – his helmet having been removed at some
point between the battlefield and the prison.

Despite the pain that rushed around his nervous
system, Kruidan lifted his slumped head off his chest
and met the vile creature's gaze. He could see the
barely suppressed excitement bubbling in those evil
eyes; there was a thirst for pain and torture shining
lasciviously over the surface of the black irises. It was
a face utterly unfamiliar with mercy, although it was
tinged with fear and insanity. For a moment, the
Mantis Warrior felt a wave of satisfaction that he
could strike a note of fear into this creature, even in
this broken and helpless form, but then he realised
that the haemonculus's fear was directed elsewhere;
it was competing against the creature's thirst for

pain, holding it in check like a leash around the neck of a wild animal.

Without warning, except for a slight dilation of its pitch-black pupils, the haemonculus brandished a long syringe, holding it up in front of Kruidan and squirting a thin toxic jet from its tip. It was dark with filth and grime, and the needle was barbed like a flaying knife. After another glint from the creature's eyes, it punched the syringe into Kruidan's neck, burying the needle all the way up to the reservoir and then emptying its contents into the Marine's bloodstream.

As the dark eldar withdrew the device, it leaned in closer to the Marine's face, as though inspecting his features for signs of change. At that moment, groggy with pain, blood loss and narcosis, Kruidan spat his defiance into the alien's face, activating his Betcher's gland subconsciously. The globule of saliva splattered against the haemonculus's face and sizzled with toxicity, burning a deep pocket into its pale, scarred skin. The alien took a sudden step backwards, its eyes wide with shock as it shrieked with pain. But then it raised its fingers to the open sore on its face and pressed its pointed nails into the wound, drawing a line of blood and hissing toxins out on its fingertips and then licking them clean. A wide grin cracked across its face as though its wildest dreams had just come true.

GAZING THROUGH THE faint lava light, Octavius could just about make out the shape of other Marines strung up against the far wall. The tentacular shape of Techmarine Sulphus was easy to discern. One of the others was roaring incoherently and thrashing against his restraints. Another was motionless with composure, but the one in the middle appeared slumped and broken. One of the dark eldar prison guards, or whatever they were, had just jammed something into his neck and he appeared to have lost consciousness as a result.

The Imperial Fists captain flexed his shoulders and grimaced against the pain that cut through his nerves. Just like the rest of his team, he was powerless to struggle against the restraints. This was not a situation to which a Space Marine was accustomed. His mind raced through the possibilities: how could their captors have known how to immobilise them so perfectly? The required knowledge of a Space Marine's physiology was beyond many of the Space Marines themselves – perhaps only the Apothecaries would really know all the specific nerve nodes. Yet, somehow, these aliens had mastered the knowledge perfectly.

Deciding to conserve his strength, Octavius let his chin sink down onto his chest. As he did so, his eyes came to rest on a pile of debris below his feet. At first he thought that it was merely a heap of rocks and ruined instruments, but as he looked more closely he realised that the remains of a body were mixed into the mound. An eldar skull was balanced on the top of the pile, and there was clearly a hand protruding from the side – a human hand.

Straining his eyes against the heat and noxious fumes that filled the chamber, Octavius could see that the hand was only one of many human body parts that had been strewn over the floor. To his horror and fury he realised that some of those parts still bore the remnants of power armour: intermixed amongst the detritus were the remains of Space Marines, tortured, dismembered and utterly violated by the Emperor-cursed aliens of Hesperax. The captain realised immediately that this was how his captors had learnt about the anatomy of the Adeptus Astartes – they had taken it apart piece by piece until they had found out what they needed to know.

'Captain?' The voice was little more than a whisper.

'Atreus?' replied Octavius, turning his head painfully to his left. The Blood Ravens librarian was clamped to the wall next to him with some kind of hood covering his face. 'Are you damaged?'

'No, but this hood is interfering with my mind, just as these pins are restraining our bodies.'

Neither of them could clearly remember how they had been captured. Their memories seemed to stop as their Thunderhawk crashed down onto the surface of Hesperax, throwing them onto the jagged rocks amidst the waiting dark eldar forces. Octavius could vaguely recall seeing Kruidan, his jump pack alive with flames, spinning above the second Thunderhawk, which had already landed, unleashing a hail of grenades over the alien warriors as they pressed in around their landing site.

After his gunship had crashed, Octavius could remember standing in the wreckage with his chainsword spluttering through xenos flesh. He could remember the pressure of numbers and the feelings of anger and despair as Sulphus and then Atreus were overwhelmed. There was another figure too, darting around the edges of his memory like a firefly through a dark forest – the shimmering white eldar Aspect Warrior had fought at his side. There had been a great explosion in the sky, and Octavius had looked up in time to see the distant Kruidan transfigured into a ball of fire.

The captain strained his neck forward, twisting his face around to look past Atreus, battling against his body's reflexive need to avoid the pain that lanced through his shoulders. On the other side of the librarian, Octavius could see the slender, white armoured figure of the eldar warrior, Dhrykna. Despite himself, he was relieved to see her alive – her eyes flashed with undiminished alertness in the darkness, and she nodded an acknowledgement to the captain.

'How did this happen, Atreus?'

'They were prepared for our arrival, captain. They knew we were coming.'

'We were not trying to surprise them, but I cannot believe that they had time to organise such a perfect reception. The corsair was only moments ahead of us.'

'Perhaps there is a breach in the integrity of the team, captain. Perhaps they were warned?'

'You mean the aliens? Why would they betray us when we are doing their bidding? Besides, they would be betraying themselves. Look.' Octavius strained his neck to indicate the immobilised, shackled forms of Dhrykna next to him and Shariele on the far wall.

'It need not have been the aliens, captain.'

Octavius looked through the heat haze towards the source of the new voice on the other side of the chamber. 'Brother Chaplain Luthar?'

'Yes, captain, it is me. Brother Kruidan is badly damaged. I am not sure what they have done to him, but they appear to be ministering to his wounds.' The Reviler was changing the subject.

'You are implying that Librarian Ashok may have had something to do with this, chaplain?' Octavius felt his ire rise. He was not sure that he trusted the Angels Sanguine librarian himself, but he would not suffer such doubts from other members of his team. 'Ashok is a fine warrior, Luthar. You will not speak in this way of a brother Marine.'

'It is odd that he is the only one not here, captain.' This time the voice belonged to Sulphus. 'Marines are not all the same, Captain Octavius, as you know. The Angels Sanguine are brothers of the flesh and, as such, they are not beyond corruption.'

'Enough,' stated Octavius. 'This is not the time for blame. We are all flesh and blood, Iron Father, whether we choose to embrace it or not. It is our humanity for which we fight. Therein lies our duty.'

There was silence, broken only by the bubbling of lava and the hiss of steam. The shuffling haemonculi appeared to have left the chamber.

'Luthar – you said that the aliens are repairing Kruidan?' asked Octavius, his mind turning back to the chaplain's earlier words.

'Yes, captain. I think so. His wounds are healing rapidly – much faster than I would expect to see on a Marine who has lost so much blood. As you know, the Larraman's organ relies on blood flow to manufacture scar tissue.'

'Why would they repair his flesh?' asked Sulphus, incredulous as much as curious.

'They want him to fight.' All eyes turned to Atreus as he spoke.

'What?'

'That is why we are still alive. The dark eldar want us to fight in their arena. It has been recorded in a number of tomes kept in the great Blood Ravens librarium of the *Omnis Arcanum* – the aliens take prisoners in order to use them as sport in their games. The greater the warriors taken, the greater the satisfaction of the game.'

'Right is he.' Dhrykna's voice was calm and even, despite the jumbled words. 'These prisoners other not enough power have.' She nodded her head, indicating the remains of the eldar artisans and dancers that were still stung up around the walls. 'Understand I do not why darklings them took. No satisfaction for Satin Throne they give.'

Octavius looked around the hellish chamber once again and realised that the Aspect Warrior was right. The other prisoners looked weak and effeminate. Most of them were already dead or dying. Their spirits were broken and they would provide no sport for the aliens at all. He recognised a couple of the eldar that were taken from Ulthwé in the last raid.

'Why would they risk their lives on raids to take these creatures?' he asked, thinking out loud.

'Bait,' said Atreus.

EIGHT HOURS WAS a long time in politics, especially in the politics of the Inquisition. Even as Perceptia made her way back towards the Hereticus librarium she noticed the increased activity in the Ramugan station. People were rushing through the corridors with more than their usual haste, bumping and bustling past each other without the conventional concerns for status and diplomacy. It was as though each and every person on Ramugan had suddenly decided that they had the most important job on the station and that everyone else was simply an obstacle to the execution of their duty. In truth, this was not far from the everyday mentality of many of the officials that called Ramugan their home, but the last few hours had seen a new and sudden urgency in their manner.

As though to confirm her observations, a faint blue warning light started to pulse in the corridor as Perceptia approached the security doors before the librarium. The warning lights were coded on Ramugan: light blue was an alert signal for the staff of the Ordo Malleus. Of course, given the nature of the station, any warning was probably of interest to everyone, so in practice the colour of the light merely indicated who was quickest on the button.

Perceptia stopped short of the doors and looked about her, pushing her spectacles higher up the bridge of her nose and peering through the vague strobe lighting at the flickering, stop start motion of the personnel around her. If Lord Aurelius had finally called an alert, that probably meant that he had decided to dispatch a team of Grey Knights to the Circuitrine nebula. At last he was acting like an inquisitor lord of the Ordo Malleus, thought Perceptia. Whatever hold Lords Seishon or Vargas had over him was clearly not enough to prevent him completely from doing his duty. Although Perceptia also realised that the disturbance around the Eye of

Terror had now grown to such proportions that it would be impossible for Aurelius to refuse to act, no matter what his arrangement with the Xenos lords. She had seen it herself using the optical enhancers provided by the viewscreen in her own personal chambers. The situation was now sufficiently obvious that it did not require the subtle mind of a Hereticus inquisitor to realise that failure to act now would look like deliberate stalling.

For a moment, Perceptia hesitated at the doors to the librarium, wondering what effect this turn of events would have on her own investigations. She was relatively sure that Caesurian would tell her that there was now no point in pursing the issue: her purpose was, surely, to force some kind of action regarding the potential threat to the Imperium. That being the case, there was no longer any need for her to continue. The Grey Knights would deal with any threats, or would at least be able to investigate their nature.

However, something gnawed at the back of Perceptia's mind and she realised with mild surprise that her concern in this case had never been about the safety of the Imperium at all, at least not directly. Her concern was with Seishon himself, and she was not prepared to drop the case now, just because the Ordo Malleus had finally decided to do its job. If Seishon was hiding something that went deep into the ranks of the Ordo Xenos on Ramugan, as the testimony of Lord Herod suggested, albeit unconvincingly at this stage, then it was potentially a greater risk to the security of the Imperium than a shifting warp signature in the lashes of the Eye of

Terror. Such things happened all the time, which was why the Ordo Malleus kept a detachment of Grey Knights on Ramugan in the first place, but a heresy in the heart of the Ordo Xenos was something else entirely. If she was lucky, the Grey Knights would do her fieldwork for her. They may uncover an unfolding plot even as she investigated its origins and dimensions in the librarium. No, this was not the time to abandon her work; it was the time to redouble her efforts.

She turned back to the unostentatious doors and smiled. She always admired the subtlety of the architects who had designed the entrance to the Hereticus librarium on this station. Nobody would guess from the small, plain, gunmetal doors that a massive, multi-levelled librarium stretched out behind them.

The purpose was not only to dissuade prying eyes from taking too much interest in the forbidden knowledge within, but it was also to understate the existence of the librarium in the first place. For many of the officials of the Ordo Xenos and Malleus, it was bad enough that they had to share Ramugan with the Ordo Hereticus. It would be almost insufferable if they were confronted each day by the massive scale of the librarium in which the Hereticus stored all their intricate records and suspicions. Small, unassuming doors suggested that there could be nothing worthy of mention on the other side – certainly nothing valuable or plentiful enough to condemn an inquisitor lord for heresy.

Muttering the password into a hidden window, Perceptia slid through the doors as they cracked open. She headed directly for the lowest levels, where she hoped to find Seye Multinus waiting for her with news of Circuitrine. The mutant curator had told her that it would take him eight hours to sift through the relevant files. It was incredible to think how much the world could change in only eight hours. Pushing her glasses back up her nose, Perceptia grinned in anticipation as she hurried down the long, winding staircase.

THE SHUFFLING HAEMONCULI had returned to the sanctorium and cut down the two eldar warriors, bundling them off with a group of wych-guards, and separating them from the mon-keigh. They were led through a maze of passageways until they reached a broad and circular chamber, where they were ushered onto a platform in the middle of the floor. Dhrykna stood shoulder to shoulder with Shariele as the circular platform rose slowly up towards the ceiling. A ring of darklings surrounded them, vicious blades jabbing forward to prevent the eldar from stepping off the gradually rising dais. The guards grinned, excitement dripping from their glinting teeth.

As the platform neared the ceiling, Dhrykna wondered for a moment whether the intention was to squash the two of them flat against the stone roof. But at the last second a crack opened up in the ceiling, widening in synchronisation with the rising dais beneath. At the same time, a blast of sound crashed down from above, pouring through the opening as though it were cut into the bottom of an ocean. There were shrieks and screams and cheers. It was like a massive wave of hysteria breaking over their heads.

With a resounding clunk, the platform slotted into place in the hole in the ceiling, pushing the two eldar warriors up into the centre of the arena above. The noise was incredible as Dhrykna looked about her and saw the extent of her predicament. The wide, roughly circular arena was bounded by stands on three sides. Thousands of darkling faces gleamed down at the two eldar from their elevated positions, braying and shrieking with anticipation and pleasure. On the fourth side of the auditorium was a sheer wall rising and vanishing into the heights above.

Cut into the frictionless surface, about half way up, was a shadow strewn platform that appeared to be bedecked in luxurious cloths and decadent furniture. An exquisitely beautiful female lay reclining on a wriggling and pulsating throne. Dhrykna could see her smile sparking across her teeth and from her dark eyes. She was flanked by a number of darkling wyches, but there were also a couple of more familiar figures.

Straining her eyes up to the platform, Dhrykna realised in horror that she recognised two of the figures that stood at the wych queen's shoulder. Shrouded in his sumptuous sapphire robes, edged in a glimmering and phosphorescent black, Bhurolyn of the Sacred Star gazed down at the beacon of brilliance that was Dhrykna – her pristine white armour shining like a sacred star in the oppressive darkness of the amphitheatre. Standing just behind the eminent seer was another Ulthwé eldar, her face hidden in the shadows but her eyes glinting visibly. They were the two seers that the council had sent the mon-keigh to recover.

Shariele–
I have seen them, Dhrykna of the Shining Spear.

The warlock's expression was grim with fury and indignation as he glowered up at the figures on the platform. In that moment, the plans of the Seer Council of Ulthwé suddenly became clear to him. Without pausing to consider his action, Shariele raised his wounded hands and threw a jagged flash of lightning up towards the platform. As the power coursed through his ruptured flesh, he roared in pain, filling his intent with agony and hatred for the darklings and the seers that had betrayed him. He poured his fury through his bleeding hands, feeling them burn and the skin melt as he screamed his rage.

The darklings in the audience brayed and shrieked with excitement at this show of power; they had become so accustomed to seeing weak and pathetic opponents in the arena that even this assault on their queen thrilled them. Meanwhile, Lelith herself did not even rise to her feet. She merely held up a hand, as though casually signalling that the streaks of sha'iel that were arcing towards her should stop their advance. Spontaneously, the warlock's joust of power ruptured and splintered, shattering into shards that scattered themselves harmlessly against the sheer wall beneath the queen's podium.

In response, Shariele roared with frustration and gazed down at his ruined hands. Whatever the haemonculi had driven through his flesh to hang him on the wall had interfered with his ability to focus energy into his fingertips. Instead his power bled over his own skin, intermingling with the blood that still streamed over his wrists.

On her feet at last, Lelith cast her eyes down on the two eldar warriors and smiled radiantly. There was a hint of mock pity in her gaze and a snarl of lust on her lips.

Greetings, eldar warriors of Ulthwé. We have been expecting you.

The audience cheered with appreciation, as though confirming the note of eager anticipation sounded by the Wych Queen of Strife.

You should consider yourselves greatly honoured by our attentions, my friends. How many lives are spent in the pursuit of death? We grant you the privilege of dying in our grand arena, from whence your souls will finally be liberated from your misguided, lightling forms. You should die knowing that you bring us great... satisfaction. You might also realise that you die to bring hope to your precious Ulthwé – although it is a fool's hope. She grinned but did not turn to face Bhurolyn. *Moreover, we owe you a debt of gratitude for bringing us our main event.* Her gaze flicked lasciviously over towards the mon-keigh warriors that were bunched together and shackled at the edge of the arena, held in a pen behind thin, black bars, where they had been brought to watch the proceedings. *And for this service we are granting you a great boon – you will be the first to do battle in our arena. It is to you that we will grant the honour of an early death.*

As her thoughts echoed into silence around the grand amphitheatre, Lelith flicked a signal to an unseen subordinate. Almost instantaneously, a massive, heavy door cracked ajar in the arena wall beneath her podium. It ground slowly open, with the heavy deliberation of weight and significance, admitting a dirty red cloud of smoke into the arena. A hideous keening sounded through the opening, and the gnashing of monstrous jaws was clearly audible, even over the eager cheers of the audience.

Shariele and Dhrykna lowered their gazes from the elevated podium and peered into the red mist that plumed out of the new opening. Vaguely familiar shapes shifted within, and the two eldar separated immediately, spontaneously deciding that they would stand a better chance if they could present more than one target for the creatures that emerged from the hellish gloom.

After a few seconds, two quadruped warp beasts lurched out of the mist into the arena, one bounding around the perimeter to the left and the other to the right, as though defining the territory of their killing zone. Before the two eldar could respond to the appearance of the gnashing beasts, two darkling wyches flipped and somersaulted their way through the dissipating, ruddy mist into the arena, glinting blades spinning in their hands. Shariele's eyes narrowed – he had encountered these two wyches before.

Finally, as the massive doors started to grind shut once again, a third darkling strode out of the settling cloud, a force whip crackling with darkness at her side and her eyes burning with a red hunger. Dhrykna and Shariele did not look at each other, but they could feel their mutual outrage feeding into a desire for combat: abandoned and alone, there was nothing left for them now other than to make their deaths worthy of Ulthwé, even if Ulthwé seemed to find their lives expendable.

'Light flashes, blood falls, death pierces the darkness,' whispered Dhrykna.

THE DEATHWATCH TEAM were pushed roughly into the barred pen at the side of the arena, prodded and jabbed from behind by the elongated blades of their captors. They moved slowly and cumbersomely, as though their own muscles were resisting the motion. Most of the nerve-pins had been removed, but a few remained in strategic points, making movement arduous and reactions slow.

Octavius tried to turn and glower at the dark eldar behind him, but his head swam nauseatingly, as though he had been drugged; it would be a rare drug indeed that could flummox the auto-immune system of a Space Marine. The guards grinned back at the unsteady captain, their eyes slit into eager, burning lines.

The Imperial Fist was the last in the line and he stopped just before the entrance to the cage. He turned his head slowly. All around the vast auditorium he could hear the braying and cheering of the audience. It was an incredible noise, crashing into his ears like an ocean. The circular space of the arena must have been three hundred metres in diameter – perhaps more.

The crowd's attention was focused in the very centre of the arena, where Octavius could see the shining white form of the female eldar warrior – Dhrykna – glittering like a pearl in the depths of a black sea. Next to her was the sinister figure of Shariele, his hands covered in dimly flickering flames. The two eldar had been removed from the

volcanic cell about an hour before the guards had
returned for the Marines. Octavius had had no idea
what was going to happen to them, and, if he was
entirely honest with himself, he hadn't really cared.
He had more than enough to think about without
concerning himself with the fates of two aliens.
Looking at them now, however, he felt an instant
pang of empathy: they stood ready for their death
like gladiators in the amphitheatre. They might be
untrustworthy and even offensive eldar, but right at
that moment they were simply warriors, alone, outnumbered, persecuted and unsupported. If he could
have broken away from his restraints and the guards,
he would have run to stand beside them.

A jab of pain punched into the small of his back as
the guards encouraged him to move into the cage.
He resisted, standing his ground and gritting his
teeth against the uncommon experience. It had been
so long since he had felt real, unadulterated pain
like this, and part of him thrilled at the parts of his
mind that had been re-awakened. Like all the Adeptus Astartes, he had not always been a Marine, but
since making the ascension his pain receptors had
been kept strictly under check, partly by implants,
partly by hypnotherapy, but mostly by raw
willpower. Somehow, the dark eldar had managed to
circumvent all of his defences and, for the first time
in nearly a century, he could remember the brutal,
vivid realities of the human condition: life was not
only war, it was also pain.

Another jab struck him in the back, this time there
was a blade sliding through the joint between the
armoured plate on his back and his utility belt. It bit

into the skin at the small of this back, penetrating his flesh and pushing in towards one of his kidneys.

The pain of the puncture wound was as nothing to the nerve induced agony that gripped Octavius's body as he snapped his arm round behind him and caught the blade in his gauntlet. He yanked it clear of his back, twisting it viciously and wrenching it out of the shocked guard's hands. In a jolting, pain riddled movement, Octavius turned to face the guards, flipping the blade so that he could grasp its hilt and brandish the killing edges.

As the disarmed guard flipped backwards, landing just out of range of Octavius's blade, the others pressed in with their weapons, surrounding the Deathwatch captain with the darkly glinting promise of death.

Octavius growled out from between gritted teeth, the pain of movement curdling his brain and making his vision swim. He roared, defying his own human frailties as much as the superior position of his enemies.

'This is not the time, captain.' The unexpected, low and almost whispering voice of Ashok came from the shadows within the cage, barely audible against the din of the auditorium. 'We will have our chance to fight soon enough.'

For a moment, the Imperial Fist hesitated. Of all the voices that he might have expected to hear urging his restraint, that of the Angel Sanguine librarian was the very last on the list. Not only had he not known that Ashok was even on the planet, but he had never heard him urge restraint on anyone. Gradually, his furious defiance began to subside and it was slowly replaced by intrigue. What was Ashok doing here?

'Remember this,' he said, forcing composure into his voice as he faced the alien guards. 'I will not always be in this cage. When I am not, you will die.' With that, he flipped the blade around once again, catching it by the tip and offering the hilt back to his captors.

The unarmed guard looked into Octavius's shining blue eyes with doubt and suspicion flickering over its features. In its entire life, it had probably never trusted anything with a weapon. After a moment of hesitation, presumably encouraged by the support of its peers, the creature reached forward to reclaim its blade.

The hapless guard would never trust anything with a weapon again. As it reached forward and grasped the hilt of its blade, Octavius wrenched the weapon back, pulling the guard off its feet and dragging it stumbling towards him. With a smooth efficiency that belied the pain that wracked his body, the Deathwatch captain spun the blade in his hand and then drove its point forward through the neck of the stumbling dark eldar. As it tripped after the abruptly withdrawn weapon, the alien lurched head first onto the suddenly inverted blade; its eyes bulged momentarily before its head, cleanly severed from its shoulders, bounced to the ground at Octavius's feet.

'Suffer not the alien to live,' murmured the captain under his breath, tossing the weapon aside and then turning to stride into the cage to join the rest of his kill-team as the guards lunged forward with their blades.

* * *

THE ANGELS SANGUINE librarian was the only one of the Marines restrained and shackled to a wall of the cage. He had been there already when the rest of the team had been pushed into the enclosure, his arms outstretched by his sides and his legs bound together, suspended about a metre off the ground by shackles that looped around the bars in the cage. His head was bowed, with his chin touching down onto his chest, the characteristically heavy hood still pulled down, obscuring his features.

The rest of the Deathwatch squad fanned out around him, staring up at the cruciform librarian with suspicion and hostility etched into their features.

'What are you doing here, librarian?' growled Sulphus, his hostility obvious and his face creased with barely disguised disgust.

'How did you get here, Angel Sanguine?' asked Pelias, suspicion transforming his question into a challenge.

Ashok made no response.

Octavius pushed his way through the ring of Marines and stood before the librarian, peering up at him in the half-light. The air was full of screams and yells from the dark eldar congregation in the stands of the amphitheatre outside, and Octavius could already taste the electric scent of energy discharges and spilt blood in the arena. In the back of his mind he realised that the Deathwatch team had probably been brought to fight in this forsaken pit, or at least to watch the fate of the two eldar warriors that had accompanied them from Ulthwé. The darkling aliens appeared to take great pleasure in knowing that their victims had to watch each other's suffering. But Ashok was foremost in his mind at that moment, and he inspected the form of the librarian closely.

Aside from a few burn marks and scrapes, there was little sign of damage on the librarian's armour. It was not clear how or whether the Angel Sanguine was properly restrained against the wall of the cage, and Octavius found it strange that he was the only one of the team that had been shackled against the bars. It seemed to him that the scene was designed specifically to give the impression that Ashok was also a prisoner when, in fact, they were all prisoners and none of them appeared in the manner of the librarian. Ashok's special restraints had clearly been dressed up to look like he had been treated even worse that the rest of them. The captain's ambiguous feelings about the mysterious librarian triggered a deep-rooted suspicion that this was all an elaborate charade.

'Are you damaged, Ashok?' he asked, peering under the folds of the librarian's heavy hood, trying to make out the expression on his hidden face.

There was no response.

'The captain asked you a question, Sanguine,' barked Sergeant Pelias, giving a voice to the tension.

'Atreus?' prompted Octavius without turning away from Ashok.

'He is suffering, captain. His mind is raging against itself, as though a great fury has been unleashed but deprived of a vent. It is consuming him.' Atreus's voice was calm and almost compassionate, but he stepped back away from the suspended figure of

Ashok, pressing his back against the bars on the opposite side of the cage as though repelled by something unseen.

'Ashok?' Octavius changed his tone, trying to lead the librarian out of his nightmare with the sound a friend. 'Ashok, can you hear me?'

With an abrupt movement, Ashok's head lurched forward. The restraints that held his arms snapped taught, rattling against the bars behind him. His contorted features snarled into Octavius's face and he breathed a gust of moisture against the captain's skin, as his head closed to within a few centimetres. Octavius did not flinch, but he met the burning and furious red gaze of the Angel Sanguine, holding the librarian's raging eyes in the complicated, sparkling blues of his own.

Ashok roared into his face, bunching the muscles of his neck as though straining against his restraints to unleash the violence that wracked his mind.

'Ashok,' whispered Octavius, his composure standing in stark contrast to the simmering energy of the librarian. 'Ashok. You are not alone here.'

'He is alone,' said Atreus with a seriousness that made the others think.

'He is not with me, that's for certain,' murmured Sulphus, turning his back on the raging Angel Sanguine and casting his attention out into the arena, where Dhrykna and Shariele were doing battle.

'Ashok,' repeated Octavius softly.

The librarian blinked and the muscles on his face writhed. Even to Octavius it was clear that a titanic internal struggle was underway in Ashok's mind. He didn't know what the dark eldar had done to the librarian, but he had seen a look like this on the face of the Angel Sanguine once before, and he knew what it meant. The last time had been in the lair of the tyranid hive tyrant on Herodian IV, when Ashok had dispatched a cluster of psyker zoanthropes all by himself.

Although Octavius could not pretend to understand the mysterious violence that sometimes raged in the simmering red eyes of the librarian, he did know that it was the source of Ashok's greatest power and his greatest fears. This was not a condition that the Angel Sanguine would have entered willingly, and the captain's suspicion about him was immediately replaced with concern.

Ashok blinked again, and the muscle tone of his face began to soften. His jaw was still clenched, but the muscles around his eyes began to relax as the red flames started to subside. After a few more seconds, his shoulders slumped and he fell back against the bars behind him, exhaling deeply as though with relief as his chin dropped down to his chest once again. At exactly that moment, a pulse of brilliant light flashed through the bars of the cage and the auditorium outside seemed to gasp into a collective silence – something unexpected had happened in the arena.

THE BODY OF the warp beast convulsed and thrashed as Shariele pressed his hands to the creature's throat. The warlock was pinned to the ground under the snarling weight of the warp spawned monster, his shoulders run through by the vicious, curved talons of the beast's forelegs. But as the dragonette gnashed down, bringing its massive jaws around to surround the eldar's elegantly elliptical head, Shariele reached up with his bleeding hands, struggling against the weight and piercing agony of the beast's claws, and clasped them to either side of the creature's monstrous skull.

Streams of crackling energy flooded out around the beast's head, cascading over its shoulders and cutting channels of burning flesh into its flanks. As one, the warlock and warp beast howled in pain as the flood became a torrent of broiling power, engulfing them both in a blaze of purpling light.

The audience was on its feet, cheering and screaming in eager delectation, eyes flaring and lips running slick with saliva. This is what they had come to see. They had grown so sick and tired of the pathetic, feeble displays of the Ulthwé artisans, dancers and poets. They had been bored to the point of despair by the cowardly fragility of the occasional mon-keigh. But now they had a real spectacle: a warlock of Ulthwé locked in the jaws of a warp beast, pumping out such quantities of barely controlled power that it would surely incinerate them both.

The other warp beast was already dead, and Quruel, mistress of the beasts, was prowling like an angry mother, sizing up the flashing white figure of the eldar Aspect Warrior as she flipped and spun around the lashes of Kroulir and Druqura. Quruel's lascivious tongue flicked around her lips, as though she could already taste the blood of the lightling, and her eyes gleamed with a perverse yet familiar mixture of thirst and violence.

Then there was an explosion of light – something that had not been seen on Hesperax for as long as anyone could remember. It was not the sickly, flickering half-light to which the darklings had grown accustomed, but rather a glorious eruption of brilliance. It blasted up from the floor of the arena, engulfing the point at which Shariele and the warp beast had been wrestling, and it brought a sudden, hushed silence into the amphitheatre, as though all the air had suddenly been sucked out.

As the light dimmed and faded, a stark and charred image began to appear in its heart. It was little more than a disfigured and incoherent lump on the ground where once Shariele and the beast had wrestled their last. It was not moving, and it was almost impossible to distinguish the shapes of two separate beings. The explosion of warp power had melted their flesh and their souls instantaneously, melding them into the picture of ruination.

Darting through the stunned silence, Dhrykna dived towards the faintly glowing remains of what she thought would be the last Ulthwé eldar that she would ever see. As she hit the ground, she rolled, flipping back up onto one knee at the side of what might once have been Shariele's head. She whispered something inaudible in a language long lost to the darklings, bowing her own head for an instant in reverence for the lost warrior. Scanning the charred remains, she realised that his waystone was also ruined, which meant that his soul was lost to Ulthwé forever – but it also meant that the darkling wych queen could not offer it as a sacrifice to the minions of the Satin Throne.

The shock of the explosive light lasted only a matter of seconds, and Dhrykna could already feel the dance-like movements of the wyches behind her as they manoeuvred for their attack. She just needed another second.

Jamming her hand into the sickly, viscous and burnt remains, the Aspect Warrior could feel the wyches drawing in around her. Even without turning, she could see them in her mind's eye, one dancing off to the left and the other to the right, like a pair of co-ordinated hunters. She was not sure where the mistress of the beasts was, but she felt certain that the senior figure would wait and see what happened to her underlings before she acted – such was the infamous cowardice of the darklings.

A shriek sounded immediately behind her as one of the wyches launched herself into a deathly lunge, stabbing forward with her delicately curving blade. At the very last moment, Dhrykna's hand found what it had been questing for. She dropped flat to ground and rolled rapidly, parrying the thrusting blade with one arm and bringing the other around into a strike as she spun. The long, barbed, dagger-like incisor that Dhrykna had yanked out of the remains of the warp beast's mouth plunged deeply into the wych's neck, puncturing her throat and severing her primary nerve cluster. The young wych barely had time for her eyes to bulge in shock before she slumped to the ground in a rapidly growing pool of her own blood.

The Shining Spear sprang back to her feet, snatching the dead wych's long, sweeping blade into her hands and spinning it in a well-practiced flourish.

She sank into a low combat stance, bracing her newly acquired weapon against her back, and she watched the movements of the two remaining dark-lings as the audience roared with excitement and hysteria. In the centre of the dark, circular auditorium of death, the Aspect Warrior seemed radiant, bursting with the brilliant white light of Khaine's own lightning spear.

'I DO NOT remember how it began, Octavius.' Ashok's speech was slurred and slow, as though the part of his brain responsible for language was functioning imperfectly. His head was still sagging down towards his chest and the tension in his out-stretched shoulders had eased. He was suspended like a martyr before his battle- brothers.

'I was aboard the craftworld, doing battle with the... aliens.' His hesitation was slight but notice-able. 'Then I was aboard a dark eldar corsair, much in the manner in which you see me now. I have been restrained like this for some time, although I have no sense of the duration. How long has it been, Octavius?'

'Too long, Ashok,' said the captain, and he meant it.

'What were you doing, Angel Sanguine? Where did they find you?' Pelias's voice was coarse, as though gravelled with doubts.

'Why did you leave us?' asked Luthar, finally giving voice to the question that was in everyone's mind.

'I did not leave you, brother-chaplain. I took the fight deeper into the craftworld. There were more enemies than merely those before us in the Hall of Khalandhriel.' The effort of speaking was almost more than the magnificent librarian could stand. Whatever his captors had done to him, they had done it perfectly.

Octavius looked up at the cruciform Angel and exhaled, weighing up the possibilities in his mind as the sounds of battle rattled through the bars and the roar of the crowd grew to a crescendo. He chanced a look into the arena and saw the startling white shape of Dhrykna springing to her feet with a new weapon in her hands, next to the crumpled form of a dead dark eldar wych. Taking a moment, he nodded his admiration for the alien warrior – she was a worthy ally on this forsaken world.

'Did you learn anything of our hosts in transit, Ashok?'

'I was not alone in the brig of that corsair, Octavius. There were also two Ulthwé seers. But they were not prisoners like me. They were passengers. They were proud and pompous, like the worst of their kind, arrogant and offensive with no self-consciousness. They bragged to me. They told me that I was being traded with their darkling cousins. They laughed. Over and over again, they laughed, chuckling about the stupidity and short-sightedness of the Imperium. They talked about the ancient Coven of Isha – they knew all about it, Octavius. They said that the coven had been sealed with a specific event in mind, and that we were now in the midst of it – an event that Eldrad Ulthran had seen clearly, but that the Imperium had been too blind to see at all. There was, in fact, a third side to the bargain, one which they assumed we knew nothing about.'

'With the dark eldar?' asked Atreus, the story beginning to resonate with what he already knew about the ways of Ulthwé.

'Yes, Blood Raven, with the darklings.' Ashok tried to nod, but his neck seemed too weak to support the weight of his head. 'The coven would provide Ulthwé with a squadron of Adeptus Astartes at exactly the time that the darklings began to demand the souls of warriors for their daemonic patrons. Instead of sacrificing its own warriors, Ulthwé could send us and then slip away through the webway.'

'The new, shifting warp signature in this sector...' pondered Octavius out loud, putting the pieces together in his head.

'Yes, it is the emergence of a Slaanesh-daemon – a princess – fed by the sacrifices of the darklings here on Hesperax.'

'Could Ulthwé not avoid this?' asked Atreus, as he struggled to tally the events with his understanding of the abilities of the eldar farseers. 'Could they not have seen it coming and moved aside?'

'Why would they?' fumed Pelias. 'This costs them nothing except our trust. And we should never have trusted them in the first place.'

Ashok coughed in agreement with the scarred and sceptical sergeant. 'Some things cannot be avoided, Atreus. Others simply are not avoided. Ulthran found a solution to this problem centuries ago, so there was no need to avoid this. We are his solution.'

'But his solution permits the emergence of a Slaanesh daemon into the Circuitrine nebula,' realised Octavius. 'It will cost millions, perhaps even billions of lives.'

'Yes. But Ulthwé will be long gone by then. The eldar will be safe, and that is his only concern.' Ashok's logic was flawless. 'The strength of our souls will release the daemon from the warp if the wych queen is able to sacrifice them appropriately. Ulthwé will be safe and the dark eldar of Hesperax will have satisfied their patrons. It is perfect.'

'What about the other Ulthwé captives? We saw the raiders taking prisoners on their sorties.' Sulphus was still suspicious, unwilling to be convinced so easily.

'Expendable, weak souls,' replied Ashok. 'They were merely bait to lure us here and to activate the coven. They were not enough to satisfy the darklings, and not significant enough for their loss to concern Ulthwé.'

Sulphus peered up at the hanging librarian and nodded slowly. It made sense. At exactly that moment, there was a massive intake of breath around the auditorium and then an abrupt and unnatural silence. Not a single voice or sound seemed audible.

The Deathwatch Marines turned away from Ashok, facing out through the bars into the arena. The scene appeared frozen, as though captured in a glorious fresco on the wall of an ancient hall of valour. There were corpses strewn over the blood-slicked ground and only one warrior remained on her feet. Dhrykna of the Shining Path stood in the centre of the arena, her glittering white armour dripping with the darkly toxic ichor that had spilt and spurted from the veins of her challengers. One foot rested on the decapitated skull of a darkling wych as she held her stolen weapon victoriously above her head. Streams of darkling blood coursed down the hilt of the blade, trickling around her hands and cascading down her arms. Pierced on the tip of the blade, held high for everyone to see, was the head of Quruel, mistress of the beasts.

The Aspect Warrior threw back her head and let out a tremendous cry, cutting through the shocked and oppressive silence that filled the amphitheatre. It was a cry of victory and despair. It was a cry of defiance. It was the bloodcurdling sound of an exarch of Khaine, the bloody-handed god. Dhrykna had found herself in the arena, and she had lost herself utterly.

THERE WAS NO mistaking the shifting warp signature now. It ballooned and blossomed like an immense weather front coasting out of the fringes of the great Eye and engulfing the neighbouring system. It showed up red and brooding on Seishon's viewscreen as the inquisitor lord regarded it in silence. His mind was racing.

A small, bright burst of light suddenly flared in the middle-distance, and Seishon fancied that he could discern the suggestion of a frigate powering its way towards the Circuitrine nebula. He couldn't really see that far. The only detail that he could discern without activating the image amplifiers was the burst of fire from the vessel's engines. But his imagination was running away from him. In his mind's eye he could see every detail of the Grey Knights' ship as it roared through the thick, soupy space on the edge of Ramugan's Reach, ploughing through the warp seepage that curdled together with the vacuum of real, material space. He could even make out the Liber Daemonica insignia on the hull, glittering and proud like a nauseating beacon of despair and hope. Even when he shut his eyes, he could see it tormenting him.

On the deck of the speeding *Titanicus Rex*, the fastest and most venerable of the Grey Knights' fleet currently birthed at Ramugan, Seishon could imagine the heroic and magnificent figure of Captain Mordia, standing with pride and resolve cut across his angular features. He would be making all possible haste towards the warp cloud that had begun to reach its vaporous tendrils into the outlying systems around the Circuitrine nebula, his will bent on uncovering and destroying the merest hint of a daemonic threat to the Imperium. In that moment, Seishon felt a surge of hatred for the valiant and honourable captain together with a wave of resentment about his simplistic view of the galaxy. If only things were really that simple.

He snorted in disgust at the lack of sophistication that he attributed to the near-legendary Grey Knight, and then his thoughts turned back to Vargas, whose lack of sophistication was itself legendary in Seishon's mind.

Throwing back another glass of rich, red wine, Seishon felt his head swim slightly. The narcotic effect of the drink was beginning to make itself felt at last, and its value as a tranquilliser started to become obvious. The inquisitor lord had always been highly strung, but the events of the last day or two had stretched his already frayed nerves to breaking point. His mind was being turned inside out, and he was no longer confident that he could trust his own judgement, let alone the counsel of that bumbling fool Vargas.

According to the chivalrous Captain Octavius, Vargas's own pet Deathwatch Marine, Librarian Ashok had vanished. This was not wholly unexpected news for Seishon, since he had directed the Angel Sanguine on a slightly different mission from the rest of the team. However, if Ashok was truly missing then this was potentially a disaster. Vargas had warned about the crucial importance of maintaining the integrity of the team, but he completely failed to understand the real importance of Ashok's disappearance. Even if the noble Octavius was successful in carrying out Vargas's will, if Ashok failed then the mission became worse than pointless.

The problem was not that the absence of Ashok weakened the team – although it surely did – since any well-chosen team should be able to withstand a few casualties. The problem, rather, was that Vargas's mission briefing was wholly inadequate for the challenges that the team would probably face. He simply failed to understand that the eldar of Ulthwé were not his friends, no matter what was written in the ancient coven.

The problem with Vargas was not his stupidity *per se*, but rather that he was simply too trusting. It was almost as though he had been enchanted by the eldar and his precious 'Lord Ulthran.' How could he really believe that the devious and cunning Eldrad

Ulthran would activate the Coven of Isha for their mutual advantage? Had he learnt nothing of that beautiful and terrible farseer over the last decades? Did he really think them so superficial and lacking in sophistication?

Before he had disappeared, Ashok had made a report that the dark eldar might be involved in the situation in some way. Again, this was not the shock to Seishon that it would have been to Vargas. The Ordo Xenos of Ramugan were not utterly naïve about the intricate web of relationships that might exist between the eldar of Ulthwé and their even darker and altogether less palatable brethren. Although he had no way of knowing the exact state of the allegiances and plans at any one time, Seishon was wily enough to anticipate that there may well be some involvement from the dark eldar, especially in that area of the sector.

In the back of his mind, he suspected that the oscillating warp signature on the edge of the Eye of Terror might have something to do with them, but he had nothing other than his paranoia to support his suspicions.

As he poured himself another glass of wine and gazed into the vanishing wake of the *Titanicus Rex*, Seishon's dizzying thoughts began to spin around the image of Ashok. Despite Vargas's faith in the valiant Captain Octavius, and despite his obvious qualities as both a commander and a warrior, Seishon began to realise that he had effectively placed the success of the mission solely into the hands of the Angels Sanguine librarian. Even if the Deathwatch team was to fulfil its duty under the terms of the coven, that was not going to be enough, and it seemed laughably naïve to think that he and Vargas had dispatched the team to Ulthwé with those orders.

They were not dealing with an ork scouring or even a tau trade dispute; this was a delegation to the eldar, and to the eldar of Ulthwé at that. In hindsight, Seishon could not believe that he had let Vargas permit that do-gooder Imperial Fist to assemble the team. What had they been thinking? His mind rushed back to the point of contact with Ulthran, and the realisation struck him like a fist: the eldar farseer had appeared only to Vargas and never to him. Unlike Seishon, Vargas had almost no psychic powers or defences – it was not inconceivable that the old fool had *actually* been enchanted by the conniving Ulthran, who had ensured that his contact was only with the weaker of the two minds.

The wine glass slipped out of Seishon's hands and smashed on the hard ground, shattering into vicious shards of glass in the pool of blood red liquid. In the Emperor's name, he cursed, what have we done? The eldar had manoeuvred him perfectly, creating a situation in which his own sense of confidence and prestige had caused him to both dispatch the Deathwatch Marines and to jeopardise the integrity of the team, producing an expedition that could fail because of his own interference and which could threaten the system even if it succeeded. On the cusp of an emerging disaster, his basic drive for self-preservation resulted in a moral crisis in which his own soul was placed in the scales of justice against those of millions of faceless subjects of the Imperium.

The *Titanicus Rex* finally vanished from view and Seishon could not stop himself from smiling. Compared to Mordia, Octavius and even Vargas, the scheming eldar were his kind of people. If he was going to be brought down, it would not be a disgrace to fall at the hands of millennia of careful planning. But it was not over yet. There was no confirmation that Ashok was lost, and Octavius himself was nothing if not tenacious.

CHAPTER TEN:
SEDITION

THE TENDRIL OF sha'iel left vapour streaked marks drawn over the immaculate curve of Lelith's pale shoulder. The wych queen felt a thrill rush through her body, like a yearning, but she squashed it immediately. This was not the time for her to lose her concentration.

After a few seconds, the tendrils that raked across her back seemed to transform into fingers, soft and delicate but tipped with long nails like razors. Despite herself, Lelith flexed her perfect shoulder blades, pulling the skin on her back taught so that she could enjoy the painful caresses even more. She could even feel herself leaning back slightly, as her body strove to press itself against the agonisingly delicate touch of the daemonic form.

The Wych Queen of Strife caught herself on the brink of the abyss and pulled her mind back into the material realms of her Seer Chamber, high up in one of the fortress towers of Sussarkh's Peak. She may be the unassailable queen of Hesperax, but she was also merely a darkling female craving the pleasures of her kind. Part of her mind longed for the visitations of the daemonic princess or even her more refined minions. Her soul cried out for their touch, and she knew that they could hear her barely suppressed screams of delectation. That was why they loved her. That was why they found her summons so powerful. That was how she could manipulate them.

The weakness of her flesh was also the strength of her soul – for she knew the perils of such temptations. She was no innocent, summoning powers about which she understood little and knew even less. She was Lelith Hesperax, Wych Queen of Strife, and the daemonic messengers of the Satin Throne held nothing that she could not anticipate.

They thought that her flesh was her weakness, but Lelith knew exactly how far she could go – she could take her pleasure from the minions of Slaanesh without abandoning herself to it. It was she who toyed with the daemons, not the other way around. This was something that they would learn to their cost if they crossed her again.

The runes etched into the curving walls of her tower chamber glowed and swirled, spinning around the walls as though trying to escape from the confines of the restricted space. Their movement seemed to stir the thick, smoky air, whisking tendrils of incense into thickening clouds of condensation until the outline of a body began to form. First its fingertips appeared, reaching out of the gathering mist as though a perfectly manicured woman was clawing its way out of the eye of a storm. After a few seconds, an elegant wrist was followed by the flawless, pale skin of a slender arm.

Cross-legged on the floor, Lelith watched the breathtaking body take shape before her, permitting herself a certain level of lustful appreciation as the last whispering fingers of vapour were absorbed into the immaculate female form. Never before had the daemon princess committed so much of herself into the material realm. Lelith was fascinated and, for a moment at least, entranced.

It is good to see you. Lelith's thoughts were slick like oil, but she had rarely meant something quite so sincerely.

The princess regarded Lelith quizzically, tilting its perfect, oval head to one side as though coy. Great cascades of translucent, shimmering hair crashed over the exposed skin of her faultless shoulder as she angled her head.

Yes. The thoughts came from nowhere and everywhere at once. *I suspect it is.*

As the apparition communicated, its mouth moved as though speaking, but the words and the movements did not coincide. Even more disconcertingly, as the image of the princess opened its mouth Lelith could see straight through it – she could see the now stationary runes burning brightly on the wall behind.

Do I please you? The princess's image seemed genuinely concerned as she cast her eyes over her own form, inspecting her body for blemishes and imperfections. She found none.

Lelith smiled. She was nobody's fool. *You are beautiful.*

At that, the princess raised her head and looked straight into Lelith's face. For the first time, Lelith could see the princess's eyes, and they were more than enough to remind her that this was all an illusion. Like her mouth, the eyes were simply pockets of nothingness – Lelith could see straight through them to the far wall of her chamber. The incongruity of the astoundingly beautiful body together with the vacuous eyes and mouth was almost physically painful for Lelith.

Yet, I am not perfect? I do not yet please… enough?

Not yet, mistress. Lelith sighed ambiguously. *But the time will come.*

Our plans are progressing as anticipated, I presume? The princess's words held a disarming mixture of coyness and self-confidence. She wore her immense power as lightly and delicately as a silken glove, like a daemon princess in the form of a fragile girl.

Yes, mistress, answered Lelith, drawn in by the intoxicating manner. *The predictable and foolish lightlings have honoured their side of our bargain, as we expected. Their sense of nobility makes them pathetically simple to read. We have the mon-keigh warriors in our cells even as we speak.*

And they will fight for me?

They will fight for themselves, mistress. The mon-keigh are even more predictable than the Ulthwé. They will fight until they draw their very last breaths – their souls will be raging and full of passion when they charge screaming into your arms.

Though they will not fight for me?

They will fight for themselves, and I will render their energy into a sacrifice for you. Fear not, mistress, they need not choose you, they need only fight – I have chosen you for them.

We need only a few more souls – just a handful of powerful lives to complete my transmigration, Lelith.

The princess used Lelith's name and the wych thrilled, feeling a wave of pleasure pulse through her nervous system like lava. For a moment, an image of the princess's perfected form flickered into Lelith's mind: her eyes burning and radiant, full of exquisite pain and ineffable places, and her mouth a haven for lascivious pleasures and utterances of death. The breathtaking image expanded into a glorious scene, with the daemon princess at the head of a treacherous and beautiful army storming out of the Eye of Terror with Lelith at her side, scything through the populations of the Imperium and harvesting their souls in an orgy of indulgence.

My power is growing, Lelith of Strife. Even the Imperium of Man can no longer be blind to it. My minions are pushing against the borders of your realm and seeping through into the materium of space. They are little more than a mist to you, but from my throne I can see them teeming and terrible, thirsty for death, conquest and agonising pleasure. Your sacrifices have brought us this far, but now we must take the last step, and we must do it now. Our secrecy is quite exploded, and we must act now. Now, Lelith… The image of the princess reached down and lifted the wych's chin with her exquisite fingernail. *Now.*

* * *

FROM THE BLOOD slicked luxury of the elevated platform that was set into the sheer wall of the
amphitheatre, Lelith and her honoured guests
watched the Deathwatch Marines being led back
into the arena. This time they were guarded by more
than thirty wyches, each wielding ceremonial,
bladed weapons. The nerve-pins had all been
removed from the vital points on the Marines' bodies, so their movements were now unrestricted and
their minds relatively uncluttered. Hence the heavier
guard. They had not been given any weapons, and
Lelith was still not sure whether she would grant
them the honour of blades when their time came to
die.

Bhurolyn of the Sacred Star stood at Lelith's shoulder, breathing in the intoxicating fragrance of her
hair as discretely as he could manage, his blue eyes
twinkling with forbidden and secret pleasure. His
companion, Xhelkisor, a minor seer who was yet to
be granted a seat on the Seer Council of Ulthwé,
stood a respectable distance behind them, her hazel
eyes fixed on the parade of mon-keigh muscle that
was crossing the arena below.

Her arms were folded across her chest, pulling her
sapphire robes close about her slight form. Despite the
fact that this was a historic moment, she was not terribly impressed: the mon-keigh looked like lumbering
primitives and the darklings were simply too unsani-
tary to be worthy of much respect. The honour of being
chosen for the mission by Thae'akzi of the Emerald
Robes herself was undermined somewhat by the utter
lack of awe that she felt when confronted with the reality of the situation. She found herself repulsed by

everything around her, and she was trying not to let anything touch her, even as subordinates busied themselves around the platform and the disgusting, semi-organic thronelings aspired to the occasional touch from Lelith's skin. Pulling her cloak even tighter around her, Xhelkisor found herself wondering how much longer she would have to put up with this.

Not long, my dear.

The thoughts were not her own, and they shocked her. They had an ineffable kind of gravity, and a smooth, sickly quality that made them hard to hang on to. As soon as she realised that they were in her head, they were gone, like oil running through her fingers. Looking around the platform, there was no obvious source – none of the wyches were even looking in her direction, and Bhurolyn's thoughts were of an entirely different consistency. Something in the darkest recesses of her soul told her that the thoughts had been those of Lelith, but the wych queen showed no signs of paying her any attention at all – she was grinning with anticipation at the spectacle of the captive mon-keigh down below.

They will make a worthy spectacle, Lelith. Bhurolyn's casual and intimate tone was inappropriately familiar; he was addressing the Wych Queen of Strife.

I have no doubts about it, seer. Lelith's thoughts eased back into Bhurolyn's mind, hissing like a snake, but she did not turn to face him. She could feel him inhaling her scent and she pretended to be preoccupied with the procession of mon-keigh.

Are you satisfied that we have upheld our end of the bargain? Never ask a darkling wych whether you have given her enough.

Very slowly, Lelith turned to face the Seer of the Sacred Star, bringing her own staggeringly beautiful features directly into his face so that he could feel her breath against his skin. She could see his excited blue eyes widen in thrilled surprise. The eldar of Ulthwé had a very different concept of personal space from the wyches of Hesperax, for whom intimacy was a proper aspect of everyday communication.

Lelith knew that a female eldar might never have stood this close to Bhurolyn in his entire life. She eyed him up and down as though for the first time, taking his measure: aside from his glorious sapphire robe, which she noticed matched that of his apprentice, he was a dishevelled and unattractive figure. His physique was poor, even for a pathetic lightling seer: he was clearly advanced in age and his sedentary lifestyle had not helped him to stay in shape.

The lightlings were usually slender and fit creatures, but this one had a belly and the remnants of what were once muscles hung loosely from his skeleton. Set deeply into his gaunt face, his eyes were bright with knowledge, but they burned with the kind of innocence that Lelith's soul cried out to violate. If this was the best that Ulthran could muster, perhaps she should not have agreed a bargain with the wily old farseer after all.

I am never satisfied. It was true.

Bhurolyn's eyebrows twitched slightly, as though the reply had surprised or titillated him. Lelith could see the strain across his features as he fought the conflicting urge to step back and the desire to remain where he stood.

As she watched him, the sense of frivolity that had pervaded her mood began to wane. This creature was not worthy of her attention, even of this kind of flippant flirtation. She simply could not believe that this was the best that Ulthran could send. He was weak and pathetic. Even standing in his face made his soul quake with emotions that he could neither recognise nor control. His mind was full of anxiety, even to the point of hysteria. This seer might be knowledgeable and useful on a council for the cowardly Ulthwé, but he was less than nothing to Lelith.

Why are you here, Bhurolyn of the Sacred Star?

I came to bring you your sacrifices, Lelith, at the request of the mighty Ulthran himself. His reply was full of pride, and Lelith even thought that she could see his chest swell slightly as he thought of the ancient farseer.

Does it not strike you as odd, seer of Ulthwé, that your prisoner required an escort? If thoughts could smile, then the vague beginnings of a grin were creeping into Lelith's.

Bhurolyn paused for a moment, thoughtful and quiet. He was finding it difficult to concentrate with Lelith's breath caressing his cheeks. *No. The psyker broke away from the rest of the mon-keigh, just as Ulthran said that he would. While Shariele and Dhrykna escorted the rest, Xhelkisor and I would escort this one. Consistency is the soul partner of good sense, after all.*

Lelith gave him an incredulous and slightly repulsed look. She often wondered how the lightlings could survive according to their pithy maxims and pathetic codes, but she had never come across any of her pale cousins who would dare to

quote them directly to her. There was only a small
logical step between such cheap wisdom and a ser-
mon on the merits of the Path of the Eldar, and if
this seer started down that road with her she would
kill him herself, Slaanesh be damned.

Before she responded, Lelith's lip curled into an
involuntary snarl as she let her mind wander
towards the laughable Path of the Eldar. She had
been there all those millennia before when the great
and the wise had constructed the path. She had seen
them bumbling and conniving in short-sighted fool-
ishness. Even now she could not believe that the
craftworld eldar had so easily and voluntarily sur-
rendered their natures and their potential, all in the
name of cowardice. Ulthran had been the worst of
them, fleeing into the darkest reaches of space and
hobbling his own people so that they could not fight
the great enemy even if the elusive craftworld of
Ulthwé was ever found. And now look what he
sends to Lelith, Wych Queen of Strife, a pathetic,
weak and feeble-minded fool.

*But why, my dear misguided Bhurolyn? Why did the
mon-keigh require escorts at all? Were not my wyches
there with you? Was it not they who captured and
restrained the primitive humans?* It was like talking to
a child.

Confusion appeared on the seer's face. It started
on his brow, furrowed and tense, and then spread
across his features, knotting crow's feet into the corners of his eyes and tweaking the edges of his
mouth.

There, thought Lelith to herself. *At last he is beginning to see.*

You mean…

Yes, I mean that you are part of the bargain, seer of Ulthwé. Your precious Lord Ulthran has sent your souls to seal the deal, although I cannot imagine that they are worth very much. It is actually rather insulting for us both.

The Seer of the Sacred Star looked dumbfounded as Lelith turned away from him dismissively and watched the Deathwatch Marines being formed into a line at the edge of the arena, awaiting her pleasure. They were an impressive if ramshackle sight – Lelith took a moment to hope that her new haemonculus had not damaged them.

Xhelkisor had advanced to the very lip of the platform and was peering down into the auditorium with an expression that suggested she saw it as little more than a pit of filth. She had been excluded from the exchange between her master, Bhurolyn, and the wych queen, and so had become bored. Now she stood with her back to them, gazing down at the blood-lined arena, waiting for something to justify her presence. In amongst the line of the mon-keigh barbarians, she could see the brilliance of Dhrykna's Aspect Armour shimmering and white like a pearl of guilt. She had not yet seen the pale shock that had descended across Bhurolyn's face. So, when she felt the gentle prod of Lelith's stiletto pointed heel push into the back of her knee, causing her leg to buckle and her balance to fail, she had no idea that she was being cast down into the repugnant arena below on purpose.

THE YOUNG SEER hit the ground hard, snapping her left leg in two places and crumpling into a bleeding heap. As she looked back up the sheer wall at the side of the arena with the jeering cries of the assembled darklings coruscating in her ears, she saw the magnificent, ceremonial robes of Bhurolyn fluttering on the lip of Lelith's platform, transforming him into the image of a massive, flightless bird. His heels were already hanging over the drop, and only the toes of his thin boots had any purchase on the wych queen's platform. For a moment, the wheeling actions of his arms seemed to defeat the force of gravity, and the Seer of the Sacred Star teetered on the brink. Xhelkisor could imagine the expression on the old eldar's face, his eyes bulging with panic as he realised that the council had betrayed him and that he was about to fall dozens of storeys into a darkling fighting pit.

Watching the flailing old seer tumble and flutter as he fell, Xhelkisor reflected that there were worse ways for a craftworld eldar to die. Although her body was broken already, and she had no hope of survival let alone victory in the arena, she knew that her death was required for the fulfilment of Lord Ulthran's grand design.

There was a kind of cold solace in the realisation that her life was not being discarded meaninglessly, even though it was being discarded by the Seer Council of Ulthwé. She had watched Shariele of the Undercouncil incinerate himself in the flames of his own power, and she had not felt even a twinge of pity. She had known that his death was necessary for the good of Ulthwé and she had known that he would have given his life willingly if only he had been asked. Standing over amid the mon-keigh,

Xhelkisor could only imagine that Dhrykna felt the same.

As Bhurolyn slammed into the ground next to her, throwing up a cloud of dust and blood, Xhelkisor considered how much better it would have been had someone actually asked them to perform this duty – but then, the council of Ulthran was never so straightforward. Deceit was part of the Eldar Way.

The darklings in the audience seemed to hold their breaths. There was a faint sniggering, but a new aura of quiet anticipation had spread around the stands.

Master Bhurolyn. Her thoughts were weak and without much hope. The old seer was weak and fragile, and she did not expect that he would have survived the fall. *Master Bhurolyn*, she repeated, pulling herself painfully up onto one foot and staring in horror at the mess that remained of her other leg.

As she limped and dragged herself over towards the cloud of dust and debris that marked her master's landing site, the sound of heavy doors grinding open made her pause and look up. A huge crack had appeared in the wall underneath Lelith's platform and the great doors were slowly rolling open – threads of putrid smoke and fragmented beams of light were already spilling out of the widening gap. The audience could not stand the anticipation any more, and they started to scream and bray like excited animals.

The cloud of dust that had been kicked up by the impact of the Seer of the Sacred Star began to settle as Xhelkisor approached it. She narrowed her eyes against the swirling grit and steam, trying to discern the broken shape of Bhurolyn inside. The ground looked uneven and broken, strewn with fragmentary objects, and for a moment Xhelkisor wondered whether her master's old, fragile body had simply disintegrated on impact, unable to withstand the trauma.

Xhelkisor. She recognised the thought tone instantly, but she could not understand where it was coming from. *Xhelkisor, we will not survive this, and it seems that we were never supposed to. But we can make an end that will be worthy of the Sacred Star and of Ulthran himself. If the farseer chose us for this purpose, he must have had his reasons.*

Xhelkisor looked around her, trying to catch a glimpse of Bhurolyn. His thoughts seemed strong and confident, in a way that she had never heard them before. The old seer was usually a bumbling mess of anxieties and conventions. Listening to the strength of his convictions, she realised that Ulthran's decision to send him to Hesperax was not merely because he was an expendable old fool. The ancient farseer could see into the souls of every eldar, and he had known Bhurolyn for longer than Xhelkisor had even been alive – if anyone could see the nature of the seer's heart, it was Ulthran. Perhaps Bhurolyn was meant to be a last surprise for Lelith?

A silent pulse rolled through the ground, rippling out from the diminishing cloud that marked the point of Bhurolyn's fall. It rolled through the arena, making its surface ripple and swell like water. Silence gripped the audience once again.

An explosion of light erupted, shrugging off the cloud of dust and filling the amphitheatre with the starkest shadows that it had seen in centuries. Hundreds of darklings gasped and shielded their eyes in admiration and horror.

The light vanished as quickly as it had appeared, as though being suddenly sucked back into its source like a kind of anti-explosion, leaving the dignified figure of Bhurolyn standing proudly in its epicentre, his long, luxurious sapphire cloak billowing out behind him. *I have grown too old, Xhelkisor. Too old and weak. The council no longer respects me. How could I have hoped for a last chance of glory like this. My lord Ulthran can see into my heart, and he does great honour to this decrepit and dying body. I will not fail him, and I will not fail myself at the last.*

With that, Bhurolyn punched forward and sent a javelin of power crackling through the arena. It slammed into the massive, slowly opening doors and blew them apart, shattering them instantly and sending shards of metal and masonry flying around the amphitheatre like hail caught in a hurricane. *Bring it on.* His thoughts were impatient and his blue eyes burnt with violence.

The crowd went wild.

The darkling guards were distracted as soon as the female seer had been pushed off the elevated platform. When the second seer crashed down into the arena with such drama, the excitable and distracted guards seemed to forget all about their prisoners, turning their backs on them to face the show: they were as good as dead anyway. If there was anything that appealed more profoundly to the soul of a dark eldar wych than the prospect of visiting violence on prisoners, it was the actual occurrence of violence itself. Next to the unfolding drama in the arena, the mon-keigh prisoners just seemed uninteresting.

The great gladiatrix gates that were set into the wall beneath the queen's podium had been grinding open with ominous weight when the sapphire seer had reduced them to rubble. Three or four somersaulting wyches had already bounded out of the widening gap, spreading themselves around the perimeter of the arena to surround the two seers in the middle. In the black shadows beyond the half-ruined gates, the sound of heavy footfalls told everyone that the wyches were just the start of the show.

For all of his apparent frailties and cowardice, the male seer was ablaze with power and defiance. His hands burned with bolts of sha'iel, which he formed into spherical projectiles before launching them around the arena at the circling wyches. After a couple of dramatic trials, he had abandoned his assault on Lelith's podium in order to turn his attention to the immediate crisis that engulfed him.

Meanwhile, the injured and lame female seer was supporting her weight on the elongated leg bone of a recently deceased warp beast, using it like a crutch under one arm. With her other hand, she was spraying a hail of sha'iel shards around the arena, imitating the discharge of a shuriken cannon.

The amphitheatre was alive with the keening of the darkling audience and the fury of escalating combat in the arena itself. High above the tumult, Lelith stood gloriously on her blood-soaked platform, surveying the scene with a wide, wild and sinister grin drawn across her unspeakably beautiful face.

The Deathwatch Marines and Dhrykna of the Shining Path stood in a line behind the distracted guards. They were unhindered by nerve-pins and were struck with amazement by the events that were unfolding around them. It seemed that the council of Ulthwé had not only double-crossed its human partners in the Coven of Isha, but it had also betrayed its own seers, leaving them to die in sacrificial combat here on Sussarkh's Peak.

Without a word, Dhrykna darted forward, her now scarred and battle damaged white armour still glinting like a fleck of sullied innocence in the enshrouding darkness. She leapt into the air, clasping her hands around the head of one of the darkling guards in front of her as she twisted and spun over into the arena; she landed crisply in front of it, facing back to where its face should have been, but she held its now detached head clutched in her hands.

A dramatic second passed before the darkling's decapitated body collapsed to the ground at Dhrykna's feet, and she snatched its darkly glinting bladed weapon from its dead hands. Sparing a moment to nod a farewell to Octavius, she turned and dashed towards the centre of the arena where her fellow sacrificial eldar were fighting a glorious but losing battle.

At precisely the moment that the rest of the darkling guards realised that something had gone wrong, the Deathwatch Marines threw themselves forward, breaking the backs, necks and limbs of the slender aliens as though they were kindling. Without the constraints of the nerve-pins, the Space Marines were far stronger than the dark eldar wyches when it came to brute power, and the shock attack from behind afforded the aliens no chance to capitalise on their great speed and skill.

Instinctively, the Marines reached down and picked up the darklings' weapons. Because there were so many more ruined guards than prisoners, the team was able to equip itself with one weapon in each hand. Without pausing for discussion, Sulphus, Pelias and Luthar turned towards the doors through which they had been ushered into the arena, set on escaping the arena of death. This battle was between the eldar and their darkling cousins; it had nothing to do with them.

Kruidan, the Mantis Warrior whose egregious wounds had been painfully but carefully healed by the haemonculi so that he might suffer more greatly in the arena, turned to follow his battle-brothers, then he stopped. Because of the attentions of the haemonculi, he was without the armour that usually covered his upper body, and his pale, intricately tattooed flesh glistened in the half-light. Octavius, Atreus and Ashok had not moved; they were standing shoulder to shoulder and staring in at the figures of the embattled eldar. In a moment of realisation, the Mantis Warrior knew what they were about to do and he returned to his captain's side.

All around the auditorium, the dark eldar audience was alive with passion, shrieking and braying like wild animals, seemingly unable to control their excitement about the ongoing battle in the arena.

Nonetheless, one or two pairs of glowering eyes had already turned towards the figures of the Death-watch Marines. Fingers were beginning to point and a new wave of hysterical excitement seemed to ripple through the crowd. Not a single dark eldar in the stands reached for a weapon or vaulted down into the arena to confront the Marines; perhaps they thought it was all part of the show.

'The sacrifice of those eldar is part of the dark queen's plan to free her daemon,' muttered Octavius, his barely audible voice tinged with disbelief about the conclusion to which his thoughts were racing. 'We must not permit the darklings to take their souls. Though they betrayed us, we are allies in this fight. There is a greater evil in the wings than the treachery of Ulthwé.'

The others said nothing. They knew that their valiant captain was right, and they simply nodded their understanding, keeping their eyes fixed on the maelstrom of shrieks, warp fire and flashing blades that had filled the arena before them. After a second, Octavius raised his blades and roared his defiance into the arena, charging forward into the fray with his weapons lashing furiously around him. Immediately, Ashok and Atreus unleashed javelins of crackling power from the tips of their blades, and then stormed after their captain. Kruidan paused for a moment, struck through with admiration for the Imperial Fists' unerring and clear-headed sense of duty. This mission was no longer about fulfilling the Coven, but about preventing its realisation.

Standing square with the field of battle, the Mantis Warrior dragged the tip of his stolen glaive diagonally across his chest, drawing a deep and symbolic gash through his flesh in the ritual manner of the Praying Mantidae. It was a sign that he was unconcerned by pain or death, even if death was ready and waiting for him. He took a breath, muttering a litany of composure and hate, and then he pounded into the arena after his battle-brothers.

Just as they reached the doors at the edge of the amphitheatre, Pelias, Luthar and Sulphus turned to see what was going on. They saw four glorious Space Marines ploughing through the thickening mire of combat, hacking and blasting their way through the wyches and snarling warp beasts, ablaze with heroism and battling towards the beleaguered eldar in the very centre of the ring. They paused as they realised what their selfless captain was doing and, one by one, they turned back into the arena, pangs of shame and disbelief intermixing with admiration in their souls.

By THE TIME the remains of the massive gladiatrix gates had finally ground open to their widest extent, the arena was already soaked with blood and strewn with the charred and hacked remains of half a dozen darkling wyches. The Deathwatch team and the eldar had formed a ring in the centre of the arena, each standing at another's back, forming a gravitational centre that seemed to suck the aliens into their doom, before scattering their bones out once again. It was as though all the darkness of Hesperax was being drawn towards them – with only the glinting shoulder plates of the Deathwatch and the radiant white of Dhrykna standing symbolically in the light.

Stolen blades flashed in the darkness, and jets of warp power lashed out of the phalanx of resistance.

'Captain!' yelled Kruidan as he ducked smoothly under the sweep of a darkling blade, the emerald greens and golds of the Chapter emblem on his shoulder whirling into streams of colour as he spun. The noise was incredible and, having been dispossessed of their helmets by the haemonculi, the Marines had no vox-beads. 'Captain!' he yelled again, stabbing one of his own blades through the neck of a scarred and sneering face as it lurched towards him, its teeth dripping with thirst.

Octavius was busy. Both of the blades that he had stolen from the guards were now shattered and broken – little more than stumps of metal in his hands. He was fending off the assault of two wyches, parrying their weapons with the armoured plates on his forearms and waiting for a gap through which he could strike back. With a sudden movement, he trapped a wych's blade between his palm and his other forearm and then spun around the point of impact as though it were a pivot, snapping the blade in the middle as he turned. Completing his rotation, he clasped the broken end of the blade and drove it into the side of the wych's head. She wailed as her eyes filled with blood, and then slumped to the ground.

At the same instant, Octavius felt a sharp, piercing cold stab into his kidney from behind. He dropped his weight, forcing his assailant to either withdraw or drop the blade, and turned sharply, bringing the stump of his remaining weapon around in a crude arc. The wych was ready for his counter, and she sprang backwards out of reach, releasing her grip on the blade that still protruded from the captain's lower back.

Even against the hideous and constant roar of the crowd, Octavius and the others could make out a distinct cheer of excitement as that blade struck home in the Imperial Fists' flesh. The assailant wych grinned maniacally, her eyes wild and burning with the thrill of combat and the narcosis of notoriety.

Pausing for a moment to take in the scene, Octavius saw that the crowd was still in the stands. They were full of excitement and approval, cheering and shrieking with ecstasy at the orgy of violence that was unfolding before them. Not one of them had descended into the arena and Octavius realised that this was exactly what they had all come to see: the human warriors doing battle against the gladiatrix wyches of Hesperax. Far from being an act of defiance, their battle was precisely what had been expected of them.

He roared in frustration. There was no way that he was going to stop fighting just to dispossess these vile creatures of their pleasure. He had spent his whole life in combat or in preparation for it, and he was not about to abandon himself to a weak and pathetic end. If these dark eldar wanted battle, he would give it to them, and he would teach them not to treat the Deathwatch as playthings in their barbaric games.

With another roar, he ripped the blade out of his flesh, tearing out a lump of abdomen and slicing off a section of his ceramite armour as he did so. The wych before him smiled, as though in approval that he had not been defeated by the poisoned surface of the curved sword. In mockery, Octavius smiled back and then hurled the sword. It spun end over end until stopping abruptly, impaled through the forehead of the still smiling wych.

Another massive cheer exploded from the stands. It was as though the crowd could hardly contain its excitement.

'Captain!'

Octavius pressed his boot against the neck of the dead wych and prised her head off his new sword before turning to find the source of the shout. It was the Mantis Warrior, his long black hair flying in a frenzy around him as the tattoos that snaked over his abdomen, neck and face seemed to writhe. Because his armour had been ruined in the fight at their landing site, much of it had been removed and discarded by the haemonculi, leaving him with only the gleaming emerald shoulder plate of his Chapter and the belt that bore the insignia of the Deathwatch on its buckle.

His pale, decorated and scarred skin shone with exertion and streams of blood. With both hands he wielded a long, double-bladed glaive, which he spun and flourished with the practiced ease of a warrior accustomed to gladiatorial practices. Not for the first time, Octavius was impressed by the first Mantis Warrior to serve the Deathwatch in a century.

With the deftest of gestures, flicking the tip of a blade as he parried and slashed, Kruidan indicated the ominous, gaping darkness that loomed between the gates to the arena. There seemed to be nothing there, except for the nauseating suggestion of dread.

The parade of wyches that had flipped and sprung their way into the amphitheatre had stopped; all of the gladiatrix darklings were already in position around the arena, prowling and menacing the Deathwatch and the eldar. So the blackness between the gates was yawning and pregnant with unseen terrors.

Standing in the midst of the fray as though utterly unconcerned by the teeming combat around him, Octavius stared over towards the open gates, focusing his gaze into the darkness beyond and trying to discern whether that was a route to salvation or doom. All around him, fighting was persisting in pockets of competition, with each Marine matched against one or two dark eldar wyches. In the absence of reinforcements, and considering the almost unbelievable reticence shown by the aliens in the crowd, Octavius began to think in terms of what to do after the Deathwatch had surmounted this challenge. It occurred to him that it would probably be best if they did not stick around to find out.

'Octavius,' boomed Ashok, unleashing a torrent of warp fire from his fists as he stepped up to the captain's shoulder. 'Octavius, we must not permit the wych queen to take the souls of those seers.' His voice was low and his intent was as dark as the shadow under his heavy hood. 'There is no way that they will survive this fight.'

The Deathwatch captain turned again. The two seers that had been thrown from the queen's podium had been separated from the rest of the group. Even the dazzling, white Aspect Warrior was no longer at their side – she was acrobatically busy with two other wyches that had cut her off from her brethren. The two seers were being hunted by five wyches, who prowled and vaulted in complicated patterns around them, easily evading the increasingly weak blasts of energy mustered by the two aging and crippled eldar. It was only a matter of time before Bhurolyn and the lame Xhelkisor would fall and the darklings would take their souls as the spoils of victory. They were too weak to survive Hesperax even if a miracle were to intervene in the arena.

Octavius nodded, acknowledging the unspoken wisdom of Ashok's words.

'See to it,' he said. 'I will investigate the gates. We need to find the spirit pool in which the queen is keeping her sacrifices. Despite all this,' he cast his arm around the scene of combat with the calm indifference of someone who was watching the conflict from a great distance, 'there is still the question of the ascension of the queen's daemon.'

Without a word, Ashok bowed curtly and then turned, striding off towards the embattled seers. He had long since abandoned the poisoned blades that he had lifted from the dark eldar guards, preferring to feel the snap of bone and the tearing of flesh in his hands, which now dripped with blood and crackled with unearthly powers. The haemonculi had not deprived him of his hood, which he now pulled deeply down over his face, hiding his reddening, glowering eyes in a new layer of shadow.

FROM THE CONTROL deck of the *Titanicus Rex*, Captain Mordia of the Grey Knights peered into the fractional future. The warp signatures around the fringes of the Eye of Terror were always tumultuous, but there was something shifting now – something threatening to emerge into the relatively heavy light of real space. He had seen it happen countless times before and he knew the signs.

Even before the ancient frigate had closed on the Circuitrine system, which lay half submerged in the lashes of the great Eye, fragments and shards of the warp were already evident, bleeding out of the unseen dimensions into the ostensible vacuum of space around it.

No alarms sounded on the *Rex*. Vessels in the service of the Grey Knights in this sector only rarely had their violation alarms active. They were constantly being dispatched into polluted space, and there was little point in rattling everyone's nerves with persistent alarms. Mordia had reflected more than once that it might be worth installing some form of purity alarm, which sounded when the vessel was no longer at risk of violation by daemonic powers. In general, however, he gave such trivial matters almost no thought at all.

From all over the ship, Mordia's squad sounded in. The *Titanicus Rex* was a sleek and elegant example of the best engineering that the Imperium could muster and it appeared massive from the outside. It was, however, smaller than a strike cruiser, but far larger than a normal rapid strike vessel. If appearances were not deceptive, it should have contained at least half a company of Marines with full support equipment. In fact, the venerable vessel was a dedicated gunship with only a single squad of Marines ensconced within, distributed throughout the vessel's decks and control centres. The greatest portion of the hull was occupied by gun batteries and relays; where there might have been stations for personnel, there were ammunition dumps and massive purification wards and the rear third of the frigate was taken up by a monumental engine, the likes of which would never be seen on a craft of a similar size anywhere else in the sector. The *Rex* was one of the finest strike vessels ever to have emerged from the great docks of Titan in the Emperor's very own solar system.

All of the gunnery emplacements around the hull were registering emergent targets. There was nothing yet solid enough for them to fire upon, but the targets were lingering on the edge of material existence, like suggestions of the future or memories of the past. As he watched the swirling patterns of ruddy mist gathering in the icy vacuum, Mordia's eyes scanned over the screen of the terminal that displayed the data from the long-range sensors. There was still nothing, not a single crisp, material signal or signature registered on the screen, despite the general background blur of activity in the warp that was spilling over into the material realm.

The *Titanicus Rex* roared onward through the thickening mire, ploughing deeper into the swirling eddies of mist that enshrouded the Circuitrine system, its gun turrets twitching and tracking constantly as potential targets oscillated in and out of existence. Whatever was waiting in the tortuous dimensions of the warp, it was pressing hard against the barriers of the material dimensions, clawing at the fabric of space-time. It could taste the promise of lives to possess and souls to steal, but it was not yet powerful enough to rip through. What was it waiting for, wondered Mordia?

Unphased by the gathering storm, Captain Mordia of the Grey Knights pressed on. After long decades of arduous training and dedicated service, he was well prepared for whatever might emerge from the unspeakable and invisible realms.

Let them come, he thought, staring out into the sullied mess of the space before his mighty and righteous vessel. Let them come, and we will show them the meaning of existence in this reality.

IT DIDN'T MATTER how many times she saw him; every time she met the curator, Perceptia had to fight against her own sense of revulsion. In an attempt to pre-empt her own instinctive discomfort, the inquisitor had removed her eyeglasses and thus transformed the two-faced creature into a somewhat featureless blur. It was a childish thing to do, and Perceptia felt sure that the four-eyed Seye Multinus would not be blind to it, but she had enough on her mind at the moment without extra, needless anxieties. The young inquisitor still found herself pushing her middle finger up along the ridge of her nose, as though to press back her glasses. In the absence of the spectacles, however, the gesture merely served to draw attention to the fact that she had removed them.

'Aah, Inquisitoror Persceptiaa. I'veve beenn waiting for youu.'

The strange echoing voice made her skin crawl. 'Greetings, Seye. Do you have anything for me?' Her voice was too perfectly controlled, making her manner seem forced and false.

'Yesyes,' hissed Seye, his two mouths spitting in excitement. He knew when he had found something important; it was what he lived for. If Perceptia had been wearing her glasses, she would have seen the barely contained eagerness glinting in the four eyes that stared back at her. 'Follow mee.'

With that, the bizarre little man turned and shuffled off through the document stacks, making almost no sound at all as his soft feet pressed against the dull, matted floor. With surprising speed, he led the inquisitor along a winding route between the innumerable shelves and bookcases until he reached the little desk at which Perceptia had been working earlier.

Perceptia's eyes widened as she emerged out of the darkness of the last aisle. Instinctively, she pressed her finger against the bridge of her nose, trying to push her glasses into place so that she could see more clearly, but they were not there. For a moment, she fumbled through her document pouch until she located her spectacles and returned them to her eyes.

'Which pile is which, Seye?' she asked, conscious that the curator's answer would be of only logistical significance at this point.

In her absence, Seye Multinus had taken all of the files, documents, and books down from the shelves along the aisle that had interested her. He had read through each and every sheet of paper and sorted them into two constellations of massive piles, one on each side of Perceptia's little desk. Casting her eyes from one side to the other, Perceptia could make out very little difference in terms of the distribution of documents or the size of the piles.

With obvious and sickly delight, Seye shuffled from one side of the desk to the other, pointing at the piles and picking out individual manuscripts whilst babbling away in his echoey and incoherent manner. After a few excited seconds, it seemed that the curator no longer knew which way to turn, so he stopped directly in front of the desk with one of his faces pointing in either direction. His mouths worked rapidly as his eyes darted over the titles along the spines of the files, but each mouth was reading a different line and the result was little more than a cacophonous outpouring of sibilance and excited, frothing spittle.

'Seye!' snapped Perceptia, trying to bring some semblance of quiet and order back to the hallowed spaces of the Hereticus librarium. She needed the quiet to be able to think properly, but she also needed Seye to calm down and explain what he had found and how he had organised the material that towered up around them.

The little curator creature flinched as though he had been struck, and he scurried off into the shadows of one of the nearby aisles, as if he were afraid that Perceptia would attack him. The long legacy of fear and abuse was not easily exorcised from his psyche, especially not in an atmosphere that was more full of suspicion and anxiety than it was of oxygen.

'Seye,' repeated Perceptia in the sudden, uncomfortable silence. Her voice dropped into a low velvet, and she did her very best to lend it an edge of compassionate appreciation. She had learnt a thousand ways to extract information from an uncooperative prisoner, but when it came to simple human communication she was rapidly reduced to being merely a bookish and socially retarded woman. Talking to people as though they were worthwhile human beings had never been Perceptia's forte, and it was even harder when she found herself talking to a two-faced, four-eyed mutant curator that was frothing from two mouths with evident over excitement.

'Seye, this looks most impressive. Can you please tell me which of the piles contain references to the Circuitrine Nebula? Time is a factor here, as you may appreciate.'

The curator slunk back out of the shadows, one of his mouths working silently as though unsure of what to say. Before it could mutter a single coherent word, the other mouth cut in. '–all off themem, inquisitoror.'

For a long moment, Perceptia did not say anything. She looked from Seye to the piles and then back again. 'All of them?'

'Yesyes,' echoed the curator, a hint of excitement returning to his voice. 'Everyy onene. Not onene withoutout Cirrtrinene. Not onene.'

'You looked at every document in that aisle?' asked Perceptia as she struggled to comprehend the implications of what Seye was saying. As she pointed down the aisle that she was talking about, her eyes followed the line of her own finger and she saw for herself that there was not a single sheet of paper left on those shelves.

Seye just nodded, his mouths smiling so broadly that they nearly cracked into a single, cavernous grin.

'Seye,' began Perceptia as her mind started to form a new string of suspicions. 'Did you know that they would all mention the Circuitrine system before you started looking?' If every confession in that section contained mention of that specific system, it seemed to Perceptia that they must have been filed in that location *because* they mentioned Circuitrine. The coincidence would simply be too unlikely.

Seye's four eyes widened in wild excitement, as though he was about to reveal the most important secret he had ever known.

To HIS SURPRISE, none of the wyches attempted to block Octavius's path towards the ruined gladiatrix gates that loomed out of the wall beneath their queen's ceremonial viewing platform. He saw some of them glance over in his direction as he strode through the arena, but not one broke off from her fight with the other Marines to intercept him.

At first, Octavius thought that this was because they dared not turn their backs on his Deathwatch battle-brothers, but then he realised that there was no panic or frustration in the looks that had been thrown at him. If anything, the manic, burning eyes of the aliens glinted with even more excitement when they saw where the captain was heading. In the crowd, a hush of anticipation had begun to settle over the hysteria. All eyes were gradually turning towards the captain, despite the other contests that still raged around the arena.

The crowd was treated to a magnificent sight: a squad of Deathwatch Marines was engaged hand-to-hand with the gladiatrix wyches of Hesperax in the grand arena of Sussarkh's Peak. The wych queen, Lelith of Hesperax, stood like an icon of terrible beauty, overseeing the ritual combat from her blood soaked throne platform; and a single mon-keigh warrior stood alone beneath her podium, defiant and proud against the impenetrable darkness that lay beyond the broken and yawning gates.

It was a scene worthy of transformation into a fresco for the halls of the Watchtower Fortress of Ramugan, or for the Hall of Lost Souls that lurked like a forgotten hell in the bowels of Sussarkh's volcanic mountain.

Octavius was unconcerned by the aesthetic quality of his dramatic pose. This was not a game for him. He paused for a moment before the yawning dark of the massive and crumbling gates, trying to discern what lay beyond, but then he simply spun his blades and strode forward. He was already cut off on an unknown planet in the fringes of the Eye of Terror, and utterly surrounded by hundreds of dark eldar warriors up in the stands. They had the high ground, and he was stranded in the bottom of a fighting pit with his team embattled and stretched.

This was no time to be concerned about strategy or calculation. This was not even the time for recourse to the *Codex*. This was the time for honour, courage and death.

As he stepped forward into the darkness, a mechanical whine and a rush of air made him dive back into the arena. He hit the ground hard, crashing down onto his back as a massive metallic talon bore down on him out of the dense shadows as though emerging from nowhere. Just in time, he rolled to one side and the reinforced point of the spike punched into the ground next to him, burying itself nearly a metre into the deck and sending debris exploding into the air.

The Imperial Fist was on his feet in an instant, dancing backwards to distance himself from the new threat and to identify it. Meanwhile, the crowd had exploded into a whole new level of frenzy. The atmosphere was dense with screams and wails of ecstasy. It was enough to make unprotected human ears ring with pain.

As he watched, a huge mechanical monstrosity emerged slowly out of the darkness beyond the gates. It was vaguely pyramidal, but with spikes, tusks and jagged angles sticking out of it like the spines of a warp beast. The protrusions were decorated with skulls and dismembered limbs, and coated in thick, bloody ichor.

From each of the two corners at the front, long pincers extended on slender mechanical arms; they reached and quested before the bizarre construction as it gently hovered forward out of the darkness and into the arena. Cut into the front of the assembly, between the two bladed arms, was a snarling metallic mouth, which gnashed and chewed continuously, venting plumes of noxious smoke each time the heavy jaws snapped shut. And from the rear of the hideous structure rose a terrible, arching talon, like the sting of a scorpion; it lashed forward, punching into the ground at Octavius's feet as he leapt clear for a second time.

The crowd thundered its maniacal thrill from the stands as Octavius looked from the slender, elegant blades in his hands to the huge, insane, torturous

device that had emerged before him. Completely surrounded and utterly outnumbered, having been
drawn into the Eye of Terror by the devious machina-
tions of the eldar and abandoned on the cursed, vile
planet of Hesperax, Octavius finally had to consider
the possibility that even a Deathwatch captain might
not be able to win every fight.

'Captain!'

The call came from behind him, but he had no time
to turn as he dived forward into a roll, ducking under
the stinging talon and coming up between the construct's forward pincers. Even before he could regain
his feet, the bladed arms lashed in at him from both
sides, forcing him to drop to the ground and roll clear
once again.

'Captain!'

There was genuine urgency in the cry from Atreus,
and Octavius thought that he could hear the pounding footfalls of the librarian charging towards him. At
the same time, the crowd roared to an incredible and
deafening pitch, just when it had seemed that they
could not possibly get any louder.

Glancing back over his shoulder as he attempted to
parry one of the lashing pincers with his feeble blade,
Octavius saw the radiant figure of the Blood Ravens
librarian storming through the arena towards him.
Out of the corner of his eye, he caught a glimpse of
another figure in the arena behind him, but before he
could look properly his blade snapped and the
mechanical pincer crashed into him, swatting him off
his feet and sending him skidding across the floor.

Rolling as he landed, Octavius craned his neck
around to see Atreus and Ashok prowling around

the new and beautiful figure in the arena, encircling her like predators around prey. She appeared undaunted and even slightly coy, with her arms folded self-consciously over her chest, and with blades held delicately in each hand. Her long black hair seemed to billow around her, as though caught in a daemonic breeze, and her exposed, pale skin glistened seductively. It was the wych queen herself – overcome by the voyeuristic thrill of combat, she had vaulted down into the arena to join in.

Her presence transformed the already blood drenched arena. The remaining wyches broke off from their engagements with the Marines, flipping and vaulting into retreat so that Lelith would be the unchallenged centre of attention as she battled the two librarians.

From his momentarily prone position, Octavius could see his team respond: Kruidan was already charging across the arena to assist his captain; Pelias and Luthar were giving chase to the fleeing wyches; and Sulphus was studying the mechanical monster that was attacking Octavius. As for the eldar, there was no sign of the two seers, so Octavius presumed that Ashok had already taken care of them, but the shimmering Aspect Warrior was slipping her way past the librarians to engage the wych queen herself.

As the new and rapidly changing situation registered in his mind, a sharp pain seared through Octavius's abdomen; something had punched down through his back as he lay on the ground distracted just for a second. Before he could respond, the huge talon erupted into a spray of spines that jabbed into his internal organs, securing itself in his flesh and yanking him up into the air. He roared in pain as the mechanical Talos construct brandished the Death-watch captain in the air like a trophy, and the crowd brayed in response, stamping their feet with thunderous approval.

Thrashing and twisting his body against the massive violations being done to it, Octavius hacked and smashed with the remains of his blade until it snapped again, collapsing under the furious violence of the captain's rage. With his weapons ruined, the Imperial Fist pounded with his hands, struggling to detach himself from the barbed talon that impaled him, but every movement simply drove the spines deeper into his flesh.

The crowd was going wild, and, even in the throes of such hideous agony, Octavius could tell that their attention was no longer being held by his own struggle with the Talos. He could hear the crackling discharge of warp energy and the metallic clatter of blades clashing. He could hear the yells as Ashok and Atreus tried to co-ordinate the attack on the wych queen, knowing that her death was their best chance of survival and victory. For the first time in his life, Octavius realised that he was little more than a sideshow, in so many ways.

KRUIDAN ARRIVED TOO late. As he launched himself through the air, driving his glaive out in front of him like a lance and punching it through the metal armour that covered the monstrous Talos, he knew that Octavius was already dead. As he ran, he had watched helplessly as the impaled captain had been flourished and brandished by the construct, thrashing him against the wall and the ground like a toy. Finally, just as the Mantis Warrior had closed with range, the Talos had ripped the captain clear of its sting, leaving a gaping hole in his stomach as the two front pincers held him up for the crowd to see one last time. Then, without ceremony, the pincers had pressed the heroic Marine between the massive, metallic, gnashing teeth in the front of the Talos, riddling him with puncture wounds before sucking him inside the terrible armoured shell. As he vanished from view, Kruidan thought that he had heard the captain's last defiant words, almost swamped in the cacophony of the arena: 'Primarch – Progenitor, to your glory and the glory of Him of Earth!'

CHAPTER ELEVEN:
FAILURE

As IT CONSUMED the captain, incarcerating him within its armoured shell and feeding on what remained of his life force, the Talos erupted into renewed frenzies of activity, thrashing its talon tail and lashing with its massive pincers. Kruidan was already upon it, climbing over its jagged shell and hanging on to the vicious spikes that stabbed out of its armour. He held his glaive in one hand, using it to jab down into the cracks between the armoured plates, trying to prise one off so that he could get inside. For some reason, he knew that there was probably no pilot in a well-hidden cockpit within – the Talos seemed to move with a will and a thirst of its own – but the Mantis Warrior didn't care. The hideous construct had taken the life of his captain, and he could not permit it to survive.

A terrible clanging and scraping noise alerted Kruidan to the presence of Sulphus, as the techmarine clambered up on top of the Talos, his various augmetic arms dragging him up over the pronged surface in the manner of a spider, clamping him securely to the machine's shell.

The Talos bucked and shook, trying to shed its unwanted passengers like a beast attempting to rid itself of parasites. Its great curving tail and its mechanical pincers started to convulse and shake, as though they were utterly out of control. The distinct hum of energy started to pulse through the metallic structure, as though being drawn into its thrashing limbs. Then, after a couple of seconds, the pincers and sting erupted with fire, spraying wild volleys of fiery projectiles around the arena.

The weapons seemed to discharge without aiming, and the Talos itself started to spin as though rotating on a central, vertical axis. Random energy blasts hailed around the arena, crashing into the walls, the ground and even into the stands. The audience screamed with delight as it scattered away from the explosions.

The spinning motion of the Talos grew faster and faster as its limbs flailed uncontrollably, spraying the amphitheatre with a random spread of lethal shards. Kruidan's grip around the spike in the construct's hull was slipping as the increasingly powerful centrifugal force threatened to throw him clear of the mechanical beast. He pushed his glaive deeper into the armoured plates and transferred his weight, but it was no good. After a few seconds the glaive's blade could no longer maintain its penetration and Kruidan was sent flying.

The Mantis Warrior spiralled through the air, flipping end over end as the incredible momentum threw him thirty metres and smashed him against the remnants of the gladiatrix gates. He slid down the wall into a heap against the floor before pulling himself back to his feet, leaning his weight against the buckled and bent glaive that he still held tightly in his hands.

The arena had changed completely. The Talos was spraying fire indiscriminately, and even the gladiatrix wyches were beginning to take some cover, although it was relatively clear that this mechanical monstrosity was part of the show. The crowd jeered at any of the surviving wyches that attempted to flee the arena, spitting their disdain and disgust and pressuring the darkling gladiatrixes to remain in the arena of death. Meanwhile, the crowd was writhing and roiling, like a single, massive organism that was struggling to avoid the errant volleys from the Talos. This was audience participation at its worst.

A little way from the spinning and convulsing Talos, Lelith was dancing with Dhrykna. The two female warriors were breathtaking in their elegance and beauty as they circled, flipped, somersaulted and spun with their blades flashing at incredible speeds. They paid almost no attention to the flurries of fire that sizzled past them or exploded at their feet; they simply turned or ducked or sprang to avoid them, integrating the movements smoothly and flawlessly into their continuously evolving dance. The scant, dark armour of the wych queen flashed with blackness, whilst the glistening white of Dhrykna's psycho-plastic armour seemed to burn with purity and brilliance. It was like watching a battle between heaven and hell.

Ashok and Atreus stood magnificently between the heavenly battle and the Talos, each unleashing tirades of warp power into the midst of both contests. With one hand they sought to support the glittering Aspect Warrior of Ulthwé, and with the other they poured destruction against the thickly armoured Talos. Their concentration was immense as they struggled to avoid striking their allies in both combats, and their own immobility rendered them into standing targets for the blasts from the Talos's weapons.

Shells and projectiles smacked into them, exploding into plumes of flame, smoke and shrapnel, but when the fireworks subsided, they could be seen standing untouched and glorious exactly where they had been before, dousing the enemies of the Emperor with streams of psychic death.

On the far side of the arena, in amongst the explosions and the relentless flashing of blades, Pelias and Luthar were engaging the remaining wyches. Their armour was cracked and chipped, and their hands ran red with blood, but they parried and punched at the darkling warriors with the fury of pride and righteousness. The hilts of daggers and swords protruded from their abdomens and limbs, where the gladiatrixes had penetrated their defences and struck home with their blades. But the Marines fought on undaunted and uncowed, their superhuman bodies able to function effectively despite the egregious wounds and the terrible pain.

They were outnumbered nearly four to one, but they stood back to back and showed the dark eldar what it meant to be part of a Deathwatch kill-team. They were in the arena to kill, not to be killed.

Looking back to the Talos, Kruidan saw that Sulphus was still clamped to its roof, his mechanical arms secured firmly to the beast's metallic shell even as the rest of his body thrashed and waved in the air above it. So close to the chassis of the mechanical monster, Sulphus was actually the only one safe from its random spray of fire.

The techmarine was beating at the roof of the Talos, pounding relentlessly at its armour with his fists and smashing at it with the adamantium fixture at the end of one his free augmetics. Eventually, the metal started to buckle and bend. The corners of the armoured plate began to lift as the centre of the panel became depressed.

As soon as there was enough of a lip for him to get a grip, Sulphus jammed his free augmetic arm into the widening crack and prised the panel up, ripping it clear of the bucking beast and throwing it aside. With a hole in its back, the Talos lurched into still more frenetic bouts of fury, vibrating, spinning and rearing in an attempt to dislodge the Iron Father that clung to its scales. But Sulphus could smell victory, and he clawed at the edges of the hole, yanking panel after panel off the beast's back until the gap was large enough for a Marine's body.

With a tremendous effort of strength that caused the servos in his mechanical limbs to whine and groan, Sulphus reeled himself in against the tortuous centrifugal force generated by the spinning

Talos. He pulled himself flat against the metallic monster's shell and transferred his weight to his human arm for a fraction of a second as he readjusted his mechanical grip, pushing his augmetic arms down inside the huge wound in the Talos's back. In that crucial instant, the centrifugal force nearly threw him clear – his human arm was simply too weak to hold him properly in place. But just as his body lifted off the surface of the shell, his augmetics found purchase in the Talos's interior and they pulled him inside.

It only took a few seconds for the techmarine to work his havoc in the interior of the mechanical beast. He had only been inside for a moment when the smooth and rapid spin started to splutter and lurch spasmodically. The Talos itself pitched forward, as though losing its balance. As the spin rate dropped abruptly, the metallic construct listed to one side and its weapons stopped firing. Then the structure seemed to gather speed, charging sideways through its sudden loss of balance, as though trying to prevent itself from falling over. It accelerated continuously until it smashed hard into the wall of the arena.

Smoke and debris plumed around the grounded Talos, but then the whole thing convulsed and detonated, blowing itself apart in a symphony of flames and red-hot metal shards. A series of secondary explosions erupted from the wreckage as the remaining ammunition blew, and a flaming inferno engulfed the surrounding area. For a few moments, there appeared to be silence in the crowd as they stared at the unprecedented destruction that was unravelling in their arena; could any of the darklings have expected the mon-keigh to survive so long? Had they ever encountered the Deathwatch before?

Through the silence and the fire emerged the tentacular figure of Sulphus, silhouetted against the raging flames. He strode out of the wreckage of the Talos, clutching something in one of his human hands. Even from his position by the ruined gates, Kruidan could see that Sulphus was holding the vivid yellow shoulder guard of an Imperial Fists captain.

As LELITH SLIPPED inside the Aspect Warrior's lunge, she grinned with appreciation. It had been so long since she had battled a truly worthy opponent, and she made a mental note to thank Thae'akzi for dispatching this glorious Shining Spear. Over the last several thousand years, she had done battle with the eldar of various craftworlds and even with the Ulthwé themselves from time to time, but she had only rarely come across warriors from the Shining Aspect. They were a rare delicacy, and Lelith was savouring every moment of the ritual of combat with this one. Despite the obvious contradictions, she found herself wishing that there were more such warriors in the galaxy.

Dhrykna's blade just glanced the immaculate skin of Lelith's sculpted stomach, drawing a hairline of near-black blood across the pale surface. Rather than withdrawing the sword, the Shining Spear followed through, darting after her own lunge and dropping low, as though anticipating a counter strike at head height. The Aspect Warrior was right, and Lelith spun at the precise moment that her stomach was cut, peeling away from the edge of the blade and bringing her own around in an elegant arc. Had Dhrykna withdrawn, the cut would have sliced through her slender neck. Instead, the exchange ended as it had begun, with the two warriors facing each other, just out of range. This time, however, a trickle of blood was running down Lelith's stomach and a few droplets were dripping down onto her leg, showing up in stark contrast to the pale skin of her right thigh.

The wych queen fixed her glistening, black eyes on Dhrykna as she ran a finger through the delicate cut in her skin, scooping out a bead of blood before licking it clean. Her eyes were wild with the thrill of combat, and her lips seemed to tremble in barely contained excitement. At that moment, all thoughts of the daemonic princess were banished from her mind – there was only the indescribable ecstasy of a worthy opponent.

She watched the Shining Spear cycling through various combat stances, flourishing her blades around her body and then above her head, slipping easily around the stray volleys of fire from the Talos. There was an effortless grace to the female's actions that filled the wych queen with admiration and thirst. She could scarcely contain her desire to ruin the shimmering perfection that danced and postured before her. To ruin something so beautiful was the highest calling in Lelith's long life – more powerful even than the temptations sent by the Satin Throne itself, although Lelith had often had reason to suspect that such ruinations would also be Slaanesh's indulgence of choice.

Running her blood tipped tongue around her pursed lips, Lelith turned a precise pirouette, spinning her two curving blades into rapidly reducing circles around her as she brought her hands together above her head. She struck a pose for an instant, letting the wild, maddened crowd admire her stretched and taught form. Then she dropped into a crouch and threw herself forward.

Dhrykna was ready for her. The Aspect Warrior spun to the side and kicked up into the air, letting Lelith's blades lash under her feet. But, at the last moment, the Shining Spear realised that she had made a mistake. As the momentum of her jump faded, Dhrykna fell back towards the ground, momentarily without strength or control. Meanwhile, Lelith had already recovered her balance after her own lunge, and she spun once again, bringing both her blades around in rapid succession. They cut into Dhrykna's back just as her feet hit the ground, slicing two thin, parallel gashes through her armour and drawing blood. Gasping, the Aspect Warrior fell forward out of range, tucking into a roll and coming up again to face the wych queen with her own blades poised.

Pain lanced across her back as the psycho-toxic poisons from Lelith's blade started to infiltrate her nervous system. She could already feel the muscles in her back beginning to spasm and stiffen as the poison started to eat them away. She howled in defiance and pain, refusing to let the injury signal the end of her resistance. In that fateful moment, everything suddenly seemed clear to the Aspect Warrior. It was as though the meaning of her life was flashing before her: she had been sacrificed by the Seer Council for the good of Ulthwé – that much was obvious enough. Part of her soul resented the fact that the council had thought that it had to trick her into making such a sacrifice, when they should have known that her sense of duty was beyond reproach and that her concern for the survival of the dwindling eldar was paramount in her mind. She shrieked in anguish, angry to be misunderstood to the last. With abrupt sweeps, she pointed her two blades out to each side, extending her pain wracked shoulders as though flexing non-existent wings.

Even worse than the pathetic and meaningless deceptions of the council, however, Dhrykna realised that Thae'akzi had chosen her on purpose. She had asked the Emerald Seer whether it might not have been better to have sent some Black Guardians or even a detachment of Dark Reapers – Truqui, the exarch, would have been a stronger and more appropriate choice. But the seer had refused to hear of it, claiming that this duty fell on the shoulders of the Shining Spears.

At the time, despite her suspicions, Dhrykna and thrilled with pride at those words, but now she could see the truth of it: Thae'akzi had never wanted her to ascend to the armour of the exarch. She had never wanted to see another exarch tending to the temple of the Shining Light. For as long as Thae'akzi had been the Emerald Seer, the Shining Spears had suffered diminishing power and numbers. Although she did not know what it was, it was clear to Dhrykna in this moment of agony and death that the Emerald Seer harboured a secret about her time in the Shining Temple, a secret that could jeopardise her position on the council and her power on Ulthwé. *The Shining Path permits no shadows.* Thae'akzi had sent Dhrykna to her doom not only as a sacrifice for Ulthwé but also as a way of ridding the craftworld of the only aspirant exarch of its smallest Aspect Temple.

'Light flashes, blood falls, death pierces the darkness!' Dhrykna howled again, trying to drag her mind back into the present for one last effort of will. Her soul was filling with a hateful desperation as she realised that her entire encounter with the monkeigh had been stage-managed from the start. The worst of it was that the humans themselves had behaved with an honour and courage worthy of her respect, but she had held them in contempt nonetheless. In reality, it seemed that it was her own people that were worthy of her contempt.

The poison was spreading quickly through her back, and she could already feel the muscles around her waist beginning to seize up. In a few moments it would be too late for her to bring about an end worthy of a Shining Spear. Summoning the last vestiges of her will and her strength, Dhrykna darted towards the dancing wych queen. Her first strike was parried easily and Lelith skipped out to the side. But Dhrykna was not finished yet: as Lelith stabbed forward with her counter, the Aspect Warrior let herself drop to the ground, letting the queen's blade pass harmlessly over her. As Lelith leant forward to catch her balance, Dhrykna stabbed upwards with both of her swords, driving them into the already blood slicked abdomen of the beautiful wych queen.

As Lelith screamed, sliding down the blades and impaling herself even further, Dhrykna howled with the defiance of victory in death. But just before the wych queen slumped down on top of the prone Aspect Warrior, she thrust her own blades down through the shimmering white figure, running her through and catching her own sliding fall at the same time. For a moment, the two female warriors gazed into each other's eyes, sharing the intensity of death, but then Lelith freed herself of the spell and pulled herself back to her feet. Dhrykna's blades still protruding from her stomach and back, she brayed up to the crowd like a wild wolf.

At exactly that moment, on the other side of the arena, the Talos construct detonated, hurling concussions, flames and shrapnel through the already death riddled space within the amphitheatre. The darklings in the crowd were beside themselves with the orgiastic pleasure of violence and voyeurism.

PICKING HIMSELF UP off the ground after the explosion, Ashok's eyes flicked automatically towards the spot where the wych queen had stood only moments before. She was gone. Lying in the blood soaked dirt where Lelith's stiletto boots had been only instants before, he could see the ruined body of the white-clad Aspect Warrior, its feet still twitching with the last signs of a collapsing nervous system.

Atreus, it's time to leave. We must find the spirit pool. Ashok's thoughts growled with discontent as he strode over to the fallen warrior, leaving the Blood Ravens librarian to conduct a survey of the situation in the arena.

The gates have closed again, librarian, but the eldar seer did them considerable damage. We should be able to get out that way. Atreus could see the cracks and holes that riddled the gladiatrix gates, not to mention the huge sections that had been completely blown away.

All around the auditorium, dark eldar warriors were vaulting down into the arena from the stands, as though they had finally realised that something other than ceremonial combat was occurring in their amphitheatre. The destruction of the Talos and the injury of their queen may well have been the turning point in the mood of the audience. It seemed that they had decided that the Deathwatch Marines should not be permitted to live out the rest of the day, despite their victories.

We have company, librarian. Atreus strode off to intercept the crowd, aiming to buy some time for his battle-brothers.

I know. Ashok appeared unconcerned about the dozens of dark eldar wyches and warriors that were flooding down from the stands into the fighting pit. Had he bothered to look around, he would have seen the blood drenched and damaged figures of Luthar and Pelias storming across the arena from the far side, just outpacing the growing crowd of aliens that raced after them. Sulphus and Kruidan were already at the great gates, ripping sections of masonry out of their weakened structure to open a gap wide enough for the team to get through.

Kneeling swiftly at the side of the lightling eldar, Ashok gazed into her fading eyes. Egregious puncture wounds were ripped into her chest and stomach, and Ashok could see the toxic poison eating away at her internal organs. Her eyes widened when she saw the Angels Sanguine librarian looming over her and then they contracted again with the pain of effort.

Please.

The word was solitary and radiant, like a sonorous, silvering chime in the murky psychic darkness of the arena. He could see the alien's eyes beseeching him with the very last vestiges of its strength.

Don't let them win.

Ashok nodded his understanding, even though he was not entirely sure about the meaning of her last four words.

'Librarian Ashok!' Luthar's voice bellowed over from the gates, where the rest of the kill-team was now assembled. His tone was urgent and filled with the anger of battle. 'There is no time!'

In the back of his mind, Ashok could remember how that same Reviler chaplain had said something similar to him on Trontium VI before this mission had begun. The librarian remained stooped over the dying eldar and showed no signs of having heard the chaplain. Involuntarily, his anger began to rise, just as it had on the mountainside on Trontium VI as he had gazed down on the injured Angels Sanguine Marine while the orks blew hell out of the mountaintop. He did not leave people behind.

We cannot save her Ashok. The words of Atreus reached behind the thickening veil of blood that was drawing over his eyes. *She is not a Marine – there is nothing we can do for her.*

The rampage of wyches was almost upon him as Ashok nodded once again to the Aspect Warrior and reached down to clasp her head in his hands. With a sudden movement, he snapped her neck, killing her instantly. He knew what her dark cousins would do to her if they took her alive, even if there was only a trace of life left in her broken body. She might not be a Marine, but he could not wish that on anything that had fought at his side.

Punching his fist through the armour on her chest, Ashok wrenched out a handful of psycho-plastic and flesh, and then he sprang to his feet. As he turned to dash back towards the gates, a blast of warp energy from Atreus seared past his face, crashing into the charging crowd behind him, making the wyches scatter and buying the Angel Sanguine time to reach his battle-brothers.

As the Deathwatch team vaulted and clambered through the ruined gates with the wyches lashing at their heels, they found Sulphus already at work on the far side. He had taken a clutch of explosive shells from the Talos whilst he had been inside, and he was busily fixing them around the frame of the gates.

Ashok was the last Marine to dive out of the arena and through into the shadowy corridor; as he cleared the mantel, Sulphus detonated the shells. A ring of explosions burst out of the walls, blowing great chunks of masonry and debris out of the supporting structures and causing lumps of rock and boulders to crash down from the lintel. By the time that Ashok had rolled back to his feet, the ruined great gates had been completely buried under a massive pile of rubble that blocked the way back into the arena.

THE DARKNESS WAS riddled with javelins of darkly glimmering light that eased their way lazily through the rubble blockade. On the far side, the Deathwatch Marines could hear the scrambling of fingers and weapons against rock, as the dark eldar strove to remove the obstacles to their hunt.

'It won't hold them for long,' murmured Sulphus, as though apologising.

'It will be long enough,' replied Ashok distractedly as he shook the eldar flesh and plastinated armour off his hand. After a second or two, he was left with a small, oval, dimly glowing gemstone in the palm of his hand. He inspected it for a second, and, momentarily, the others could see the faint reflection of its phantasmagoric light spark in the depths of his black eyes. Without knowing why, it held their attention in reverential silence as Ashok dropped it into a pouch on his belt, where they could hear it clink up against two others.

'This way,' murmured Ashok as he strode deeper into the darkness, away from the makeshift barricade. It was not an order, but merely an observation of fact: this was the way he was going. It was not clear to the others whether the Angel Sanguine had been addressing them or not, but they fell in behind him automatically. In any case, there did not appear to be anywhere else to go.

The corridor quickly narrowed and lowered as it snaked deeper into the mountain, growing hotter and stuffier with every abrupt corner and sweeping bend. There were dozens of tributary tunnels leading in and out of the main shaft, and Ashok strode confidently from one to the next, pushing onwards as though certain of his direction. From time to time, they could hear the cackling voices of dark eldar wyches or the trampling of warriors' feet echoing through the passageways, but they encountered very few aliens. They couldn't tell whether the crowd of wyches that had been scraping at the rubble in the gateway to the arena had given up or whether they had broken through and simply lost track of the group.

After what seemed like nearly half an hour of steady progress, the team emerged into a wide, cavernous chamber. It was roughly spherical in structure, and dozens of passageways led out of it in every direction, some cut into the walls, others into the floor and still others into the domed ceiling.

The Deathwatch Marines fanned out, inspecting the unusual space but realising that it was an impossible chamber to secure. There were simply too many entrances, and there was not a single point from which an individual could monitor them all. As they made their way through the cave, the Marines noticed that some of the passage mouths were actually reflective pools of energy. From a distance, they were indistinguishable from gaps and corridors, but close up the images rippled and sparkled like liquid.

'What is this place?' asked Sulphus, his curiosity genuinely aroused by the bizarre feat of engineering.

'It is a nodal chamber,' answered Ashok matter-of-factly, as he strode from one pool to the next, peering into each carefully as he went.

'What?' snapped Luthar. The Reviler was quite accustomed to infiltrating enemy positions and working behind enemy lines, but he had never come across anything like this before. 'What do you know about this Blood Angel?'

'It is a kind of navigation point,' explained Ashok, seemingly oblivious to the accusatory tone in the chaplain's voice. 'Each of these pools is an access point to a form of transportation network. I'm not exactly sure how it works, but I would guess that it is analogous to the eldar webway. These pools are portals that can transport us instantaneously to various linked points.'

The Angel Sanguine librarian had stopped next to one of the pools and was kneeling at its side. He was peering into the rippling image with concentration written across his hidden features.

'How do you know all this, librarian?' asked Atreus. The erudition of the Blood Ravens was legendary, but he had never heard of anything like this before. There was certainly no mention of such a transport system in the great library aboard the magnificent battle barge, *Omnis Arcanum*.

Ashok stood to his feet, as though reaching a decision, and then turned to face Atreus. 'This is the one,' he said, as though the previous conversation had been going on in the background and had nothing to do with him. 'We need to go through here.'

The Blood Raven regarded him carefully. 'I think that you should tell us what you know, Ashok. You are not the commander of this mission, and we need a reason to follow you. Our sense of duty will take us only so far.'

The two librarians faced each other in silence for what seemed like an age. Meanwhile, the other Marines kept up the surveillance, ensuring the integrity of the chamber while the situation was resolved. The Deathwatch team had entertained various doubts about the mysterious Angel Sanguine librarian, and Atreus had taken on the task of mediating the question of trust. In the absence of Octavius, the mantle of command should naturally fall to one or other of the librarians.

Eventually, Ashok spoke. 'You're right, Atreus. This is not the time for secrets. This nodal chamber is similar to one in the heart of Ulthwé, which I discovered during my infiltration mission on the craftworld. At that time, I was searching for an access point to the craftworld's infinity circuit – the reservoir of Ulthwé's lost souls. I found it. It corresponds with this portal,' said Ashok, indicating the pool behind him. 'I believe that this should lead us to the spirit pool of the dark eldar wych. We cannot leave it intact, Atreus. We should blow it before we leave this place in order to prevent the souls therein from being presented to the queen's daemonic princess.'

Atreus said nothing for a long moment, as he considered his brother-librarian's words. 'What makes you think that the dark eldar technology is the same as that used on Ulthwé?' It was a practical question, and it suggested that Atreus was convinced by the rest of the story.

'It is not identical, Atreus, but it is similar enough. The technology of these systems is ancient beyond reckoning, and Inquisitor Lord Seishon is confident that both species of alien developed it at the same time, possibly at a time when they lived in co-operation with each other.'

The Blood Raven librarian nodded and strode over to the pool behind Ashok. Peering into the swirling, oily image, he looked up at the rest of the team and nodded. The explanation was imperfect but it matched various documents that he had read in the past. The sources he had in mind were far from reliable, but at least he could corroborate the current story with some familiar records. No matter what his previous suspicions may have been, at that particular moment, Ashok's word was as good as proof for the scholar warrior.

'Let's get this over with,' he said as he stepped onto the surface of the pool and sunk like a stone, vanishing completely from view. Without hesitation, Ashok dived in after the Blood Raven, and the others followed suit, one by one.

THE CONTROL ROOM of the *Titanicus Rex* was a haven of calm. Captain Mordia's expression showed no signs of emotion as he directed the serfs through their combat manoeuvres. All around the decks and control centres of the gunship, the other Marines in Mordia's Grey Knights squad were doing the same thing. From the inside, the *Rex* showed almost no signs of the fury that was being unleashed in the thick, eddying mess of space in the lashes of the Eye of Terror outside.

As the ancient and venerable vessel had pressed further into the Circuitrine system, tendrils of the warp had started to reach through from the unspeakable, immaterial realms. What had started out as merely wisps of red mist, permeating out of the daemonic dimensions like oil being pushed through a sieve, had thickened and grown more viscous as the *Titanicus Rex* ploughed through the curdling shapes, whipping them into tentacles and arms that reached out for the vessel, dragging their ethereal fingers across the ageless and sleek hull. The caresses grew more prolonged and lustful, but the *Rex* shrugged them off, repelling them with its warp shields like unwanted and lecherous advances.

The shapes that swam and struggled into existence were barely recognisable as figures or faces. They were little more than suggestions of nightmares or dreams. Hands reached, fingers touched, and tendrils draped themselves against the smooth sides of the *Titanicus Rex*. But despite the monstrously seductive atmosphere that oozed and tore itself into the strictly governed dimensions of real space, the guns of the *Rex* were firing continuously. The forward cannons and the las-arrays spluttered with constant discharge, splintering and dispersing the daemonic images as they were forming, preventing them from solidifying any further.

Through the main viewscreen on the control deck, Mordia could see the streams of fire pouring out of his gunship, ripping through the warp spawned quagmire that was thickening into a soupy consistency before them. For a while, the *Titanicus* had been picking off the occasional apparition in the manner of a frigate blasting its way through an asteroid field. However, as the concentration of warp energy increased, the lashes of fire power from the gunship were acting more like battering rams or ploughs, clearing a passage in the mire for the ship to slip through, enabling the *Rex* to sail through the predictabilities of real space for as long as possible.

Despite the relentless and constant firefight that was raging on all sides of the Grey Knights' vessel,

Mordia had not yet come into contact with an identifiable daemonic force or presence. The persistence
and quantity of warp energy bleeding into normal
space was certainly unusual, but it did sometimes
happen in this part of the sector, so close to the
lashes of the Eye of Terror. The great Eye – a huge,
raging warp storm caught on the cusp of reality –
was always changing shape and dimensions, and
parts of the Circuitrine nebula were swallowed up
from time to time. It was for exactly this reason that
the outlying worlds were no longer inhabited. Not
even the inquisitor lords of the Ordo Malleus could
predict or explain the behaviour of the warp storms
in this region.

Nonetheless, as the *Titanicus Rex* ploughed onward
through the gathering warp mist, Mordia's eyes kept
flicking back to the warp density readings on one of
the terminals. The display had been showing a gradually ascending line for the last hour, reflecting the
increasing permeability of reality outside. This meant
one of two things to Mordia: either the Eye had shifted
orientation and he was now taking his gunship deeper
and deeper into it, or there was something massive
and powerful lurking in the immaterium struggling to
break through into material space – something growing stronger all the time, and just teetering on the very
edge of the necessary power.

Taking a couple of strides towards the viewscreen,
Mordia brought his face to within a few centimetres
of the glass and peered into the red, curdling mess
that lay in wait before his ship. Over his long years
of service, Mordia had learnt to trust his well-honed
and highly disciplined instincts, and something told

him that this was more than just a routine warp mist seeping from the fringes of the swirling Eye. For a split second, he thought that he could see the contours of a beautiful female form haze into focus in the clouds, but it dissipated as quickly as it formed.

'I TOLD YOU not to return until you had proof, Perceptia.' Hereticus Lord Caesurian was seated in the luxurious padded armchair in her chambers, with her back to the door. She did not rise or turn when the door opened to reveal Perceptia standing in the corridor outside. 'If you have found something, then you had better come in,' she added, issuing her first ever invitation to the bookish and irritating young inquisitor.

Taking a deep breath to steady her nerves and snatching her glasses off her face so that she wouldn't be tempted to play with them once she had stepped inside, Perceptia moved quietly into the room. As soon as she cleared the threshold, the door slid firmly closed behind her, sealing the chamber. Simultaneously, she thought that she could hear the hum of numerous privacy devices activating all around the room.

Her first step into Caesurian's personal sanctum was like a step into another world. Most of the living quarters on Ramugan were sparse, particularly amongst the personnel of the Ordo Hereticus, who could not afford to be seen to be lapsing into hedonism or indulgence. However, Caesurian's rooms were the picture of affluence and comfort. The floor was covered in a deep red, thick pile carpet that cushioned Perceptia's feet into silence. She had never seen anything like it, and for a moment she felt disorientated as the spongy floor upset her sense of balance. The walls were covered in images and paintings that the inquisitor lord had collected on her various travels. For the first time, Perceptia could see an array of items that might be interpreted as being heretical, had she found them in the possession of anyone else. The elaborate, hand-fashioned deathmask of a Trogeth witch cultist hung in a place of honour on the wall next to the door, positioned so that it was only visible from inside the room.

As she took in the myriad decorations and ornaments around the room, Perceptia let her mind flick back to the two-faced, mutant curator hidden away in the secret depths of the librarium. She realised for the first time that Caesurian was a collector. The older woman had spent the best part of her life charging around the galaxy, punishing heretics and aberrations, but it seemed that she had also been collecting mementoes. She had brought fragments of each heretic back with her and installed them in her own chambers, or in the lowest levels of the librarium. Perceptia had never heard of an inquisitor interpreting her mandate in such a touristic manner before, and she wondered what it all meant.

'You have a lovely chamber, Lord Caesurian,' hissed Perceptia, her voice betraying her discomfort. She felt as though she had to say something.

'Thank you, inquisitor.' Caesurian's voice had lost none of its usual composure; it was deep and velvety, like the carpet. 'But I hope that you did not come here to discuss interior decorating.'

'No, lord. I came… I came to ask a question.' It was as difficult to say the words as she had anticipated.

'I am sure that I told you not to return without proof of your suspicions,' countered Caesurian smoothly. 'I had expected information rather than questions.'

'A question is itself a type of information, my lord. You taught me that yourself.'

'Ah yes, Perceptia the perfect student. I should be very careful what I say to you in future if you are going to remember it all so closely.' Perceptia couldn't tell if the inquisitor lord was smiling; she was still seated in her plush chair, facing the other way. 'Nevertheless, you are right. What is your question?'

'I have been in the librarium since last we spoke, lord. I have found a large number of documents connecting senior inquisitors in the Ramugan Ordo Xenos to a number of events in the Circuitrine system. It seems that the Xenos inquisitors have shown interest in that sector for many centuries, my lord – Seishon is not the first.'

Perceptia paused, waiting for some kind of response so that she could judge how to continue.

'This sounds suspiciously like information, young Perceptia. I thought that you wanted to ask a question.'

That was not quite the response that she was expecting. 'Yes, my lord. I am getting to the question. You see,' she continued, nervously twisting the frames of her glasses in her hands. 'You see, I asked Seye Multinus to survey the documents in part of level 67b. As you know, one of the aisles there is dedicated to records about Ordo Xenos confessions. I wondered how many of the confessions would contain mention of Circuitrine…'

As Perceptia spoke, the inquisitor lord's chair began to rotate very slowly, bringing the older woman's face into view for the first time. Her figure was bathed in shadows but her eyes shone brightly as they inspected the young inquisitor who was standing inside her rooms for the first time.

'Continue,' she said simply.

'Yes, my lord.' Despite herself, Perceptia performed a little bow to indicate her respect. Even in the current circumstances, Caesurian was a formidable and intimidating woman. 'I asked Seye to sort the documents according to whether they mentioned that system, hoping to find one or two extra sources to corroborate my theory, so that I could come back to you with some more detailed findings. I have to confess that I had very little in the way of a working hypothesis – I wasn't sure exactly what I was looking for. Having read and reread the confession of Lord Herod and matched parts of it against the *Legend of Hourian*, I had a vague idea that the eldar might be involved somehow.'

'Ah yes, of course,' said Caesurian with a tone of affirmation. 'Hourian was set in the Circuitrine system. I had almost forgotten.' As she spoke, the inquisitor lord tilted her head slightly to indicate a large painting that hung on the wall behind Perceptia, on the opposite side of the door from the Trogethian witch's mask.

Perceptia turned her head gingerly, half expecting to find a silent and deadly death cultist standing behind her. Instead, she saw the painting, but its presence on Caesurian's wall sent a whole raft of confused and conflicting emotions crashing through her mind. In the centre of the picture was a near-life-size depiction of Hourian himself. He was crouched onto one knee, on which was balanced the bloodied remains of an eerily beautiful child, half human and half eldar. Hourian was weeping in the foreground while an immense space battle raged in the background, where the red glow of the distant Eye of Terror dominated the scene.

'What was it you wanted to ask, inquisitor?' prompted Caesurian, as though the sight of the painting should have already exploded any questions of reticence.

'Seye discovered that every document in that section of the library contained some kind of mention of the Circuitrine system.' Perceptia paused to reformulate her words. 'That is to say, Seye *knew* that every document would mention Circuitrine. It seems that he had already been instructed to create an annex dedicated to such files. It seems, in other words, that I am not the first Hereticus inquisitor to investigate along these lines.'

'I still cannot hear a question, my dear,' said Caesurian in her characteristically smooth tone. There was nothing defensive in her voice, despite the implied accusations in what Perceptia was saying.

'Did you authorise the creation of that collection, Inquisitor Lord Caesurian?' That was as direct and formal as Perceptia could muster.

'Yes, I did, Inquisitor Perceptia.' The answer was immediate and unselfconscious. The unapologetic confidence took Perceptia by surprise. She had expected to have a fight on her hands, trying to extract that information from her one-time mentor.

'Then you admit it freely?'

'Of course. I am an inquisitor lord of the Ordo Hereticus here on Ramugan. It is my right as well as my duty to ensure that our most sensitive records are kept appropriately ordered and appropriately… discreet.'

This was not going quite as Perceptia had planned. 'Then I have another question, my lord. *Why* did you request those records to be assembled into a discreet annex?'

'That is a much better question, my young inquisitor, but it is not one that a lord need answer.' There was a new air of superiority flowing around the chamber, as though Caesurian was enjoying seeing the young inquisitor rail against her own unassailable position. 'You do not yet have enough evidence to force me to answer that question, my dear Perceptia. You have suspicions, yes, and I have told you many times before to trust your instincts. They serve you well. However, the fact that I have assembled this collection is only as suspicious as the fact that you have also sought to assemble it. I just got there first, many years ago. The difference between our positions, of course, is that you are responding to a concrete event and the atypical actions of Xenos Lord Seishon. I, it seems, had my own reasons for being interested in this system. If your suspicions about Seishon and about me are correct, then Lord Aurelius's valiant Captain Mordia will find the proof you require, for he is already on his way to the Circuitrine system. If, on the other hand, Mordia finds nothing, then you should be aware that levelling accusations of heresy at senior Hereticus and Xenos lords will land you in a great deal of trouble.'

'I have made no accusations, my lord,' muttered Perceptia, surprised to hear that the steps of her argument had been so clearly pre-empted by the inquisitor lord.

'Oh but you have, my child. And you are right to make such accusations. Your reasoning is sound and your instincts are crisp. Being right, however, is only half the battle. Now you have to demonstrate that you are right. Now it is simply a question of power. I did warn you not to return to me without proof. The warning was for your own good.'

Perceptia bowed, acknowledging the talent of her opponent. Caesurian had basically confessed to being involved in whatever relationship the Ordo Xenos had with the eldar in the Circuitrine system, but the inquisitor lord need have no fear of such a confession to her. She was right that Perceptia had insufficient evidence and power to condemn her own mentor, whether she was right or not. Everything now rested on the Grey Knight captain; only he was in a position to discover what was really going on out there.

Turning her back on the inquisitor lord, Perceptia faced the sealed door and waited for it to open to let her out. She waited for what seemed like a long time, expecting at every moment to feel the cold sliver of an assassin's blade slip into her back. Anticipation was often the worst kind of torture. But then the door slid open smoothly and the young inquisitor swept out into the brightness of the corridor outside; Caesurian had apparently seen no point in terminating the inquisitor's investigation. Insulted, frustrated and inspired, Perceptia pushed her glasses back into place and rushed off back to the librarium. Perhaps she had overlooked something?

By THE TIME Kruidan spilled out of the portal, the battle was already underway. It seemed that Lelith had anticipated their plan, and she was lying in wait in the vast cavern that housed the spirit pool of Sussarkh's Peak. For long centuries the wych queen had been accumulating the souls of warriors from various species and storing them up for a magnificent sacrifice.

Her shadowy and delectable patron princess had already granted Lelith numerous favours and had offered her assistance to ensure the longevity of the wych queen's rule on Hesperax itself. In return, Lelith had promised her enough souls to push her Slaaneshi army out of the infernal dimensions and into the material realm. As it turned out, she was still a vital few short.

Atreus and Ashok had emerged first, and they were defending the mouth of the portal, each standing like colossi, unleashing the fury of the warp against the wyches that ran and sprang around the cavern, trying to close in on the glorious librarians. Behind them, the rest of the Deathwatch team was emerging one by one. Kruidan tumbled out onto the ground, rolling back up onto his feet, still clutching the buckled and bent glaive that he had taken from the

guards in the arena. Sulphus stepped confidently out
of the shimmering pool in the wall, his arms twitching and probing the liquid substance as though he
was testing its composition. Luthar and Pelias
vaulted out together, each braced and ready for
whatever lay in wait.

'This is not a battle that we can win,' growled
Luthar as the magnitude of the challenge began to
sink in. His armour was shattered, cracked and broken, and the ruined plates were slick with blood –
alien blood intermixed with rivers of his own. The
battle in the arena had almost finished him, and it
looked fairly certain that the teeming cavern would
finish the job.

'We do not have to win, brother-chaplain,' replied
Pelias, his voice deep with gravel and fury. 'But we
do need to take some of these vermin with us when
we go.' Just like Luthar, the Black Consul's armour
was tattered and broken where it had begun to
buckle under the onslaught that it had suffered in
the arena. His already scarred face was coated with
ichor and blood, and a fresh gash had ripped down
across his left eye, leaving the socket ruptured and
gory.

'Pelias is right,' hissed Kruidan, drawing himself
up to his full height. The Mantis Warrior's tattoos
were now barely visible beneath the patchwork of
cuts and gashes that laced over his exposed
abdomen. So much blood covered his chest and
arms that it appeared as though his skin was of the
deepest red, flecked all over with traces of pale scars
and cursive, black ceremonial tattoos. Even with
most of his armour missing, Kruidan cut an

imposing and powerful figure, like a barbarian
warrior poised to do battle with the terrible beasts
of myth and legend.

'No,' said Ashok, his low, calm voice commanding
instant respect and attention. 'This is not a battle
that we need to win. We just need to survive for a few
moments; just for long enough to give Sulphus a
chance to rig that thing for destruction.'

The face of the Angel Sanguine librarian was still
hidden under his shroud, but his voice was powerful
and clear, as though it did not require the medium
of air to travel into the heads of his Deathwatch
brethren. His armour was scarred and scored, showing signs of the frenzied combat in the arena, but it
was unbroken. Compared with Pelias and Luthar,
the librarian's dark appearance was immaculate, as
though he were dressed for the parade ground in the
Watchtower Fortress itself.

Sulphus nodded his understanding and looked
across the cavern at the immense and intricate
device that dominated the centre of the cave. It was
roughly conical in shape, with its point touching
down into the ground and its base stretched out
across the ceiling. It was laced with a complicated
array of tubes and wires, but the focus of it was a
huge sphere of darkness, like a large black pearl,
which was set into the translucent cone near the
roof. It pulsed and shimmered with a black light that
hurt his eyes.

Lined up in front of the spirit pool was a bank of
wyches. There must have been twenty or thirty of
them arranged in haphazard rows of five or six. Each
was armed with an array of ugly beautiful weapons

– no longer merely the simple poisoned blades used in the ceremonial arena. Standing before them, quite alone in the no-man's-land between her retinue and the Deathwatch, was Lelith herself. The wounds in her stomach still ran with blood, sending streams of sickly darkness cascading down her perfect legs. She was grinning with menace and composure, as though this was the best day she had experienced in centuries.

'She's mine,' whispered Ashok, stepping forward of the group and holding his arms out to block the others from following. 'You see to the spirit pool,' he said to Atreus, turning his head to face the Blood Raven.

For the first time since they had encountered him, the Deathwatch kill-team saw Ashok reach up slowly and push back his hood. He revealed a completely shaven head, laced with scars and lined with signs of hardship and suffering. A row of golden service studs glinted above his eyebrow, but it was the glow emanating from his eyes that caught everyone's attention. As they stared, they could see the fathomless black eyes begin to flicker and sheen, as though a red mist were curdling across his vision. After less than a second, the burning red had engulfed his eyeballs completely, and they raged with a flaming radiance that made the others recoil.

With an abrupt nod to the team, Ashok turned and charged towards the Wych Queen of Strife. He roared an incoherent battle cry, dedicating his efforts to Sanguinius and to the Emperor, as his hands erupted into fireballs.

In response, the wyches scattered, reorganising their lines to accommodate the terrifying figure that was charging towards them. Lelith herself grinned and darted forward to meet the rampaging librarian head on.

As the strategic situation shifted, Atreus broke into a run, leading the Deathwatch team in an arc around the side of the cavern, looking for an angle of approach towards the spirit pool. His fingertips were alive with fire, lashing out at the wyches and trying to clear a path. But there were simply too many of the dark eldar foes.

Focusing his will, the Blood Ravens librarian unleashed a massive javelin of power through the constantly shifting lines of wyches. A couple of shrieks told him that he had hit his mark, but most of the darting warriors flipped aside, evading the tirade of warp power. However, evasion was enough, since it opened up a brief channel in their lines. It was enough for Sulphus and Kruidan to charge forward, hacking their way through the closing ranks until they stumbled up against the inverted point of the spirit pool itself.

Their charge had cut them off from the others, but the wyches were now caught between two smaller forces of Deathwatch Marines, forcing them to divide their attentions and to re-orientate their strategy once again.

Pelias and Luthar were not about to give the wyches time to reorganise, and they stormed forward into the lines, throwing their weight and their blades into the thick of combat once again. Atreus followed their lead, vaulting into the mix and setting his burning hands against the flickering whips, hydraknives and impalers brandished by the wyches. In only a matter of seconds, the Deathwatch had engaged the wych queen and her retinue in the very heart of her lair.

CHAPTER TWELVE

SULPHUS DETACHED HIS vice-like grip and dropped off the inverted conical structure, crunching down onto the shoulders of one of the battling wyches below. He shattered the alien's spine and crushed her under his weight as he ground his boots into the broken ruins of her body. He thrashed his arms around him, clattering them against the forest of blades that lunged in.

'We have to get out of here!' he yelled, his voice booming and resonant in the cavernous space.

The Marines around him reacted as one, forming into a wedge and driving out from the centre of the chamber towards the portal in the far wall. They parried and hacked with their swords, meeting the skilful attacks of the wyches with brute power and will. Ahead of them, Kruidan could see the unfolding duel between Ashok and Lelith. A group of wyches had formed a ring around the combat to ensure that none of the others interfered with their queen's enjoyment.

The two warriors circled one another without caution. Every few seconds, one of them would throw themselves forward, lunging at the other with crackling lances of power. The other would meet the attack head on, each refusing to appear cowed by the powers of the other. Great eruptions of warp energy sparked and exploded from each and every clash between the magnificent fighters, riddling the cavern with hails of warp shards.

Even as they fought their way around the arena of the duel, the Deathwatch Marines could see the reckless passion raging in their librarian's eyes as he threw himself into the contest with no thought of his own survival. His fury was reflected back at him, but it was twisted and perverted into a sick kind of euphoria as Lelith's terrible and beautiful face displayed a daemonic smile. Her teeth were glinting and she was biting down on her tongue, drawing an excited bead of blood across her grinning lips.

'Ashok!' yelled Atreus as the team deployed around the portal, attempting to hold the position for long enough for their maverick librarian to break away from the magnificent queen. But the Angel Sanguine showed no signs of having heard the Blood Raven. His eyes continued to burn and he prowled menacingly around the dancing and swirling wych queen.

'Ashok!' repeated Atreus as he parried a flashing blade and then pressed his other palm against the sneering face of a thrusting wych. A burst of power exploded from his hand and incinerated the dark eldar's head, but her place in the line was immediately filled by another wych, eager to prove her worth in combat against the Marines.

'Ashok, there is no time for this. We are leaving now, with or without you!' With that, the Blood Raven flicked a signal to the others, indicating that they should throw themselves through the shimmering surface of the portal.

With a crisp nod of acknowledgement, Chaplain Luthar hacked and sliced a few last times with his chipped and blood coated sword, and then he turned and dived into the portal, vanishing immediately. Sulphus was close behind him, striding confidently into the sheen of liquid as though oblivious to the fury of battle that he was leaving behind.

Meanwhile, a flicker of recognition seemed to flash over Ashok's face. The burning light in his eyes appeared to flash and then fade into a simmer. He stole a glance back to Atreus, who stood in a blaze of blue and white flames, holding back the pressing line of wyches as the blood-red back of Kruidan vanished into the portal behind him.

The sound of a small explosion in the centre of the chamber dragged Ashok's attention back around in time for him to see Lelith's curving blade arching towards his neck. Instinctively, he threw out his arm to meet the slash, but he was already staring past the breathtaking visage of the wych queen, inspecting the puff of flame and smoke that had just blown out of the top of the conical spirit pool. Instantaneously, another explosion sounded and then another, strafing around the soul reservoir in a flurry of chain reactions.

Lelith's blade cut deeply into Ashok's arm, slicing straight through the ceramite armour on his forearm and burying itself in his bone. The librarian did not let out a sound, but he yanked his arm away from the wych, dragging the hilt of the blade out of her hand as its edge was lodged firmly in his flesh. Punching forward with his other hand, he threw a concentrated ball of fire into the wych's stomach from close range, blowing her back off her feet.

Grasping the opportunity, Ashok turned on his heel and pounded towards the portal and Atreus, ploughing his way through the lines of wyches, taking them by surprise from behind. As he ran, he could hear the staccato of explosions behind him growing to a crescendo. Throwing himself headlong into the portal, Ashok felt the concussion of a massive explosion engulf him and propel him even faster. An instant later, and everything was black and silent.

As THE TITANICUS REX ploughed on into the asteroid field on the edge of the Circuitrine system, the quagmire of warp taint had grown so thick that the vessel's instruments were beginning to give conflicting readouts. The machine-spirit was uncertain about whether the *Rex* was in real space or whether it had dropped into the warp.

The gunnery stations were working continuously, disrupting each wispy signature of the warp before it could fully form in the material realms. Meanwhile, the forward cannons were occupied with clearing a path through the asteroids. As the *Titanicus* roared onwards, it was surrounded by a relentless barrage of fire, flames and burning warp energy.

'Captain,' reported one the serfs on the control deck. 'We are detecting a massive energy build-up on the other side of one of the larger asteroids.'

'Show me,' replied Mordia, his voice calm and without emotion.

The viewscreen flickered rapidly as the image switched and then magnified, bringing the tumbling shape of a moon-sized asteroid into focus. Threads of warp mist had been pulled into orbit around the spinning rock, as though drawn in by its trace gravity, forming ruddy, red rings around its axis. For a moment, Mordia felt that he was gazing upon the formation of a Chaos world as the great Eye started to consume the asteroid field.

As the huge asteroid rolled over, a shimmering energy field swung into view. It was anchored to the rock by a series of metallic fixtures around the horizon, and it appeared to be stretched over a massive cavity that had been excavated from the interior of the asteroid. The surface of the energy field rippled like a colossal lake, and Mordia could see the suggestion of images swimming in its depths.

'Distance?' he asked, his voice betraying no signs of the tension that had suddenly lurched into his mind.

'Two thousand metres and closing, captain. We will be upon it in a matter of seconds.'

'What will be its orientation when we reach it?'

'The energy field will be on the dark side, captain, but only briefly.'

'Very good. Hold the present course and alert the gunners that the asteroid should not be fired upon until I give the word. Ensure that they are ready. We may have to act quickly.'

As the *Titanicus Rex* cut its way through the roiling space between it and the asteroid, Mordia kept his eyes locked on the tumbling rock. The energy field looked like a warp gate of some kind and, judging by its position, it was probably a gateway deeper into the Eye itself. It would be an incredible coincidence if the shifting warp signature in this region had nothing to do with the architects of that gate.

'The energy surge is growing, captain,' cautioned the serf as the *Rex* closed on the position of the asteroid. Its image now filled the viewscreen, and Mordia could see each and every crater that had been blown into its surface as it rotated around in front of him.

'Hold here. Ready the forward torpedoes.'

After a few seconds, the edge of the energy field emerged over the horizon at the top of the screen. It was shimmering with reflected light, and the screen hazed for a moment as the imaging relays struggled to cope with the sudden contrast. By the time the picture on the screen had returned to crispness, the shimmering pool of energy was already dominating the image.

In the ripple obscured depths of the lake of energy, Mordia could just about make out the shape of a space craft. Its outline was vague and malformed, as though it was little more than a ghost, but it looked distinctly like an Imperial vessel.

'Enhance that quadrant. Hold off with the torpedoes,' barked the Grey Knight, the tension finally showing in his voice. If there was really an Astartes frigate through that gate, he could hardly destroy it without finding out what it was and what it was doing there.

The image amplifiers kicked in and dragged the ghostly ship closer to the *Rex*. It was still obscured by the rippling effect of the energy field, but it was definitely a Nova-class frigate. And it was getting closer.

'Stop the magnifiers,' commanded Mordia as the vessel started to dominate the screen.

'They are stopped, captain. The field is surging. Something is coming out.'

'Throne!' barked Mordia. 'Pull us back! Get us clear of this portal before that thing rips out of there!'

It was too late. The warp gate erupted suddenly, vomiting sheets of warp power which crashed out over the *Titanicus Rex*, throwing it back through the asteroid field like a sailing ship onto rocks.

For the first time, the control deck of the Grey Knights frigate lurched into turmoil. The serfs were thrown from their terminals and scattered over the floor as the ship listed and pitched. Even Mordia had to check his footing as he struggled to maintain his view of the screen.

Outside, the crashing tide of the warp broke against the hull of the *Rex* and then a frigate roared out of the portal with its engines pouring fire out in its wake. It was powering along at full speed, as though fleeing from the grasp of death itself. Blasting over the tumbling *Rex* and bathing it in fire from its exhaust, the frigate instantly opened up with its guns, clearing a path through the warp mist and asteroids as it flashed away towards the centre of the Circuitrine system.

As Mordia caught his balance he cursed. The unidentified frigate had torn past the *Rex* without

him being able to get a clear view of it. It had been
too close and too fast, and the muddying distortions
of the waves of warp had made its features indistinguishable.

'Scanners?' he barked, demanding that the serfs
should get back to their sensor terminals more
quickly as the control deck continued to rock and
reel. 'Give me an ID on that vessel. Pilot, give us
some stability here!'

The serfs chorused their acknowledgements as
they scrambled back to their stations. But just as the
control deck appeared to be returning to normality,
a second blast smacked into the stricken frigate. A
massive explosion rushed out of the warp gate. Great
plumes of flame and smoke jetted out of the asteroid, as though they had been compressed and forced
through a nozzle.

The rush of discharge crashed around the *Rex,*
sending it sprawling once again and engulfing it in a
superheated cloud of burning warp. After a second,
it became clear that the structure of the asteroid
could not bear the pressure that was being forced
through it. Bits of rock started to break off and scatter, and cracks ripped through it. Finally, it could
withstand the pressure no longer and the asteroid
itself exploded, sending chunks of rock and debris
shooting through the surrounding space in a spray
of projectiles. They pounded against the armoured
panels of the *Titanicus Rex,* smacking relentlessly
into it like a meteor shower.

It took several minutes for the control deck to
come back on line, and even then its instrumenta-
tion was damaged and only partially active. Smoke

plumed out of a number of the terminals, and electricity arced across ruptured circuits. There were several small fires burning in the cogitator banks, and damage reports were flooding in from all around the ship. Mordia cycled through the remaining, functional scanners, bringing up image after image on the viewscreen. The *Rex* was badly damaged, but its situation had changed profoundly: the warp gate and asteroid had been utterly destroyed; the frigate that had emerged from its depths had vanished without a trace; and the thick, soupy mire of warp mist seemed to have evaporated completely. The *Titanicus Rex* was alone and free-floating in the middle of an asteroid field, on the cusp of the Circuitrine system, which was now quite free of incursions from the nearby Eye of Terror.

THE PASSAGEWAYS CONVULSED with flames and concussive blasts of thermal energy as the Deathwatch team stormed through the corridors and tunnels in the heart of Lelith's lair. Plumes of dirty green fire licked at their heels, and the ground shuddered, as though the mountain itself was riddled with nausea. Whatever Sulphus had done to the wych queen's spirit pool, it was having a chain reaction through the network of portals that interlaced the structure of Sussarkh's Peak, like the veins and arteries of a massive body.

Although they never looked back into the raging inferno that chased them through the hellish realm, the Marines knew that the dark eldar were not pursing them. There was no way that anything could survive in the midst of those flames. They did not even pause to wonder whether Lelith herself had escaped – their mission here was already complete.

As he ran, leaving his duel with Lelith far behind him, Ashok's smouldering eyes gradually returned to a depthless black. He could hear voices in the fiery hounds that snapped at his heels, as though long tortured souls were screaming through the conflagration, caught in the sudden ecstasy of liberation and the abrupt agony of incineration at the same time. The passageways were alive with whispers and screams, and the flames seemed to reach at the backs of the Marines, like the hands of drowning men.

On both sides of him, the rest of the team rushed through the corridors, ducking under the low ceilings, vaulting the sudden cracks that ripped into the ground, and filing through bottlenecks with unquestioned and silent determination. But it was clear to Ashok that some of the Marines were suffering. For the first time in his long service, Ashok was concerned that the enhanced physiology of the Adeptus Astartes may not be enough for the challenge.

The Mantis Warrior, Kruidan, was without the support and protection of his armour; his skin was bloodied, raw, and thick with filth, and his long, matted hair whipped around his face as he ran. But his face was set with resolve and he showed no signs of slowing. In fact, the Mantis Warrior was at the head of the group, leaping and sprinting through the labyrinthine tunnels, leading the others with the power of his courage.

Luthar and Pelias were not in much better shape. Their armour was cracked and ruined, with sections of ceramite hacked away and others shattered beyond usefulness. The gnarled face of Pelias was taught with aggression and hostility; he was no longer a young Marine, and he had put his body through so much already. The conflagration of fiery souls clawed at his back and scorched the skin of his neck and head as he brought up the rear of the group.

Just as Ashok began to think that they were not going to make it, the team tumbled out of the passageway and fell into the bowled floor of one of the wide, portal filled nodal chambers. Flames and smoke plumed in from all directions, vomiting out of the mouths of other tunnels and pluming out of dozens of the portals. As Ashok hit the ground and rolled back to his feet, he looked back and up, just in time to see the dirty flames explode out of the tunnel mouth through which the team had just fallen.

They were utterly surrounded by the fiery screams of desperate souls.

'Ashok!' called Kruidan, his voice emerging like a ghost from the smoke.

Ashok and the others snapped their heads round to look at the Mantis Warrior, but he was nowhere to be seen. Great clouds of smoke and curdling gas roiled through the chamber, swirling and eddying in the thermal currents whipped up by the explosions of flame and the hot air being blasted through the tunnels.

'Ashok, this way is clear!'

As the words thundered and echoed around the chamber, the billowing smoke shifted and the unarmoured shape of Kruidan could be seen standing over a portal on the farside, his long hair lashing in the air currents, his emerald eyes flashing with clarity, and the tattoos snaking over his bloody shoulders.

Without pausing for discussion, Ashok broke into a run. He vaulted through the pillars of fire that jetted out of the other portals on the ground, and sidestepped the yawning infernos that raged through the other tunnel mouths. Behind him, he could feel the rest of the team keeping pace. As he closed on Kruidan's portal, he noticed that the Mantis Warrior was waiting for them, standing like a beacon of confidence and heroism, armourless and surrounded by the infernal warp fires of Hesperax.

The Angel Sanguine librarian brought himself up short of the portal and stepped to the side, allowing Sulphus, Atreus, Luthar and then Pelias to pass him and dive through.

For a moment, standing on the cusp of the shimmering, watery portal as the cavern started to melt and collapse around them, Ashok and Kruidan held each other's eyes, sharing an unspoken understanding.

THE LAST PORTAL dumped the Marines into the barren, frozen wastes under the roiling sky outside, ejecting them beyond the confines of Sussarkh's Peak on the crest of a massive wave of fiery energy. They dived out, rolling free onto the sharp, icy rocks of the planet's surface as the mouth of the portal disintegrated and collapsed behind them.

On their feet and running immediately, the Deathwatch team did not look back. Instead, their thoughts had turned to the surviving Thunderhawk. Although Octavius's ship had been destroyed, Kruidan's vessel had made it down into one of the craters. The Imperial Fists captain had insisted that the team brought two of them, in case one was destroyed, and yet again they were thankful for their fallen captain's understanding of the *Codex*. But none of them even dared to hope that the dark eldar would have left the downed Thunderhawk unmolested for all this time.

And yet there it was.

As the Deathwatch Marines clambered up the bank of icy, black debris and boulders around the edge of the crater, they could see the gunship still sitting in the bottom of the pit, exactly where the team had left it. There were not even any guards around.

As Ashok strode up the ramp into the gunship, he whispered a prayer of thanks to the spirit of the deceased Octavius, and he offered a silent prayer of gratitude for the arrogance of the eldar and their dark brethren. He could think of no other species in the galaxy that would have left the gunship untouched: only the eldar would be so certain of their victory in the amphitheatre and so dismissive of the technological capabilities of the ugly gunship. It was insulting, of course, but Ashok smiled, happy to disillusion the aliens. They had clearly never dealt with the Deathwatch before.

As THE GUNSHIP had blasted up out of the thick, curdling atmosphere of the dark planet, the Marines had collapsed into their harnesses, teetering on the point of exhaustion. Without his armour to augment his

strength, the heroic Mantis Warrior had been almost
dead on his feet. His skin was bloodied and raw, and
his muscles burned with over exertion. Luthar and
Pelias had not been in much better shape. Their
armour was broken and cracked, with sections missing or ruined beyond repair. The two librarians had
sat in silent meditation while Sulphus, the almost
entirely mechanical techmarine, piloted the vessel up
and away.

It was not until they were a couple of thousand
metres in the air that they had finally looked back
and seen the volcano erupting. It appeared to be
venting massive amounts of sickly green and red
energy, as though the souls that had been contained
within were finally visiting their violence against the
structures that had imprisoned them. The explosions reached right up into the stratosphere, chasing
the fleeing Thunderhawk like packs of flaming warp
beasts or hellhounds, just as the Marines themselves
had been chased through the labyrinthine tunnels
inside the volcano itself.

Even when they were back aboard the *Lance of
Darkness*, its engines pouring fire out behind it to
blast it away from the disintegrating planet, the team
had not been free of the explosive fury of Lelith,
Wych Queen of Strife. Huge columns of warp fire
lanced out of the massive volcano as though the
deathly planet had been hurling its infernal soul
into the chase, wrenching the stomach of its core
and vomiting vast swathes of daemonic energy into
the wake of the speeding vessel.

Just as the *Lance of Darkness* had plunged into the
warp gate and lurched out of the moon-like asteroid

in the fringes of the Circuitrine system, the tide of warp energy had crashed against its engine blocks, hurling it forward at an incredible and impossible speed. The *Lance* had burst out of the warp gate into material space like a torpedo from a barrel, firing straight through the rest of the asteroid field.

As they had emerged from the gate, the Marines had detected the briefest blip on their sensors, indicating the presence of another Astartes vessel in the immediate vicinity, but by the time the *Lance of Darkness* had slowed to normal speeds, the signature had vanished from their instruments, and the *Lance* must have been beyond the range of the other vessel's sensors too.

When they finally limped back to the previous location of Ulthwé, their engines spluttering and ruined after the warp inferno had scorched them to the point of destruction, Ashok was unsurprised to discover that the craftworld was no longer there. There was no way that the arrogant and conceited eldar would have expected the Deathwatch to survive their ordeal on Hesperax. They had been sacrificed and abandoned, just like the seers and the eldar warriors that were sent as bait. Ashok had never entertained any illusions about the honour of the deceitful aliens, but he knew that Octavius would have insisted that they at least attempt to make contact with Ulthran, had the honourable captain survived to make such an insistence.

Standing on the small control deck, Ashok, Atreus and Sulphus surveyed the stars before them. The tainted, ruddy, red fog of the warp had dissipated, as Lelith and the Slaaneshi princess's plans had been

foiled. And now the stars shone with their customary clarity and brilliance. Not far off, however, the
lashes of the Eye of Terror were already reaching
back into the system, like a creeping and insidious
cancer. Something about the momentarily pristine
light of the stars made Ashok think of Dhrykna and
the way her shining white armour had glared like a
beacon on that dark and forsaken world. Instinctively, he moved his hand to the pouch on his belt,
tapping the side to hear the chinking of three eldar
waystones.

THE DOORS SLID open with a perfunctory hiss, and
the ragged, bloody Deathwatch Marines strode forward into the conference chamber. Where it was still
in evidence at all, their armour was in tatters. Where
it was visible beneath the thick layer of congealed
blood and grime, their skin was scarred and cut.
Without their helmets, their faces were etched with
dirt and creased with suffering, while their hair was
matted and thick with ichor. They looked more like
a ragtag bunch of renegades than a squad of the
finest Space Marines in the galaxy.

Inquisitor Lord Vargas looked up from his customary chair, his delicate crystal wine glass poised
precisely at his lips. An involuntary look of revulsion
passed across his features as he saw the filthy group.
He didn't bother to stand up, but he did put his glass
down on the table, giving the impression that he
couldn't possibly drink in the presence of such pollution. Sitting across from him at the table
experiencing none of his reticence about drinking,
was the Hereticus Lord Caesurian. She nodded a

swift acknowledgement to Librarian Ashok, as though they were already on familiar terms.

Lord Seishon hurried over to greet them.

'Librarian Ashok, when you disappeared, we feared the worst, I'm afraid.'

'I doubt that,' replied Ashok gravely. 'The worst is probably more terrible than you can imagine.' His black eyes danced from Seishon to Caesurian and back again.

Seishon stared at him for a moment, peering into the deep shadows that hid the librarian's eyes under the folds of his hood. 'Lord Aurelius dispatched the Grey Knights to investigate the shifting warp signatures around Circuitrine. What do you suppose that Captain Mordia might find?'

'It is nothing,' replied Ashok without a hint of irony. 'Just a temporary storm. It appears to have burnt itself out now.' Although he was responding to Seishon, he addressed his words to Caesurian, who smiled knowingly in response.

Seishon nodded quickly, but the anxiety dropped slowly out of his shoulders.

'And what of our Captain Octavius?' asked Vargas, picking his glass up again and deciding to take the risk of a quick mouthful.

With heavy solemnity, Sulphus stepped out of the line and approached the table, his mechanical limbs twitching and whirring as the burnt out servos struggled to support their movement. Vargas recoiled slightly, pushing himself further back in his seat and trying to hide behind his wine glass.

Without even a clatter, Sulphus lay the Imperial Fist's shoulder plate carefully and reverentially onto the conference table. He did not say a word – no further comment was necessary – and the rest of the Deathwatch team hung their heads in a moment of respect.

'I see,' said Vargas at last. 'He will be missed, of course.'

The sentiments of the inquisitor lord were utterly inadequate. 'He was a great captain and a magnificent warrior. His honour was beyond reproach, and he died as he would have wished, in the fulfilment of his duty. We will not see his like again,' intoned Ashok, offended by Vargas's casual words.

He could imagine how the inquisitor lords had sat around this table drinking wine and fretting about the chances that their little pact with the aliens would be discovered. It made him sick. They were as cowardly and treacherous as the eldar themselves. The loss of a Deathwatch captain like Octavius was a terrible price to pay for their games.

'You see, Vargas,' snapped Seishon with a flicker of childish glee. 'Your precious Octavius was not the key to this problem after all.' He turned to Ashok and held out his hand. 'Do you have anything for me, librarian?'

The Angel Sanguine paused for a moment, as though weighing up whether to give the inquisitor lord what he wanted. But then he flicked open the pouch on his belt and handed over the waystones that he had taken from the two seers in the arena. His finger toyed with the last stone, still hidden in his pocket, but he hesitated, as though considering his next move, before closing the pouch again. 'As requested,' he said. 'These are from the Ulthwé seers.'

'Excellent, Ashok. Thank you,' Seishon was beaming, like a child that was winning a contest against his best friend. 'Can I also assume that you placed our beacon into the infinity circuit of Ulthwé when you "vanished" from the team?' He shot a significant and sarcastic look over to Vargas, as though to rub in the old inquisitor's naivety. The old fool still seemed to think that the mission had been all about fulfilling their duty under the terms of the ancient coven.

'Yes, Lord Seishon, you may assume that this has been done.' Ashok could feel that the other Death-watch Marines were surprised and discomforted by this new revelation, but they maintained their discipline. He had lied to them, after all, and he could not blame them for their sudden resentment.

'Excellent,' repeated Seishon. 'Then everything has gone exactly according to plan. Next time we have some dealings with the conniving and treacherous eldar of Ulthwé, we will have some extra cards to bring to the table. It is not only the alien farseers who can play these games, is it Vargas?'

'No indeed, my Lord Hourian,' growled Ashok, turning in disgust and striding out of the conference chamber. 'It seems that the keepers of the Coven of Isha are not so very different from the eldar themselves.'

ABOUT THE AUTHOR

C S Goto has published short fiction in
Inferno! and elsewhere. His previous
novels for the Black Library include the
Warhammer 40,000 epics *Dawn of War*
and *Dawn of War: Ascension,* the first
Deathwatch novel *Warrior Brood* and the
Necromunda novel *Salvation.*

WARRIOR BROOD

Check out the first action-packed novel in
the Deathwatch series!

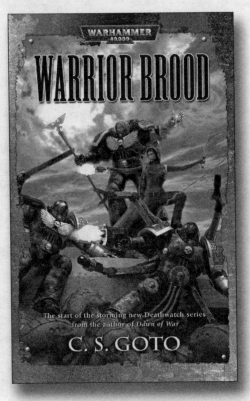

1-84416-234-6

www.blacklibrary.com

THE ART OF WAR!

For the artwork of Warrior Brood and many other
awesome art prints visit *www.blacklibrary.com*

THE BLACK LIBRARY

**More action from the Warhammer 40,000 universe
based on the hit computer games from THQ!**

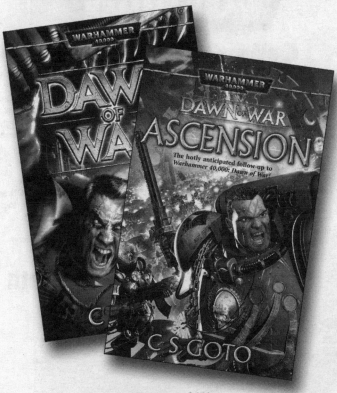

Dawn of War
1-84416-152-8

Dawn of War: Ascension
1-84416-285-0

www.blacklibrary.com

Collectible Card Game

Go deeper into the action with Dark Millennium – The Warhammer 40,000 Collectible Card Game. Take up the struggle as the defenders of the Imperium or one of the many alien races wanting to destroy it!

With participation events that actually change the fate of entire planets, YOU are in command! What will you do with such power?

Check out *www.sabertoothgames.com* for more information!

Sabertooth Games™

THE BLACK LIBRARY

GAUNT'S GHOSTS

In the war-torn Sabbat system, the massed ranks of the Imperial Guard battle against Chaos invaders in an epic struggle to liberate the enslaved worlds. Amidst this carnage, Commissar Ibram Gaunt and the men of the Tanith First-and-Only must survive against a relentless enemy as well as the bitter in-fighting from rival regiments.

Get right into the action with Dan Abnett's awesome series from the grim far-future!

www.blacklibrary.com/gauntsghosts

COMMISSAR CIAPHAS CAIN

THE GALAXY NEEDS A HERO, WHETHER HE WANTS THE JOB OR NOT

Follow the outrageous adventures of the Imperium's
unlikeliest hero in these all-action novels!

For the Emperor
ISBN: 1-84416-050-5

Caves of Ice
ISBN: 1-84416-070-X

The Traitor's Hand
ISBN: 1-84416-187-0

Death or Glory
ISBN: 1-84416-287-7